Nic let out a long, slow breath, rubbing his hand across the back of his neck.

For a minute Lily wondered if she'd completely misread what had been going on between them—maybe he was more interested in just being friends?

She risked a glance up at him, and all her doubts fled. The heat in his eyes told her everything she needed to know about how he felt—and it was a lot more than friendly. She felt that heat travel to the depths of her belly, warming her from the inside until it reached her face as a smile. He pulled gently on her hand, bringing her close to him, and planted his other hand on her hip.

"Is this a good idea?" she asked, knowing the answer, knowing just as well that it wasn't going to stop them.

"Terrible," Nic answered, dropping her hand, his palm finding her cheek. "Want to stop?"

Stop? How could they stop? They'd tried to avoid it—they'd talked about exactly why it was a bad idea. Looking deep into Nic's eyes now, she could see that he still had reservations, that he still didn't fully believe this was a ~~~~~~~~~~ to do...
but st~~~~~~

"No."

NEWBORN ON HER DOORSTEP

BY
ELLIE DARKINS

Published in Great Britain 2015
by Mills & Boon, an imprint of Harlequin (UK) Limited,
Eton House, 18-24 Paradise Road, Richmond, Surrey, TW9 1SR

© 2015 Ellie Darkins

ISBN: 978-0-263-25167-8

23-0915

Harlequin (UK) Limited's policy is to use papers that are natural, renewable and recyclable products and made from wood grown in sustainable forests. The logging and manufacturing processes conform to the legal environmental regulations of the country of origin.

Printed and bound in Spain
by CPI, Barcelona

Ellie Darkins spent her formative years devouring romance novels, and after completing her English degree she decided to make a living from her love of books. As a writer and editor her work now entails dreaming up romantic proposals, hot dates with alpha males and trips to the past with dashing heroes. When she's not working she can usually be found at her local library or out for a run.

For Rosie and Lucy

CHAPTER ONE

LILY TUCKED HER pencil behind her ear as she headed for the door. She almost had this website design finished, with a whole day to go before the client's deadline. She was privately amazed that she'd managed to get the thing done on time, given the chaos in her house. Even now she could hear chisels and hammers and God knew what else in her kitchen, as the builders ripped out the old units ready for work on the extension to start.

The ring of the doorbell had been welcome, actually. When she'd glanced at her watch she'd realised that she'd not taken a break since settling down in her home office at six. She was overdue a cup of coffee— and no doubt the builders would appreciate one, too.

A glance through the hallway window afforded a glimpse of a taxi heading up the road, but she couldn't see anyone waiting behind the frosted glass of the front door. Strange… she thought as she turned the key and pulled the door open.

No one there.

Kids? she wondered, but she'd lived in this house almost all of her life, and she couldn't remember a single case of knock-door-run.

She was just about to shut the door and head back inside when a kitten-like mewl caught her attention and she glanced down.

Not a kitten.

A Moses basket was tucked into the corner of the porch, out of the spring breeze. Wrapped tight inside, with just eyes and the tip of a soft pink nose showing from the yellow blanket... A baby.

Lily dropped to her knees out of instinct, and scooped the baby up from the floor, nestling her against her shoulder. Making sure the blanket was tucked tight, she walked down to the front gate, looking left and right for any sign of someone who might have just left a baby on her doorstep.

Nothing.

She moved the baby into the crook of her arm as she tried to think, her brain struggling to catch up with this sudden appearance. And as she moved the baby she heard a papery crackle. When she pulled the corner of the blanket aside she found a scribbled note on a page torn from a notebook. The writing was as familiar as her own, and unmistakable.

Please look after her.

Which left all the questions she already had unanswered and asked a million more.

She walked again to the gate, wondering if she could still catch sight of that taxi—if she had time to run and stop her half-sister before she did something irreversible. But as much as she strained her eyes, the car was gone.

She stood paralysed with shock for a moment on

the front path, unsure whether to run for help or to take the baby inside. What sort of trouble would her half-sister have to be in to do this? Was she leaving her here forever? Or was she going to turn up in a few minutes and explain?

For the first time Lily took a deep breath, looked down into the clear blue eyes of her little niece—and fell instantly in love.

His feet pounded the footpath hard, driving out thought, emotion, reason. All he knew was the rhythm of his shoes on the ground, the steady in-out of his breath as he let his legs and his lungs settle in to their pace.

The sun was drying the dew on the grassy verges by the road, and the last few commuters were making their way into the tube station. The morning commute was a small price to pay to live in this quiet, leafy part of London, he guessed.

He noted these things objectively, as he did the admiring looks from a couple of women he passed. But none of it mattered to him. This was the one time of the day when he could just concentrate on something he was completely in control of. So, no music, no stopping for admiring glances—just him and the road. Nothing could spoil the hour he spent shutting out the horrors of the world—great and small—that he had encountered in his work over the years.

Tomorrow he'd be able to find a solitary path through the Richmond Park, but this morning he was dodging café tables and pedestrians as he watched the street names, looking out for the address his sister had texted to him. She'd been taking furniture deliveries for him before he flew home, and had left the keys to his new place with a friend of hers who worked from home.

He turned the corner into a quiet side street, and suddenly the fierce cry of a newborn baby ahead skewed his consciousness and he stumbled, his toe somehow finding a crack in the footpath.

He tried to keep running for a few strides, to ignore the sound, but found it was impossible. Instead he concentrated on counting the house numbers—anything to keep his mind off the wailing infant. But as the numbers climbed he felt a sense of growing inevitability. The closer he drew to the sound of the baby, the more he wished that he could get away—and the more certain he became that he wouldn't be able to.

The rhythm and focus that had always come as easily as breathing when he pulled on his running shoes was gone. His body fought him, sending awareness of the baby to his ears. Another side street loomed on his left, and for a moment he willed himself to turn away, to *run* away, but his feet wouldn't obey. Instead they picked up their pace and carried straight on, towards a dazed-looking woman and the wailing baby standing in the porch of one of the houses ahead.

He glanced at the house number and knew that he'd been right. His sister had sent him to a house with a baby—without a word of warning.

'Hi,' he said to the woman, approaching and speaking with caution. Lily, he thought her name was. 'Is everything okay?' He couldn't help but ask—not when she was standing there with a distressed baby and looking as if she'd just been thunderstruck.

Her blonde hair was pulled back into a loose ponytail so shiny that he could almost feel the warmth of the sunlight reflecting off it. Her eyes were blue, clear and wide—but filled with a shock and a panic that stopped him short.

She stared at him blankly and he held out his hands in a show of innocence. 'I'm Nic,' he said, realising she had no idea who he was. 'Dominic—Kate's brother. She said to drop by and pick up my keys?'

'Oh, God,' she said. 'I'd completely forgotten.'

But still she didn't move. Her eyes did, though, dropping to his vest and running shorts, moving as far down as his ankles before her eyes met his again. There was interest there, he could see, even behind her confusion and distress.

'Is everything all right?' he asked again, though everything about her—her posture, her expression—told him that it wasn't.

'Oh, fine,' she said.

He could see the effort it took to pull the muscles of her face into a brave smile, but it wasn't enough to cover the undercurrents of worry that lay beneath. There was something about that contrast that made him curious—more than curious—to know the layers of this woman.

'*My* sister...' she said, boldly attempting nonchalance. 'She never gives me much notice when she needs a babysitter.'

Which was about five per cent of the truth, if he had to guess. He found himself looking deep into her eyes, trying to see her truths, all the things that she wasn't saying. Was there some sort of trick here? Was this something Kate had set up? Surely she'd never be so cruel, never willingly expose him to so much pain?

But he wanted to know more about this woman, he acknowledged. Wanted to untangle her mysteries.

Then he could ignore the screams of the baby no longer, and knew that he mustn't even think it. He should turn and walk away from her and the little bundle of trouble now. Before he got drawn in, before wounds that had taken a decade to become numb were reopened.

But he couldn't, *wouldn't* walk away from someone so obviously in trouble. Couldn't abandon a child, however much it might hurt him. He'd discovered that on his first trip to India, when he'd seen children used as slave labour, making clothes to be sold on British high streets. He'd not been able to leave without doing *something*, without working to improve the shattered lives that he'd witnessed.

Now, ten years later, the charity he'd founded had helped hundreds, thousands of children from exploitation or worse. But that didn't make him any more able to ignore this single child's cries.

Distressed children needed help—whoever they were, wherever they were living. He finally forced himself to look at the crying baby—and felt the bottom fall out of all his worries. He was in serious trouble, and any thoughts of walking away became an impossibility. That was a newborn baby…as in hours-old new. Completely helpless, completely vulnerable and—by the look on Lily's face—a complete surprise.

The baby's crying picked up another notch and Lily bounced it optimistically. But, if he had to guess, she didn't have what that baby needed.

'Did your sister leave some milk? Or some formula?'

She looked up and held his gaze, her eyes still a complicated screen of half-truths. There was something dangerously attractive in that expression, something drawing him in against his better judgement. There was a bond growing between himself and Lily—he could feel it. And some connection with this baby's story was at the heart of it. It was dangerous, and he wanted nothing to do with it, but still he didn't walk away.

'She asked me to pick some up,' she replied, obviously thinking on her feet. 'Thanks for stopping, but I have to get to the shop.'

He chose his next words carefully, knowing that he mustn't scare her off, but seeing by the shocked look on her face that she hadn't quite grasped yet the trouble that this newborn baby might be in. Who left an hours-old baby with a relative who clearly wasn't expecting her? There was more, much more, to this story, and he suspected that there were layers of complications that neither of them yet understood.

'That's quite a noise she's making. How about to be on the safe side we get her checked by a doctor? I saw that the hospital round the corner has a walk-in clinic.'

At that, Lily physically shook herself, pulled her shoulders back and grabbed the baby a little tighter. There was something about seeing the obvious concern and turmoil in her expression that made him want to wrap his arms around her and promise her that everything would be okay. But he was the last person on earth who could promise her that, who could even believe that it might be true.

'Maybe you're right,' she said, walking away from the open front door and through the garden gate.

'Kate's keys are in the top drawer in the hall. Can you pull the door closed on your way out?'

And then she was speed-walking down the street, the baby still clutched tightly to her, still wailing. He glanced at the house and hesitated. He needed his keys, but he could hardly leave Lily's house with the door wide open—the woman hadn't even picked up her handbag. Did she have her own keys? Her wallet? So he had no choice but to grab her bag and his keys and jog in the direction of those newborn wails.

He just wanted to be sure that the baby was going to be okay, he told himself.

'I'll walk with you,' he said as he caught Lily up.

The words were out of his mouth before he had a chance to stop them. However much he might wish he hadn't stumbled on this little family drama, he had. He might be wrong, but gut instinct and not a little circumstantial evidence told him that this child had just been abandoned—which meant, of course, that both mother and baby could be in danger.

He tried to focus on practicalities, tried to put thoughts of what might have been had he and Lily met on any other sunny day out of his mind. He should call Kate. And maybe the police—they were the best people to ensure that the baby's mother was safe and well. But he couldn't ignore the fascination that he felt about Lily. There was an energy that seemed to pull him towards her and push him away at the same time— it had him curious, had him interested.

CHAPTER TWO

LILY EYED NIC, where he leaned against the wall by the door—a position he'd adopted almost as soon as they'd been shown into this room. He looked at the door often, as if reminding himself that it was there. That he could use it any time. So why was he still here?

Under normal circumstances she'd say that an attractive man, background-checked by her BFF, somewhat scantily clad, could involve himself in her life at any time he chose—as long as she had the option of checking out those long, lean thighs. But he really had killer timing.

She didn't have time to ogle; she didn't have time for his prying questions. All she could think about was her sister, Helen, and the baby, and what she needed to do to take care of both of them.

She paced the room, glancing over at the baby and wondering what on earth they were doing to her. Had they found something wrong? If everything was okay, surely someone would have told her by now. She hadn't wanted to hand her over to the doctors, but she'd had no choice.

It was becoming a pattern, this letting go, this watching from afar. She'd lost her father before she was born, to nothing more dramatic than disinterest and a lost phone number. Her mother had died the year that Lily had turned thirteen, and it seemed her sister had been drifting further and further from her since that day. All she wanted was a family to take care of, to take care of her, and yet that seemed too much to ask from the universe.

And now someone had called the police, and her sister was going to be in more trouble than ever, pushed further from her. She tried not to think of the alternative. Of Helen out there needing help and not getting it. If it took the authorities getting involved to get her safe and well, then Lily was all for it.

She started pacing again, craning her neck each time she passed the baby to try and get a glimpse of what was happening.

'Just a couple of tests,' the doctor had said. How could that possibly take this long?

She glanced across at Nic, and then quickly away. How had she never met Kate's brother before? Surely there should be some sort of declaration when you became best friends with someone about any seriously attractive siblings. He'd been abroad, she remembered Kate saying. He ran a charity that tried to improve conditions for child workers in factories in the developing world. He'd recently been headhunted by one of the big retailers that he'd campaigned against, and would be sitting on their board, in charge of cleaning up their supply chain. So attractive, humanitarian, and with a job in retail. There should definitely be a disclaimer for this sort of thing.

But there was something about him that made her nervous—some tension in his body and his voice that told her this man had secrets too: secrets that she couldn't understand. It was telling her to stay away. That he was off-limits. A warning she didn't need.

Nic came to stand beside her. 'Try not to worry. I'm sure that everything is fine—they're just being thorough.'

Lily bit her lip and nodded. She knew that he was right. He gestured her back to a seat and cleared his throat, giving her a rare direct look.

She continued pacing the room, waiting for news—until she heard a shriek, and then she was by the bed, her arms out, already reaching for the baby.

The doctor barely looked up from where he was pricking the little one's heel with a needle.

'I'm sorry, we're not quite done.'

'You're hurting her!'

Lily scooped the baby into her arms as she wiped away the spot of blood from her foot and cooed soothing noises, gently rocking her. Back in Lily's embrace, the baby stopped crying and nuzzled closer. Lily leaned over, instinctively shielding the baby from the doctor who had hurt her, until she felt the little body relax. She kissed the baby's forehead, leaving her own face close for a moment, breathing in her baby smell. Once she was satisfied that she was calmed she looked up at the doctor, and instantly stiffened her resolve at the look of disapproval on his face.

'I'm her aunt,' she stated, as if that were explanation enough for everything. 'Have you finished with the tests? It looks as if she's had enough for now.'

She stared him down until he conceded that they had everything they needed. That was when she spotted Nic, looking grey and decidedly ill by the door.

'When she cried out...' he said. 'I thought...'

Whatever he had thought had scared him witless, she realised, instinctively taking a step towards him.

'She's fine. We're fine,' she told him, in the same soothing tone she'd used with the baby. She turned her towards him. 'Look, she's settled now.'

He breathed a sigh of relief and Lily could almost see the adrenaline leaching from his body, leaving him limp and drawn. She met his eyes, looking for answers there, but instead saw only pain. An old pain, she guessed, one that had been lived with a long time and had become so familiar it was hardly noticed. Until something happened—a baby screamed—and it felt like new again.

For a moment she wished that she could soothe him as easily as she had the baby—smooth those creases from his face and the pain from his body. But something told her that taking this man in her arms would bring him anything but peace. She pressed herself back against the wall, trying to put whatever space she could between them.

'Is everything okay?' she asked.

'Fine.'

Nic's reply was terse, sharper than she'd expected, and she saw the fear and hurt in his expression being carefully shut down, stowed away.

'I need to grab a cup of coffee. Do you want to find the canteen? We've been here for hours.'

And leave the baby alone with strangers? 'I'm fine, thanks. I don't want to leave her.'

He gave her a shrewd look. 'I'll go, then,' he said, pushing himself away from the wall.

He looked better now, as he had in her front garden, all bronzed skin and taut muscles. No sign now of the man who had looked as if he might slide down the wall from fear.

When he returned with coffee and cake his manner was brisk and his eyes guarded. *Goodå,* Lily thought. *Guarded is good. If we're both being careful, both backing away slowly from whatever this energy between us is, then we're safe.*

'I've got to go,' he said. 'I promised that I'd meet Kate and she's not answering her phone so I can't cancel. I don't want to leave her stranded.'

And then he was off—out of their lives, and no doubt relieved to be so. She held in her heavy sigh until he'd slipped out of the door with her polite words of thanks.

CHAPTER THREE

KATE BURST THROUGH the door of the treatment room, wearing her air of drama queen as if it was this season's must-have.

Lily smiled at the arrival of her best friend. If anyone was going to help her make sense of this situation it would be Kate, with her remarkable ability to see through half-truths and get straight to the point.

'So I get back from court and pop in to see my brother in his new flat, and he's got this crazy story about your dear sister and a baby and a hospital. I didn't have a clue what was going on, so I thought I'd better get down here and find out just what he's talking about. Explain, Lily! Where's this flippin' baby come from? What are you doing here? And why does my brother look so cagey whenever I mention your name?'

Lily couldn't help but laugh—trust Kate to boil this down to the bare essentials.

'She's Helen's baby. Helen left her on my doorstep with a note. Your brother was passing by to pick up his keys and…and kept us company while we were waiting here.'

It was rare that she saw Kate lost for words, but she dropped into a chair now, silent, and Lily could practically see the thoughts being processed behind her eyes. Her barrister's brain was reading all the evidence, everything that Lily was saying, and everything she wasn't.

'Okay, give it to me again. And this time with details.'

Lily sighed and took a breath, wondering how many times she would have to repeat everything that had happened. But when she came to talking about Nic her words stumbled and faltered.

'Nic turned up to collect his keys just as I'd been left literally holding the baby and was freaking out. He suggested we walk over here and have her checked out.'

'And then he waited with you? How long for?'

Lily glanced at her watch. 'A couple of hours, I guess.'

Kate blew out a deliberate breath, and Lily raised her eyebrows.

'What?'

'Nothing…nothing,' Kate said, but Lily had known her long enough to know that she was hiding something.

'Not nothing,' she told her best friend. 'Definitely *something*.'

Kate looked at her for a long time before she replied.

'Something,' she agreed, nodding, her eyes sad. 'But not my something to tell. Can we leave it at that?'

Lily nodded. Though she was intrigued, her friend's rare sombre tone had pulled her up short and warned her to stop digging.

'So you and my brother, then…?'

'It's not like that.' The denial came to Lily's lips as soon as she realised what Kate was getting at. 'I don't think he wanted to be here at all. He looked like he was going to bolt the whole time.'

'So why didn't he?'

True to form, Kate had hit on the one question that Lily had been searching for an answer to—to no avail.

'I've no idea.'

'I've got one or two,' Kate said with a sly grin. 'So what happens with the baby now?'

Another question Lily had no answer to.

No doubt between the hospital staff and the police someone would be arranging for a social worker to visit her. But she had no intention of letting her niece be looked after by anyone but herself. She knew that she could look after her—she already ran a business from home, and had flexibility in her hours and her work. It was one of the things that she enjoyed most about her job as a freelance web designer—the chance to balance work and home life. She'd manage her work commitments around caring for the baby—whatever it took to keep the little girl safe and with her family.

'She's coming home with me.'

Lily gulped at the baldness of that statement, and backtracked.

'Until we can find Helen.'

'Right. And then you're going to hand her over to a woman who's been living God-knows-where and doing God-knows-what for years?'

'Helen's her mother—'

'And she seems pretty clear about who she wants taking care of her daughter. I'm not saying that taking her home is a bad thing—she's family. Of course you want to look after her. I'm just saying it looks like it might be slightly more commitment than a regular babysitting gig. Are you ready for that?'

Ready for a family? It was what she'd wanted for as long as she could remember. She'd been lucky after her mother had died. She'd been placed with a wonderful foster family who had slowly and gently helped her to come to terms with her grief. She'd certainly been luckier than her sister, who, at sixteen, had decided that she was old enough to look after herself.

They'd exchanged letters and emails, but over the years they'd become less and less frequent, until now she couldn't even rely on a card at Christmas. All she wanted was a family of her own. To recapture something of what the three of them—herself, her mum and Helen—had had before the accident.

She'd even looked into ways to build that family. After her own experience of foster care she'd thought of offering her house to children who might need it.

The old family home had seemed echoey and empty when she'd moved back in when she was eighteen. Her mother's will had protected it in a trust for her and her sister, but it had been lonely with no one to share it with. But she'd never considered she'd ever be handed a newborn baby and asked if she was ready to be a parent.

'We have to find Helen,' Lily said. 'That's as far as I can think right now.'

'There is one slight flaw in that plan,' Kate said.

'Only one?' Lily asked, only half joking.

'Your house. It's currently a building site, and—unless I'm much mistaken—not exactly ready for a newborn…whether she's going to be there permanently or not.'

Lily's face fell. In all the drama she'd somehow managed to forget the chaotic state of her house. There was no way that she could take a baby back there. And if she couldn't take care of her niece that left only one option. Letting social services place her with strangers. Her gut recoiled at the thought of losing another member of her family, of her and Helen and their past being fractured even further.

'Don't look like that,' Kate said. 'This is not insurmountable. We can sort this out—'

'That's really kind,' Lily said, her mind still racing, 'but your place barely has enough room for me to pull out the sofa bed. I'm not sure that—'

'Not *me*!' Kate exclaimed. 'Good God, no. We'd lose the baby under a stack of briefs or something. Nic's place—it's perfect.'

Lily gave a little choke.

'Nic's place? I couldn't possibly impose…'

She couldn't share a flat with that man—not when she felt drawn to him and afraid of that attraction in equal measure. When her skin tingled just from being in the same room as him.

'Honestly, you should see his place. It's ridiculous. A penthouse—overlooking the river, naturally. He told me it was something to do with investing his golden handshake money, and London property prices, and being able to do so much more with the money once he sold up. Personally, I think it might have something to do with sleeping in hostels for the best part of a decade. It's huge, and he's barely ever there.'

Even the thought of a Thameside penthouse couldn't convince her that spending more time with a man who had her wanting him and wanting to run from him was a good idea. But what choice did she have? If she wanted to take care of her niece she couldn't afford to be picky about what help she accepted. And, anyway, what she thought was probably irrelevant…

'Nic would never—'

'Nic will be travelling on and off for the next few months. He's due to fly out again tomorrow, I think. You won't see each other much. And if the man who's preached charity and child welfare at me for the past ten years can't see it in his heart to give an abandoned baby a home for a few months, then I'll disown him.'

Somehow Lily didn't think that was a threat that would carry much weight for Nic.

'*And* trash his lovely new apartment,' she added.

'Okay, ask him,' Lily said eventually. What choice did she have?

An awkward silence fell for a few moments, until Kate obviously couldn't stand the quiet any longer.

'So, does this little one have a name, or what?'

Lily shook her head. 'Helen didn't exactly say.'

'Well, that's just not right, is it? She's had a rough enough start in life already, without ending up being named just Baby Girl. So what are we going to go for: naming her after a pop star or a soap star. Or we could go big and Hollywood?'

Lily raised an eyebrow.

'Okay, so I'm guessing that's a no. What do *you* suggest?'

Lily looked closely at the baby, trying to work out who she was. 'Look at her,' Lily said. 'All pretty and pink and fresh and soft…like a flower. A rose. What about Rosie?'

'I think it's perfect,' Kate agreed. 'Little Rosie— welcome to the world.'

Nic's feet pounded on the pavement as he tried to get thoughts of Lily Baker out of his head—with zero success. Since the moment he'd met her she'd invaded all of his thoughts, forcing him to keep busy, keep working, keep running. But even two days on his body still wouldn't co-operate, refusing to find the quiet place in his mind where he could retreat from the world.

His sister wasn't exactly helping, with her pointed remarks and regular updates on how baby and aunt were faring. Did she think he couldn't see what she was doing? That the strings of her puppeteering were somehow invisible? But he *did* wonder how the baby was. Kate had said that she was doing well, and the doctors hadn't seemed worried when he'd left the hospital, but he knew better than most how precarious a new life was, how quickly it might be lost.

Turning for home, he tried to find his usual rhythm, but his feet carried him faster than he wanted, rushing him.

His mobile rang as he reached his flat, and Kate's latest unsubtle update gave him all he needed to know. No news on the missing sister. Baby apparently doing well in hospital. But somehow it wasn't enough. What did that mean anyway? 'Doing well in hospital.' Surely if the baby was 'doing well' then she wouldn't be in hospital at all. She'd be home, tucked into a cot, safe. And this time Kate had not said anything about Lily.

He hadn't been able to think of a way to ask about

her without raising suspicious eyebrows. He could hardly say, *And how about the aunt? The one with the glowing skin and the complicated expressions and the fierce independence? How's she getting on?*

But he was desperate to know. Lily Baker seemed to have soaked into his mind until his every thought was coloured by her. It was no good. The only way he was going to get this woman and her niece out of his mind was to get some answers, some closure.

He saw her as soon as he walked onto the ward. He should have known that she would have been there all night. Had been there for two nights, he guessed. Her hair was mussed, rubbing up against the side of the chair she'd curled into, but her face was relaxed, looking so different from when she'd worn that troubled, burdened expression before.

He knocked on the door, aware that he didn't want to answer the questions that being caught watching her sleep would give rise to. Lily sat bolt upright at the sound, her hand instinctively reaching for the cot, eyes flying towards the baby. Only once she was satisfied that she was sleeping soundly did she turn towards the door. Her eyes widened in surprise, and he realised how unguarded she was in the moment after waking—how her expression shifted as her eyes skimmed over him appreciatively.

There was no mistaking the interest there, and his stomach tightened in response as he fought down his instinctive reaction. Eventually her eyes reached his, and he saw her barriers start to build as she emerged properly from sleep. Her back straightened and her face grew composed.

The rational, sensible, *thinking* part of his brain

breathed a sigh of relief. He was glad that she was as wary as he was of this energy he felt flowing and sparking between them, the pull that he felt between their bodies. Much as he might find her attractive, he would never act on that. He wasn't the kind of man she needed in her life. When she found someone she'd need a partner—a father for this child and the ones that would come in the future. She would need someone she could rely on, and he knew that he wasn't capable of being that man.

But the part of his brain less removed from his primal ancestors groaned, trying to persuade him to get that dreamy look back on her face, to seduce her into softness.

'Morning,' he said, rather more briskly than he'd intended. 'I brought coffee. I know the stuff here's awful.'

'Morning. Thanks…'

Her voice was as wary as her expression, and he guessed that he wasn't the only one who'd thought that they would never see each other again after he'd left the hospital. He wondered if she'd found it as impossible not to think of him as he had of her. Of course not, he reasoned. She had the baby to think about—there was probably no room in her life right now for anything other than feeding, nappies and sleep.

At the sound of her voice the baby had started to stir, and Lily automatically reached out a hand to stroke her cheek.

'How is she?'

'She's fine…good. They've said that I can take her home today.'

Home. So that settled it, then. Kate had been right

the other day—Lily was going to look after the baby as her sister had asked. And that meant he'd been right to fight off this attraction. Because if there was one thing he was certain of it was that he could never get involved with someone who had a child. He could never again open himself up to that sort of hurt.

Even if Lily's sister returned, he couldn't imagine that Lily saw a future without children. He'd seen the melting look in her eye as she'd gazed down at her niece—there was no hiding her maternal instincts.

'That's good. I'm glad she's okay.' Now that he had his answer he felt awkward, not sure why he had come. No doubt Lily was wondering what he was doing there, too. Or perhaps not. Perhaps his real interest was as transparent to her as it had been opaque to him.

Perhaps he had imagined this energy and attraction—imagined the way her eyes widened whenever her skin brushed against his, the way she flushed in those rare moments when they both risked eye contact. Maybe she saw him as nothing other than the Good Samaritan who had happened to be there when she'd needed someone. If only she knew that when someone else had really needed him, when they'd relied on him to be there for them, he'd let them down.

He glanced up at the name plate above the crib and realised that the little girl was no longer Baby Baker.

'Rosie?' he asked, surprise in his voice. Kate hadn't mentioned that.

'It seemed to suit her,' Lily said with a shrug. 'It's not official yet. If Helen doesn't like it…'

'It's pretty.'

'Look, I hate to ask this when you're already doing so much for us…'

Lily glanced at the door and Nic guessed what was coming. Instantly he wished himself anywhere in the world but here. But Lily was still speaking, and he knew that it was too late.

'...just for fifteen minutes or so, while I grab a shower. I know the nurses are listening out for her, but I hate the thought of her being alone. I know I can trust you with her.'

A lump blocked his throat and he couldn't force the word *no* out past it. He'd not been responsible for a child since the morning he'd found his son, cold and still in his crib. But the look on Lily's face—the trust that he saw there—touched his heart in a way he hadn't realised was even still possible. And more than anything he wanted to know that the baby—little Rosie—was going to be okay. That was why he'd dragged himself down here, after all. Fifteen minutes alone with a sleeping baby—surely he could manage that, could ensure that she was safe while Lily was away?

He nodded. 'Sure, go ahead. You look like you could do with a break.'

Her smile held for a moment before her face fell. Oh, God, that wasn't what he'd meant at all. He'd all but said, *You look awful,* hadn't he? What was it about this woman that made it so impossible for him to function anything like normal?

He started back-pedalling fast. 'Sorry, I didn't mean it like that at all. You look fine. I mean—I just meant you've slept in that chair two nights in a row, and I bet you're tired. You look great.'

This wasn't getting any better. But Lily grinned at him, probably enjoying his discomfort, and the fact that he didn't seem at all able to remove his foot from his mouth.

A disconcerting noise and a very bad smell halted Nic's apology in its tracks, and as he caught Lily's eyes they both laughed.

'Well, perhaps if you change her I might find it in my heart to forgive you.'

Before he had a chance to argue she was out of the room, leaving him alone with the baby. This was not at all what he'd expected when he'd reluctantly agreed to watch a sleeping baby for fifteen minutes, but he reached for the nappies and the cotton wool, acting on instinct.

He narrowed his eyes, trying not to see Rosie's little pink cheeks or her tiny fingers. He just had to concentrate on the task in hand, and he could do that without really looking at her, without thinking about the fact that this little body was a whole new life—maybe a hundred years of potential all contained in seven pounds of toes and belly and new baby smell. Without thinking about his son.

He had nearly finished the nappy when Rosie began to fuss. As he fastened the poppers on her Babygro and washed his hands, he silently pleaded with her not to start crying. But her face screwed up and the tears started, and her banshee-like wail was impossible to ignore. He shut his eyes as he scooped a hand under her head and another under her bottom and lifted her to his shoulder, making soothing noises that he hoped would quiet her. He tried not to think at all as he bounced her gently, waiting for her tears to stop, tried not to think of the first time he had held his son, Max.

Or the last time.

The memory made him clutch Rosie a little tighter, hold her a little safer, knowing how precarious a young life could be. Eventually her cries slowed to sniffles as she snuggled closer to his shoulder and started looking for a source of food. He looked around the room, wondering where he'd lay his hands on formula and a bottle. He could ask the nurses, he supposed.

He transferred Rosie to the crook of one arm, only flinching momentarily at the remembered familiarity of the movement, and headed for the door. As it opened he was greeted by the sight of Lily, fresh from the shower, with no make-up and her hair pulled back, and it took his breath away.

Any chance of kidding himself that his interest was only in Rosie's welfare was lost. It was more than that. It was...*her*. He just couldn't stop thinking about her. But that was the problem. If he'd met Lily just one day earlier, before her sister had turned up with a baby, he wouldn't have hesitated to explore this connection between them, to imagine Lily looking as she did now—all fresh and pink and polished from the shower. But the shower would have been in his flat, and she'd have just left his bed.

Everything about her fascinated him. But she'd taken in her sister's child without a thought. And because of that he knew that they could never be happy together. He could see from her every look at Rosie that Lily was born to be a mother. She wanted a family, and he could never give her that—nor could he ask her to sacrifice it for him. There was no point considering a brief fling, either: a taste of her would never be enough—and if he started to fall for her then how would he make himself stop? And all that was even without the added complication of his sister's unspoken threats to hurt him in a *very* sensitive place if he messed with her best friend.

'I was just going to try and find her a bottle.'

Lily waved the bottle of formula she was carrying. 'No need. I see you couldn't resist a cuddle? I don't blame you—she's very squeezable.'

'It's not like that,' he replied instinctively. 'She was crying, that's all. Here—take her.' He almost shoved the baby at her, alarmed at how quickly he'd adapted, how natural it had felt to hold her.

'What's wrong?' Lily asked, her eyes wary. 'I don't mind you holding her.'

'I know.' Nic breathed slowly, trying to fight the urge to run from the room, knowing that he should explain his harsh words to Lily. Hating the wary, guarded look that had just entered her eyes. 'I'm just not good around babies.'

She glanced down at Rosie, who looked happy and content. 'Seems like you're pretty good to me.'

An awkward silence fell between them, and Lily looked as if she was trying to find the right words to say something. Suddenly he wanted out of the room. Her face was serious, and he wondered if she had guessed about his past, or if Kate had told her about it. His heart started racing as he remembered all the times he had failed at that in the past. All the broken conversations, the broken relationships that had followed.

'Nic, I don't know how to thank you for being there for us the other day. And Kate told me—'

Before he knew it he was reaching for her, wanting to stem the flow of her words. He didn't want to know what Kate had told her of his failings as a father and a partner.

He'd do anything to stop her speaking.

His lips pressed against hers as his fingers cradled her jaw, and for just a second he wondered what would happen if she opened her mouth to him, if her body softened and relaxed against him. If this kiss changed from a desperate plea for mercy to something softer, something more passionate. But he pulled away before it had the chance.

'I'm sorry,' he said, shutting his eyes against the confusion on her face and heading towards the door. 'I shouldn't have done that.'

Lily stood shell-shocked in the middle of the hospital room, the baby in one arm and the bottle held loosely in her other hand. What on earth had just happened? She'd been about to thank him for letting them stay with him—just until the work on her house was finished. But the cornered look in his eyes had stopped her words, and the kiss he'd pressed against her lips had stopped her thoughts.

It had been difficult enough to see herself living in his apartment. How was she meant to do it now, with this kiss between them, dragging up every fantasy she'd been forcing herself to bury? If she'd had any other option she'd have jumped at it. But Kate had been right. This was her only choice—kiss or no kiss.

She wondered at the expression on Nic's face, at the way he had cradled Rosie in one arm as if it was the most natural thing in the world. He'd obviously been around babies before. Had he been a father once? Was that what was behind the fear and the pain she saw in him? She couldn't imagine that anything but the loss of a child could draw such a picture of grief on someone's face. He carried a pain that was still raw and devastating—so why on earth had he agreed to let her live with him?

She spun at the sound of a knock to the door, wondering for an instant if it was Nic, back to rescind his invitation, to tell her she wasn't welcome anywhere near him. But instead of Nic it was her social worker standing in the doorway, case file in hand and a smile on her face.

CHAPTER FOUR

LILY LEANT AGAINST the wall of the lift as it climbed to the top of the building and snuck another look at Rosie, sleeping in her pram, not quite believing that she was really going to do this. But Kate had promised her that Nic was okay with it. He would be away on a business trip for the next week at least, so she'd have plenty of time to settle in and find her feet before she had to think about him. Or that kiss.

What had he been thinking? Perhaps the same as her—nothing. Perhaps the touch of their lips had banished all rational thought and left him as confused as she was.

At least all the paperwork and everything in officialdom was ticking along nicely. It was just a case of getting the right legal papers in order, and making sure that Helen had the medical help—both physical and mental—that she needed to get and stay well. There had been no talk of prosecution for abandonment—only concern for Helen and Rosie's welfare.

A stack of half-opened parcels littered the hallway, making the apartment look less bachelor sophisticated and more like a second hand sale. Kate must have beaten her here and picked up all the internet shopping that Lily had done while she was in the hospital with Rosie. They had some work ahead of them to get the apartment baby-ready—that was clear.

She peeked into the living room and was tempted to shiver at the abundance of black leather, smoked glass and chrome. Everything in the room shone, and Lily wondered if Nic was quite mad for letting them stay here. One thing was for sure: even with Rosie on her best behaviour it wasn't going to be easy keeping the place looking this show-home perfect.

'Kate?' Lily called out as she stood in the living room with Rosie in her arms, her eyes drawn to the glass walls with a view out over the river. 'Are you here?'

A voice sounded from the end of the hallway.

'In here!' she shouted. 'I'm just doing battle with the cot.'

Lily followed the sound of Kate's swearing and found herself in a luxurious bedroom. Between the doorway and the enormous pillow-topped bed Kate's curly head was just visible between the bars of a half-built cot.

'Are you winning?' Lily asked with a laugh.

'Depends on who's keeping score,' came the reply, along with another string of expletives.

Lily covered Rosie's ears and tutted.

'Sorry, Rosie,' Kate said, finally dropping the screwdriver and climbing out from the pile of flat-packed pieces. 'How are we doing?' she asked as she crossed the room to give Rosie a squeeze and Lily a kiss on the cheek.

'She's fine,' Lily told her. 'Clean bill of health. Thanks so much for getting started with this.' She waved a hand towards the cot.

'Don't be daft. It's nothing. Now, are you going to put the baby down and give me a hand?'

'Let me just grab her carrycot and I'll see if she'll go down.'

As Lily walked back into the hallway she jumped against the wall at the sight of a man's dark shadow up ahead of her.

'Nic…?' she said, holding Rosie a little tighter to her.

As Nic took a step forward his face came into the light and she could see the shock and surprise written across his features.

'Lily, what the hell—?'

'Kate!'

She wasn't sure which of them shouted first, but as it became apparent that Nic had had no idea she was going to be there Lily felt flames of embarrassment lick up her cheeks, colouring her skin. Oh, Kate had some explaining to do.

Kate at least had the good grace to look sheepish when she emerged into the hallway.

'What the hell is *she* doing here?'

Lily's gaze snapped back to Nic at the anger in his voice and she felt herself physically recoil. She was as surprised to see him there as he was to find them both in the flat—Kate had promised her he would be out of town for at least a week yet—but the venom in his voice was unexpected and more than a little offensive.

'Nic!' Kate admonished. 'Don't talk about Lily like that. I promise you, I can explain. You're not meant to *be* here.'

'It's my home, Kate. Where else would I be?'

'Well, India, for a start. And then Bangladesh. And Rome. And…'

'And I decided to spend a few weeks in the office before I go abroad again. I pushed some of my trips back. Not that I need to explain myself—*I'm* not the one who's in the wrong here.'

He threw a look at Lily that was impossible to mis-interpret.

'Look…' Kate was using her best lawyer voice, and Lily suddenly felt a pang of sympathy for Nic. When she took that tone there was little doubt that she was going to get her own way.

But it didn't matter how Kate was planning on sweet-talking her way out of 'stretching the truth', as she was bound to call it. There was no way she could stay here—not with the looks of pure anger that Nic was sending their way.

'This is how I see things: Lily needs somewhere to stay. Rosie can't go back to Lily's as it has no kitchen, no back wall, isn't warm or even watertight. You have a big, ridiculous apartment that was *meant* to be empty for at least the next week, and which even when you're here has more available square footage than most de-tached family homes.'

Nic opened his mouth to argue, but Kate held up a hand, cutting him off.

'You, Mr Humanitarian, having spent the last de-cade saving the world one child factory worker at a time, have the opportunity to practise what you preach here. Charity begins at home, you know.'

Lily rolled her eyes at the cliché, and from the cor-ner of her eye caught just the hint of a smirk starting at the corner of Nic's lips. When she built up the courage to look at him straight she saw that the tension had dropped from his face and he was smiling openly at his sister.

'Oh, you're good,' he said. '*Very* good. I hope they're paying you well.'

'And I'm worth every penny,' she confirmed. 'Now, seeing as you're home, I don't want to step on any toes.' She thrust the screwdriver into his hand and Nic had no choice but to take it. 'I'll leave you two to work out the details.'

And before Lily could pick up her jaw from the floor Kate had disappeared out of the front door, leaving her holding the baby and Nic staring at the screwdriver.

'I'm *so* sorry,' she said, rushing to put Rosie down in her pram and take the screwdriver from Nic's hand. 'She told me that you'd okayed it, but I should have guessed...I'll pack our stuff up and order a cab and we'll be out of your hair.'

Nic gave her a long look, and she watched, fascinated, as emotions chased over his face, first creasing his forehead and his eyes, then smoothing across his cheeks with something like resignation.

'Where will you go?'

'Oh...' Lily flapped a hand, hoping that the distraction would cover the fact that she didn't have a clue what her next move was. 'Back to mine, of course. It's not that bad. I'm sure I can come up with another plan.'

Nic rubbed his hand across his forehead.

'What plan?'

'A hotel,' Lily said, improvising wildly. 'Maybe a temporary rental.'

He let out a long sigh and shook his head slowly.

'Stay here.'

'Nic, I couldn't—'

Lily started to speak, but Nic's raised hand stopped her.

'Kate's right. You need a place to stay. I have loads of room here.'

A warm flood of relief passed through Lily. For a moment she'd thought that she might be out on the streets—worse, that she wouldn't be able to provide Rosie with the home she so desperately needed. And it was the thought that Rosie needed somewhere safe to stay that had her swallowing her pride and nodding to agree with what was almost certainly a terrible idea.

'Thank you. I promise we'll keep out of your way.'

Lily stood in the kitchen, coffee cup in hand, surveying the vast array of knobs and buttons on the espresso machine built into the kitchen wall. She'd already boiled the kettle, intimidated by the levers and chrome of the machine, but in the absence of a jar of good old instant coffee she was going to have to do battle with this beast. She tried the sleek-looking knob on the left— and jumped back from the torrent of steam that leapt from the nozzle hidden beneath. Thank God she'd left Rosie safely sleeping in their room.

A lightly haired forearm appeared over her shoulder and turned off the knob, shutting down the steam and leaving her red-faced and perspiring.

'Here,' Nic said, taking the cup from her hand. 'Let me.'

'Thanks.' Lily handed over coffee responsibility gratefully, and leaned back against the kitchen counter.

Embarrassment sat in the air between them, and Lily's mind couldn't help but fly back to that kiss in the hospital. The way that Nic's lips had pressed so firmly against hers, as if he was fighting himself even as he was kissing her. He'd known that it was a bad idea at the time—she was sure of that. And yet he'd done it anyway. Now they were living together—and apparently they were just going to ignore that it had happened. But even with them saying nothing, it was there, in the atmosphere between them, making them awkward with each other.

She wondered whether she should say something, try and clear the air, but then she heard a cry from the bedroom.

'You go and get Rosie. I'll sort the coffee.'

Was that an invitation? Were they going to sit down and drink a cup of coffee like civilised adults? And if they did would he bring up the kiss? Would she? Surely they couldn't just carry on as if nothing had happened. It was making her clumsy around him, and she could never feel relaxed or at home unless they both loosened up. Maybe that was what he was hoping for. That he'd be able to make things awkward enough that she'd have no choice but to leave. Then he'd get his apartment back without having to be the big bad wolf in the story.

Lily had returned to the kitchen with the baby in one arm, and set about making up a bottle for her. Nic watched them carefully, knowing that a gentleman would offer to help, but finding himself not quite able to live up to that ideal.

'It's good we've got a chance to sit down and talk,' he said as he carried their coffees over to the kitchen island. 'I wanted to apologise for the other day. The…

the kiss. And the way I left things. I know I was a bit abrupt.'

'It's fine—' Lily started, but he held up a hand to stop her.

The memory of the confusion on her face had been haunting him, and he knew that if they were to live together, even if it was only temporarily, he had to make sure she knew exactly why that kiss had been such a mistake. Why she shouldn't hope for or expect another.

They had only known each other for a few days, but after that parting shot at the hospital he wouldn't be able to blame her if she'd misinterpreted things—if she'd read more into that kiss than he'd ever wanted to give. She deserved better than that…better than a man with his limitations. And with Rosie in her life she was going to have to demand more. Demand someone who would support her family life whatever happened. He'd already been tested on that front and found wanting. It was only fair that Lily knew where they both stood.

'Please,' he continued, 'I want to explain.'

A line appeared between her brows, as if she had suddenly realised that this was a conversation neither of them would enjoy. The suggestion that she was hurt pained him physically, but he forced himself to continue—for both their sakes.

'There's no need to explain anything, but I'll listen if you want me to.'

She glanced over at the counter, her edginess showing in the way she was fidgeting with her coffee cup. The anxious expression on her face told him so much. She'd guessed something of his history. Guessed, at least, how hard it was for him to be around Rosie. Had she seen how impossible it would be for them even to be friends?

Not that *friends* would ever have really worked, he mused, when the sight of her running a hand through her hair made him desperate to reach across and see if it felt as silky as it looked. When he'd lain awake every night since they'd last met remembering the feel of her lips under his, imagining the softness of her skin and the suppleness of her body.

He kept his eyes on Lily, never dropping them to the little girl in her arms, not risking the pain that would assault him if he even glanced at Rosie or acknowledged that she was there. The way Lily looked at him, her clear blue gaze, gave him no room to lie or evade. He knew that faced with that open, honest look he'd be able to speak nothing but the truth.

'There's something I need to tell you…' he started.

His voice held the hint of a croak, and he felt the cold climbing his chest, wondered how on earth he was meant to get these words out. How he was meant to relive the darkest days of his life with this woman who a week ago had been a stranger.

'I know there's something between us—at least I know that I've started to feel something for you. But I need you to know that I won't act again on what I feel.'

He kept his voice deliberately flat, forcing the emotion from it as he'd had to do when faced with people living and working in inhuman conditions. And he looked down at the table, unable to bear her sympathetic scrutiny. Or what if he had read this wrong— what if there was nothing between them at all? What if he'd imagined the chemistry that kept drawing them together even as it hurt him? It wasn't as if he'd even given her a chance to return his kiss. He risked a glance up at her. Her lip was caught between her teeth and the line had reappeared on her forehead. But he wasn't sure what he was seeing on her face. Not clear disappointment. Definitely not surprise.

'It's fine, Nic. You don't need to say any more.'

'I do.'

He wanted her to know, wanted to acknowledge his feelings even if just this once. Wanted her to understand that it was nothing about *her* that was holding him back. And he wanted her to understand him in a way that he'd never wanted before. He'd never opened up and talked about what had happened. But now he had been faced with the consequences of the choices he'd made so many years ago he wanted to acknowledge what he had felt, what he felt now.

'I want to explain. For you to understand. Look, it's not you, Lily.' He cringed when he heard for himself how clichéd that sounded. 'It's…it's Rosie. It's the way that you look at her. I won't ever have children, Lily. And I know that I cannot be in a relationship—any relationship—because of that.'

'Nic, we barely know each other. Don't you think that you're being—?'

He was thinking too far ahead. Of course he was. But if he didn't put an end to this now he wasn't sure how or if he ever could. What he had to say needed to be said out loud. He needed to hear it to make sure that he could never go back, never find himself getting closer to Lily and unable to get away.

'Maybe. Maybe I'm jumping to a million different conclusions here, and maybe I've got this all wrong. But the thing is, Lily, I'm never going to want to have children. Ever. And I don't think it would be right for me to leave you in any doubt about that, given your current situation.'

He allowed himself a quick look down at Rosie, and the painful clench of his heart at the sight of her round cheeks and intense concentration reminded him that he was doing the right thing. It was easier to say that it was because of the baby. Of course that was a big part of it. But there was more—there were things that he couldn't say. Things that he had been ashamed of for so long that he wasn't sure he could even bear to think of them properly, never mind share them with someone else.

'Well, thanks for telling me.'

She was fiddling with her coffee cup again, stirring it rapidly, sloshing some of the rich dark liquid over the side. He'd offended her—and what else did he expect, just telling half the story? All he'd basically done so far was break up with a woman he wasn't even dating.

'Lily, I'm sorry I'm not making much sense. It's just hard for me to talk about… The reason I don't want children…I was a father once. I lost my son, and it broke my heart, and I know that I can never put myself at risk of going through that again.'

And if she was going to take this gamble, raise her sister's child with no idea of what the future held, then she needed someone in her life she could rely on. Someone who would support her with whatever she needed. Who wouldn't let her down. He hadn't been able to do that when Max had died, hadn't been the man his partner had needed, and he'd lost his girlfriend as well as his son.

A hush fell between them and Nic realised he

had raised his voice until it was almost a shout. Lily dropped the bottle and Rosie gave a mew of discontent. But Nic's eyes were all on Lily, watching her face as she realised what he had said, as the significance of his words sank in.

She reached out and touched his hand. He should have flinched away. It was the reason he had told her everything, after all. But he couldn't. He turned his hand and grabbed hold of hers, anchoring himself to the present, saving himself from drowning in memories.

Now that he had told her, surely the danger was over. Now she would be as wary of these feelings as he was. He just wanted to finish this conversation—make sure that she knew that this wasn't personal, it wasn't about her. If Rosie had never turned up...if he'd never had a son... But there was no point thinking that way. No point in what-ifs and maybes.

'Nic, I'm so sorry. I don't know what to say, but I'd like to hear more about your son. If you want to talk about it.'

He breathed out a long sigh, his forehead pressed into the heels of his hands, but then he looked up to meet her gaze and she could see the pain, the loss, the confusion in his eyes.

'It won't change anything.'

She reached for his hand again, offering comfort, nothing more—however much she might want to.

'I know, but if you want to talk then I'd like to listen.'

He stared at the counter a little longer, until eventually, with a slight shake of his head, he started to speak.

'I was nineteen and naïve when I met this girl—

Clare—at a university party. We hit it off, and soon we were living in each other's pockets, spending all our time together. We were both in our first year, neither of us thinking about the future. We were having fun, and I thought I was falling in love with her.'

Lily was shocked at the strength of her jealousy over something that had happened a decade ago, and fought down the hint of nausea that his tale had provoked.

'Well, we were young and silly and in love, and we took risks that we shouldn't have.'

It didn't take a genius to see where this was going but, knowing that the story had a tragic end, Lily felt a pall of dread as she waited for Nic's next words.

'When Clare told me she was pregnant I was shocked. I mean, a few months beforehand we'd been living with our parents, and now we were going to be parents ourselves… But as the shock wore off we got more and more excited—'

His voice finally broke, and Lily couldn't help squeezing his hand. There was nothing sexual in it. Nothing romantic. All she wanted was to offer comfort, hope.

'By the time the baby was due we'd moved in together, even started to talk about getting married. So there I was: nineteen, as good as engaged, and with a baby on the way.'

His eyes widened and his jaw slackened, as if he couldn't understand how he had got from there to here—how the life that still lit up his face when he described it had disintegrated.

'The day Max was born was the best of my life. As soon as I held him in my arms I knew that I loved him. Everyone tells you that happens, but you never believe them until you experience it. He was so perfect, this tiny human being. For three weeks we were the perfect little family. I washed him, changed his nappies, fed him, just sat there and breathed in his smell and watched him sleep. I've never been so intoxicated by another person. Never held anything so precious in my arms.'

His face should have glowed at that. He should have radiated happiness, talking about the very happiest time of his life. But already the demons were incoming, cracking his voice and lining his face, and Lily held her breath, bracing herself.

'When he was three weeks old we woke one day to sunlight streaming into the bedroom and instantly knew that something was wrong. He'd not woken for his early feed. And when I went to his crib…'

He didn't have to say it. All of a sudden Lily wished that he wouldn't, that he would spare her this. But *he* hadn't been spared; *he* hadn't been shown mercy. He'd had his heart broken, his life torn apart in the most painful way imaginable. She couldn't make herself want to share that pain with him, but she wanted to help ease it if she could. She'd do just about anything to lift that blanket of despair from his face.

'He was gone. Already cold. I picked him up and shouted for Clare, held him in my arms until the ambulance arrived, but it was no good. Nothing I could have done would have helped him. They all told me that. They told me that for days and weeks afterwards. Until they started to forget. Or maybe they thought that *I* was forgetting. But I haven't, Lily.'

For the first time since he'd started speaking he

looked up and met her gaze head-on. There was solid determination there.

'I can never forget. And when I see Rosie…'

It all became clear: the way he turned away from the baby, the way he flinched if he had to interact with her, the stricken look on his face the one time he'd had to hold her. Seeing Rosie—seeing any baby—brought him unimaginable pain. There could be no children in his future, no family. And so she completely understood why it was he was fighting this attraction. Why he pushed away from their chemistry, trying to protect himself. Knowing that there could never be anything between them didn't make it easier, though. The finality of it hurt.

But there was one part of the story he hadn't finished.

'And…Clare?'

He dropped his head back into his hands and she knew that he was hiding tears. It was a couple of minutes before he could speak again.

'We were broken,' he said simply. 'We tried for a while. But whatever it was that had brought us together—it died with our baby. She needed… I couldn't…I saw her a couple of years ago, actually, in the supermarket, of all places, by the baked beans. We exchanged polite hellos, because what else could we say: *Remember when we lost our son and our world fell apart and could never be put back together? Remember when you needed me to be there for you, to help you through your grief, and I couldn't do it?*'

Lily choked back a sob. She couldn't imagine, never *wanted* to imagine, what this man had been through. She wanted to reach out and comfort him, to do anything she could to take his pain away, but she knew there was nothing to be done. Nothing that could undo what had happened, undo his pain. All she could do was be there for him, if that was what he wanted.

But it wasn't.

'So now you know why getting close to Rosie scares me—why getting close to you both can never happen. I can't go through that pain again, Lily. Just the idea of it terrifies me. How could I cope with another loss like that?'

Lily didn't have the answer to any of it. Of course she could say that the chances of it happening again were slim, but she couldn't promise it. No one could. And how could she blame him for wanting to spare himself that?

She didn't say anything when Nic stood from the table, only reached out a hand and rested it gently on his arm.

'Thank you,' she said. 'For everything. And I wish you all the best, Nic, I really do. I hope you can be happy again some day.'

CHAPTER FIVE

THREE WEEKS AFTER her sister had dropped her little surprise off on her doorstep Lily still hadn't heard anything from her. Social services seemed happy that Lily was being well cared for by her aunt, and were trawling through the appropriate paperwork. To begin with she'd thought it must be temporary, that one of these days Helen would call and ask for her daughter back. But so far—nothing.

And barely a word from Nic, either. Not that she had expected much after the way things had been left, but it was strange living with someone who could barely say more than good morning to her. A part of her had hoped, she supposed, that he might rethink things. That he might think that she—they—were worth taking a risk on. And then she remembered the look on his face when he told her about losing his son and knew that it couldn't happen. Knew that he wouldn't risk feeling like that again.

She lifted her head from the pillow and looked over at Rosie, still tucked in her crib, fast asleep again after her six o'clock feed. Lily listened to her breaths, to the steady whoosh of air moving in and out of her lungs. Rosie was the same age now as Nic's son had been when he died. After three weeks together, Lily could no longer imagine life without Rosie—couldn't imagine the pain of being torn from her.

So what would happen if Helen wanted her back? How could she keep mother and daughter apart, knowing how much it hurt to want a family and have them disappear from your life?

She collapsed back into her pillows and threw her arms over her face, blocking out the world, fed up with the circles her mind was spinning her in. She wanted to make sure that Helen was well and happy, but would that mean handing Rosie over? Accepting the fact that Helen might take off again, leaving her missing Rosie as she missed the rest of her family?

Much as she had tried to remember that she wasn't Rosie's mother, somewhere the line had become blurred. Because Helen hadn't just nipped to the shops, and Lily wasn't just being a helpful aunt: she was almost her legal guardian. It was Helen who had blurred this line, and Lily wasn't sure how she would cope if she suddenly turned everything on its head.

Thoughts still racing around her mind, she swung her legs out of bed and reached for her dressing gown. She'd learnt that if Rosie was sleeping she'd better shut her eyes, too, but this morning that was a luxury she couldn't afford. She had managed to put off a couple of her deadlines when she'd told her clients what had happened—sparing them most of the details—but she couldn't put them off for ever.

She had beta designs for two sites to finish, and while Rosie was sleeping she couldn't justify not working. Then there was the fact that she'd not bothered with the dishes last night, the fridge was looking decidedly bare, and when Rosie woke up she'd want milk, clean clothes and a clean nappy. The round of chores was endless, even with Nic's generosity, and she sometimes felt she'd been walking through fog since Rosie had arrived. A joyful fog, obviously, but an endlessly draining one, too.

She padded into the kitchen and hit the button on the kettle—still too foggy to attempt espresso—knowing that she needed coffee this morning, and wondering how breastfeeding mums coped with the newborn stage without caffeine. She felt as if she was flailing, barely keeping her head above water, and she wasn't even recovering from giving birth.

Over the rumbling of the kettle coming to the boil she heard her mobile ringing in the bedroom and ran to get it, hoping that she could reach it and hit 'silence' before it woke the baby.

When she got to it Rosie was already mewling quietly, and Lily scooped her up quickly before swiping to answer her phone.

'Hello?' she said, as quietly as possible, rocking Rosie in the vain hope that she'd decide to go back to sleep.

When her social worker told her the news she couldn't think of an answer. *Why* couldn't she think of an answer? So many times these past weeks she'd wondered how her sister was, whether she'd ever be ready to be part of a family again, and now here was the proof that she might want that one day. She wanted to see Lily—and her daughter—that morning.

'Okay,' she told the social worker eventually. 'I'll bring Rosie to her.'

As soon as she ended the call tears were threatening behind her eyes. Irrational tears? she wondered. Through the sleep deprivation she was finding it hard to remember what was reasonable and what wasn't. She needed Kate and her no-nonsense way of seeing the world, her way of cutting through the mess and making the world simple.

She dialled her number and waited, rocking slightly on the bed. 'Come on, pick up…pick up…' She walked back through to the kitchen as the ringing continued on the other end of the phone. 'Come on, Kate. *Please* pick up…'

'Everything okay?'

Not Kate. At the sound of Nic's voice she spun around and the tears started in earnest, though she couldn't rationalise why. Too much family drama. Too little sleep.

'Any idea where your sister is?'

'Not sure,' he told her, and she could hear concern for her in his voice. 'But I know that the Jackson case is coming to trial this week. My guess would be chambers or court. Is everything okay? Rosie?'

'She's fine,' Lily told him, though she couldn't stop the tears.

She still clutched Rosie tight against her, her every instinct telling her that she must protect the baby at all costs. But protecting her didn't mean keeping her from her own mother, if seeing her was what she wanted.

'Look, I've got to go out, but please can you find Kate and tell her to meet me at the Sanctuary Clinic as soon as possible?'

He paced the corridor of the clinic, asking himself for the thousandth time what he was doing there. The sense of déjà vu was almost overwhelming. It had been only a couple of weeks ago that he'd paced a similar corridor, asking himself a similar question.

Lily.

She had been the reason then, and she was the reason now. Her voice, so quiet and shocked, but filled with a fierce protectiveness for Rosie. *Find Kate*, she'd said.

But he hadn't been able to. When Kate was embroiled in a case there was no telling when she might emerge for sunlight and fresh air. All she could see was her duty to her client. Just as impossible as getting his sister on the phone was the thought of leaving Lily alone. She'd been so stoic, but he had heard the vulnerability in her voice and been unable to ignore it. The way she'd sounded—those intriguing layers of vulnerability and strength—had made him want to be here for her, *with* her. She could do this on her own, he had no doubt of that, but that didn't mean he wanted her to have to.

He was just relieved for now that Lily's sister was safe and well—he knew how much Lily had worried about her, how much she'd hoped to have her back in her life.

Lily emerged from the bathroom with Rosie smelling fresh, but there was a fearful look on her face. When they were halfway down the corridor, without thinking, he wrapped an arm around her. Holding her close to him, he could feel her body trembling.

'Here—' he gestured to some seats set against the wall '—do you want to sit for a minute? Get your breath? Helen's not going anywhere, and nor is Rosie.'

She sat in a chair and he pulled his arm back, suddenly self-conscious, aware of the line that he had crossed.

'Do you want to talk about it?'

Lily shook her head, but spoke anyway.

'Helen's been staying here since she left Rosie with me. She's not wanted to see us before now, but she's decided she's ready.'

'And you and Rosie—are *you* ready?'

She sat silent for a long moment. 'She's my sister. She's Rosie's mum. She's family. I don't want to lose her.'

'But you're the one making decisions for Rosie. Helen asked you to do that. If you're not ready...'

'*I'm* ready,' she said, with sudden steely determination. 'But I want to see Helen alone first, before I decide whether I'm ready for her to meet Rosie. I can't get hold of Kate and there's no one else. I know that I shouldn't ask. That after everything we've spoken about—'

'It's fine.' The words surprised him. He'd been all too ready to agree that she shouldn't ask, that it *was* too much, that he couldn't... But he'd looked down at Rosie, and he'd looked up at her aunt, and he'd known that this family had touched him. That Lily had touched him. And that much as he wanted to pretend he had never met them, that was impossible now.

It had been impossible from the moment he'd found Lily on her doorstep, babe in arms and already with a fierce determination to protect. It had been impossible when he'd laid out the hardest and most painful parts of his past, hoping that it would scare her off, hoping that the pain the conversation dredged up would be enough to scare *him* off. But it hadn't. He'd spent all that time questioning what he'd done. Wondering how he was going to live life full of the regret that he felt when he thought of Lily. Wondering if he could be brave enough to try and live another way.

And when he had reached out just now and taken her in his arms he'd had his answer. He didn't have a choice. The feelings he had for Lily weren't going to go away. Trying to convince her—convince himself—that they shouldn't do this hadn't made the pain less. It had made it worse. Walking away from Lily would leave another hole in a life that was already too empty.

'I'll watch her for you.'

'Are you sure?'

Her disbelief was written plainly on her face, and when he nodded he thought he saw a flash of hope there, of anticipation. He smiled in response—they had a lot to talk about later.

'We'll be fine. Your sister needs you now.'

Lily hesitated outside the door. She'd waited patiently for her sister to be ready, hoping every day that she would come back into their lives, but feeling terrified at the same time that she might ask for Rosie back, take her away. And then Lily would have lost a niece—almost a daughter—as well as her sister.

She took a deep breath and pushed open the door.

At the sight of her sister in the bed, pale and skinny, all her fears left her. As long as they were all safe and well, the rest of it didn't matter. She'd hoped so many times that she'd have a chance to reconnect with Helen. She couldn't be anything but pleased that she had somehow found her way back again.

'Lily?'

Lily hadn't realised that Helen was awake, but she reached out a hand to her with tears in her eyes.

'I'm so happy to see you,' she told her.

Helen sniffed, her expression cautious. 'I thought you might be angry.'

'I'm not angry—I've been so worried. I'm just glad that you're okay.'

'But what I did…'

'We don't need to talk about that now. The most important thing is to get you well again. Everything else we can talk about later.'

A tear slipped from the corner of Helen's eye and Lily wiped it away with a gentle swipe of her thumb.

'I knew that I couldn't look after her,' Helen went on, her tears picking up pace.

And even though Lily hushed her, told her that they didn't have to talk about it now, she carried on as if the words were backed up behind a failing dam and nothing could stop them surging forward.

'The house that I was living in—it wasn't safe. Not for me or her. And I couldn't think of another way, Lily. I knew that she'd be better off with you.'

'You did the right thing,' Lily reassured her. 'And your daughter's fine. She's doing really well.'

At that the dam finally broke, and Helen's face was drowned in tears.

'I…was…so…scared.' She choked the words out between sobs. 'After I left her with you I realised I couldn't go back to where I had been living, but I couldn't come home to you, either.'

'That's not true, Helen. You can come home any time. The house is yours just as much as it is mine. And I know that we both want what's best for Rosie.'

'Rosie?'

Lily gulped. She hadn't meant to use her name, knowing that she'd taken something of a liberty by choosing one in the first place. But there had been no one else to do it.

'If you don't like it...'

'No, it's perfect. I love it.' Helen's tears slowed. 'It just goes to show that I was right. You're the right person to look after her, Lily. I know that the way I did it wasn't right—just dumping her and running—but I didn't make a mistake. I can't be the one to raise her.'

Lily took a deep breath, feeling the thinness of the ice beneath her feet, knowing that one misstep could ruin her relationship with her sister for ever, could lose her Rosie.

'You've not been well,' she said gently. 'And you don't need to make big decisions right now or all at once. There'll be plenty of time to talk about this.'

Helen nodded, her features peaceful for the first time since Lily had arrived. 'I want to be part of her life—and yours, too, if you'll still have me. But I'm not going to change my mind. You're the best person to look after Rosie. I'm not ready to be a mother, Lily. I might never be. I'm not going to change my mind about this.'

Lily just squeezed her hand, lost for words.

'And maybe I will want to come home one day—but not yet, Lily. I can't do that until I'm really properly well, and that's going to take me some time.'

'I could—'

'I know you want to do everything for us, Lily. But you're already doing so much. I have to get better on my own, and I need space to do that.'

Space? How much space did she need? She'd given her nothing *but* space for years, and where had that got her? Living somewhere she didn't feel safe with a baby she couldn't care for.

'Will you do it? Will you take care of Rosie.'

There had never been any question about that.

'Of course I will. She's here, you know. If you'd like to see her.'

Pain crossed Helen's features for a moment. 'I thought I was ready, but…I'm not, Lily. It would hurt too much to see her. So what do you say? I'm not talking about a few weeks or months, Lily. I need to know that she'll be safe for *ever*. That I can concentrate on getting well without the pressure of… I know it's selfish.'

It wasn't. It might have been the most self*less* thing Lily had ever heard. Because the yearning and the love in Helen's face was clear. She hadn't abandoned Rosie because she was an inconvenience, or too much hard work, or because she cried too much. She'd done it because she loved her. She'd broken her own heart in order to give her child the best start in life, and Lily couldn't judge her for that.

'It's not selfish. And of course I'll take care of Rosie.' Her voice was choked as she said the words. 'I love her, Helen. You don't have to worry. I'll keep her safe.'

Some of the tension left Helen's body, and Lily could tell that she needed some of that space she'd been talking about.

She gave her hand another squeeze. 'I'll come back and visit again when you're ready. Rest now.'

'Thanks, sis,' Helen said, drifting off. 'You were always going to be an amazing mum.'

Back in the corridor, Lily leaned her forehead against the wall and took a couple of deep breaths, wanting to compose herself before she saw Rosie, not wanting her to sense that she had been upset.

She glanced down the corridor and saw that she was no longer in her car seat but on Nic's knee, being fed from a bottle. Lily couldn't help but smile. While she had been talking to her sister she'd almost forgotten that Nic had stayed, and the look on his face when she'd asked him to watch Rosie even though she'd known that she shouldn't. But the fear and the panic that she'd been expecting to see there hadn't emerged. Instead there had been something different, something new, and it had given her hope.

Now, seeing him holding the baby, she wondered what this meant. After everything that he'd said to her back at his flat, the harrowing story of his loss, she'd thought they'd said all that needed to be said about their feelings, their future. But here he was.

'Thank you so much for this,' she said as she reached the chairs and sat beside him. 'I can take her if you want.'

'She's fine. Let her finish her bottle.'

His words suggested that he was comfortable, but his body language was telling a different story. He was sitting bolt upright on the plastic chair, his shoulders and arms completely stiff. Rosie was more perched on him than snuggled against him, but that hadn't stopped her staring up at him with her big blue gaze locked onto his face as she fed.

I wish I could look at him like that, Lily thought. *With no need to hide what I feel, no need to look away when I realise that he's seen me.* How simple life must seem to Rosie, with no idea of the impact her birth had had on her whole family.

'How was it?' Nic asked her at last.

Lily blew out a breath. 'I don't really know—it's not like I have a lot to compare it to. But okay, I think.'

'That's good…'

'It's good that she wants to get better. But I wish she'd come home, that she'd let me take care of her. It's what I've been hoping for for years. But…'

'But you're worried about what will happen to Rosie if she gets well?'

She nodded, the lump in her throat preventing the words from coming.

'You know I can't tell you for definite what will happen.' The tone of his voice was soft and measured. 'But everyone involved will want what's best for Rosie.'

She nodded, still not trusting herself to speak.

At the beginning she had genuinely believed, when she'd said she would look after Rosie, that she was only taking care of her temporarily, until Helen was back and better. Now she couldn't imagine watching someone else sing her to sleep, someone else comfort her when she was upset. She was a little jealous just watching Nic giving her a bottle.

'So, are you heading home?' he asked when Rosie had finished.

'I thought I might walk through the park first, as the sun's out. I think me and Rosie need some fresh air. The smell of hospitals…'

'I'll walk with you, if that's okay?'

CHAPTER SIX

WALKING THROUGH THE PARK, just the three of them, Nic couldn't shake the feeling that he had wandered into someone else's life. To anyone else they would look like a family—a loving husband and wife, perhaps—taking a stroll with their baby, talking together, making plans for the future. This had been his life once, and it had left him so scarred that he had sworn he would never let himself come close to it again.

Until he had met Lily and been unable to forget her. And now was the moment he had to decide. It wasn't fair on Lily to keep pushing her away and then changing his mind. If he was going to take this chance, he had to commit to it.

'So...' he started as they exited the park. 'Have you got plans for dinner?'

She looked a little panic-stricken for a second.

'There're a few bits and pieces in the fridge. I was just going to rustle up something simple. Or maybe order something in...'

He could see the doubt in her eyes as she finally looked up at him, and he cursed himself for the confusion he must have caused her over the past days. He was more aware than anyone of how hot and cold he had blown. He wanted to reach out and smooth the lines of concern from her face. Instead he offered an encouraging smile, urging her to take a risk—as he had—and invite him in.

'We could order something together?' she suggested at last.

'I'd love to,' he agreed, opening the gate for her.

Back in the apartment, Nic reached across for another slice of pizza and asked the question that had been nagging at him since they had left the hospital.

'So, did your sister say anything about what her plans are…with Rosie?'

'It's still early days. I don't think she's really in a position to decide anything yet.' Lily took a long drink of her cola. 'But…'

'But?'

'She said that she wants me to take care of Rosie permanently. If I don't want to, or can't, I don't know what will happen. She'll go into care, I suppose.'

'And how do you feel about that?'

'About Rosie going into care?' She fought off a wave of panic and nausea, reminding herself that the social worker had told her that they tried their hardest to keep families together. That Rosie being taken away completely would be a last resort. 'Honestly, the thought of it makes it hard to breathe.'

Nic looked at her closely and she dropped her eyes, not enjoying the depth of his scrutiny, feeling as if he was seeing all too much of her.

'There must be a lot of fantastic foster parents out there. And couples waiting to adopt. All you ever hear on the news is the horror stories, but every type of family has those. I'm sure that Rosie would find a happy home if that's what you and Helen decide is best.'

Lily shook her head, not trusting herself to speak for a moment. After a long breath, she chose her words carefully. 'But she should be with her family. I *have* to look after her.'

'Why do I feel there's more to this story?' Nic asked.

'What do you mean? I just want to take care of my family.'

'It's not all your responsibility.'

He was using his careful voice again, and she read the implication in that loud and clear. He thought she was being irrational, that she needed talking down like some drunk about to lose her temper. Well, if he carried on like this…

'It's okay to admit that maybe sometimes you need help.'

'I don't need help to look after my niece, thank you very much. I'm sorry if that's not what you want to hear. If you were hoping that maybe I'd wake up one day soon unencumbered by a baby. It's not exactly what I had in mind for the next few years, but she's my responsibility and I'm not handing her over to strangers.'

He held his hands palms up and sat back on his stool, surprise showing in his raised eyebrows and baffled expression. 'Whoa! I'm sorry, Lily. That's not what I meant at all. I'm not going to lie and say that Rosie doesn't make things complicated, but I'd never expect you to give her up. I'd never want that.'

'Then what *do* you want? Because I've got to tell you I'm struggling to keep up. The last time we talked you were very clear that I was nothing more to you than a temporary lodger—and not even a very welcome one at that. But now here we are, strolling through the park and sharing dinner. Why?'

She hadn't meant to get mad at him, but he'd already squashed her every romantic and X-rated fantasy, when she'd only just started to realise the feelings she was developing, and it was suddenly all too much. She'd held back before—keeping her feelings at the back of her mind, not questioning his—and she'd had enough. They were both grown-ups. If he was man enough to have these feelings then he'd damn well better be man enough to talk about them.

'Because I can't make myself *not* want this. And I've tried, Lily. I've tried for both of us. Because I'm not the right guy for you. I've tried to keep my distance because I know that this isn't good for either of us—I can't be the person you need me to be. But something keeps throwing us back together and I don't know if I can fight it any more.'

Man enough, then.

Lily froze with a slice of pizza halfway to her mouth. Complete and utter honesty was what she had been hoping for, but really the last thing she'd been expecting. The raw power of his words made her want to move closer and pull away at the same time. He'd just told her that he wasn't sure he was ready. He was taking a big gamble with her feelings and with his, and she wasn't sure that was a game she wanted to play. Had he really thought this through?

'I'm not sure, Nic. I barely have the time or the brain capacity to think beyond the next bottle and nappy-change. I'm not sure that I can even *think* about a relationship. And you know me and Rosie come as a package deal, right? I don't know what's going to happen with Helen in the future. I don't know whether I'll be Rosie's caregiver for the next week, the next month, or the rest of her life. There are no guarantees either way.'

She let out a long, slow breath.

'I'm sorry, but I don't think I can even consider a relationship right now. If you want to be friends, I'd like that.'

He gave her a long, searching look, before sighing. 'Of course. You're right. But friends sounds good. I'd like that.'

'That's exactly what I need.' She offered him a small, tentative smile, feeling her hackles gradually smooth.

'I guess I could take that as a compliment. But how about we leave off over-analysing getting to know each other and change the subject? If we're going to be friends, then talking over pizza and a glass of wine seems like something we should master.'

'Agreed. So, Dominic Johnson, in the spirit of getting to know each other, tell me something about you I don't already know. Please, let's talk about something completely normal for a change.'

She took a bite of her pizza while she waited for him to reply, trying to make her body relax. Instead all it was interested in was Nic—his smell, his nearness, the fact that he was tearing down barriers she'd been counting on for weeks.

'There's not really much to tell.'

His words snapped her attention back, and she listened intently, trying to school her resistant body.

'I grew up with Mum and Dad and Kate in the suburbs of Manchester. Completely unremarkable childhood. Kate and I still get dragged back there regularly for family Sunday lunches.'

'Sounds lovely,' Lily said. She *knew* it was lovely, actually, and had been up there with Kate more than once. 'You're lucky,' she told Nic.

He nodded in agreement. 'How about you?'

Lily took a deep breath, realising too late that of course her question had been bound to lead to this. In wanting to hear something completely unremarkable about his life she'd led them to talking about the most painful parts of hers.

'Uh-uh.' She shook her head as she reached for the last dough ball, wondering how best to deflect his question. 'I'm not done grilling you.'

She thought around for a topic of conversation that wouldn't lead back to her family, and her failure to hold things together at the heart of it.

'How did you start your charity? Why did you decide that you wanted to spend your life improving the conditions of child factory workers? It seems like a bit of a leap the suburbs.'

He smiled softly, obviously resigned to being the subject of her questioning for now.

'It never really seemed like a choice. I travelled after…after Max, and I was horrified by some of the things that I saw. I had nothing to come home to—or that's what it felt like at the time—so I stayed and tried to do something about it.'

'And was it what you expected?'

'It was worse—and better,' he replied. 'I saw things that I wish I could forget, and I saw people's lives saved because of my work. But what I loved most was that it was so all-consuming. It exhausted me physically and mentally. It didn't leave room for me to think about anything else. It was exactly what I needed.'

'And now? Is it still all-consuming?' Because there wasn't room for anyone else in what he'd just described.

'It can be on the days I want it to be,' he said, thoughtfully and with a direct look. 'There've been a few of those lately… But usually, no, it doesn't have to be. That's part of the reason I took the job in London. I knew that I couldn't carry on the way I had been. And I knew that my parents wanted me to be closer to home. I've spent the last ten years trying to change these companies from the outside—I thought trying from the inside might work better.'

She watched him closely, wondering whether she had been part of the reason he'd needed a distraction lately. Or was it just his grief he didn't want to face?

She sat back on her stool and rubbed her belly as Nic eyed the last slice of pizza speculatively. 'I'm done,' she declared. 'It's all yours.'

They fell into an easy silence as Nic ate, and Lily smiled up at him, feeling suddenly shy, and also shattered. Rosie's feeds through the night and her early starts were catching up with her, and much as she was loath to admit it suddenly all she could think about was her duvet, her pillow, and the fact that Rosie would be awake and hungry almost before she managed to get to them.

For half a second she thought about Nic being under that duvet with her, about seeing his head on the pillow when she woke in the morning.

Something of her thoughts must have shown on her face, because Nic raised an eyebrow.

'What?' he asked. 'What did I miss?'

'Nothing!' Lily declared, far too earnestly. 'Nothing...'

'Something,' Nic stated, watching her carefully. 'But if you don't want to share that's fine.'

'Good. Because your reverse psychology doesn't work on me.'

Nic laughed. 'Busted. I want to know what you were thinking!'

'And I'm not going to tell.'

He looked triumphant at that. 'Well, then, I'll choose to interpret that look however I want to, and there's nothing you can do about it.'

Lily shook her head, laughing. 'Right, that's enough.' She stood good-naturedly, clearing away the pizza box and their glasses. 'I'm going to bed.'

He walked through to the hall with her, and she hesitated outside her door.

'This was nice,' she said eventually, feeling suddenly nervous, unable to articulate anything more than that blatant understatement.

He grinned, though, his smile lighting his whole face. Maybe he'd heard all the things she hadn't said.

'I'm glad we talked.'

So he could do understatement too. On purpose? Or was he feeling awkward as well?

Lily reached for the door handle, but as her hand touched cold metal warm skin brushed her cheek, and she drew in a breath of surprise. Nic nudged her to look up at him as he took a step closer. The heat of his body seemed to jump the space between them, urging her closer, flushing her skin. She looked up and met his gaze. His eyes swam with a myriad of emotions.

Desire, need, relief, hope… All were reflected in her own heart. But they couldn't have timed this worse. She'd meant what she said earlier. Friendship was all she had space for in her life.

She closed her eyes as she stretched up on tiptoe and let her lips brush against his cheek. Soft skin rasped against sharp stubble and for a moment she rested her cheek against his, breathing in his smell, reminding herself that even if she did drag him inside to her bed she'd be snoring before he even got his shirt off.

Nic's other hand found the small of her back and pressed her gently to him, appreciative rather than demanding. She let out a long sigh as she dropped her forehead to his shoulder, and then finally turned the door handle.

'Goodnight…?'

There was still the hint of a question in Nic's farewell, and she smiled.

'Goodnight.'

CHAPTER SEVEN

HE BARELY HAD a foot through the front door when Lily flew past him. Shirtless and running.

'Everything okay?' he called to her retreating back, knowing that he should drag his eyes away from the curve of her waist and the smoothness of her skin, but finding that his moral compass wasn't as refined as he'd always hoped. There was something about the way the light played on her skin, the way it seemed to glow, to luminesce…

'I'm sorry,' she called over her shoulder as she ran into her bedroom. 'Spectacular timing. I'll be right out.'

Rosie was in a bouncy chair in the kitchen, wearing most of her last bottle, he guessed, and had clearly been hastily and inadequately mopped up by the kitchen roll on the counter. Lily turned suddenly and he threw his gaze away—anywhere but at her. His mind was filled by the image of her bare skin, the sweep of her shoulder, the curve of her…

No. To ogle a shoulder was one thing, but there were lines he shouldn't cross.

Instead he went into the kitchen and looked at Rosie and at the dribble of milk trickling down her chin. With

mock exasperation he grabbed a muslin square and
started mopping. He kept it objective, detached. There
was no need to pick her up, but it wasn't really fair to
leave her damp and uncomfortable, either. If he was
going to be spending more time with Lily, he couldn't
ignore Rosie completely.

Lily emerged a moment later, pulling down a T-shirt
to cover that last inch of pale flesh above her jeans.

'Thanks for doing that. I started, but I seemed to be
getting messier from trying to clean her up. Seemed
one of us should be clean, at least.'

'It's no problem,' he said, holding out the muslin,
handing back responsibility. His eyes were fixed just
above her T-shirt, where shoulder met collarbone and
collarbone met the soft skin of her neck.

And then it was hidden behind Rosie's soft-haired
head and he was forced to look away again. He wondered how he could pinch Rosie's spot, how he could
get his lips behind Lily's ear, breathe in her smell as
Rosie was doing.

For another whole week, while he'd been putting
in fourteen-hour days at the office, all he'd had to remember was that brief kiss on the cheek, the press of
her soft warm skin against his, the fruity scent of her
shampoo and the heat that had travelled from her body
to his without them even touching. The long nights
had been filled with plans he knew would never be
fulfilled: for picking up where that kiss had left off,
for having her cheek against his again, but this time
turning her, finding her mouth with his, scooping her
up in his arms and heading straight for her bedroom,
or the couch, or the kitchen table…

'I'm so sorry. I know I said I'd cook tonight, but

I haven't got started on dinner yet,' she said, bouncing Rosie and trying to snatch up tissues and muslins from the kitchen counter and shuffling dirty pots from the breakfast bar. 'I just don't know what happens to the hours.'

Rosie was showing no sign of settling, so he grabbed ingredients from the fridge and tried to fire his imagination.

'You don't have to do that,' she told him, still bouncing and rocking. 'I'll be on it in just a minute.'

'Don't worry—let me,' he insisted. 'I like to cook.'

She looked up at him in surprise. 'Hidden depths?'

He took a few steps closer to her, pulled the muslin from her hand and stopped her rocking for just a minute. For the first time since that too-brief kiss on the cheek she met his eyes, and he relaxed into her gaze.

'There's a lot you don't know.'

She wanted to find out, she realised. She wanted his secrets.

'I'm pretty sure that you'd rather not arrive home to a strange woman in your apartment, baby spit-up, no sign of dinner, and—'

'It's not so bad,' he said with a grin.

It was true, he realised as he spoke. And he wanted her any way she came—baby spit-up and all. Because for this scene to be any different, *she* would have to be different. *Not* the sort of woman who took in a vulnerable child. *Not* the sort of woman who put feeding that child before her own appearance. He wanted her just as she was.

He looked down at the top of Rosie's head, at the way she was nuzzling against Lily's shoulder, the way she'd started to snuffle again since he'd stopped

Lily moving. If he wanted her to be that woman, if he wanted to be *with* that woman, then he was going to have to learn to be patient. If these few weeks had taught him anything, it was how to wait for Lily.

'She needs you,' he said. 'I'll look after dinner. And then, when she's sleeping, we can…'

She looked up again, this time with a blush and a smile.

'We can eat. And talk.'

The smile spread into a grin—and a knowing one at that.

He started chopping an onion, and had to bat away Lily's one-handed attempts to help. Ten minutes later he had a sauce bubbling on the stove, and had to snatch the wooden spoon from Lily's hand as she attempted to stir it.

'Did you never hear the one about too many cooks? Out.' He threatened her clean T-shirt with the sauce-covered spoon until he could close the door behind her.

Finally, after she'd popped her head around the door twice, just to 'check' there was nothing she could do, they had Rosie asleep in her Moses basket and dinner on the table. Conversation flowed easily between them as he shared stories of his client meetings, and told her about his plans for the new product lines he'd like to stock. They talked about what she'd been up to, but she managed to deflect most of his questions.

He wondered how much of it was her trying to protect him, shielding him from Rosie because she knew the baby caused him pain.

He couldn't remember which of them had suggested watching a movie, but now, in the dark, sharing a couch with her, he wanted to curse whoever it had been.

He felt like a teenager again. Even their choice of a comedy, hoping to steer clear of the romantic, seemed hopelessly naïve. And, like the awkward fifteen-year-old he vaguely remembered being once, he was thinking tactics. How to break their silence and separation? Trying to guess whether she was watching the film or if—like his—her line of thought was on something rather different.

They had agreed to be just friends, but his week of long days in the office—giving her the space she needed—had proved to him that keeping his feelings friendly was going to be anything but easy. Especially knowing that she was attracted to him too. She hadn't denied that before, after all. Only said that the timing wasn't right. Well, when was it *ever* right? Had she missed him, too, this week? Rethought their very grown-up and very gruelling decision to keep things platonic?

As he glanced across at her Lily turned to him, lips parted and words clearly on the tip of her tongue.

'I was just going to…to get a drink. Do you want anything from the kitchen?'

Her cheeks were rosy again, and he wondered if that was really what she had planned on saying. But most importantly she'd hit 'pause' on the movie, broken the stalemate. He watched her retreat to the kitchen and relaxed back into the cushions of the sofa. How was he meant to make it through the rest of this movie? It was torture. Pure torture. She *must* be feeling this tension as much as he was. Was she as intrigued by the attraction between them as he?

She emerged from the kitchen with a couple of glasses, balancing a plate of cakes. She'd pulled her hair back, exposing even more of the soft skin of her neck, and it took every ounce of his self-control not to sneak his arm along the back of the sofa until his hand found it, touched it. He knew that if he did his whole experience of the world would be reduced to the very tips of his fingers, and he'd be able to think about nothing other than how much he wanted her.

Her face was turned up to his, and when he breathed in it was all *her*, fruity and fresh. She smiled, and the sight of it filled him with resolve. She didn't want more than this. He would never be everything she needed in a partner, a husband. They were doing the right thing.

But when he closed his eyes he imagined her hand on his jaw, pulling him close, her tongue teasing, him opening his mouth to her and taking control. One hand would wind in her hair, tilting her head and caressing her jaw. He could practically hear her gasp as he pulled her into his lap. He knew the sound would reach his bones.

But even in his fantasy there was something else: a hesitancy, a caution that he couldn't overcome. He opened his eyes to find her watching him from the other end of the couch. He knew that his fantasy was written on his face, and other parts of his body.

'Nic...'

'Don't,' he said, holding up a hand to stop her. 'Nothing's changed since last time we talked about this. Apart from the fact that I've not been able to stop thinking about you... But it doesn't matter. We're doing the right thing. I know that. One of these days Rosie's going to need a dad—or a father figure, at least. You'll meet someone amazing who can give you the family life you deserve.'

He could never be that man.

'It's been a long week,' he told her, faking a yawn. 'I think I'm going to hit the sack.'

And with that he left her, staring after him as he practically ran from the room.

CHAPTER EIGHT

'RIGHT THEN, MISS. Are you going to tell me what's going on? Because Nic is being annoyingly discreet. I don't know what's got into him.'

'And I have no idea what you're talking about.'

'Oh, like hell you don't. The pair of you have been making doe eyes at each other since the day he pitched up on your doorstep. I can forgive *him* not telling me what's going on: he's my brother, and a bloke, and he has been irritating me for as long as I can remember. It's like a vocation for him. But you're my best friend and you have a new man in your life and you're telling me *nothing*. That's just not acceptable by anyone's standards of friendship.'

Lily groaned as she tipped the pram back and lifted it onto the pavement. 'A nice walk in the park,' Kate had said. 'Fresh air and a catch-up,' Kate had said. Since Rosie had landed they'd barely had the chance for more than a hello. It was her own fault for not realising that what she'd actually meant was *I will be grilling you for details about my brother.*

Well, if that was what she wanted…

'Okay, if it's details about the wild, sweaty sex I've been having with your brother you want you should have said. I hope you've got all afternoon free, though. Because that boy has stamina—and imagination.'

Kate's squeal had an elderly couple by the pond swivelling to stare at them and pigeons taking off from the path.

'That is all kinds of disgusting. I don't want details. But the fact that you've been doing the dirty with my brother and not telling me...*that* we need to talk about.'

Lily laughed at the look of horror on Kate's face. 'Calm it down, Kate. There has been no dirty. I'm winding you up.'

'You're— Oh, I'm going to kill you. *And* him. I've not decided yet which I'm going to enjoy more. So there's nothing going on?'

'Nothing.'

It was absolutely the truth. The fact that they were both *thinking* about what might be going on was beside the point.

'Then why are you blushing?'

Damn her pale skin—always getting her into trouble.

'I know that he likes you.'

Lily took a deep breath. 'I know he does too. But it's more complicated than that.'

'You don't like *him*?'

'Of course I like him. You've met your brother, right? Tall, good-looking, kind—all "I have a brilliant business brain but I choose to use it saving the world"?'

'Then what's the problem?'

What was the problem? There was the fact that she'd just become solely responsible for raising a brand-new human without even the usual nine-month notice period. There was the fact that Nic was still so scarred from losing his own son that he couldn't look at Rosie without flinching. There was the fact that she fell asleep any time she sat down for more than six minutes at a time, and the fact that her life was threatening to overwhelm her. It was hard to imagine how anything more complicated with Nic *wouldn't* push her over the edge.

And there was more that he hadn't told her. It wasn't just Rosie he was fighting. When he looked at Lily she saw something else—doubt. He'd told her that he wasn't the right man for her, but she failed to see why. Not wanting a life with a baby in it was one thing, but there was more to it than that. He warned her away whenever they got close, as if he couldn't trust himself.

What really tipped the situation over from difficult to impossible was the fact that she didn't want to care about any of that. That all the time she was walking around sleep-deprived and zombified her thoughts went in one direction only—straight to Nic.

'We're just friends—it's all we can handle right now. Honestly, Kate, if there was more to tell you I would. But we're still trying to work it out ourselves.'

Kate gave her a long look, but then her face softened and Lily knew that she was backing down and the grilling was over—for now, at least.

'And how are things with Rosie. Any word from Helen?'

'Nothing more yet—only that she's still at the clinic and doing well. Social services are happy with how things are going with Rosie, so it looks like this is it. Once they've decided Helen's well enough to make a final decision I guess we'll have more paperwork to do.'

'And you're still sure you're making the right decision?'

'I can't see what other decision I could make. She's my family. We should be together.'

Kate gave her a long look. 'I know you miss your mum, and your sister, but that doesn't mean—'

Lily stopped walking and held up a hand to stop Kate. 'Please—don't. I promise you I've thought about this. I've asked myself again and again if I'm doing the right thing and I honestly believe that I am. I *want* to do this. I love Rosie, and we're having a great time.'

'Well, she *is* completely adorable. I can't blame you—totally worth turning your life upside down for.'

Lily looked down at the pram, where Rosie had been sleeping soundly for over an hour. When she was like this, how could she disagree?

She'd just got the baby fed, changed and sleeping when the front door opened. She backed out of the bedroom on tiptoes, holding her breath to avoid waking Rosie. Nic was standing in the hall, bearing a bunch of flowers and a grin.

'Hi.'

He bent forward to kiss her on the cheek—strictly friendly—and she sneakily soaked up the smell of his aftershave and the warmth of his body.

'Hi, yourself. You look good. Did you do something different with your hair?'

She knew for a fact that there was milk in her hair, and that she'd pulled on this T-shirt from where she'd tossed it by the side of the bed last night. What a gentleman.

'How was it?' Lily asked as they walked through

to the kitchen. 'Did you manage to clear your desk for rest of the weekend?'

He'd been working and travelling non-stop since he'd arrived back in London, and had declared last night that he was ready for a break. He'd suggested a touristy day, sightseeing, and had volunteered *her* as tour guide.

'All sorted. I'm free till Monday morning. Are you still on for today?' He thrust the flowers at her. 'I'm banking on you saying yes, and these are a thank-you in advance.'

Lily thought about it—a few hours in the sunshine in one of the parks, perhaps the Tower of London or the London Eye to really up the cheesy tourist factor.

'Of course we're still on. Do I have time to change?'

'An hour before the car arrives. Is that enough? I can always call and delay.'

'An hour's perfect.'

She left Nic in the kitchen while she dived into the shower and grabbed jeans and a clean shirt. Rosie didn't stir in her crib, and Lily kept an eye on the clock, wondering when she'd wake for her next feed. She'd been sleeping for an hour already, which meant that she'd be waking up…just as the car reached them. *Not* perfect, then—far from it.

Maybe she should just tell Nic that they needed to leave a little later—but he'd seen too much of her struggling already, and she didn't want to admit that an hour wasn't enough time to get two people ready and out of the house. She'd just have to wake Rosie early from her sleep and feed her before they set off. Hopefully she'd pop straight off back to sleep afterwards.

Clean from the shower, Lily headed back out to the

kitchen, to find Nic immersed in stacking the dish-washer.

'Nic! You shouldn't! Leave those and I'll do them when we get back.'

'It's no problem,' he insisted as Lily gathered up sterilised bottles and cartons of ready-mixed formula, trying to work out how many bottles they would need to get them through the day.

Nic finished the washing up, despite her contin-ued protests, and with twenty minutes to go until the car arrived the kitchen was looking more like a home than a bomb site.

'Right, then—anything else I can do to help?' Nic asked.

'Absolutely not. I just need to give Rosie a quick feed and then we're all good.'

She cracked open the curtains in the bedroom slightly—just enough so that it wouldn't feel like night to Rosie—and then lifted her from the crib, tickling her fingers up and down her spine and over the soles of her feet. When her eyes started to open Lily moved her face closer and smiled at her, holding eye contact.

'Morning, sleepyhead,' she crooned. 'Time for some-thing to eat, and then we're going on an adventure!'

She swiped a bottle from the kitchen on her way, and then settled into a big comfy chair in the living room, where Nic had turned on some music.

'So, am I allowed to know what's in store for us today?' Lily asked once Rosie had started to feed.

'I can tell you if you really want to know, but I thought a surprise…'

Lily grinned. She couldn't remember the last time someone had organised a surprise for her, and after weeks of being enslaved to a demanding newborn, the thought of being spoilt for the day was irresistible.

'A surprise sounds divine. Though I'm not sure how I'm meant to play tour guide if I don't know where we're going.'

'Without giving too much away, let's just say that you don't have to worry too much about that. You're doing enough, indulging my need to see the tourist hotspots. I don't expect you to sing for your supper, too.'

Lily was distracted by Rosie spitting out the bottle, but managed to rearrange the muslin square before she got a direct hit on her clean shirt. She tried to get her to take the bottle again, but she turned her head and pursed her lips. Lily gave a small sigh. Perhaps choosing this morning to try waking her for a feed for the first time wasn't the best idea she'd ever had—it seemed Rosie wasn't a big fan of spontaneity.

She sat her up and rubbed between her shoulder-blades, hoping that she just had some wind and could be persuaded to take the rest of her bottle.

'Everything okay?' Nic asked, when she gave a small huff of exasperation.

'Just fussing,' Lily told him, not wanting to admit that her mistake was probably to blame.

'There's no hurry, you know. We can move the car back.'

'It's fine—honestly.' The damage had been done now, after all.

She offered Rosie the bottle again, but she absolutely refused it, and Lily knew that she was being unfair on her when all she wanted to do was sleep. Cursing whatever instinct it was that had kept her quiet when she could so easily have asked Nic to change their plans, she rocked the baby back to sleep and wondered when she'd wake next—when she'd be hungry next. She couldn't shake the feeling that she'd just played Russian roulette with their day.

The doorbell rang just as Rosie dropped off and Lily held her breath for a moment, wondering if the sound would wake her, but it seemed they'd got away with it. She lowered her gently into her car seat and hefted her to the hallway—for a tiny bundle she was certainly starting to feel like a heck of a weight to carry around.

Nic answered the door to a driver in a smart-looking uniform, and for a second Lily was surprised. She'd heard 'car' and thought local minicab, but it seemed Nic's idea of a day's sightseeing might be somewhat different to her own. She glanced down at the plimsolls she'd been about to pull on and wondered whether she ought to go for something smarter.

'Should I change?' she asked Nic. 'I'm in the dark about what we're doing, but if I need to be...'

'You look perfect as you are,' he told her, and she smiled, but still wasn't entirely at ease.

Lily watched out of the window as they headed down towards the river, trying to work out where they were going. They zoomed past a couple of parks, which ruled those out, and by the time they pulled up at a wharf Lily had to admit defeat. She had no idea where they were going.

'We're here?' she asked Nic, and he grinned by way of an answer. 'What are we doing?'

'Wait and see,' he told her with child-like enthusiasm. 'But it should be amazing.'

She pulled Rosie's car seat out and looked up at

Nic, hoping for some guidance. He nodded towards the water, where a sleek white and silver yacht was moored.

'Are we going aboard?' she asked.

'We are indeed.'

He was practically bouncing now—and no wonder. The yacht was magnificent—all flowing lines and shiny chrome, and decks scrubbed to within an inch of their lives. She could see through the expanse of glass that a dining room had been set with sparkling crystal and polished silverware. It looked as if they were in for a treat.

'Would you like the pram, madam?' the driver asked as he opened the boot of the car.

She glanced at the gangplank and the yacht's decks, and for a shivery moment had visions of a runaway pram rolling towards the railings that edged the decks.

'I think I'll take the sling instead.'

Nic grabbed the changing bag from the boot and hefted it to his shoulder. Climbing up onto the gangplank, he held out a hand to her. As his fingers closed around her palm warmth spread through her hand, and she had to remind herself sternly of the very sensible decision that they'd both taken to remain just friends. But with the fancy dining room and the glamorous yacht this was starting to look more like a date than temporary flatmates hanging out for the afternoon.

'Welcome, sir, madam—and to the little one. You're very welcome on board. Luncheon will be served in thirty minutes. In the meantime feel free to explore the decks or take a drink in the champagne bar on the upper deck.'

Lily smiled at the man as he discreetly retreated

from them, though she couldn't help a little twist of anxiety. Luncheon, champagne bar… She'd had take-away sandwiches in mind when Nic had first mentioned something to eat and sightseeing, and she wondered if he had higher expectations of the day than he'd let on. This was looking less and less like a casual day out and more like a seduction.

She looked up at Nic, wondering whether she'd glean any clue from his expression. But his beaming smile didn't give much away.

'Nic, this is amazing,' she said. 'If a little unex-pected…'

'I know…I know. It's a bit over the top. But I wanted to see London from the water, and my new assistant said the food on board was not to be missed. There's nothing wrong with treating ourselves, is there?'

She searched for double meanings, but found none in his words or in his eyes. She was worrying about nothing. It was no surprise, really. After he'd ended up cooking for them both these last few weeks, he wanted a slightly more refined dining experience.

'So, what will it be?' he asked. 'Exploring or the champagne bar?'

Lily thought about it for a second, measuring the rocking of the boat under her feet and the weight of the baby in her arms. 'Exploring, I think,' she said with a smile.

They walked the decks, gasping over the unrivalled luxury of the vessel, the attention to detail and the de-votion to function and aesthetics in every line. Pol-ished chrome and barely there glass provided a barrier between them and the water, but as they climbed step after step Lily's head grew dizzier and her feet a little less steady.

When she had to pause for a moment, at the top of the highest step, Nic gave her a concerned look. 'You okay?' he asked, with a gentle arm around her shoulder.

'Fine,' she told him, shrugging off his arm.

It was making it too hard to think, and she needed to focus all her energy on keeping herself on her feet at the moment.

Nic's face fell—just for a second, before he caught it—and she knew that she had hurt his feelings. She'd opened her mouth, without being entirely sure what she would say, when a liveried steward came up the steps behind them and asked that they take their seats in the dining room. With just a quick glance at Nic, Lily shot down the stairs, glad of the moment to clear her head.

It wasn't that she hadn't wanted Nic's support. God knew it had felt good to have his arm around her. But there was the problem. It was *too* good. It would be too easy to forget all the very sensible, grown-up reasons that they were staying friends and friends only. And it wasn't as if Nic had meant anything by it; he'd just been trying to help when he'd seen that she needed it. It was her overactive libido that was complicating things—having her jumping like a cat every time he came near her.

There were about a dozen tables in the dining room, each set for two with a shining silver candelabra and fresh-cut roses in crystal.

'Wow,' Nic said behind her. 'This is…'

She turned round to look at him, not sure how to interpret the wavering in his voice.

Go on, she urged him silently. Because this dining room had 'romance' written all over it, and right now she was struggling. Struggling to see how they were meant to stay friends if Nic was going to spring romance on her with no warning. Struggling to know what he wanted from her if this was where he thought they were in their 'friendship'.

'This is…unexpected,' he said.

The candlelight made it hard to tell, but she was sure there was a little more colour in his cheeks than normal. She let out a sigh of relief. Okay, so she was worrying over nothing. This wasn't some grand seduction—just a lunch that was turning out to be a little more romantic than either of them had been expecting.

Lily watched the other diners taking their seats as they were shown to a table by the window, tucked into a corner of the room. Light flooded in through the floor-to-ceiling windows, throwing patterns and shapes from the crystal and the flatware.

Nic tucked the changing bag under the table as they sat, and Lily reached down to adjust Rosie in her carrier. She'd slept through their tour of the vessel and Lily glanced at her watch, not sure what time she would wake.

Nic looked determinedly out of the window, Lily noticed, and was careful to make sure that his eyes never landed on Rosie.

'Come on, then,' he said, gesturing at the window. 'What are we looking at? I can't waste the fact that I'm out here with a genuine Londoner.'

'How have you never been sightseeing in London?' she asked with wonder. 'Never mind the fact that your sister has lived here for years, you've been to —what?—six different cities in the past couple of months alone. You don't honestly need me to point out the OXO Tower, do you?'

'And in not one of those other cities did I have a tour guide. Or time off for lunch, for that matter. What can I say? Maybe I've packed in too much work and not enough fun.'

'Well, we'll make today all about fun, then. What else have you got planned for us?'

'Nope—still not telling.'

She laughed, and then looked down as she felt Rosie rubbing her head against her chest, a sure sign that she was about to wake up and demand a bottle. She was just going to suggest that they find a way to heat up some formula when the maître d' appeared.

Seemed everybody was ready to eat.

As a team of waiting staff paraded into the dining room, carrying their starters, Lily dug through her bags and found a bottle and a carton of ready-mixed formula.

'Excuse me,' she said to their waitress, once she'd placed their starters in front of them, 'could I have some hot water to heat a bottle?'

The girl shot Rosie a look that was fifty per cent fear of the baby and fifty per cent disdain. It turned out that diners under one weren't exactly flavour of the month on luxury restaurant cruises.

'Is she okay?' Nic asked, as Rosie started to mewl like a mildly discontented kitten.

'Just hungry, I think,' Lily said, rubbing her back and trying to get her to settle.

If only her fusspot of a niece would take a cold bottle—but she had tried that before, with no success. She tried again now anyway, hoping that maybe she'd be hungry enough not to care, but after screwing up her face she spat out a mouthful of milk and Lily knew they had no choice but to wait for the hot water. She really ought to get one of those portable bottle warmers…

The doors to the dining room swung open, and Lily looked up, hoping to see a steaming pot of water heading her way. Instead the waitress was carrying bottles of wine, topping up the glasses on the table nearest the kitchen. Rosie chose that moment to let out a scream, and every head in the room turned towards her—Nic's included.

'I think maybe I should take her out… Just for a few minutes…until she settles.'

'If you think that's best,' Nic replied, his expression hovering somewhere around concerned. 'Is there anything I can do?'

'If you could get that bottle warm, that would be amazing. Sure you don't mind?'

She'd have done it herself—marched into the kitchen and found a kettle—but from the looks she was getting a hasty retreat seemed like the safer option.

'Course. I'll grab someone. Want me to bring it out to you? Or will you come back in?'

She should have an answer to that. But all she could think was, What was he asking *her* for? *He* was the one who'd done this before—*he* was the one with experience of being a parent, having had months to prepare for it and classes to learn about it.

But she couldn't ask him about any of that.

She pushed through the heavy door and went out onto the deck, taking in a deep lungful of breeze and spray. She let the breath out slowly, her eyes closed, focussing on calming thoughts, knowing that it would help Rosie settle.

Could everyone still hear her? She risked a glance at the windows. Whether they could hear her or not, she was still providing the entertainment, it seemed, as more than one pair of eyes was still fixed on her. It was hard to tell, though, what normal volume was with her eardrums about to rupture.

She rolled her eyes in the face of their disapproval. As if none of *them* had ever had to deal with a hungry baby. Smiling, she looked down at Rosie, determined to stay cheerful in the face of her cries. She was still cooing at her when she realised that Nic had left their table, and she only had a moment to wonder where he was before he emerged through the double doors with a steaming jug of water and the bottle.

What a hero. She could kiss him.

Well, actually, that pretty much felt like her default setting these days. But she was more grateful than ever to have him in her life right at that second. She watched him walk towards her as if he were carrying the Holy Grail.

'One bottle,' he declared as he closed the door to the deck behind him and passed it over to her.

She'd expected him to be sprinting back through the doors as soon as he'd offloaded his cargo, but instead he dropped down onto a bench, spreading his arms across the back. Lily sat beside him as Rosie started sucking on the bottle, quiet at last.

'Why don't you go in and eat?' she said to him. 'It seems a shame for us both to be missing out on lunch.'

'I don't mind—'

'Honestly—go and eat. She's perfectly happy now, so I'll be back in soon.'

He hesitated for a second, but then stood and headed for the door. Lily leaned back against the bench and closed her eyes for a moment, letting herself drift with the rhythmic rocking of the boat. At the sound of the deck doors opening her eyes flew open—to see Nic juggling glasses and plates as he fought to shut the door behind him.

'If Rosie's picnicking out here, seems only fair that we get to as well,' he said with a grin.

Lily risked a glance into the dining room and could see that more than one set of eyes was disapprovingly set in their direction.

'Open up.'

A forkful of delicate tartlet appeared in front of her nose and Lily hesitated, meeting Nic's eyes as he offered the food to her. *Definitely* too intimate for friends. But Rosie's weight in her arms reminded her that this wasn't romance, it was practicality, and she opened her mouth, let her lips close around the cold tines of the fork.

Closing her eyes seemed too decadent, too sensuous. But holding Nic's gaze as he fed her so intimately seemed like a greater danger. As balsamic vinegar hit her palate she smiled. With food this good, why let herself be distracted by anything else?

She sat looking out across the water, enjoying seeing the city that was so familiar to her with the unfamiliar smells and sounds of the boat. Nic's arm was still stretched across the back of the bench, but she didn't move away. It was too easy, too comfortable to sit like this, enjoying the moments of quiet and savouring their lunch.

Eventually, when both plates were cleared and Rosie had finished her formula, Nic nodded towards the dining room.

'Think we can risk human company again?'

CHAPTER NINE

NIC LOOKED DOWN at Rosie, milk-drunk and sleepy again.

'I think we should be safe,' Lily said, setting the bottle down beside them, lifting Rosie to her shoulder and starting to rub her back.

'Let me do that,' Nic offered, already reaching for Rosie.

He hadn't meant to: he'd been clear with himself that the only way he could let himself explore this connection with Lily was if he remembered to keep his distance with Rosie. But he could hardly invite them out for the day and not expect to help. It was what any friend would do, he told himself. Friendship wasn't just offering the parts of yourself that were easy. Taking the parts of the other person that fitted with your life. It meant taking the hard bits too, exposing yourself to hurt, trusting that the other person was looking out for you.

They'd agreed that a relationship was too much to take on, but if they were going to be friends he was going to be a *good* friend.

He nestled the baby on his shoulder as they walked back inside, and for a moment he was caught by her new baby smell—a scent that threw him back ten years, to the happiest and hardest moments of his life. His eyes closed and his steps faltered for a second, but he forced himself forward, pushing through the pain of his past and reminding himself that Rosie wasn't Max, and Lily wasn't Clare.

As they reached the table their main courses arrived, and he slid into his seat with Rosie still happy on his shoulder.

'This looks amazing,' declared Lily, looking down at the plates of perfectly pink lamb and buttery potatoes. She reached for her knife and fork, but then hesitated. 'Are you sure you don't want me to take her?'

'You can if you want,' Nic told her, wary of overstepping some line. 'But I don't mind.'

Lily's eyes dropped to Rosie again as she thought for a minute.

'No, you're right. It would be silly to disturb her when she's settled.'

He picked up his fork, wondering how he was meant to tackle a rack of lamb one-handed.

'Here,' Lily said, with a smile and a sparkle in her eye. She pinned the meat with a fork while he cut it, and when she caught the maître d's shocked expression, she laughed out loud. 'I don't think I've ever caused such a scandal before,' she whispered to him.

He laughed in return, relieved to feel the tension leaching from the air.

'I feel like we're doing him a service. His life must have been very sheltered if we're so shocking to him. Maybe we should up the ante? Give him something to really disapprove of…?'

Oh, did he like the sound of *that*. His skin prickled,

his grin widened and he leaned closer across the table. 'What exactly did you have in mind?'

Lily blushed.

God, it was such a turn-on when she did that—when the evidence of her desire chased across her skin like watercolours on a damp page.

'I...I...I don't think I really thought that sentence through,' she said at last with a coy smile.

He laughed again, feeling his shoulders relax, leaning back in his chair as they seemed to find common ground again...as he started to feel the subtle pull and heat between them that had brought them together in the first place.

'Maybe I'll ask you again another time,' he suggested, unable to resist this spark between them. 'When we've a little more privacy and a little less company.'

She looked up at him from under her lashes—a look, he suspected, not entirely uncalculated.

'Maybe I'll give it a little thought this afternoon.'

For a moment the silence spanned warm and comfortable between them, and he held her gaze as gently and sensuously as if he was reaching out and touching her.

A little choking sound from the baby he'd almost forgotten was in his arms drew his attention and he smiled down at her, so exposed from the conversation with Lily that he didn't have a moment to try and defend himself, had no chance of raising any sort of resistance to those adorably round cheeks or her big blue eyes.

'Sorry, little Rosie,' he told her, mopping her up automatically and shifting her to his other shoulder. 'I guess we weren't paying you enough attention.'

Lily gave him a complicated smile, but then with one more bite of potato she dropped her knife and fork.

'That was incredible—truly,' she told him. 'The closest thing to heaven I've ever eaten.'

'Agreed,' he said, looking a little longingly at the lamb still on his plate.

'I'll take her back,' Lily told him, her tone brooking no argument this time. 'Seriously—you'll kick yourself if you don't eat every bite.'

CHAPTER TEN

THE BOAT SLOWED as they approached the wharf and Lily could practically feel the collective sigh of relief from everyone on board. Not that she cared. The three of them had enjoyed another picnic out on deck, when Rosie had been testy again during dessert, and she couldn't help but think that it had been nicer, anyway, to be out in the fresh air than in that dining room, with its candles that spoke of a romance they were definitely *not* going to be pursuing.

Part of her had wanted to explain to the other diners —to confess that she'd thought more than once that maybe if she was Rosie's real mum she might be better at this. She might be flailing a little less at the prospect of a baby whose needs were really pretty simple if only she could work out the code that everyone else seemed to understand. She couldn't really blame them for being annoyed. No doubt they'd paid handsomely for their lunch, and hadn't expected to encounter a crying baby while they enjoyed it. But their silent judgement was cutting nonetheless.

At least she'd had a partner in crime.

Nic had actually taken the baby today. Offered to help and then cooed at her and rocked her until she was calm. Though the ghost of pain and doubt etched into his every feature was enough to show her that, romantic as the setting was, his thoughts were anything but. There was nothing more likely to put him off, she thought, than being reminded of the realities of parenting.

'You okay there?' Nic asked, breaking into her reverie. 'You look a million miles away.'

The car had met them as they'd disembarked and they were crawling through London traffic again, on their way to sightseeing event number two.

The car stopped outside the Tower of London, and she sent Nic a questioning glance. She couldn't hide her deep breath of apprehension. The last time she'd been to the Tower had been years ago, and she'd had to fight her way through crowds, elbow her way into a picnic spot and strain her ears to hear the commentary from the obligatory Beefeater. She couldn't imagine it being any more relaxing with Rosie strapped to her chest.

'We're here,' Nic announced with a smile.

He reached for her hand to help her out of the car, and then reached in after her to take Rosie from her seat. He handed the baby straight over, but she couldn't help seeing a tiny bit of progress.

They were met at the gate by a uniformed Beefeater, and as she passed through the entrance she realised how different it felt from the last time she'd been there. Looking around her, she realised why. The place was deserted. How on earth had he pulled *this* off?

The Beefeater puffed up his chest as he turned round and launched into a clearly well-practised speech, welcoming them to Her Majesty's Royal Palace and Fortress, The Tower of London. 'There's a thousand years

of history here, sir, madam: more than you could dis-
cover in a week. So what would you like to see? The
armouries? The torture display? The Crown Jewels?'

Lily gave an involuntary gasp at the mention of the
jewels. The day of her teenaged visit the Jewel House
had been packed and sweaty. She'd managed to get
stuck behind someone with a huge backpack on the
moving conveyor, and had passed through without getting one decent look at a crown.

She looked up at Nic, who laughed. 'Looks like the
Crown Jewels it is,' he declared to their Yeoman Guard.

'You're sure you don't mind? I'd understand if diamonds weren't your thing.'

'That look on your face is exactly my thing,' he told
her quietly as their guide discreetly moved away. 'And
if it's a diamond that gets it there...'

His sentence trailed into silence, but his gaze never
faltered from hers. He *was* talking about diamonds?
Had he realised what he'd said? Of course he didn't
mean a *diamond* diamond—the type that led you up
the aisle and towards happy-ever-after. But if he'd
meant nothing by it, why wasn't he looking away.
Why was he reaching out and touching her face, as if
trying to see something, touch something, that wasn't
quite there?

His hand dropped gently to cup the back of Rosie's
head, then lower still to Lily's waist, pulling her towards him. She closed her eyes as he leaned in for a
kiss, and felt the lightest, gentlest brush of lips over
hers. For a moment she couldn't move. Not even to kiss
him back or push him away. In that moment she didn't
know which she wanted more—which she was more
scared of. Because this kiss was something different.

It wasn't the desperate press of his lips on hers at the hospital, or that regretfully friendly kiss on the cheek. This kiss was the start of something new. Something more than they'd had before…something more serious…something more frightening.

Rosie let out a squawk, clearly less than impressed at being trapped between the two of them, and Nic backed off a little, his smile more of a slow-burning candle than a full-beam sun.

He called over to their guide and let him know that they were ready.

Rosie started to whimper a little as they headed over to the Jewel House, and their guide slowed a little.

'Aw, is she out of sorts? She looks just the same age as my granddaughter—and that girl has a pair of lungs on her, I can tell you. Do you want to sit somewhere quiet with her for a while?'

'Thank you, but she's just tired. I think if we keep walking she'll send herself off.'

'Of course. Mum knows best,' he told her with a wink. 'Though if you ask me…' he gave her a careful look '…it's probably Dad's turn.'

He carried on speaking, but Lily couldn't make out what he was saying. Her focus was pinned entirely on Nic as his face fell, then paled, and then as he slowly put himself back together. His eyes refocused, and his jaw returned to its usual position.

'Here,' he said, just as Lily caught something about Colonel Blood in 1671 from their guide. 'He's right. My turn.'

He held his hands out for her, and Lily sent him the clearest *Are you sure?* look she could manage without speaking out loud. He took Rosie in his arms and lifted her to his chin, then leaned down and pressed a kiss to the top of her head. He closed his eyes for a moment and Lily knew that he was remembering. But then he looked up at her with a brave smile, grabbed her hand and squeezed.

They followed the guard, and she tried to listen to his stories, tried to take in the information, but really she just wanted to look. And not at the diamonds or the gold or the ancient artefacts. She wanted to watch Nic with Rosie. Wanted to witness the way he was resisting his hurt and his past and trying to endure, trying to move on. And he was doing it for her.

When they emerged from the Jewel House the evening was starting to draw in. Car headlights were lighting up Tower Bridge, and the banks of the river were bustling with tourists calling it a day mixed with commuters heading home.

'A walk along the river before we head home?' Nic asked. 'I had thought maybe dinner, but...'

Lily burst out laughing, remembering how they'd spent barely half an hour of their lunch actually in the dining room. With a few hours' distance suddenly the whole cruise seemed like a farce. For dinner she wanted nothing more than a sofa and a cheese sandwich. Michelin-starred cuisine was all well and good, but you couldn't exactly eat it in your pyjamas. Or with a baby nearby, apparently.

'I think we'd better quit while we're ahead,' she said. 'Lunch was spectacular, in so many ways, but I think Rosie needs her bed. Enough excitement for her for one day.'

'I understand. We should probably head back.'

Lily nodded, suddenly feeling sombre. The prospect

of an evening together in the apartment was suddenly overwhelming. That kiss—there'd be nowhere to hide from it once they got home.

In the privacy and seclusion of the car, nipping through London traffic, Lily's thoughts were heading in one direction and one direction only—behind the so far firmly shut door of her bedroom. She risked a glance up at Nic, wondering whether her feelings were showing on her face. Were they going to talk about this again? Put aside all their good intentions to do the sensible thing? That kiss had promised so much that couldn't be unsaid.

But she stayed silent—as did Nic. Silent in the car, silent in the lift, silent until Rosie was settled in her cot and they were alone in the living room—with nothing and no one standing between them and the conversation they were avoiding.

Nic let out a long, slow breath, rubbing his hand across the back of his neck, and for a minute Lily wondered if she'd completely misread what had been going on between them—maybe he was happy with things as they were? Maybe he was only interested in being friends?

She risked a glance up at him and all her doubts fled. The heat in his eyes told her everything she needed to know about how he felt—and it was a lot more than friendly. She felt that heat travel to the depths of her belly, warming her from the inside until it reached her face as a smile. He pulled gently on her hand, bringing her close to him, and planted his other hand on her hip.

'Is this a good idea?' she asked, knowing the answer…knowing just as well that it wasn't going to stop them.

'Terrible,' Nic answered, dropping her hand and finding her cheek with his palm. 'Want to stop?'

It took considerable effort not to laugh in his face. Stop? How *could* they stop? They'd tried to avoid this. They'd talked about exactly why this was a bad idea. Looking deep into Nic's eyes, she could see that he still had reservations, that he still didn't fully believe this was the right thing to do. But stop…?

'No.'

'Everything we said, Lily—it still stands. I've not changed who I am, what happened…'

'I know. But what are we meant to do—just ignore this? I can't, Nic. It feels too…big. Too important. So let's see where it goes. No guarantees. No promises. Let's just stop fight—'

His lips captured hers before the word was even out, and she knew that they were lost. They'd been crazy to think that they could live here, together, and pretend that this wasn't happening—that their bodies hadn't been dragging them towards each other, however unwillingly, since the moment that they'd met.

With her spine wedged against a console table and her feet barely on the floor, Lily thought how easy it would be to surrender completely. To let Nic literally sweep her off her feet, caveman-style if he wanted, and really see where they could take this.

But as his hands found the sensitive skin at the back of her knees, lifting her until her legs wrapped around his waist, she knew that the easy road wasn't the right one.

'Nic…' she gasped into his ear, not able to articulate more than that one syllable.

But he'd perched her gently on the table and now, although his breathing was still ragged, he pulled back—just an inch…just enough to give her the space she needed to clear her head. His expression held all his questions without him having to say a word.

'Slower,' Lily said eventually, when she'd regained the power of speech. 'That was…I want to see where this will go, but…slower. Slower than that.'

She could barely believe that she'd managed to get the words out, and even as she was saying them she was already half regretting that she wasn't more fearless. But she couldn't be. Just because they had decided to stop fighting, it didn't mean that she had decided to be stupid. There was no happy ending in sight—no easy way to set aside everything they'd convinced each other was good reason to stay apart.

They'd still have to work through it…whatever it was that made Nic's eyes dim at the most unexpected times. It wasn't all going to disappear because they wanted things to be easy. And until they were more sure of each other there was only so far she could take this.

CHAPTER ELEVEN

SUNDAY MORNING, LILY WOKE to sunshine at the curtains and Rosie gurgling happily in her crib. She stared at the wall opposite, trying to picture Nic just on the other side of it, sprawled across the king-size bed she'd seen when she'd sneaked a look at his room. And she could be in there with him now, she thought, rather than be trying to conjure the feeling of his arms around her waist, the warmth of his chest warming her back as she turned on the pillow and drifted back to sleep...

If only she hadn't been so darned sensible last night.

Much as she was cursing herself, she was glad, really, that she'd made the decision she had. Sure, daybreak wrapped in Nic sounded like perfection—but then what about breakfast? Lunch? All the conversations they hadn't had yet? The things that needed to be said before they decided if whatever it was between them could turn from 'let's see where this goes' into something more real, more lasting?

Footsteps padded down the hallway, and as they approached her room she held her breath, wondering whether they would stop—whether Nic wanted to pick up where they'd left that kiss last night. But they faded again, towards the front door, until she heard a key turn in the lock and then silence.

He'd just gone! Without a word! A cold shiver traced her spine. But she forced herself out of bed and into the kitchen, determined not to read too much into it. He often went for a run at this time of day, before the streets were busy. But it was a Sunday—and, more than that, it was the morning after *that* kiss, when she had a million things to say and no idea where to start. Was that what he was avoiding?

She shook her head as she boiled the kettle and scooped formula. Who said he was avoiding anything?

When he strolled into the apartment at half past ten, still in his running gear, she'd just got Rosie down for a sleep and was thinking of following her back to bed. But the sight of Nic's legs in his scantily cut running shorts gave her second thoughts.

'Good run?' she asked, having still not entirely shaken the worry that he'd left early that morning to avoid her. But he was smiling—beaming, actually— as he fiddled with the coffee machine.

'Brilliant—really good. What about you? Good morning?'

'Milk, nappies, sleep. Pretty much standard.' She said it with a smile, and she could hear the dreamy edge in her voice. It might be hard work, but she would be hard pressed to think of another job that was more worth it.

'I stopped by the office,' Nic said as he placed a cup of coffee in front of her. 'Had a bit of a brainwave when I was running…'

Lily's eyebrows drew together.

'What sort of idea?'

'What have you got planned this week?'

She gave it a moment's thought. One tiny design job that she had to finish and email to her client, and other than that more milk, more nappies, more sleep.

'Just the usual.'

'Then come to Rome with me.'

He was still talking, but a crash of thoughts drowned out his words as she tried to process what he'd just said. A trip to Rome with the man she knew she was rapidly falling for? How could she say no? *Why* would she say no?

Nic squeezed her hand.

'Lily? Still with me?'

'I am—sorry. I think that's an incredible idea, but…'

Even as she was saying the words the real world began to intrude.

'But you're worried about the practicalities and about Rosie? I know—of course you are. But she'll have everything she needs. The logistics might not be easy, but they're not impossible.'

'She doesn't even have a passport.'

'No, but she does have an appointment at the passport office tomorrow. *If* you decide it's what you want,' he hastened to add. 'There'd be a skycot on the flight, and a cot in your room at the hotel. Formula, nappies… I've organised a pram and a car seat—the same ones as you have here—to use while we're there. I think I've thought of everything—if not the hotel's concierge is on standby for anything baby-related. We can even organise a nanny, if you want one.'

Lily slumped back in her chair, her mouth agape.

'I don't know what to say.'

'Say *yes*,' Nic said with a boyish eagerness. 'Have you been to Italy before?'

'No, I've never been to Italy…' she said, her words coming out slowly as her brain fought to catch up. 'But I'm not sure that really comes into my decision. I've got to think practically.'

'You can think practically if you want, but I swear it's all taken care of. Instead you could think about Rome: sipping coffee in a quiet *piazza*, genuine Italian cuisine, the shopping…'

'You're a great salesman—very persuasive. No wonder you were head-hunted.'

'What can I say? I'm only human. Now, stop changing the subject. If you need time to think about it, that's fine.'

Would she use the time to think about it? Or would she use it to talk herself out of it? *Rome*. It was hardly the sort of opportunity that came along every day. And the opportunity to take a spur-of-the-moment trip to a romantic city with Nic seemed like a once-in-a-lifetime sort of thing. She'd be mad to say no.

'Okay, yes. I'd love to.' She could feel the smile spreading across her cheeks, feel the warmth in the pit of her stomach rising to glow in her chest and her heart. '*Rome*, Nic. I don't know where to start being excited about that!'

Nic simply sat and watched as Lily enthused about Rome, so pleased that he'd been able to convince her to come with him. He'd had a flash of inspiration this morning and not been able to rest until he'd got the details in place. His trip had been booked for a while— a meeting with a fabric supplier he'd been in contact with several times over the years. And now that he and Lily had decided to see where this chemistry between them might go, Rome seemed like too good an opportunity to miss.

For a brief moment—just a split second—he'd been tempted to call his sister and ask if she'd babysit Rosie for a night. But he'd stopped himself. He wanted Lily and everything that came with her. He couldn't pretend—didn't want to pretend—that Rosie wasn't going to be a part of their life together. He'd made a few calls, pulled in a few favours, and had plans for the trip underway before he'd even got to the office.

'You know, you don't talk about your family much,' he remarked, once they'd exhausted all possible Roman topics of conversation.

'There's not a lot to tell,' Lily said with a shrug, but the shadow that darkened her eyes told him a different story.

'I know how sad it makes you that you and your sister aren't close…'

He wasn't sure why he was pushing the issue. Maybe it was because he wanted to be close to her, to *really* know her. He'd laid bare the darkest parts of his own history, but he knew so little about her. How could they try and be something more than friends to one another if he didn't really know her?

'It does,' she admitted. 'But maybe now… Maybe things will be better.'

'Was there a big falling-out?'

Lily shook her head as she drank her coffee. A drop caught on her lower lip and he watched, entranced, as her tongue sneaked out to rescue it.

'Nothing dramatic.'

'How do your parents feel about it?'

She caught her breath in a gasp, and though she tried to cover it he knew that he'd just stumbled into dangerous waters.

'Actually, my parents aren't around. My dad never was, and my mum died when I was twelve.'

He felt a gut-wrenching stab of pain on her behalf, and at the same time wanted to kick himself for causing her distress. What an idiot he was to go stumbling around in her past. If she'd wanted to talk about her family she would have brought it up. But then he was sure he'd heard Kate say something about her visiting her family. If not her sister or her parents, then who?

'I'm sorry, Lily. I didn't mean to pry. We don't have to—'

'It's fine,' she told him, settling her mug on the table. 'I don't mind talking about her. It's nice, actually, to have a reminder occasionally.'

'What was she like?'

'She was lovely—and amazing. That doesn't seem like enough, but I'm not sure how else…' Her voice trailed off and she rested her chin on her hand, leaning on the table. 'It was all rather wonderful when I was growing up—which, knowing what I do now about what it is to bring up a child on your own…'

She still had no idea how her mother had done it. Every day she spent battling to keep her head above water with Rosie was another day when her respect for her mother grew exponentially. And when she found herself looking at her own efforts and wondering why she found it so hard…

'And I had a big sister to look out for me. But then Mum was in a car accident and everything changed.'

'I'm so sorry.'

He couldn't believe that he hadn't known this about her before now. That she'd let him talk about his loss and his grief while never hinting that there were people she loved missing from her own life.

'It's not as bad as all that,' she said, catching his eye and giving a little smile. 'At the time, obviously, it was horrendous. But I was placed with a wonderful foster family who helped me come to terms with losing my mother. Helped me so that I could remember her with love, remember the wonderful family that we were. I was lucky to find a second set of people to love me and take care of me.'

He marvelled at her composure, but sensed that her sister's story was somewhat different.

'And Helen?'

'Helen's older,' she said. 'She was sixteen when we lost Mum—too old for foster care. Not that that was what she wanted anyway. After Mum was gone it was like she wanted to prove that she didn't need her. She wanted to do her own thing, take care of herself. She was always welcome with my foster family, and we all tried hard to make her feel included, but it wasn't what she wanted. With our mum gone, the "half" part of being her half-sister suddenly seemed to matter more than ever.'

There were only so many times that he could say he was sorry before it started to sound trite. He couldn't fathom the way Lily had dealt with these blows—how she had come out the other side able to smile fondly when she thought about the family she'd once belonged to but which had since fallen apart. When he'd lost his son and then his fiancée, it had been as if the world had changed overnight. As if the warmth of the sun had stopped reaching him. He'd stopped living. Whereas Lily had grieved and then moved on.

'You didn't stay in touch?'

'We tried. *I* tried. I'd write to her—letters at first, then emails. Sometimes she'd reply and sometimes not. Eventually my letters started coming back to me and the emails started bouncing. She'd drop me a line occasionally, but the message was pretty clear. She was happier without me in her life—I think I was a reminder of what she'd lost.'

'But when she was really in trouble it was you she came to. She must trust you—love you—a lot.'

'I've thought about that. A lot, actually. And done a little bit of reading. I'm not sure that was why she left Rosie with me. Perhaps it was just because we're related. Maybe she didn't want Rosie in the care system. Hadn't completely decided what she wanted for her. Perhaps she thought that if she left her with me and changed her mind she could get her back. It didn't matter *who* I was—it only mattered that we had the same mother.'

'Oh, Lily.' He reached for her hand, turned it under his and threaded their fingers together. 'I can't believe that's true. I think she knows just what a special person you are—that you'll take care of her daughter without even questioning it. That you'll give her the happy childhood Helen remembers having.'

'Perhaps…'

Lily smiled, though he could see that there were tears gathering in her eyes.

'So, what's happening with…?' He wasn't sure what to call it. The Rosie Situation? 'With your guardianship? Have you had any update from the social worker?'

Lily explained the situation—that it was looking more and more likely that she would become Rosie's permanent guardian—and he tried hard to pin down how he felt. Tried to judge the proportions of fear, trepidation, excitement and affection that seemed constantly to battle for supremacy in his heart.

He wasn't sure that he could admit it to Lily, but maybe he could admit it to himself. In those early days, when he'd first been getting to know her, despite her fierce protection of Rosie, he'd managed to convince himself that her guardianship would only be temporary. That he could let himself fantasise because one day Rosie's mother would return, Lily would be a simple aunt again, and the baby's presence in her life would fade to the background. Then there would be nothing to come between him and Lily.

Now he knew that wasn't going to be the case. And it was too late—way too late—to stop falling for her. But what would happen when he hit the ground? He tried to imagine that life and it still filled him with a cold dread. He wanted to embrace all the possibilities that a relationship with Lily might bring, but when he allowed himself to think about the certainties of it he was filled with fear.

He watched her across the table and saw how she became shy under his gaze, dipping her eyes and concentrating far more than she needed to on sipping her coffee. She still wasn't sure of him—and with good reason. She deserved a lover who had no reservations, who was ready for a commitment to her, and he wasn't sure that was him—not yet.

For the first time he questioned whether he'd done the right thing in inviting her to Rome, whether that was leading her on—but, no. Rome was different. It was a way for them to get to know each other better, not a promise.

Three days to plan and she was just thinking about waxing her legs *now*? She glanced at her watch. Not a hope. Nic would be back from work in half an hour, her hair was still wet, and dinner was at least an hour off going in the oven. In fact most of it was still in the supermarket. Rosie was overdue a bath and it was veering dangerously close to being past her bedtime.

Where had three days gone? And how was it that she found it so impossible to do something as simple as cook dinner? Since the moment Rosie had turned up all she'd wanted to do was be a good mum…aunt… sister. To make a family for Rosie and for herself. But it seemed as if every time she thought she had it sorted she found herself in the middle of a disaster of her own making. They sneaked up on her and were suddenly right in front of her eyes.

She heard his key in the lock just as she had Rosie stripped off and ready for her bath. Cursing his bad timing, she wrapped the baby in a towel and carried her with her as she went to the door. Her plan had been to have an uninterrupted bedtime routine for Rosie this evening—to have her down and sleeping before Nic got home, so they could enjoy dinner together before heading off on their trip first thing tomorrow. But Rosie had slept late this afternoon. So she'd fed late and played late. And now—almost—she was being bathed late.

And then Nic was there, and in a moment her stress fell away. The width of his smile created fine lines of pleasure around his eyes as he leaned in to kiss her without hesitation.

'Hi,' she breathed, letting her eyes shut and enjoying that simple pleasure.

When she opened them she realised that the man was not only absurdly good-looking and radiating charm, he was also brandishing carrier bags and a bottle of red wine. It was almost enough to have her crying into Rosie's towel.

'I've interrupted bathtime,' he said, pointing out the obvious. 'I thought I'd leave a bit early and make a start on dinner. Couldn't wait to get home to you, actually, kick off our holiday tonight instead of in the morning.'

There were no games, no subtexts.

'You ladies get back to it, and I'll have dinner ready when you're done.'

Lily opened her mouth to argue: she'd promised him dinner and wine on the table when he got home—a small way of thanking him for the holiday.

'You're a hero,' she told him, meeting his honesty with her own. 'A genuine, real-life hero. Are you sure you don't mind?'

'My pleasure,' he said, already opening drawers and cupboards and emptying the carrier bags onto the worktop.

She shut the bathroom door behind her and checked the temperature of the water, smiling to herself when she found it was still warm enough—no time wasted there. She slid Rosie into the bath and soaped her, distracting her with bubbles as she washed her hair and ran a flannel over her face, rubbing away the last few remnants of milk.

And as she went through their bathtime routine her mind strayed to the man in the kitchen, wondering what his expectations were for this evening…wondering how well prepared he had come. Had he replayed their conversations as often as she had? Had he wondered when would be the right time to take their relationship further? When 'slow' would become impossible?

And what would that next step mean?

Of course she was hoping that they would make love, but doing something like that didn't come without strings attached for Lily. For her it would be a commitment—but did Nic feel the same?

She left the bathroom with Rosie all clean and fresh and tucked into her pyjamas, wishing that she looked half as good herself. Unfortunately she knew that she looked little less than crazed. And, while she couldn't *see* any stains on her T-shirt, the laws of parenting probability meant that there had to be one there somewhere.

When she reached the kitchen Nic was cooking up a storm, but everything seemed to be perfectly under control. What did *that* feel like? She tried to remember a time when her life had felt like her own, when she had been confident that she knew exactly what she was doing and that she was doing a good job. Some time in the haze her pre-Rosie life had become, she assumed.

The paradox plagued her. It was the time when she most wanted to pull her family together, to prove that she could be mother and sister and aunt with the best of them, and it all seemed entirely out of her hands. The more she fought to show that she could do this—

be the matriarch, hold it all together—the faster things spun around her.

Nic stopped stirring the sauce on the hob for long enough to steal a quick kiss, and Lily plonked herself on a stool at the breakfast bar, watching him for a moment.

The kettle clicked and she noticed the bottle and tin of formula standing next to it, ready to be made up.

'I figured if the grown-ups are hungry then Rosie might well be too,' he said.

He'd dropped the wooden spoon and now stood leaning against the counter, hands in pockets. Lily looked at him closely, observing the slight change in his posture, the tension that had sneaked into his body and was holding him a little stiffer. Still trying, still struggling, she deduced. But he kept coming back for more. Not only that, he'd come carrying dinner and was helping to make bottles. She couldn't judge him for still finding things hard: he had earned her respect for trying despite that.

'So, what's for dinner?' Lily asked, placing Rosie in her bouncy chair and making up the bottle.

'Not very exciting, I'm afraid. Gnocchi, pancetta, cream sauce, a bit of salad—I've brought a little of Italy home with me.'

'You are the consummate domestic goddess,' she told him with a smile, hoping that it would cover the twinge of—what? Resentment that that had been *her* role, *her* talent, until she was faced with her first real challenge?

He must see how much she was struggling. Must have guessed that she wouldn't be able to put dinner on the table for him. Not that she was even *trying* for

Stepford-wife-style Cordon Bleu cuisine. She'd have settled for managing to get oven chips ready.

Something of her fears must have shown on her face, because Nic pushed himself up from the counter, hands no longer in his pockets. Instead they were reaching for her waist and pulling her into him. Suddenly emotional, Lily kept her eyes lowered, not wanting to look up and show him how upset she was that she was *still* not getting this right.

'I'm sorry if I did the wrong thing,' he said. 'I only wanted us to have a nice relaxed night. I've been looking forward to this, and the last thing I wanted was to cause you more work, more stress.'

He palmed her cheek and she turned into the warmth of his skin instinctively, and then slowly looked up.

'It wasn't a criticism, or a judgement.' He leaned in further, and pressed a quick kiss to her lips. 'You're doing an amazing job with Rosie, and I just wanted to do my bit.'

Another kiss and her limbs started to feel loose and languid, her body like a gel that wanted to mould to him.

Nic pulled away slightly and rested his forehead on hers. 'I've been thinking about that all day. *Every* day, actually,' he admitted. 'The least you can do after keeping me awake three nights in a row is let me make you dinner.'

She smiled. He was good—she'd give him that.

'Thank you,' she said. 'It's a lovely thought. And, for the record, I *might* have thought about you too. Just once or twice.'

He broke into a grin at that, and swooped a kiss onto her cheek.

True to his word, once Rosie was in bed Nic set two places at the dining table, lit the candles, served Lily an enormous portion of gnocchi and filled up their wine glasses.

'This is incredible,' Lily said as she sat down.

'I wouldn't get carried away,' Nic told her with a self-effacing smile. 'It's just gnocchi and sauce.'

'It's gnocchi, sauce, good wine and better company. It's like being in an alien land, and it's divine.'

'Well, I can drink to that,' Nic said, raising his glass in a toast and clinking it against hers. 'So, what have I missed?'

He'd been in the office until late the last couple of nights, making sure that everything was in place for his trip.

'Well, I have two big pieces of news—Rosie lifted her head for the first time today, and then I thought she smiled at me...but it turned out to be gas. It's been hectic!' She laughed, wondering what he'd make of her day.

'I'm sure it *was* a smile,' Nic said. 'Most likely because she's got such a wonderful aunt to take care of her.'

Lily smiled, bashful, acknowledging his praise with a blush, if not his knowledge of development milestones.

'And did you get the work done that you needed to?' Nic asked.

'Only just,' Lily admitted. 'But it's done now. I've not got anything else lined up for the next few weeks so I can concentrate on Rosie. I'm sure I'll miss it soon enough, and want something to challenge me. A *different* sort of challenge,' she clarified, just in case he'd missed the point that Rosie was an Olympic-sized challenge in herself. 'I'm only going to take on small commissions for now, but it's good to keep my eye in… keep my skills ticking over.'

'I'm impressed,' Nic told her.

Lily shrugged off the compliment.

'No, seriously.' He reached out for her hand as she tried again to brush off his words. 'I'm actually in awe—I can't even think how you find time in the day for it all.'

Lily laughed. 'Oh, it's easy. You just forget the laundry, and mopping the floor, and filing your nails, and…'

'And focus on what's important. Like I said, you're incredible.'

Lily held her hands up and shook her head. 'Okay, that's officially as much as I can take. We're going to have to change the subject or I'll become unbearable. What about you? Did you get everything sorted that you needed to?'

'Everything's taken care of. All we have to do to-morrow is get in the car when it shows up.'

And then make some pretty huge decisions about their future.

That bit didn't need saying, but after the careful way they'd spent the last few days she thought they both knew that that was what Rome was really going to be about. About finding out what they wanted to be to each other. What risks they were prepared to take and what hopes they were going to nurture.

They lingered over their coffee, neither of them making a move to go to bed—alone or otherwise.

But as Lily stifled a yawn Nic stood and cleared

away the last few dishes. 'You look done in,' he said over his shoulder. 'And I'm ready to turn in. I guess we should call it a night.'

So he wasn't going to suggest it. Well, she shouldn't be surprised. She was the one who had insisted on 'slower' the last time things had got out of hand. The ball was really in her court now.

'If you're sure…' Lily said, aiming the lilt in her voice at pure temptation.

But he didn't look as if he was wavering.

'We've an early start tomorrow,' he said, but the tense lines of his forehead told her he was struggling to do the noble thing. 'It's probably best if we call it a night.'

'Of course.' Lily stood up, but the slight shake of her legs revealed her hidden emotions.

Nic stood too, and rested his hands lightly on her waist. 'It's not just that…' he told her.

He surprised her with his sudden honesty. But she supposed they *were* trying to see if they had any hope of a future together. If they couldn't talk to each other, be honest with each other now, at the outset, then what hope did they have?

'Don't think for a second that it's because I don't want to take you to bed—that I haven't been imagining it every day.' He was rewarded with a flash of colour in her cheeks, and he traced the colour with his fingertips and then his lips. 'But once we take that step I'm yours, Lily. Everything I am will belong to you. We both have a lot to think about…a lot to decide… Let's not rush. We have as much time as we want and as we need.'

She nodded, the smile on her lips now genuine, if a little wary.

He walked her to her bedroom door and grabbed her hands as she reached for the handle. 'Still time to say a proper goodnight,' he said, pulling her close and running the backs of his fingers down the soft skin of her arm. From there he rested his hands on her waist, until there was nothing between them but their heavy breaths.

He dipped his head and brushed his lips gently against hers, testing. But she smiled against him, yielding to him for a moment and then drawing back, yielding and drawing back—until one of his hands was at the nape of her neck, the other was clamped at her waist, and he was backing her slowly against the hard wood of the door. He was desperate for more, to feel her giving herself wholly to him. For her to stop her teasing and give him everything she was…to demand all of him in return.

When she opened her mouth to him and touched his tongue with hers he let out a low groan, his hand fisting behind her back. He leaned back and smiled at her flushed face, laughed a little breathily.

'Oh, you're good,' he said. 'Really, *really* good. But I'll see you in the morning.'

She nodded, biting her lip.

'If you're sure…' she said, with a minxy little smile. 'I guess I'll see you then.'

'I've never been less sure about anything in my life,' he said, and his voice had a little gravel in it as he tried to pull her closer again.

But her hands had found his chest and were pushing

gently. 'No, I won't take advantage,' she said. Then, more seriously, 'You're right. I want us to be sure.'

He nodded, reason starting to return to him as the blood returned to his brain. 'So I'll see you in the morning?'

'I'll be waiting.'

CHAPTER TWELVE

LILY LIFTED THE delicate espresso cup to her lips and savoured the full, rich flavour as it touched her lips. Nic hadn't made it up to the hotel suite yet, but the smell had been so tempting she'd not been able to wait. There was a lot of that going on at the moment, she realised, still not sure what to make of Nic's decision last night to go to his own bed—alone.

It was gentlemanly of him, and deep down of course she knew that it had been the right decision. There was too much at stake, too many ways they could get hurt, for them to rush a decision like that. But... But nothing. The fact that she'd been desperate for him since the moment he'd left her last night shouldn't be a part of their decision-making process.

Well, if you were going to try and temper a girl's disappointment a suite in a five-star hotel in the Piazza di Spagna was a good start. She wandered around the living area of the suite now, stopping to admire the artwork adorning the walls and the artfully placed side tables. It was exquisite—unlike anywhere she'd seen before, never mind stayed. Rosie was still fast asleep in her carrycot, as she had been since they had left the airport. True to his word, Nic had arranged everything they needed, and they had been whisked from house to car to airport to hotel with barely a whimper from Rosie and barely any intervention from her.

There were two doors leading off the living area and she crossed to the one on her left, still a little awestruck by her surroundings. She tried the handle to the door and found it unlocked. She nudged the door open, feeling as if she was about to be caught snooping. An enormous bed—king-size? Emperor? Bigger?—dominated the room, draped with rich silky curtains and topped with crisp white sheets. Her room? she wondered. Or Nic's? Then she spotted the cot in the corner and her question was answered. Her room. And Rosie's. For a moment she wished she'd wake, so that she could share her excitement with her, waltz her around the suite and wow her with all the finery she couldn't yet understand.

But she'd woken her early once before, and that hadn't exactly gone well. She took another sip of her coffee, wondering where Nic had got to. He'd wanted a quick word with the concierge—that was all he'd told her as he'd encouraged her to go straight up to the room. The coffee had been awaiting them, along with fruit and pastries. She'd intended to wait for Nic to arrive before she indulged further, but now she questioned that decision. Well, if he was going to leave her here, he had only himself to blame.

She'd just selected the lightest pastry from the platter when the door opened and she was caught red-handed.

'Glad to see you're settling in,' Nic said, tossing his carry-on bag onto the couch and crossing to the table to grab a pastry for himself. 'These are incredible,' he said, devouring the morsel in a few quick bites. 'Worth flying out for these alone.'

'The coffee's not bad,' Lily said, with a smile to show she was joking. 'And the room's just about adequate.'

He surprised her with a quick kiss to the lips.

'I'm glad you like it,' he said. 'I've not stayed here before, but I've heard great things.'

'Not your usual haunt?'

'No, I normally stay somewhere a little more…rustic. But I promised you girls an adventure in Rome, and I don't think that Nonna Lucia's *pensione* really fits the bill.'

'Nonna Lucia?'

'She looks after me when I'm here—seems to rather like having someone to fuss over.'

'Won't she be offended that we're not staying with her?'

'Actually, I already ran it by her. I knew she'd be offended if she found out somehow. I explained that I was bringing a friend with me, and that we'd need some more space, and she nodded in a very knowing way and said, "Of course." I think maybe I've given her the wrong idea…'

Lily laughed, delighted with this description. 'Will I get to meet her?'

'If you'd like to. I know that we'd be welcome any time. I was just speaking to the concierge about dinner, and he was making some enquiries, but if you'd rather—?'

She thought back to how well a fancy meal had gone last time and didn't hesitate. 'I'd love to. I'd like to see what your life is like when you're travelling,' she said. 'If it's not all five-star suites and divine coffee.'

'Oh, Nonna's coffee is second to none,' he reassured her. 'I'll call her to arrange tonight—if you're sure you don't want to go somewhere more…?'

'I'm sure,' she told him.

'Well, that's dinner sorted, then. What do you fancy doing in the meantime? Settle in here a little longer? Or head out for some sightseeing?'

She glanced around the room, caught sight of the bed in the other room, and suddenly lost her nerve. 'Let's go out,' she said. 'I don't want to waste a minute of this trip.'

'Brilliant,' Nic replied. 'What about Rosie? I don't want to wake her if she's not ready, but Rome's not known for being pushchair-friendly. There should be a baby carrier around here somewhere, though.'

Torn, Lily tried to decide what to do. She didn't want to wake the baby, and risk her grumping through the afternoon, but the whole of Rome was waiting for them and she couldn't wait to see it. She glanced at her watch, wondering how much longer she would sleep. Perhaps another half an hour…

'What about this?' Nic said. 'We head up to the roof terrace—I can carry the carrycot. We take in Rome from above, and once she wakes we hit the town.'

'Perfect.'

An hour later Rosie was awake, looking from Nic to Lily, wondering who was most likely to give her attention and a cuddle. Lily got to her first, reaching down to the carrycot, which Nic had tucked into a shady corner, and scooping Lily into her arms.

'What do you think she makes of it so far?' Nic asked.

Lily laughed. 'She's been asleep since we left the airport! But I'm sure she'll love it as much as I will.'

'Shall we dig out that baby carrier and find out?'

They wandered out from the hotel with Rosie strapped to Lily's front, and the heat of the summer afternoon hit them hard. The roof terrace had been shaded, with creeping plants over gazebos, but out on the street there was nothing more than her wide-brimmed hat to protect her and Rosie's pale skin from the burn of the sun.

'You okay?' Nic asked.

'I didn't realise how hot it is,' she told him, fanning her face. 'The terrace was so shady.'

'Let's keep off the main streets, then,' Nic said, taking her hand and leading her down one of the winding side streets that led off the main drag.

She breathed out a sigh of relief as they walked along in the shadow of the buildings, the blare of car horns and buzzing mopeds fading behind them.

'Better?' he asked.

'This is lovely.' She squeezed his hand as they passed a sleepy-looking restaurant, its owners still at their siesta, perhaps.

'So, what do you want to see? The Colosseum? The Vatican? Trevi Fountain? We can start wherever you like.'

'They all sound nice…' Lily started.

'But…?'

'But this is nice too,' she finished, smiling up at him as he pulled her to a stop.

The lane had meandered past delicious-smelling

bakeries and traditional-looking *trattorie* until it had become no more than a sun-dappled alleyway, with apartments on either side, their balconies spilling colour and texture as flowers hung down from the walls.

'Seeing Rome like this…it's something I never really imagined. But what I'm most looking forward to about this trip—' She bit her lip, looking for the confidence she needed to make this confession. Then she remembered his honesty the night before, and knew that she owed him nothing less than the truth. 'I want to spend it with *you*. Whether we do that at the Colosseum or here—and frankly this is the prettiest little street I've ever seen—doesn't seem that important.'

She watched him carefully, wondering what he had made of her words. The expression on his face left her none the wiser. Then, instead of speaking, he dropped his head and his lips landed on hers, soft and gentle. Their warmth, his taste, was becoming deliciously familiar. With each time they kissed she felt more comfortable, and that heat in her belly grew, leaving her wanting more and more. The backs of his fingers brushed the skin of her neck, her collarbone, and it was only as she instinctively moved closer that she remembered that Rosie was there between them—physically as well as emotionally.

With a smile, she pulled away. Nic met her gaze and held it for a few seconds, then, with his eyes on hers until the last minute, he dropped his head slowly and kissed Rosie on the top of her head.

He straightened, meeting Lily's eyes with an intense look. 'I want to make you promises, Lily. I want to tell you that I'll be everything you deserve. But I can't.'

Lily froze, not wanting to break the intensity of the moment, knowing that Nic had more to say.

'I've been here before, Lily. I've tried to be the family man, tried to support a partner and a family, and it didn't end well.'

'Nic, you can't blame yourself for what happened to Max.'

'If that was all I had to feel guilty about…' His voice was filled with anguish and his eyes were faraway, lost in the past. 'It wasn't just Max I let down, Lily. It was Clare. After what happened she needed me. Needed her fiancé to be there for her, to talk to her about what had just happened. To try and find a way to get past it. I couldn't do it.'

'Nic, everyone copes in different ways.'

'That's no excuse. She needed something from me—something very simple—and I couldn't give it to her. It was *my* fault that our relationship broke down after Max died. *My* fault that we fell apart when she thought she was already at rock bottom. You need to know this, Lily, before you decide where you want this to go. You need to know that if—God forbid—it all goes wrong, and you lose Rosie, I can't promise to be there for you. You deserve someone who can.'

Lily stood and stared at him for a moment, and shivered even in the thirty-degree heat. This was what he'd been hiding, then—this was the shadow she'd glimpsed and never understood.

'Nic, I can't believe that it was all your responsibility. I'm sure you tried your hardest.'

'You're right—I did,' he said, his voice steadier now. 'I tried my hardest and it wasn't enough. I like you—a hell of a lot. I don't want to keep fighting it. But if we're doing this you deserve to know what you're getting into.'

Lily placed her hands either side of his face and reached up on tiptoes to press a kiss to his lips. 'Nic, I trust you. You've done more for me these past few weeks than just about anyone else I can think of. You can say what you like, but if there's a crisis heading my way I know I want you there with me. Nothing you tell me about your past is going to change that.'

His face softened slightly, and she let herself hope for a moment that she'd got through to him.

'I want to do this,' she went on. 'I want us to take these feelings seriously. I'm not talking about sitting back and seeing what happens. I'm talking about working hard to make each other happy.'

He closed his eyes for a brief moment, and then leaned forward and kissed her quickly, sweetly.

'Can we walk?' he asked, keeping hold of her hand as he started moving again, towards the arch of sunlight at the end of the lane.

She said nothing, knowing that he was still working through his feelings.

'I don't know how I thought I could stop myself,' he said at last.

Lily bit her lip, wondering whether she was supposed to understand that enigmatic sentence.

'Falling for you, I mean.'

She risked a glance up at him and saw that it wasn't only tears that had made his eyes bright. There was a light there—something bright and shining. A smile that hadn't quite reached his lips yet but was lighting his face in a way that she recognised.

'You're sure that you don't want to get out now? Because I'd understand.'

'I'm going nowhere, Nic. But are *you* sure you're ready for his? Because I come as a package deal, remember?'

'I know that. I don't know how I thought I could fall for you without falling for Rosie as well, but I tried—and I failed. I want you for everything you are. And that includes the way you care for Rosie.'

'And you're okay with that?'

By his own admission he'd been fighting it, and fighting it hard. How could he be so sure now?

'I'm not going to lie and say that it doesn't hurt. Sometimes when I look at Rosie, growing all bonny and fat and healthy, it does make me think of my son and everything that he and I missed. But it's too late, Lily. She's a part of you, and I feel like she's becoming a part of me too.'

She was falling for him too—she knew that. The feelings that had been growing these past few weeks had only one possible end point. She smiled up at him and saw relief wash over his features as she reached up to kiss him, pressing her lips hard against his, trying to show with her body what she couldn't find the words to express.

They wandered the city hand in hand for another hour or two, with Rosie alternately snoozing or cooing from her baby carrier. The Trevi Fountain was magical, even packed with tourists, and the coffee in a little *piazza* café was hot and strong—but it was the light in Nic's eyes that made the afternoon perfect…the way he sneaked touches and kisses when they found themselves alone, the promise in his eyes and his body and the feelings for her that he had already declared.

When Rosie began to grumble, a little tired, they headed back to the hotel. Once she was tucked into her carrycot, all ready to be clipped into her pram when they went out for dinner, Lily headed out into the living room, a little nervous to be alone in a hotel room with Nic after all that had been said, all that had been resolved between them. She found Nic by the sofa, pouring glasses of something deliciously cold and sparkling.

'Something to start our evening off with a bit of a pop,' he said as she approached. 'Nonna's expecting us in about an hour, but if you need a bit more time…?'

Lily glanced at her watch. 'I think Rosie will sleep for another two hours at least, so as long as we don't have to disturb her that should be perfect. Just enough time to shower and change.'

Nic raised an eyebrow. 'You know you look perfect as you are.'

Lily had to laugh. He must have it bad, she thought, knowing full well that there was formula on her T-shirt and that she'd perspired more than was strictly lady-like during their walk.

'Don't give me that look,' Nic admonished. 'You could go out without doing a thing and be the envy of every woman in Rome.'

'Flattery will get you everywhere.'

She said the words without thinking, with a chuckle and a sip of her wine. But when she lowered her glass and met Nic's eyes it was to find them full of the passion they'd barely been suppressing all afternoon.

'An hour?' she asked, thinking of everything they could do in that time—all the possibilities open to them now they had admitted what they were feeling for one another.

'An hour's not nearly enough time for everything I've been thinking of,' Nic said, his face full of promise. 'And I think I might want a good meal first...'

Now, *that* sounded encouraging: the sort of evening one needed to carbo-load for.

Nic crossed the room until he was by her side and took the glass of Prosecco from her hands, placing it carefully on a side table before taking her in his arms. One hand sneaked up her spine and rested at the nape of her neck, the other settled in the small of her back, pulling her close against his hard body.

She let out a breathless sigh, wondering how they were meant to make it out of this hotel room without things getting out of hand. Reaching up, she cupped Nic's face in her palm, enjoying the rasp of his stubble against the smooth pads of her fingers, the hardness of his jaw and the softness of his cheeks. When her fingertips found his mouth, he kissed first one finger then the next.

With her thumb she explored the fullness of his bottom lip and the cleft of his chin. When she felt she knew every inch of his face she stretched up on tiptoes and traced the path of her fingers with her lips. Butterfly kisses that teased and promised more, but she wanted to savour every moment. They had all night to explore one another. And while there were parts of him she was desperate to know better, she was determined to make the most of every minute with him. Not to rush a single second of the experience.

For so many years she had waited, wondering when it would be her turn to have a family of her own. Now that she had found it she wanted to remember every moment, appreciate every sensation. Finally her lips found his, and she brushed a gentle kiss across his top lip, and then the bottom. Nic's fingers flexed behind her head, twisting strands of hair but not pressing her closer, not taking what she wasn't ready to give.

His body was strung like a bow, and with every caress she felt more tension in his muscles, more possession in his hold at the small of her back. When her thumb brushed the sensitive skin behind his ear his mouth opened in a groan, and she could resist temptation no longer.

She explored the warmth of his mouth, tested the limits of his restraint, measuring the desperation in his hold. The man was determined—she had to give him that. He'd said they should wait, and it seemed that wait they would. But she had only just started exploring, and at a guess they still had a good forty minutes before they had to leave.

When her tongue touched his, the fire she'd banked in his veins burst free. With the passion she'd seen in him earlier he possessed her mouth, his hands roaming now, rather than settling her against him. One dropped to the curve of her buttock, alternately caressing, exploring and pressing her against him. The other moved from nape to collarbone, and then lower. When his thumb brushed against her breast she moaned into his mouth, sure that at last she was going to get everything she had been fantasising about for the past month.

But he broke off their kiss, moved fractionally backwards until there was a good inch of space between them.

'You…are an absolute…siren.'

She gave him her most minxy smile as he struggled to speak, his voice ragged and breathless.

'And I am going to make you pay for that later. But for now a shower—a cold one, I suggest—and then let's go to dinner.'

'Spoilsport.'

But she couldn't be disappointed really—not when she'd seen the effect she'd had on him, and now knew better than ever what she had in store when they got home. Waiting had done nothing to temper their passion before now, and another couple of hours could only make them more ardent.

She hadn't known what to expect of Nonna's *pensione*, and at times when they'd passed by the brightly lit windows of the Trastevere area she'd feared that they would find themselves in either a fine dining restaurant, where she would feel awkward and out of place, or one of the *trattorie* designed to trap tourists—all plastic vegetables and fake bonhomie. But when she walked through the door of Nonna's her fears instantly vanished.

This was neither pretentious nor tacky. It was—almost instantly—*home*. The moment they walked through the door she found herself enfolded in a generous matronly bosom and kissed on both her cheeks. Nic had pushed the pram across the challenging Roman cobbles and was now wrestling it up the front steps, leaving Lily undefended against this friendly onslaught.

'*Bella*, you are the friend of Nico. You are so very welcome tonight,' she said, kissing her again on both cheeks.

'Signora Lucia, it's a pleasure to meet you.'

'*Tsch*, you must call me Nonna—like my Nico.'

At that, Nic finally made it up the steps with the carrycot, and Nonna's attention was lost completely as she peered into the carrycot and spoke in a loud whisper.

'And your *bambina*. She is a beauty. Nico told me this and now I see. *Bella*—like her *mamma*.'

Lily blushed, both from the compliment and the mix-up. But she was distracted from correcting her by the sensation of Nic's arm settling across her shoulders. The gesture was comforting, possessive, natural, and she turned into the warmth of his body.

Nonna bent over the pram again and Lily held her breath, hoping that the baby wouldn't wake up and fret through their dinner, but Nonna only stroked her cheek and muttered a string of Italian babytalk.

'Come—I have lovely table for this lovely family,' she said, and she stood and led them to a table set for two, tucked in a private corner. A candle flickered on the crisply ironed cloth and Nonna pulled up a bench for them to set the carrycot on.

'When she wakes up you call me and I come see her, okay?'

Lily was filled with such a sense of warmth and welcome that she felt tears welling behind her eyes.

'You didn't correct her,' Nic said, his voice carefully casual, and Lily knew he was referring to Nonna's use of the word *'mamma'*.

'I didn't really know what to say…how to explain… Anyway, you distracted me.'

'Me? What did I do?'

'That casual arm around the shoulder. I couldn't think for a minute.'

'An *arm*? After what you tried earlier, you couldn't think because of an arm?'

She laughed. 'Well, maybe the arm brought back a memory or two,' she clarified. 'What must she think of me? A mum with a new baby, out for dinner with a man who's not the father. Wait—she knows you're not Rosie's dad, right?'

Nic took a sip of the Prosecco that Nonna had poured when she'd shown them to their table. 'She knows. And I think it's as clear to you as it is to me that she already adores you both. She doesn't care about the details of how Rosie came into our life any more than I do. She can see that you love her like a mother.'

'But I'm not, am I? Rosie and I have spent all this time getting to know each other, trying to see how our lives can fit together, and it could all have been for nothing. We could get back to London and find that everything's changed. I could lose Rosie—and then what?'

'First,' Nic said, pressing her hand into his, 'I'm sure that whatever happens with Helen you're never going to lose Rosie completely. I think that your sister loves you, and loves Rosie, and she knows that you're both better off with each other in your lives. If Helen was to turn up tomorrow and take Rosie away—we'd try and cope…together.'

She took a deep breath, forcing her body to relax. She wasn't sure where the sudden surge of fear and apprehension had come from. Perhaps it was inevitable, she thought. With things going so well in one part of her life now that she and Nic seemed to be finally finding their way towards happiness, some other aspect of it had to fall apart. Surely this was too good to be true—

a kind, handsome man, a romantic getaway in Rome, a beautiful niece whom she thought of as a daughter...

'Are you okay?' Nic asked, concern creasing his forehead.

Lily nodded, determined to throw off this sense that it was all going too well. It would be unforgivable to ruin this evening just because of some strange sense of foreboding. There was no such thing as karma. The universe wasn't going to punish her for being happy with Nic by taking Rosie away.

'Better than okay,' she said, and after glancing around to check that no one was looking she sneaked a quick kiss. 'Sorry—just a wobble. I guess I'm still not quite sure what I am to Rosie—mum or aunty. It's going to take a little time to get used to what other people might think.'

'It doesn't matter what anyone else thinks. What matters is that you and Rosie are happy.'

'Well, we are. Blissfully,' she replied honestly. 'This has been just a perfect day, Nic. I don't know how to thank you.'

'Oh, well, I can think of an idea or two,' he replied with a cheeky grin. 'But there's no need to thank me. The pleasure of your company for today is thanks enough.'

She smiled back, and then turned her head as Rosie stirred in her cot.

'Will she wake soon?' Nic asked.

'Maybe just for a feed, but she normally goes back to sleep after a bit of a cuddle.'

'She's changing so quickly,' Nic said, watching her as she wriggled awake.

Lily reached out and touched his arm, knowing that

he was thinking of Max. But he wasn't frowning when she looked up at him. Instead he had the same soppy, dopey expression that she normally wore when she was talking about Rosie.

'It's amazing to watch her, you know. I feel very lucky to be a part of it.'

'We feel pretty lucky too,' Lily told him. 'I know how hard you've found it, but having you here for me these past few weeks…I'm not sure what I would have done without you.'

'You'd have done fine,' he told her. 'But you're right. Some things are better when you can share them with someone.'

'I'm glad you said that,' Lily said, trying to lighten the mood. 'Because I have to nip to the bathroom. Are you okay with her for a minute?'

Before today she'd have watched him carefully, trying to judge his reaction to the thought of being left alone with Rosie. But now she trusted him to tell her what he was feeling. To tell her if she was asking too much.

'Of course.'

He pulled her down for a brief kiss as she passed him, and she was filled with a sense of warmth and well-being.

When she returned from the bathroom it was to find Nonna seated at their table with the baby on her lap drinking from her bottle and lapping up the attention. She moved to stand beside Nic, but when she arrived Nonna stood, offering her her seat back.

'I cannot resist such a beautiful baby,' she told Lily. 'Nico tells me she's hungry and I find myself sitting

like this. I think I'll never put her down. She is so wonderful I keep her for ever.'

'I hope she wasn't causing trouble?' Lily replied.

'Not at all,' Nic reassured her. 'Nonna just couldn't
resist. I hope that's okay?'

She told him that of course it was, and when a shout
emerged from the kitchen both Nic and Lily held out
their hands to take the baby.

Lily could almost feel the weight of her in her hands,
but Nonna passed her to Nic instead, and Lily was left
watching as Rosie settled happily into his arms.

'Ah... Daddy's girl, I think you say. I must go back
to the kitchen now, but if she cries I will come straight
away and take her. You two need a quiet dinner. Lots
of talking,' Nonna commented sagely, before bustling
in the direction of the kitchen.

Lily watched as Nonna walked away, her mouth
slightly open in surprise.

'What can I say?' Nick commented with a laugh.
'She's quite a force. I'm always too terrified to argue
with her. I think she's crazy about you, though.'

'Crazy, perhaps,' Lily agreed. 'You didn't even
flinch,' she said, 'when she said Daddy.'

He took a deep breath, and Lily knew that he was
working up to something.

'You know that I've never thought about having any
more children, but when Nonna said that my initial reaction wasn't horror or fear. Instead I thought about
how much I liked being a dad. How I might like that
again one day.'

Lily couldn't speak. She'd paused with her glass
halfway to her lips and now found that she couldn't
move. Was he talking about starting a family? With

her? For a fleeting second she could see it—the three of them, the four of them…God, maybe even more—but then a gentle panic started to nag. Things were moving too quickly, surely, to be talking about this now.

'I didn't mean right away,' he said, interpreting her expression. 'I just meant that one day I think I might want it again. And I've never thought that before.'

Lily finally took the sip of her wine, buying herself a few more moments to calm herself.

'I'm glad if me and Rosie have helped.'

The words sounded trite, even to her, and she wondered how she had wandered into this politeness— wondered at the distance that seemed to have sprung from nowhere.

She *wanted* Nic to want a family. Deep down, she wanted Nic to be part of *her* family. Surely that was what it was all about? Getting to know someone, exploring a relationship. She'd always envisaged marriage, a husband. Equal partners. But now she wondered if she'd really thought about what that would mean. She'd never considered that her family growing meant that she was a smaller constituent part. Since Rosie had landed on her doorstep she'd been everything to her, and it was going to take some getting used to if she wanted Rosie to share her affections with someone else.

She wanted to show that she could do it herself. Wanted to build a family and keep it close. What did it say about her if she couldn't do it? If one day she wasn't the person Rosie turned to?

Their starters arrived and she ate, watching Nic and Rosie, despising the curl of jealousy she couldn't deny, despite the fact that she knew it was ridiculous. She pasted on a smile, not wanting Nic to guess that her thoughts were still dwelling on Rosie's willingness to go to him. It was just one bottle, she reminded herself. Not a competition, or anything.

Rosie finished her bottle with an enthusiastic gurgle, and the familiar sound broke Lily's tense mood.

'Do you want to take her?' Nic asked, looking a little hesitant.

Well, maybe she hadn't hidden her worries as well as she had hoped.

'You cuddle a little longer if you want to,' Lily said—and meant it. How could she begrudge these two some time together? Rosie deserved this full-on attention—deserved the full force of Nic's smile and the warmth and comfort of his arms. There was a connection between the two of them, Lily acknowledged, and she was glad of it.

'So, did you tell your sister about this little excursion?' Lily asked, finding it a little strange that Kate hadn't called for a run-down of the latest developments.

'Well, it all happened so fast…' Nic said with an expression of insincere innocence. 'I only just managed to tell her that I had to go away. There simply wasn't time to tell her that you two were coming as well.'

'By which I take it to mean you were too scared to confess?'

He laughed. 'The woman's capacity for inappropriate questions knows no bounds,' he said, holding up his hands in defeat. 'It takes a stronger man than I am to volunteer for that sort of grilling.'

'Oh, gee, thanks—so you leave me to handle the fall-out when we get back?'

'Is there a chance that she might just conveniently never find out?' Nic asked, looking hopeful.

'Not any chance, I'm afraid. You're right—she sniffs these things out, and if she ever discovered that I'd kept it from her there'd be hell to pay. *So* not worth it. She has to forgive *you*—you're her brother. If I held back on her I'm not sure that she'd ever take me back.'

Nic laughed. 'I'm not so sure about that. Some of the lectures I've endured—I think she's rather more concerned with you than with me.'

Lily could imagine. Kate was protective of her friends at the best of times, but since Rosie had come on the scene, and Lily's life had become at least twenty-seven thousand times more complicated, she'd stepped things up a level. Lily had tried telling her that she didn't need to worry so much, but Kate seemed determined to be the gatekeeper to Lily's life.

Conversation flowed like wine through the rest of their dinner, and by the time Nonna was cooing over Rosie as she brought over their coffees the earlier tension had disappeared completely. Well, not *disappeared*, exactly. It had morphed into a different sort of tension.

The sort that drew her close to Nic's side as he manoeuvred the pram back to the hotel. The sort that had her up on her tiptoes and stealing a quick, hard kiss in the hotel lift. And the sort that made her draw away from him, a little shy, once they'd reached the privacy of their suite.

But her kiss in the lift had clearly fired something in Nic, and the moment they were through the door his arms were around her, lifting her and moulding her, until his lean body was perfectly fitted to her soft curves and his lips had found hers in a kiss that stole her breath.

All thoughts of shyness fled under the onslaught of sensation: hips and lips on hers, his hands in her hair, the cold wood of the door behind her back contrasting with the heat of his body. She tore her lips away and tilted her head, inviting him to kiss the soft skin of her neck. He responded greedily, nuzzling at her collarbone, sipping kisses from behind her ear, biting gently on her shoulder.

She let out a groan as she let her body loosen, her weight held entirely by door and man, and instead focussed her energy on Nic, on kissing and exploring and reaching bare skin.

Until a snuffle from the pram behind him drew her up short.

Her body froze instantly and Nic backed away, a question in his eyes.

'Sorry…' she gasped, fighting for reason as much as she was for breath. 'I nearly forgot…' How could she have forgotten that Rosie was right there? That she was responsible for a little human life before giving in to her own needs and desires?

But Nic didn't look concerned, or even shocked that she had put her own passions above her responsibility to Rosie.

'Don't worry about it,' he said, kissing her again on the lips, but gently this time. 'She was fast asleep and perfectly safe. You didn't do anything wrong.'

She let out a long breath, thankful to have this understanding, intelligent man in her life. Someone who saw her worst fears even more clearly than she saw them herself.

'Why don't you get her settled? Take your time,' he added, with an expression full of dark, seductive promise. 'I'm not going anywhere.'

Take your time. Why had he said that? It seemed as if she'd been in her bedroom for an age, and he paced the living room, waiting for her to return. He could hear Rosie, grizzling slightly—disturbed, he guessed, by the move from warm pram to cold cot. *Settle quickly*, he pleaded with her silently, desperate to pick up where he and Lily had left off.

He poured wine, for the sake of something to do, though he knew that they wouldn't touch it. He'd sipped one glass all night and Lily had barely started hers.

Finally the door to Lily's room opened, and he turned on the spot to see her closing it softly, peeking through at the last minute to make sure that Rosie was okay. With barely a whisper the latch closed, and they were alone at last.

He forced himself to stay where he was—not to rush over and hold her against the wall as he had earlier. He'd moved quickly—too quickly—when they'd first arrived back, and she'd ended up looking uncertain and concerned. He couldn't risk that again. Instead he'd wait for her to come to him, as she had before they'd gone out for dinner, teasing him with her kisses and caresses.

She crossed the room to stand in front of him, but kept her body from him still. He stood firm, determined that she must reach for him and not the other way around. She'd dropped her eyes. He loved to see bashfulness warring with passion in her posture and in her features. Was she having second thoughts? God knew *he'd* had enough over the past few weeks. But none tonight. He wouldn't ever again, he suspected, after his revelation this afternoon of what she'd come to mean to him.

Caving at last, unable to keep himself from touching her, he brushed his lips gently across her cheek. 'Everything okay?' he asked gently.

'Fine,' Lily said, finally looking up.

Her smile was brave, but not entirely genuine. There was still something troubling her, he knew.

'What is it?' he asked, pulling on her hand until she dropped down next to him on the sofa.

'Nothing's wrong,' she said, but then paused. 'It's just hard…trying to do what's right for Rosie and what I want for me.'

'Those two things aren't mutually exclusive, you know,' he told her gently.

'I know. But when we came in just now I just wasn't thinking. I mean *at all*. Anything could have happened and I'd have been completely oblivious.'

The smug smile was halfway to his lips before he got it under control.

'That's not true, Lily,' he reminded her. 'As soon as she made a peep you were right there. You can do a good job of taking care of her *and* have a life of your own as well. Trust me,' he said, wrapping an arm around her shoulder. 'You're doing an amazing job. But if you want to turn in now, cuddle up just the two of you in your room, then I would understand.'

She thought about it for a long minute.

'It's not what I want,' she told him, her voice carrying a slight waver. 'I know what I want—you.'

He breathed a long sigh of relief. He'd meant what

he'd said—he would have kissed her gently goodnight and watched her shut her bedroom door behind her—but, God, was he glad that he didn't have to.

He'd wrapped his arm around her shoulder to comfort her, but as his fingers brushed across the soft skin of her upper arm the caress turned from soothing to sensual, and his fingertips crackled with the electricity that surged between them.

Lily turned to him, but he knew the next move had to come from her. If she'd had doubts—if she *still* had doubts—he'd understand, and he wouldn't rush her.

Slowly, quietly, she moved closer to him, until her lips were just an inch from his, the lower one caught between her teeth. He could bite it for her, he thought, imagining the warmth and moistness of her mouth. She looked from his eyes to his lips and reached out her hand. Her thumb caught his lower lip, as it had earlier, caressing gently. He opened his mouth to her, inviting her in, and finally, excruciatingly, she leaned forward and pressed her lips to his. But it wasn't surrender on her part—it was triumph as she kissed and tasted and explored.

He ran his hands down to her hips, pulling her closer to him, and swallowed the satisfied groan that emerged from her mouth. Now, with no distractions, no limits on their time, no reason not to do everything he had ever imagined…it was intoxicating. He pulled her closer still, until she was nestled onto his lap, her arms around his neck. When he could hold back no longer he stood, lifting her as if she weighed no more than a feather, and started towards his bedroom.

She pulled back for a moment and gazed into his

eyes. 'Yes?' he asked, hoping with every part of his being that he had judged this right.

'Oh, God, yes,' Lily replied, her voice barely more than a husky murmur. *'Yes.'*

CHAPTER THIRTEEN

LILY CRACKED AN eyelid and glanced at the clock on the bedside table—it was nearly six. Rosie would be up again soon, and Lily didn't want her to wake up alone in a strange place. She eased herself out from under Nic's arm, careful not to wake him, and threw on what she could find of her clothes. She sneaked out of the room, closing the door softly behind her.

Rosie was awake when she went into their room, happily gurgling in her cot. 'Morning, sunshine,' she whispered as she got closer. 'Did you remember we're on holiday?'

She picked up the phone and arranged for hot water to be brought up, then started digging in Rosie's bag for formula and a bottle.

Once she'd answered the discreet knock at the door and made up Rosie's breakfast she wasn't sure what to do next. In the night she'd fed Rosie in bed, and then crept back to Nic and initiated round two, and three… What if Nic woke this time and found her gone? It didn't seem like the right way to start their day. But bringing Rosie into their bed—it screamed *family*, and she wasn't sure if they were ready for that.

I'll go back to him, she decided eventually. It might

not be the right thing to do—there was no way to know until she did it—but getting back into her cold bed alone didn't seem like the right thing, either.

She tiptoed back into Nic's room, trying not to wake him as she eased herself under the blankets without dropping either baby or bottle.

She settled into the pillows and looked around her. This was it, she thought. Beautiful baby...beautiful man. This was how she had always imagined Sunday mornings would be. Admittedly, their path to here had been a little unconventional, and, yes, it was a Thursday, but now she was here it seemed pretty perfect to her.

It was almost impossible not to reach out and touch Nic. She wondered whether it was possible to wake him just by staring at him. Apparently not. But Rosie didn't have the same scruples as Lily and was more than happy to wake Nic up, practising a raspberry noise with a mouthful of milk. Lily tried to mop up without waking him, but the stirring hand beneath the sheet gave him away and she knew that Rosie had managed what she hadn't dared.

She watched his face as he swam up from sleep. A lazy smile lifted his lips as he realised she was there: he'd forgotten, perhaps. Though how he couldn't remember last night, when it was seared on her memory, she had no idea. His face fell when he spotted Rosie and he pulled himself up on the pillows, blinking rapidly and wiping sleep from his eyes with the heels of his hands.

'Morning.'

His voice was gruff, and not entirely friendly. She instinctively pulled the blankets a little tighter around them, feeling suddenly vulnerable under his scornful gaze. Was it her presence or Rosie's that was the problem? She knew the answer to that—he'd been more than happy to see *her*, it had only been when he'd spotted the baby that his face had turned to stone. And when his face had dropped, so had Lily's.

'Sorry, we didn't mean to wake you.'

She *was* sorry for waking him, but she didn't see that she really had anything else to apologise for. Nic was the one who had told her he was ready for this. That he'd struggled in the past but wanted her and Rosie to be a part of his life. He couldn't have expected her to sneak back to her own bed this morning as if nothing had happened, could he? Or to leave Rosie where she was and pretend that this wasn't the reality of her life?

Nic tried pasting a smile back on to his face but it was too late: the damage was done. The cracks were showing anyway, and Lily knew that however much he might say otherwise he wasn't as ready for this as he'd said he was. He would have been happier not to find them both there this morning, and that cracked Lily's heart more than just a little.

'No, it's fine—just a surprise, that's all.'

A surprise? It shouldn't have been. If he really understood her life—and how could he decide if he wanted to be a part of it if he didn't understand it?— then surely he should have expected this.

She hadn't known when she'd woken in the dawn light what to expect of this morning—whether they would be awkward, or whether the natural-as-breathing intimacy of last night would carry through to today.

The last thing she'd expected was this: the sight of
Nic climbing from the bed and pulling running shorts
from a drawer.

'I think I might make the most of the early-morn-
ing temperature,' he said, not meeting her eye. 'Fit
in a quick jog before it hits thirty degrees. You don't
mind, do you?'

Did it matter what she thought? It was pretty obvious that he was going, either way.

As the door to the bathroom shut she looked down
at Rosie and breathed out a long sigh. Last night everything had seemed so perfect, so right. She had known
even then that it was too good to be true.

Nic counted his breaths in and out as his feet struck
the unfamiliar cobbles, trying to pace himself around
the irregular maze of streets and alleyways. That was
maybe the most cowardly thing he'd ever done, and
no number of heel-strikes was going to make him any
less ashamed of it. The look on Lily's face had been
heartbreaking. A mixture of confusion and sorrow.

He pushed himself harder and checked his watch:
he'd been gone forty-five minutes. The guilt was more
than a twinge—it was closer to a knife in his gut. He
really should go back. But what to say to her?

He'd seen her face. How could he make her see
that he'd meant everything he'd said to her yesterday? When he'd told her he was falling for her, that
he wanted both her *and* Rosie in his life, he'd meant
it—and he'd thought he'd known what he was taking
on.

But nothing had quite prepared him for the sight

of them both when he was barely awake, barely conscious. There had been a split second when he'd seen a different baby, when he'd been in a different bed. And the thought of what had happened, of the different reality that he was waking up to, had crushed his heart for a moment.

This was harder than he'd expected, but that didn't mean he was giving up. Anything worth having was worth fighting for. Hard. But how could Lily know that he felt that way? He'd already told her that he didn't know if she could rely on him, and now he'd gone and proved it—he'd bailed at the first opportunity. As far as she was concerned he'd got what he'd been looking for and then left her alone in his bed while he pulled on clothes and headed out through the door.

He turned back to the hotel, wondering what he'd find when he got there. Her bags packed, perhaps. Or the suite empty, her clothes gone from the wardrobe and her lotions missing from the bathroom.

He let himself into the suite and was relieved to hear her singing in her bedroom, Rosie gurgling along. There was clearly something about the combination of nursery rhymes and power ballads that was irresistible to that girl.

Obviously encouraged, Lily turned up the volume and sang even louder. The door was open and he crossed the living room, resting his shoulder against the frame as he watched her dancing around, pulling faces to try and make Rosie smile. Despite his serious mood, he found himself smiling too.

But he knew that he was intruding on something personal, so he cleared his throat, drawing her attention. Colour rose on her cheeks as she turned towards him, and she stopped singing instantly.

'You're back.'

'Yes. And I'm sorry for leaving like that.'

She dropped her gaze, but not before he could see the hurt in her eyes. He had a lot of explaining to do—and a lot of making up. For weeks they'd been moving so slowly, feeling their way towards trusting each other, and then with one rash move—running instead of staying and explaining—he'd destroyed something of the bond they'd built. Had he learnt nothing from the way things had ended with Clare?

'Are you hungry?' he asked. 'I thought we could call down for some breakfast and eat up here. I know that I've upset you, and I think it would be good to talk.'

She didn't answer for a moment; instead she picked up Rosie from the bed and held her against her chest. Her arms were firm around her, and Nic knew that the cuddle was more for Lily's comfort than for Rosie's.

'Sure,' she said eventually. 'I'll order something while you take a shower.'

He washed quickly. Part of him wanted to delay this conversation—delay the moment when he had to look at Lily and know how much his selfishness had hurt her. But it wasn't fair on her to make her wait longer than she already had for his apology and his explanation. So he grabbed a towel and dragged it over his limbs.

The softness of the cotton reminded him of her tender caresses last night—the way that every sensation had been heightened until even the brush of the sheet against his back had driven him to heights he hadn't recognised.

He glanced at the clock as he walked towards his wardrobe. He had meetings today—it was why he was here, after all—but the thought that he'd have to leave in an hour, whether things were settled or not, twisted that knife in his gut.

When he arrived back in the living room a waiter was laying a breakfast of pastries, cold meat and absurdly good-smelling coffee on the table by the window. Lily was standing, looking out over the city, Rosie still in her arms. She had grabbed a handful of Lily's hair, and Lily was gently teasing her as she eased it out of her grasp.

She turned—must have heard his footsteps—and the smile dropped from her face at the sight of him. She looked guarded, wary, as if about to do battle.

'This looks nice,' he told her, and could have kicked himself for hiding behind pleasantries.

She just nodded—didn't even answer as she settled Rosie into the bouncy chair by the table and then sat herself.

'Lily, I'm sorry,' he said as soon as the waiter had left the room. 'I shouldn't have just taken off like that. You have every right to be angry with me.'

She nodded—which didn't do much to help the guilt in his belly.

'I should have stayed to talk to you, to explain what I was feeling.'

She met his gaze head-on and nodded. It was everything he'd feared. Everything he'd warned her of. He'd let her down.

'Right. You should.'

Good. She wasn't going to make this easy on him. He didn't deserve *easy*. He deserved to see how his actions had affected her. This was what he wanted. To be Lily's lover and partner. Maybe—if he could fix this unholy mess he'd made—more. He couldn't expect all that without giving everything of himself in return.

'Why did you go?' she asked.

He tried to find the right words to express what he had felt, to tell her that he'd been hurt but it hadn't been her fault.

'It was seeing you and Rosie like that, when I was barely awake. It just brought back…memories.'

Her face softened and relief swept through him like a wave. She understood. He'd known deep down that she would. She wouldn't be the woman he thought she was if she wasn't able to sympathise with another person's pain. But that didn't make what he'd done right. He should have spoken to her, explained what he was feeling, rather than running from the pain and from her. That was what he'd done at the start, when he'd first met her. If he couldn't show her that things had changed, if he *hadn't* changed, then what chance would he have of showing her that they could be happy together.

She nodded. 'I understand,' she said.

And maybe she did. But that didn't mean she'd forgiven him. She picked at her pastry, and he knew that hurt was still simmering under the surface.

'But you could have asked for my help, my support.' She gave him a long look before she spoke again. 'What are we to each other if we can't do that?'

What are we to each other? Genuinely, he didn't know. Had he been naïve, thinking that they could make a relationship out of good intentions? Maybe there was too much history, too much pain. After all, he'd been tested once and hadn't come out of it well. But the only way to know was by trying, and so far things weren't looking great.

'This is why me and Clare...' he started. 'I couldn't talk. She needed me to. I tried. I couldn't.'

She let out an exasperated sigh. 'I don't want to hear again that you let Clare down because you wouldn't talk to her about how you were feeling. It wasn't fair of her to expect you to grieve the way she wanted you to. I wasn't planning on making you do anything you weren't comfortable with this morning. But instead of finding that out you decided to bail. You don't have to talk to me about your feelings for your son, but if we can't find a way to communicate with each other then we're lost before we've even really started.'

Her words made him stop his pacing. He'd never considered that maybe there was another side to what had happened in his last relationship. That perhaps he wasn't entirely to blame. If only the same could be said about this morning.

From the corner of his eye he caught sight of the clock on the wall and cursed under his breath.

Lily followed his eyeline. 'Your meeting,' she said, remembering.

'I don't have to leave just yet.'

'But you'll be late if you leave it much longer. It wouldn't exactly give the right impression. If you don't get this contract signed then what was the point of us coming here? You should go.'

What was the point of them coming here? Could she not see that the whole thing had been his—clearly misjudged—way of contriving to find some time for them to get to know each other? The whole point of this trip was *them*, not the business.

But she was already heading back to her room, and he didn't have to ask to know that he wasn't invited to follow her.

CHAPTER FOURTEEN

THE HOTEL DOOR closed behind Nic and she breathed out a long sigh—disappointment? Relief? She wasn't sure. Her heart had started hurting the moment he'd left the suite earlier that morning and hadn't stopped since. His brief return and apology hadn't helped. It wasn't that she didn't forgive him—he'd clearly been in pain, and she could understand and sympathise with that. But instead of asking her to face that pain *with* him, trying to find a way to get past those feelings *together*, he had turned from her. Literally run from her.

Twenty-four hours in Rome. Well, their time was nearly up. By the time Nic got back from his meeting she'd need her bags packed and ready to go, and they'd have to go straight to the airport. There was no time to fix this before they had to leave, and her shoulders slumped with sadness that a day as sweet and as perfect as yesterday could be tarnished so soon.

Rosie had gone back to sleep, so she moved around the room quietly, tucking her belongings into bags and cases, checking under the bed and in the bathroom drawers.

Rosie gave a whimpering little cry in her sleep, a sound Lily didn't recognise, and she stopped her packing and crossed to the cot. Whatever had upset her hadn't been enough to wake her properly, and she'd settled herself back to sleep, but Lily watched her a little longer, feeling a swell of trepidation. It was just the remnants of her disagreement with Nic, she reasoned. Making her see trouble where there was none.

Rosie gave another sniffle, and this time Lily reached into her cot to check that she wasn't too hot. The air-con was on, and the thermostat was showing a perfect eighteen degrees, but her skin was just a little clammy and warm. Lily pulled the blanket back, so that Rosie was left under just a sheet, and then dug the thermometer out of the first aid kit she had brought with her.

Rosie's temperature was on the high side of normal. Maybe she'd picked up a cold, Lily thought, trying not to let her mind race ahead. She had some infant paracetamol in her case, and she woke the baby to feed her some. She barely opened her eyes, but swallowed down the medicine, and Lily told herself just to keep an eye on things and not to panic as she rocked her gently.

Nic arrived back from his meeting and she could see from his face that it had gone according to plan. That was something, at least. And the paracetamol had seemed to do the trick with Rosie. Her temperature had returned to normal, and she seemed to be sleeping easier.

A maid had turned up to pack Nic's things, so by the time he was back they were all but ready to go. They stood in the living room, their cases at their feet as they waited for a porter, and Lily wondered if they would ever rediscover the intimacy they had felt yesterday. Perhaps she had overreacted when Nic had left this morning, but it wasn't just her sadness and disappointment that was between them. It was more than that. At the first instance of something hard in their relationship Nic had decided to leave rather than work at it.

Yesterday they had been full of optimism about the future—aware of the challenges they might face, but ready to tackle them together. This morning had shattered that illusion.

Nic wanted to face his demons alone, and so must she.

She'd worked so hard to be a good mother to Rosie that she knew she could do it alone, that she didn't need Nic by her side to be a good parent, to hold her and Rosie together in their little family. She just needed to remember that. Remember that the most important thing in all of this was to be a good mother. Everything else came second. If that meant protecting Rosie from someone who wasn't ready to be in her life then she would have to do that, however much it hurt.

The flight had been short and uneventful, their way smoothed by Nic's charm and first-class tickets. Again his preparations had been thorough, and the onboard staff had responded to everything Rosie had needed, though she had slept for most of the flight. Lily had kept thermometer and paracetamol in her handbag, and kept a careful eye on her, looking out for any signs that this might be more than a cold.

Nic had asked her more than once if she was okay, if Rosie was okay, if there was anything that he could do. She'd smiled and said no thanks, needing to focus on Rosie. With her baby still grizzly and unhappy there was no time or space in her head to tackle this frosty wasteland that was expanding between them.

Now, in the luggage hall, Rosie started crying feebly, and it didn't seem to matter what Lily did—she paced, she rocked, she bounced—she wouldn't stop. She took her temperature again, and as soon as she saw the number on the little digital display—nearly two degrees higher than when she'd last taken it—she was reaching for the phone.

She dialled the NHS urgent helpline and bit her lip with nerves as she waited for her call to be taken. Nic guided her through the airport and out to their car as she answered the operator's questions, telling her what Rosie's temperature was and how sleepy she'd been.

The car pulled away from the airport and she barely even noticed. She had no time or energy to mark the end of their trip. Her ear was glued to her phone, and her eyes flitted between Rosie and the thermometer. She cast Nic the occasional glance and noted that he looked grey, drawn. No wonder, she thought, given everything he had been through.

But she had to focus on Rosie. She had to funnel out Nic's pain and concentrate on her girl.

Finally, after running through a seemingly endless list of questions, the operator spoke in a calming, measured voice that made Lily instantly terrified.

'Now, I know that you're in the car, so what I'm going to suggest is that you go to the nearest hospital with an Accident and Emergency department. If you can give me your location I'll be able to let you know where that is. Or if you want to pull over I'll arrange for an ambulance to come to you.'

Lily had never believed that a person could feel their

own heart stop, but in that moment she could have sworn her every bodily function ceased. She didn't breathe, blood stopped flowing in her veins, she stilled completely.

'Lily, love, are you still there?'

She nodded, before finding her voice and asking the driver for their exact location, then relaying it to the operator on the phone.

Lily thanked her for her help and hung up. She turned back to Rosie, who was sleepy, but still grizzling in her car seat.

'Lily?'

She could barely bring herself to look at Nic, because she needed to focus with everything that she had on Rosie. She had to give her her full attention. She couldn't bear to lose another member of her family— and this time she knew if it happened she would be the only one to blame. She was solely responsible for taking care of Rosie, and she had to make sure that she got better. If she didn't…it wouldn't just be Rosie she was losing. How could she ever face her sister again if she let anything happen to her?

'Lily, what's going on?' Nic asked.

She turned towards him but couldn't meet his eye. Instead she kept her gaze around his jaw, noted the tension there, and the pallor of his skin, but couldn't let herself worry about that now. Couldn't let herself think of anything but Rosie.

'We have to go straight to a hospital,' she told him. 'They didn't say what they thought might be wrong, but they want her checked out asap.'

'Three minutes,' their driver called from the front seat. 'Hospital's just up ahead and there's no traffic.'

Lily couldn't allow herself an ounce of relief. She had to stay alert, stay ready, make sure that she was focussed only on her little girl.

Nic reached for her hand and squeezed it gently. 'Lily, I'm sure they're just being cautious. Rosie's going to be fine.'

She opened her mouth to answer, but her voice wasn't there. Instead tears were welling in her eyes and threatening a flood. She couldn't do this. Not with him here. Not with his fear of the worst-case scenario written so plainly on his features. Her only responsibility was taking care of her family, and Nic had told her and then proved this morning that when things were tough he wasn't going to be there for her.

Lily unbuckled her seatbelt and put her hands on the straps of Rosie's car seat, ready to have her out of there as soon as the car pulled up outside A&E.

The click of Nic's seatbelt being unbuckled drew her attention, and she glanced over at him. 'You don't need to come in.'

'It's okay,' he said, though the dread and fear in his face told a different story.

'No.' Lily took a deep breath, knowing that she had to do this—for her niece, for her family, for herself. 'I can do this on my own,' she said firmly.

Nic stared at her, clearly shocked. Was there relief there too? she wondered. There must be. He'd never wanted to get involved with a family...never wanted to expose himself to the hurt and pain that might be waiting for them around the corner. She couldn't make him do this for her, and she couldn't walk into that hospital with someone who might bail on her at any moment. It was better to do this now, end things here, and know exactly where she stood, exactly who she could rely on as she walked into the hospital.

'I'll come in with you, Lily. You shouldn't have to do this by yourself.'

But she didn't want him there out of duty or obligation—didn't want him there against his better judgement. She wanted him there because he was part of her, part of Rosie. Because they were a family. He was offering half-measures, and that just wasn't good enough. Not for her, and not for Rosie.

'No!' Lily shouted this time, the tears finally spilling onto her cheeks. 'We're better off on our own,' she blurted. 'And not just today. We made a mistake, Nic. This was never going to work. We're better off accepting that now, before it goes any further. You know I'm right. You know that you don't want to be inside that hospital with us. I'm sorry, but it's for the best. It's over, Nic.'

As they came to an abrupt halt Lily grabbed for Rosie, lifting her out of the car seat. The driver opened the door behind her and she ran from the car, focussing on Rosie's face, refusing to look back.

CHAPTER FIFTEEN

LILY UNLOCKED THE door to Kate's flat one-handed while Rosie slept peacefully at last in the crook of her arm. She'd never used her friend's key without asking before, but with her own place still a building site and her relationship with Nic in tatters she had nowhere else to go.

It had been a long couple of days. She wished she could curl up like Rosie, block out the world and sleep through the day. The last seventy-two hours had consisted of nail-biting terror and endless waiting while doctors drew blood, ran tests, muttered together in corners.

Until this morning, when a smiling junior doctor had come to give her the news—all clear. They had been worried about meningitis, they'd told her when she'd arrived at the hospital, and had run a slew of tests. But every one had come back negative. It seemed that Rosie had been battling a nasty case of flu, and after three days of topping her up with fluids and paracetamol they were happy for her to be discharged.

After settling Rosie in her carrycot she plugged in her phone, dreading what might be waiting for her there. Nic had called a couple of times, and then passed the baton on to Kate. But Lily had found that she didn't know what to say. She'd breathed a sigh of relief when the phone's battery had died and she'd not had to think about it any more.

But now that she was back, and Rosie was on the mend, she knew that she had some thinking to do. And—she suspected—some apologising. Kate, for one, would be furious that she'd been incommunicado for more than twenty-four hours. And Nic…?

She had no idea what she could expect from him— if anything. Looking back at that car journey, she was ashamed of the way she had behaved, and saw in her behaviour a reflection of his, of everything she had criticised him for that very morning. She'd not talked about what was scaring her; she'd not tried to explain. Instead she'd decided that she had to do things on her own, in her own way, and left him out in the cold while she got on with it.

But the thing really twisting the knife in her stomach was the fact that she knew he had been hurting already. Seeing Rosie sick, the trip to the hospital, the not knowing what was happening… It must have brought back so many memories. And instead of trying to help, or even to understand, she'd pushed him away.

Just as she was putting on the kettle, hoping that coffee would make this awful day better, a key turned in the front door. Kate, home from work. Or Nic? she thought suddenly, with a stab of guilt in her belly. Did he have a key to his sister's place?

She thought for a moment about trying to sneak out the back way. But her best friend and her brother had stood by her these last few weeks—the most challenging of her life—and it would be cruel of her to push them away now. The thought of facing Nic's hurt and Kate's disapproval was terrifying, but it couldn't be put off for ever, she knew.

She breathed a sigh of relief when Kate's curls appeared around the door.

'Lily!' she exclaimed with a double-take. 'You scared me half to death. What are you doing here?'

The blunt words were muffled as her face was trapped in a cloud of curly hair and she was squeezed in a tight hug.

Pulling back, Kate held her at arm's distance as she gave her an assessing look.

'Of course you're here—stupid of me. How are you doing?' she asked, though Lily knew from her tone that she wasn't expecting an answer. 'Not great, I imagine, from everything that I've heard. Rosie okay?'

Lily nodded, unable to speak after being shown such kindness when she'd been expecting the opposite.

'Now, I need coffee, and I need some sort of baked goods, and then we're going to talk,' Kate carried on, steering Lily back into the kitchen and pulling mugs from the cupboard as the kettle came to the boil. 'That brother of mine has been walking around with a face like a month of wet Sundays, and you're not looking much better yourself. And as it seems like neither of you knows how to operate a telephone or carry out a conversation—despite you having clocked up almost sixty years on this planet between you—an intervention is required.'

Lily dropped onto a stool and opened her mouth to speak.

But Kate stopped her with a pointed finger. 'Uh-uh. I'm talking first. You're sitting like a good girl and listening while I tell you just why *you're* an idiot for pushing my brother away, and *he's* an idiot for letting you and for somehow managing to screw up a romantic whirlwind trip to Rome. And then you're *both* going to apologise and find a way to make this work before your twin glum faces drive me mad. Am I clear?'

Lily didn't know what else to do but nod and accept the coffee that Kate placed in front of her, some of the hot black liquid sloshing over the side of her cup with her enthusiasm.

Despite her rousing sentiments, and her insistence on speaking first, Kate sat and listened quietly as Lily gave her a summed-up version of what had happened in Rome—skirting very quickly round the 'sex with your brother' part and instead focussing on the 'thinking we were falling for each other and then he freaked out and left' part.

Not for the first time she wished she could have fallen for someone else—anyone other than her best friend's brother. Maybe then she could have just spilled out all her worst pain, everything Nic had done wrong, every way he had hurt her and upset her. But knowing how much Kate loved him, how much she knew that he was really a good guy, she couldn't do it.

She couldn't explain what had happened without seeing for herself how much responsibility they both carried for the way things had fallen apart. No, Nic *shouldn't* have left with barely a word the morning after they had made love for the first time. But she should have given him the space he'd needed. Recognised that grieving was a long process, full of setbacks and surprises. That he must have been as taken aback by the turn of events that morning as she had.

And she couldn't deny that pushing him away when he must have been every bit as frightened for Rosie as she had been had been cruel. She just hoped that it wasn't unforgivable.

'So you're both idiots—that's what you're telling me?'

Once again Kate had managed to find a way to compress their entire torturous, complicated lives into one simple sentence.

Lily nodded. 'Though I'm pretty sure I'm the bigger one.'

'You both want to make this up. You're both sitting at home moping rather than doing something about it. Seems pretty equal to me. You know that he wouldn't leave the hospital, right? Slept that first night across a couple of chairs in the A&E waiting room? It wasn't until you texted me that Rosie was fine and I passed it on to him that he would leave. He wanted to be there... just in case.'

Lily dropped her head into her hands, her heart swelling and breaking a little at the same time, ashamed of the way she had behaved, but pleased at this demonstration of Nic's commitment to her—and to Rosie.

'So what do I do about it?'

'Do you want him back? Really?'

She was surprised Kate could ask her that after everything that had just been said—after she'd explained how much she felt for him, how stupid she had been. But in the words she could hear more than a hint of sisterly protection, and Lily knew that she was crossing some sort of rubicon. Say yes now and she wasn't just committing to Nic, she was committing to his family. She was promising not one but two of the people she cared for most in the world that she was committed to them, that she wouldn't hurt them.

'I do,' she said seriously. 'I want us to try again.'

Kate leaned over and gave her a hug with uncharacteristic gentleness, both in her body and her words. 'Glad to hear it. Now, you go borrow my room and get some sleep—you look hideous—and we'll talk again tomorrow.'

Lily felt her body growing heavier. The lack of sleep these past days was catching up with her, and she knew that Kate was right. She needed rest, needed to recharge. And then, when Rosie was better, she'd call Nic, beg his forgiveness, and see if there was any way to rescue what they had so briefly found in Rome.

A few days later Lily reached across to the coffee table, trying to grab her phone without disturbing Rosie, who was asleep on her lap.

It was a message from Kate.

I have a plan. I'll be home in an hour—make sure you're in.

Lily glanced down at the sleeping baby and thought for the millionth time how lucky she was to have her safe and well in her arms—the doctors had given her a clean bill of health, her temperature was gone, and she was feeding and sleeping as normal. The only reason she was being cuddled to sleep instead of drifting off on her own in her cot was because Lily was still nervous of letting her go, still haunted by her worst fears.

It was how Nic must feel every day, she thought, unable to shake the unease of knowing how easily a child could be lost, how impossible it would be to fill the void she would leave.

The doorbell rang, and Lily softly cursed Kate. How could a grown woman, a successful barrister, forget her own house keys on a daily basis?

She set Rosie down, careful not to wake her, and picked her way across the living room. She threw open the door, and had already half turned back when she realised what was wrong with the scene. Kate's slight shoulders wouldn't block the sunshine, wouldn't cast a shadow that was solid and masculine and...

'Nic?'

CHAPTER SIXTEEN

'Hi.'

In that moment he knew he'd done the right thing: 'borrowing' his sister's phone, sending that text, coming to see her. Her voice brought memories flooding back…their one night in Rome, their walks around the city, the way she'd heard him confess his darkest fears about his character and told him that she still trusted him. What they'd found together was too important to let it go without a fight.

But maybe Lily was tired of fighting. She looked tired: black bags under her eyes, her shirt unironed, her skin pale. But none of that mattered. Because all he could see was what made her beautiful to him.

How had they managed to get it all so wrong? He thought back to that night in Rome—he couldn't even remember how long ago that was. Four nights? Five? It felt like a lifetime… Everything had seemed right with the world. He'd had the woman he loved, relaxed and happy and contented in his arms. He'd felt peaceful at last, after a decade of running from his memories.

And then in a half waking moment of confusion he'd pushed her away. That one push had spiralled and had a butterfly effect on everything—until he hadn't even recognised who they were to each other any more.

He'd been in so much pain—watching her suffer, watching Rosie suffer—and utterly paralysed with fear that he would lose them both. He should have argued when she'd told him that she wanted to face it alone. Should have told her that he *knew* this pain, *knew* this fear, and that they would be stronger if they faced it together. All he'd been able to do was wait, haunt the hospital waiting room until he'd known that Rosie was going to be okay.

'Come in,' she said, though her voice was hesitant.

He followed her through to the kitchen anyway. He couldn't bear the thought of leaving without things between them being back where they had been. Without her knowing what he'd realised as he'd sat in the hospital, waiting for news, wanting to be nearby just in case she needed him. He loved her. That was why he hadn't been able to go home to his huge, empty apartment. It was why his heart had felt empty for days— why he hadn't been able to sleep or think straight until he'd made the decision to come here and fight for what he wanted. He just hoped it was what she wanted too.

He took a moment to watch her, to refamiliarise himself with her features, with the colour of her hair, the line of her nose and the angle of her smile. Did she know how much he had missed her? How he had missed Rosie as well? Missed the mess and the noise of the two of them at home?

Lily was hovering by the table, and he realised that in his eagerness to look at them both he'd not yet spoken. She looked uncertain, as if she might bolt at any moment, and with that his anger towards her dissipated.

He'd been furious for a while that she wouldn't even answer his texts, that she had left him sitting and wondering whether Rosie was even alive, but seeing her now, seeing the evidence of the emotional toll of the past few days, he found that he couldn't add his anger to her list of troubles.

'The text was from you?' she asked, her voice tremulous.

'I wasn't sure you'd see me. I'm sorry.'

'I would have,' she said. 'I wanted to call…to talk. But after the way I behaved I…I couldn't.'

'You *could*,' he told her. 'That's what you've been trying to show me, isn't it? That we should be finding ways to support each other? I'd have supported you, Lily, if you'd let me. So how is she?' he asked at last, and suddenly his arms felt empty, light, as if they needed the weight of the baby in them to know that she was okay.

Lily wasn't the only one who'd become part of his heart, and he knew that could never be undone.

Never mind his arms, his heart had felt empty these last few days, missing its other half, missing that which made him whole. At first he'd thought it was just the memories making him sad—the thought of another funeral, another tiny white coffin. But when the feeling had persisted long after he'd known that Rosie was in the clear he'd known there was another cause.

Knowing how that felt, knowing what it was to be without her, it suddenly seemed stupid of him to be angry, to hold a grudge. Why jeopardise this? Why risk the chance of being happy?

He met her eyes and tried to show her everything with that look. Everything that he had felt and thought and hoped and feared since he'd last seen her. But it wasn't enough. He had to be sure that she understood.

'I'm sorry,' he said. 'I'm sorry for leaving that morning. I'm sorry that you didn't think you could rely on me when Rosie was sick. I'm sorry it's taken me all week for us to get to this point. I love you, Lily, and I want us to fix this.'

She stared at him for a moment. He wasn't sure what she'd been expecting, but it was clear from her expression that it hadn't been this.

'*I'm* the one who should be apologising,' she said. 'I shouldn't have judged you so harshly when we were in Rome. I shouldn't have pushed you away when Rosie was sick because I was still angry with you.'

'You don't have to apologise,' he said, reaching for her hand and allowing himself a small smile when she didn't pull back. 'You were so worried about her—you had to do what you thought was right at the time.'

'It doesn't make the way I acted any better.'

Nic shrugged. 'We can't change what happened—what we said or did. But if you still want to we can forgive each other. See if we can try harder, do better.'

She smiled, although it still looked tentative. 'I'd like that.'

'I can't promise that I won't have another day like that one in Rome,' he warned. 'There will be times when I feel sad. When I look at Rosie and remember Max. Things might not be smooth sailing just because we want them to be.'

Lily nodded. 'And I can't promise I'm not going to make mistakes, either. It's quite a lot to get used to, this parenting thing. I might need help. Sometimes I might need space.'

'I *can* promise that I will always love you, though. That I will always want you—want you both—in my life.'

'Then I can promise to remember that. Even when I'm upset and angry. I love you, Nic.'

A tear sneaked from the corner of her eye and he reached out with his thumb to wipe it away. The last tear she would shed over him, he hoped.

Rosie started to stir in the bedroom and Nic smiled. 'Can I?' he asked.

Lily nodded and he went to pick the baby up, moved himself beside Lily on the sofa.

'She's really okay?' he asked.

'Right as rain. They were just being cautious. Absolutely the right thing, of course. But it did give me seventy-two hours I'd very much like to wipe from my memory.'

'Just as long as she's okay. And as long as *we* are.'

He placed a tentative arm around her shoulders and his whole body relaxed when she turned into him, burying her face in his neck for a long moment and taking a deep breath. He wished they were at home, that there wasn't a chance his sister might walk through the door at any moment.

Taking advantage of the privacy, temporary as it might be, he dropped a kiss on the top of Lily's head. When she looked up at him he caught her lips with his, holding her there in a long kiss, pouring all the emotion of the last week into it. She moaned as she opened her mouth, and he sensed her longing, her love for him.

As they leaned back in the sofa, nestling together, their little family of three, a thought came to him—and a question…

when? She asked.

EPILOGUE

LILY LOOKED IN the mirror. As with pretty much everything else in her life, this wasn't exactly what she'd had
in mind. She had always thought she would walk down
the aisle on her wedding day looking like something
out of one of those bridal magazines. She had never
expected to do it eight months pregnant.

The day she'd found out she was expecting their
baby had been one of the happiest of their lives. But
when they'd sat down and worked out the due date
they'd realised that, as always, things were a little complicated. The church and the venue had been booked,
and everything had been planned for months. It had
seemed silly and vain to change the date of their wedding just so that Lily could buy a gown in the size that
she wanted.

After the briefest knock on the door Kate appeared,
Rosie propped on one hip and a grin on her face. 'How's
the blushing bride getting on?' she asked. 'Better than
my brother, I hope. The poor guy's so nervous he can't
even eat. Don't know what he's worrying about, personally. Not like you can run very fast in your condition. If you tried to ditch him he'd catch up with you
and drag you back.'

'And hi to you too.' Lily laughed, accepting a glass of something sparkling and a kiss on the cheek. 'I'm fine. Better than fine. I'm flippin' brilliant and I cannot wait to be officially your sister. How long have I got?'

Kate checked the time on her phone. 'Three minutes. Right—have we got everything? Old, new, borrowed, blue?'

Lily nodded. Not that she needed any of those things. As long as she had her family she had everything she wanted.

'Let's get you hitched, then.'

She walked into the church and saw Nic waiting for her at the end of the aisle. Any nerves she might have been hiding fell away. She had never felt so happy and in love and safe and secure in her life.

As she turned to look at her guests she saw Helen in the second row, a tissue pressed to her eyes. Her sister looked well, *really* well, better than she'd seen her for a long time. She was making tentative steps to get to know Rosie, and focussing on looking after her own health.

Rosie, still in Kate's arms, went ahead of her up the aisle, so when she reached Nic her little family was all together. Looking around her, Lily felt more lucky than she ever had, and knew as she said 'I do' that nothing could make this moment more perfect.

* * * * *

"Where's my daughter?" Missy asked, hating the huskiness of her voice.

Liam moved to the edge of the porch. Despite the passage of time, he looked the same, like an older version of the boy she'd known. He was impossibly handsome in jeans, a long-sleeved dress shirt with the cuffs folded back to his elbows and cowboy boots.

Always cowboy boots.

His gaze lit on her, but the setting sun and deep shadows of the porch made it impossible to see his expression as he thanked the driver who'd placed her suitcases on the porch. She tore her gaze from him and thanked the man as well when he walked past her. When it was just the two of them again, she returned her focus to Liam, who hadn't moved other than to cross his arms over his chest.

The defensive pose spoke volumes about his state of mind.

Fine, but right now she wanted to see for herself that Casey was okay. "I asked you—"

"Is it true?" The words were out of his mouth as she reached for the stair railing, freezing her on the first step. "Is Casey my daughter?" he demanded.

* * *

Welcome to Destiny:
Where fate leads to falling in love

DESTINED TO
BE A DAD

BY
CHRISTYNE BUTLER

MILLS &
BOON

Published in Great Britain 2015
by Mills & Boon, an imprint of Harlequin (UK) Limited,
Eton House, 18-24 Paradise Road, Richmond, Surrey, TW9 1SR

© 2015 Christyne Butilier

ISBN: 978-0-263-25167-8

23-0915

Harlequin (UK) Limited's policy is to use papers that are natural, renewable and recyclable products and made from wood grown in sustainable forests. The logging and manufacturing processes conform to the legal environmental regulations of the country of origin.

Printed and bound in Spain
by CPI, Barcelona

Christyne Butler is a *USA TODAY* bestselling author who fell in love with romance novels while serving in the US Navy and started writing her own stories in 2002. She writes contemporary romances that are full of life, love and a hint of laughter. She lives with her family in central Massachusetts and loves to hear from her readers at www.christynebutler.com.

To the following extraordinary authors…you have no idea how much your books mean to me, as a fan who spends many hours lost in the pleasure of reading them and as a writer for the inspiration you provide.
Thank you!

Donna Alward
Rachel Gibson
Kristan Higgins
Shirley Jump
Virginia Kantra
Laura Kaye
Susan Mallery
Catherine Mann
Sarah Morgan
Molly O'Keefe
Christine Rimmer
Jill Shalvis
Roxanne St. Claire
Karen Templeton

Chapter One

"Wankers! You cowboys promised to take me to Liam Murphy, not show me the back side of some bloody barn!"

The lilting British accent, rarely heard here in the small town of Destiny, Wyoming, floated on the hot August morning breeze. It came from somewhere behind him and despite the voices bickering on the other end of this endless phone call—and the fact she'd said his name—the inflection kicked Liam square in the gut.

He should have been used to it by now.

His family's business, Murphy Mountain Log Homes, was celebrating its twentieth year in business with a growing following in the United Kingdom, thanks to securing a contract to build a log home—scratch that, a twenty-thousand-square-foot log mansion—for a popular movie actor based in Scotland.

Meaning as company president, Liam spent a lot of time on the phone and in meetings with people who spoke the

Queen's English. Still, whenever he heard that soft and silvery accent spoken by a female voice, it never failed to take him back.

To another place, another time when he'd thought he could have it all.

Aw, hell, that was a lifetime ago.

"Are you daft?" The girlish voice came again, cutting into Liam's thoughts. "Not bloody happening!"

Hmm, not so soft this time.

She sounded young and her words were angry, but there was a hint of fear laced through as well. Liam didn't know what was going on, but he had a pretty good idea.

Ending his call, he pocketed his phone, backtracked a few steps and headed for the far end of a nearby barn.

The first-ever Destiny rodeo was in full swing, and campers and horse trailers filled this area of the fairgrounds. It'd taken a lot of hard work by a lot of people to pull this event together. His family's company was a major sponsor, and while it might only be a one-day event, the prize money was good, ensuring participants and fans alike packed the arena and the town.

The last thing they needed was trouble.

Liam spotted the trio as soon as he rounded the corner. Dressed in jeans, plaid shirts and Stetsons, two cowboys stood with a young girl sandwiched between them. He wasn't sure about the men, but the female definitely looked to be under eighteen. That made the six-pack of beer held by one of the cowboys—who didn't have a valid alcohol wristband—even more of a concern. And it wasn't even noon yet.

"Come on, darlin'. Let's enjoy a cold brew in our camper." One of the cowboys encircled the girl's waist with his arm. "Then we'll track down that Murphy guy for ya."

"No need to go far." Liam kept his voice light as he

strolled toward the group, despite his anger spiking at the scene before him. "I'm right here."

The three jerked around, surprise on the faces of the cowboys, relief in the girl's eyes. And there was something else about their dark navy coloring that hit him as hard as her voice had.

"What can I help you with?" he continued, joining their circle. "Something related to the rodeo, perhaps?"

The first cowboy took a step back, dropping his hold on the young girl, whose gaze darted from the booklet she held to Liam and back again. Twice.

Liam looked down and saw she had the rodeo program folded back to the pages that featured his photo. Great. That's why she was looking for him.

He and his brothers had all grown up on horseback, competing in local rodeos before they were even teenagers. But it'd been Liam who'd made it to the professional circuit as a saddle bronc rider when he'd turned eighteen, finishing in the top five at the National Rodeo Finals his first two years out. His third—and what would end up being his final—season had ended early when he destroyed his left shoulder. He never rode professionally again.

That had been thirteen years ago.

When the Destiny rodeo committee had wanted him for the cover of the program based on his past accomplishments, he'd balked but finally given in and agreed to be included inside, never thinking they'd make him a damn centerfold.

"Ah, Mr. Murphy, we were j-just looking for you," the younger of the two cowboys said.

So now he was Mr. Murphy. Well, that could work in his favor. "What's with the beer?" Liam gestured at the kid with the six-pack under his arm. "You're not twenty-one."

"I, um…"

"It's mine. He's carrying it for me," said the taller cow-boy, giving his left hand a quick shake before he dropped his hands to his side and planted his feet in a wide stance. "We're on our way back to our camper."

Liam turned, picking up on the wristband and the atti-tude. At thirty-four, the last thing he needed was a roll in the dirt with a kid more than a decade younger than him. "Then I suggest you carry it. Be less trouble that way."

Their gazes held for a long moment, but the cowboy backed down, making a show of taking the alcohol, and then slapped the younger guy on the shoulder. "Come on, bro. Let's get out of here."

Liam watched them leave, making a mental note to check in with the sheriff. Gage Steele and his deputies were patrolling the fairgrounds, but Liam hadn't seen any-one back this way yet.

He turned his attention back to the girl. Shoulder-length blond hair, streaked with bright patches of blue and pink, fell over her face as she stood studying the program again. "Are you okay?" he asked. "They didn't hurt you?"

She lifted her gaze, her eyes raking from the top of his Stetson to the tips of his boots before she looked him in the eye. "Are you really him?"

A bit uncomfortable at her scrutiny, Liam looked at where she jabbed a finger at the picture of his winning ride that first year. "Yes, but that was a long time ago." He spotted a small duffel bag lying nearby in the grass. Mov-ing past her, he grabbed it. "Is this yours?"

"Yeah, thanks."

He watched her walk toward him, studying her again and wondering if there might be another reason she'd been looking for him. She was pretty, if one got past the crazy-colored hair, dark eye makeup and…was that a diamond chip on the side of her nose?

She had a slew of earrings dangling from both ears, her black T-shirt displayed a bright purple skull surrounded by flowers and she wore skintight jeans tucked into brown leather boots accented with bright turquoise embroidery that looked new.

Brand-new, from the way she hobbled. "You buy those today?"

She nodded, looking at her feet. "Not hard to spot, huh? They hurt bloody awful."

Her accent pulled at him again, making him frown. "The vendor should've given you a pair of boot socks."

"They did." She shrugged. "But I already had socks. See?"

Balancing on one foot, she tried to pull the other from inside the boot but gasped, a wince creasing her features, and she froze.

"I think we should get you to the first-aid tent," Liam said, looking at the row of vendors not too far away. The tent set up by the local clinic was at the end closest to them. "Can you make it there?"

"Do I have a choice?" She yanked the bag from his grip and started to shuffle across the grass, the frightened girl from moments ago long gone. "Last time I listen to an American cowboy. They're all a bunch of nutters."

"Not all of us." Liam joined her, grinning at her quicksilver mood change. She reminded him of his niece, Abby, who had turned sixteen earlier this year. His older brother had his hands full with that one, not to mention his twin sons, who were a few years younger. "You need to be more careful who you make friends with."

"Ya think? Jeez, you sound just like my—oh!" She stumbled, one boot catching on a rock, but she caught herself before ending up on her backside. "Bollocks! That hurt!"

"Can I make another suggestion?"

She pushed her hair off her face, swiping hard at one eye before glaring at him. "Sure, why not?"

Liam's chest tightened at the tear she hadn't managed to brush away. "How about I give you a lift? The sooner we get your foot looked at, the better you'll feel."

"A lift?" Her brows scrunched together over the top of her nose in a way that was so familiar, Liam could only stare. Before he could decide why, understanding dawned on her face. Her expression turned disbelieving. "You mean carry me?"

"If that would be all right with you."

She hugged her bag to her chest and studied him again.

Damn, maybe that wasn't such a good idea. More and more people were milling around the vendor tents. He'd already spotted a few giving the two of them some speculative looks. Gossip was a favorite pastime in Destiny, and the Murphy family always seemed to supply plenty of fodder, whether they wanted to or not.

The town was still buzzing over Liam's brother Devlin taking off to London back in June with his newest lady love, a girl he'd only known a few months.

Then three weeks ago, both Liam and Nolan had participated in a bachelor auction to raise money for the town's summer camp. The fact that Liam had gone for one of the highest bids to nearby Laramie's pretty city attorney had actually ended up in the local newspaper. Good thing they hadn't gotten wind of their date last week—which had been nice but spark-free—or else that would've made the headlines as well.

"Okay." She shrugged with a feigned carelessness that reminded him again of his niece.

Liam smiled, forgetting about the crowd. There was so much going on at today's events, he doubted anyone would even notice them during the short stroll to the first-aid tent. Seconds later, he had one arm beneath her knees and the other secured just beneath her shoulders.

Cradling her bag in her lap, she wrapped the other hand around his neck as he started walking. "Do I weigh a lot?" she asked.

Liam resisted the urge to roll his eyes. No matter the age, the female species never stopped asking loaded questions. "Of course not. I bet you don't weigh a hundred pounds."

"Forty-four kilos."

He did the math in his head. "Ninety-seven pounds. See? I was right."

"For a Yank you did that conversion pretty fast."

She smiled and that punch to his gut returned. "Well, I'm a pretty smart guy."

Ducking her head, she whispered, "I hope so."

Having no idea what she meant by that, Liam covered the distance to the tent in a matter of minutes and once inside, placed the girl on an empty chair. It took one of the volunteers a few moments to tend to the blisters on her feet. Liam used that time to study her again, positive now that he knew her from someplace. But where? Could she be a friend of his niece's or a daughter of one of the guys on his construction crew? With that accent?

"You're staring at me."

Liam blinked, realizing she was right. "Ah, sorry. You know, you never did say why you were looking for me."

She tugged her boots back on, over a thick pair of socks this time, her gaze darting around the tent. Other than a few people at the far end, they were alone.

. "Do I look familiar to you?" she finally asked. "At all?"

"You…" His voice trailed off. He had a feeling she

wanted him to say yes. He almost did, but the truth was he had no idea who she was. "No, I'm sorry, you don't."

She heaved a dramatic sigh and then rooted around inside her duffel bag, digging out a cell phone. "Bloody thing is about out of juice, but maybe…" Her fingers flew over the screen, her thumb flipping through a long string of photos before she turned the phone to him.

"How about her?" she asked. "Does *she* look familiar?"

His breath disappeared. Every muscle in his body tensed and his knees automatically locked to keep him upright.

Stay back, stiff rein, set feet, squeeze and stay on.

Liam had created his own personal mantra back when he was a teenager, and he silently recited those words every time he climbed on the back of a horse.

A horse determined to buck him off and send him crashing to the dirt.

A lot of people thought saddle bronc riding was only about trying to hang on. It wasn't. There were specific locations a rider's feet needed to be from the moment the chute gate opened if one expected to last the required eight seconds to garner a score.

It was a perfectly choreographed dance of man working to remain synchronized with each twist and turn and jump the horse made. All while keeping his free hand from touching the animal or himself so he wasn't disqualified.

Now, that same chant raced through his head as he stared at a picture of Missy Ellington, his very own heartbreak girl.

Missy had come over as an exchange student from London during his senior year of high school, and from the moment he'd first seen her, he'd fallen hard.

And she'd been just as smitten with him. They'd been inseparable until things ended badly the summer after graduation. A nasty fight over each other's plans for their shared future. Plans they had never bothered to talk about, plans that had turned out to be vastly different. He'd said some stupid things and the next thing he knew, Missy had flown home to London.

He never saw or spoke to her again. He thought about her sometimes though. An old country song would come on the radio, or he'd catch a whiff of a peach-scented perfume or hear a woman speak in a British accent.

And back in the spring, when Devlin had made a crack about Liam's dismal track record at marriage and how a long-ago girlfriend had been the love of his life, Liam had quickly corrected him, stating emphatically that he had no such love.

He'd been lying. She had been the love of his life, at least back then.

In the photograph, Missy looked much as she had the last time he'd seen her. Long blond hair, beautiful porcelain skin. Soft blue eyes. Only instead of smiling at the camera, her eyes were focused on the infant she held in her arms.

"That was taken fifteen years ago this past April." The girl turned the phone back and looked at the image, that same smile—Missy's smile—on her face. "I was only a couple of weeks old at the time."

Fifteen years ago.

The months and years rushed through his head, the numbers making his brain go into a serious meltdown. The imaginary rein he'd been holding onto slipped from his grip, the wild beast beneath him disappeared and he was flying through the air.

"Missy…" he rasped, determined to push the words past the restricted confines of his dry throat. "Missy Ellington is your mother?"

"Abso-bloody-lutely." The girl's gaze was serious as she looked up at him again. "And you're my father."

* * *

Blimey, he still looked good.

After sixteen years, Missy Dobbs had thought he would have changed, but no, Liam Murphy had only grown more handsome than the boy who'd stolen her heart all those years ago.

She pulled in a deep breath. She had to do this. There was no gray area to fill with *could she* or *should she* when it came to this decision. The certainty of what lay ahead outweighed the fear, although not by much.

The hustle and bustle of the busy airport gate continued on around her as she waited for a flight that would take her to the last place on earth she'd ever thought she would see again.

Destiny, Wyoming.

She tightened her grip on the tablet as she stared again at Liam's picture on the website for his family's company. She tried to reconcile the wild and crazy cowboy she'd known as a teen with the serious man looking impossibly dashing in a business suit. The dark-framed glasses he wore couldn't hide the sparkle in his eyes and his hair was shorter now, but a wayward curl or two still threatened to spill down over his forehead.

Her former love had done well for himself. CEO and president of his family's business. She wasn't surprised. Liam had been cut out for more than being a rodeo star, but at eighteen that had been his dream.

A dream that had torn them apart.

A dream that had sent her running home and into a fateful one-night stand with a former boyfriend. A man she'd ended up marrying because she believed—she'd been told—he was the true father of her child after finding out she was pregnant a few months later. Only now—after many years, she knew the truth.

Liam Murphy was her daughter's father.

What a bloody mess!

She hadn't even talked to Casey about what she'd learned before heading to Los Angeles on a last-minute work assignment. No, there'd only been time for a heated argument with her mother, who'd known the truth about Casey's paternity all along.

That had been two weeks ago.

Her job on the film set had finished late yesterday and Casey was set to fly in on Monday to join Missy for an extended holiday here in the States. That meant Missy had the weekend to fly to Destiny, knock on Liam's door with the hope he remembered her and break the news to him that he'd fathered a child.

The gentle chiming of her mobile phone came from deep within her purse. She didn't recognize the number and offered a quick prayer that it wasn't anything work related that would cancel her plans.

"Hello?"

"Mum, it's me. Casey."

Missy slammed the tablet's cover closed, almost as if her daughter could see what she'd been looking at.

Other than texting back and forth, they hadn't talked in the last few days. And when they had chatted during Missy's stay in Los Angeles, she hadn't mentioned anything about what she'd discovered to her daughter. Sharing the news about Casey's real father had to wait until they were together again, face-to-face.

"Ah, hello, sweetie. Why aren't you calling me from your mobile?"

"It died. Completely. I've got it charging at the moment."

The airport's loudspeaker came to life, blaring out information. Missy turned to the wall and ducked her head in hopes of muffling the noise. She quickly figured the time difference between California and London. It was after dinnertime there. "Are you home now? You need to start packing."

"Not…exactly."

Two words—and the nervous hitch in her daughter's voice—sent a shiver of maternal alertness through Missy. "Laundry might be your least favorite chore for a Friday night, sweetie, but you can't wait until the last minute to figure out what to bring for our holiday—"

Her daughter's words cut her off midsentence. "Mum, I don't have to worry about packing because I'm already here."

Here? In Los Angeles?

Missy jerked to her feet, her leather tote swinging from her shoulder. She scanned the gate area for an airport map. "What do you mean, *here*? Are you at the LAX international terminal?"

"No, I'm in Wyoming."

What?

Missy's precarious hold on a reality that had been spinning out of control over the last few weeks slipped away. She dropped to the unyielding airport seat beneath her, the ability to stand gone as the blood drained from her head.

"Mum? Did you hear me?" Casey asked. "Mum?"

"How did—why are—" Missy pushed the words past her lips, unable to complete either question. She finally managed to squeak out, "Why on earth would you fly to Wyoming? Alone?"

"I was planning to fly to LA alone, wasn't I? Blimey, it's not like it's the first time I've traveled by myself."

Yes, Casey had started joining her at film locations during school breaks a few years ago, but those were always nonstop flights around Europe.

"Of course, but again, why—" Missy's heart pounded in her chest, the truth already settling like a rock in her belly. "Why are you in—"

"Why do you think? I overheard bits and bobs when you and Grandmum fought the night before you flew to California. About what you found in Granddad's desk. I can't believe they did that to you! To us!" Her daughter's words came fast. "And you didn't talk to me before your flight or the few times we've chatted since. Not one word!"

Oh, this was not how she wanted this to go. "Sweetie, I—"

"Not that I blame you, really. I mean, it's not exactly a topic for casual conversation," Casey barreled on. "I heard you say a man's name and a town in Wyoming during your argument, so after some online searching I decided to change my flight plans. I arrived in Cheyenne this morning."

Missy tried to keep up, but her daughter's words blended with the loud rushing in her ears and the announcement that her flight was boarding. She gathered her items and got in line, the boarding pass shaking in a mad fit in her fingers.

Casey was in Wyoming. She knew about Liam.

Fix this! Fix this! Fix this!

The words thundered inside Missy's brain as she made her way to her first-class seat, trying to think of what to say—what to do—next.

Casey could wait for her at the airport. They'd get a hotel room and talk. She'd figure out a way to get in touch with Liam tomorrow.

Slightly calmer after her hastily thought up plan, Missy said, "Okay, I want you to stay at the airport. I'm on a flight—"

"Mum, I'm not in Cheyenne anymore. I'm in Destiny!

And guess what?" Casey's voice rose in excitement before it dropped to a loud whisper. "I found him."

Destiny! Missy's impetuous daughter had traveled from London to a small ranching community in the American West and found the man who was her true father.

Missy dropped into her seat, staring numbly at the seat in front of her.

"Mum? Are you still there? Mum?"

She needed to answer her daughter, needed to know what had happened in the last twenty-four hours. Needed to know how Liam had reacted to the bombshell her—their—daughter had dropped at his feet today. But there wasn't time. She would have to end this call soon and Casey still didn't know Missy was making her way to Wyoming.

Pulling in a deep breath through her nose, she released it in a soft wisp past her lips. By the third one she was able to speak. "Honey, we need to talk."

"I couldn't agree more."

Missy gasped. The same deep, gravelly, sexy voice she remembered from her youth filled her ear and stole her breath. A heated flush that made no sense at all started in the center of her chest and rushed to every part of her body.

How could he sound exactly the same after all this time?

"Liam."

She heard a swift intake of breath, and then silence filled the distance—both in miles and years—that stretched between them.

Up until the last few weeks, she hadn't spoken his name aloud in a long time. Not when she and her girlfriends would gather for drinks and a chat, not to her daughter when they talked about things like boys and dating and growing up, and never to her parents.

Sometimes it felt as if that year in her life had happened to someone else.

"Casey tells me you've been in Los Angeles for the last few weeks." Liam's voice was clipped and businesslike now. "If you let me know where you're staying, I'll make arrangements to get you to the airport and on a flight to Wyoming right away."

Bristling at his authoritative tone, she said, "I'm on a flight to Cheyenne scheduled to depart in a few minutes, actually. I land at half past five, local time."

There was more silence as he processed her news. Was he surprised she'd already been on her way? How much had her daughter told him about the night Missy—and she—had learned the truth?

"I'll be there when your plane lands," he finally said.

Of course he would. And since she hadn't thought far enough ahead to figure out how she would travel to Destiny, she wouldn't fight him. Getting to Casey was the most important thing at the moment. "May I speak to my daughter again?"

His voice dropped away, and then Casey's voice came back on the line. "You're flying here? Like right now?"

"Yes, sweetie, and I promise we'll talk about everything when I see you." Missy tried to keep her voice light. "Including you changing your transatlantic flight. Please don't cause any trouble for…for Liam in the meanwhile."

"You're a tad late for that bit of advice, Mum." Casey offered a staged sigh, an expression the teen had perfected in the last few years. "I'd say me showing up out of the blue is just the start of trouble."

Missy popped a breath mint into her mouth and made stopping by the loo her first priority as soon as she landed in Cheyenne.

After using the facilities and washing her hands, she redid her hair, making neat the messy chignon style she favored. When she found herself leaning toward the mirror to reapply her lipstick, she froze.

Did she care what Liam Murphy thought of her after all this time?

Not wanting to answer that question, she hurried to the baggage claim area and found her case still circling the carousel. She retrieved it and then checked her phone. No calls or texts from her daughter or Liam. With a thirty-minute stopover in Denver, she'd only had time to ring her mother and have their first real conversation since Missy had left London.

Wise enough to keep her opinions of Casey's actions to herself, her mother had insisted she had no idea what her granddaughter had been up to. But Elizabeth Ellington had been shocked to find out Missy was also on her way to Wyoming. Before she could say anything more, Missy had ended the call with a curt promise to get in touch as soon as she found a place for her and Casey to stay for the weekend.

"Ms. Dobbs?"

Missy spun around and found a gentleman dressed in a dark suit holding a placard with her name on it. She'd traveled enough over the years to recognize a car service when she saw one.

Liam wasn't here. She should be grateful for more time before she saw him again, but it bothered her more than she cared to admit that he hadn't kept his word. "Yes?"

"Mr. Murphy was unavoidably detained in Destiny due to business," he said. "I'm to make sure you arrive safely. I have a car waiting outside."

Resentment burned that not only had Liam stood her up, but he hadn't sent Casey along to meet her either. Bollocks! What did he think she'd do? Grab her daughter and take the next flight out of here?

"Could you give me a moment, please?" she asked.

The gentleman nodded and stepped away. Missy found a quiet corner and called Casey's mobile. It went straight to voice mail. She left a message that she'd landed and was on her way to Destiny. She then tried the number her daughter had used when she'd called earlier today, assuming it was for Liam's cell phone, but it just rang and rang.

Seeing as she didn't have any other choice, she followed the driver outside and moments later was seated in the back of a luxury town car. They soon were out of the city and on the motorway. Out the window the land was flat and wide and empty with a blue sky that seemed to go on forever.

So different from the hustle and bustle of London, where she'd lived all her life. She remembered feeling very lost and vulnerable when she'd first arrived in Wyoming all those years ago.

She'd almost cut her visit short after a trip home for Christmas, but had decided to return to Destiny.

Because of one boy. The one she'd been crushing on from the time she'd seen him in the school hallway the very first week.

Liam Murphy, a real cowboy who spent his weekends riding in rodeos, had finally asked her to dance during the last slow song at the winter semiformal, and she had promptly tripped over his boots—

No!

Missy gave her head a quick shake. There would be no trips down memory lane. It was bad enough she'd spent the last few weeks remembering how she and Liam had met, started dating and fallen in love.

Of course, steering clear of their shared history wasn't going to be easy. Goodness knew what kind of questions Casey was going to have for her—for them—over the next few days.

Missy tried once more to reach her daughter, but again she got only voice mail. She grew more nervous as they arrived in Destiny, which she had to admit looked much the same as the last time she was here.

They drove down the charming main street with its many businesses, around the gazebo in the center of town, past the firehouse and the sheriff's office and the Blue Creek Saloon, a bar and restaurant whose roots went back to the town's founding in the late 1800s, a fact that had fascinated Missy the first time she'd been there.

When the car passed over the rushing waters of the blue creek the town landmark was named after, she realized the turnoff to Liam's family ranch and business headquarters was just ahead.

She tensed, expecting a large crowd. Liam was one of six boys, most of whom worked for the log-home business as well, so there must be wives and other children in the family by now. Would they be here? What about his parents? Were they still alive and living here, too?

When the car bypassed the oversize parking lot and slowed to a stop in the half circle drive in front of the massive two-story log home, only one figure waited on the front porch that ran the length of the building.

Liam.

From her own memories and the candid photographs on the company's website showing the Murphy family at work and at play, the brothers were all good-looking men with similar features, but she knew it was him.

Missy couldn't take her eyes off the man as she exited the car and pushed her tote bag to one shoulder, her fingers clenching her phone as the memories she'd tried so hard to keep at bay washed over her.

Memories of falling in love for the first time, and all the joy and wonder that came with that experience. But then the pain—a truly aching, physical pain—when he had broken her heart.

How, after all this time, could those feelings still be powerful enough to bring a piercing sting to the back of her eyes?

Blinking hard, she wished she'd thought to grab her sunglasses from her bag. Regardless, she started forward, suddenly needing to see Casey. She made her way up the elaborate brick pathway, bordered with a colorful array of flowers that also ran along the front of the house.

"Where's my daughter?" she asked when she reached the stairs, hating the huskiness of her voice.

Liam moved to the edge of the porch and she couldn't help but note that the picture online must've been taken recently. Despite the passage of time, he did look the same, just an older version of the boy she'd known. Impossibly handsome in jeans, a long-sleeved dress shirt with the cuffs folded back to his elbows and cowboy boots.

Always cowboy boots.

His gaze lit on her, but the setting sun and deep shadows of the porch made it impossible to see his expression as he thanked the driver, who'd placed her suitcases on the porch. She tore her gaze from him and thanked the man as well when he walked past her.

When it was just the two of them again, she returned her focus to Liam, who hadn't moved other than to cross his arms over his chest.

The defensive pose spoke volumes about his state of mind. Fine, but right now she wanted to see for herself that Casey was okay.

"I asked you—"

"Is it true?" The words were out of his mouth as she reached for the stair railing, freezing her on the first step. "Is Casey my daughter?" he demanded.

Chapter Two

Liam hadn't meant to sound so rude. He'd figured once Missy arrived at the house they'd sit down like adults, catch up on the last sixteen years and talk about the craziness that had descended on his life today.

Craziness in the form of his supposed daughter. But first, he had to know.

"Is she mine?" he asked again, his voice softer now.

He waited for her to answer, not having felt this rush of fear, excitement and adrenaline since his bronc-riding days. No, that was a lie. The moment Casey had shocked him with her announcement, he'd felt something far beyond anything he'd ever experienced on the back of a horse.

The sensation now returned in full force. The feeling that he was about to take the ride of his life.

"Yes," Missy finally said, "she is."

He dropped his arms. The almost desperate need to

believe her was so foreign he brushed it away. Could he accept what she was saying as the truth? He'd admit the numbers made sense and according to his mother, Casey shared the same eyes—right down to the dark blue coloring—as him, but he was having a hard time believing the girl's rambling story.

None of this made sense. How? Why?

"I'd like to see her," Missy continued, her lilting voice laced with a condescending tone. "Now. If that's all right with you."

"You can't."

Realizing again how bad mannered that sounded, Liam tried once more to soften his tone. "She's at the rodeo with her gran—with my folks. My family. She had a good time today and didn't want to miss the finals, presentations to the winners or the fireworks afterward."

"Hmm, yes, I remember well how a rodeo works." Missy's smile was rueful as she continued up the steps toward him. "How can a mother compete with all that?"

She remembered because of him. Because of their time together. That thought caused a burst of heat to ignite right in the center of his chest.

"They also figured you and I would appreciate the opportunity to talk privately about…well, about everything."

"Saying we have quite a bit to discuss seems a bit of an understatement, doesn't it?"

Liam stepped back when she joined him on the porch but not before a summery floral scent with a hint of peach invaded his head. Damn, she still wore the same perfume. Swallowing hard against the rush of memories, he took a step back and gestured toward a seating area set up at the far end of the porch.

She moved past him, walking in that same graceful way she'd had as a teenager. Years of ballet training, she'd once told him. Her hair was the same honey-blond color, but she wore it up off her neck, a few long pieces curling around her face. He wondered if it was as long as it'd once been, halfway down her back.

As if she could read his mind, Missy paused when she reached the wicker sofa, one hand tucking back a strand of hair that had fallen free as her chin rose in an almost regal attitude before she sat.

Yeah, she still possessed that British reserve that had made it hard for her to make friends when she first came to Destiny all those years ago.

He'd noticed her the first day of his senior year in high school. Every guy had. She'd been so different from the rest of the girls in their class. Some of his friends had made fools of themselves, trying to capture her attention, but the more they tried, the more she shot them down.

As someone who never had any problem getting a pretty girl to notice him, he'd liked that about her.

After a few months of watching her, he'd been determined to melt that icy reserve—and brave enough to try thanks to a dare from his buddies at the winter semiformal.

It'd taken until the night was almost over before he asked her to dance. She'd surprised him by accepting, and like a klutz, he'd tangled his boots with her delicate shoes. She'd laughed it off, stepped into his arms and he'd been a goner.

"You're staring at me."

Her words—the same ones spoken by her daughter earlier today—had him shaking off the memories as he joined her, taking one of the chairs. "I'm sorry. After all these years...to see you again. I guess I'm comparing the photos Casey showed me to the real thing."

Missy rolled her eyes. "Her and that mobile. I think she must have five hundred pictures on it."

"Many of them are of the two of you. Some going back years."

She nodded, a soft smile on her face, and then her gaze met his again. "You look just like your photo, too."

It took him a moment to figure out where she might have seen a picture of him. Online. Thanks to their office manager's insistence, the company's site had been updated this summer with new pictures, including formal portraits of the management team.

Liam liked that she had done a Google search on him. "You visited the Murphy Mountain Log Homes website."

"Very corporate looking." Her gaze traveled over him. "You look good in Hugo Boss."

"They cut a good suit."

Silence stretched between them as they studied each other in the fading light of the sunset. Was she looking for the cowboy he'd been back then? Wild and reckless and so full of himself he couldn't see beyond his own wants and needs? His own dreams?

She looked exactly the same. Older, yes, but still the same ethereal beauty as when he'd last seen her. It was easy to see the features she shared with her daughter.

Their daughter.

His throat suddenly dry, Liam rose and went to the antique dresser that held pitchers of tea, water, an ice bucket and glasses, all thanks to his mother. "I'm sorry, I should've asked. Would you like something to drink?"

Missy let loose with a delicate humph from behind him. "Do you have anything a wee bit stronger? I think you're going to need it."

He shot her a look over his shoulder, and then opened the door below and pulled out a bottle of wine and his drink of choice, whiskey. She gestured for the wine and he poured her a glass, then whiskey for himself.

"You know, Casey tried to explain how she'd only found out a few weeks ago about me being her…" His voice trailed off as he returned to his seat, handing Missy her wine. "The more she talked, the more upset she became. I gather from your shock at her announcing she'd traveled to Destiny and found me that you hadn't shared this news with her yet?"

Missy placed her cell phone on the table and took the glass. "No, I didn't have the chance before my job had me flying to Los Angeles. I've barely had time to absorb everything myself. After all these years…to think, it never occurred to me to question the test results—"

It was at that moment his cell phone chirped from inside his pants pocket, cutting her off. Damn, now was not the time for business. He ignored the phone and it went silent for a moment, but came back to life again right away.

"You can get that," she said. "If you need to."

He probably should. A typical day for him ran long past five o'clock, especially for a select few clients who had his direct line. Or was it someone from the rodeo committee looking for him, despite his hasty explanation about a business emergency?

"It might be Casey," he said, the thought just coming to him.

Missy flipped over her phone, checking it. "I tried to ring her when I landed. All I got was voice mail."

He pulled the now silent phone out and looked. Two missed calls, both from the same client, who wouldn't hesitate to move on to his brother Nolan if he couldn't reach Liam. A press of a button and the phone would stay quiet.

"It was work, but it can wait," he said. "Now, you were saying something about test results? Casey mentioned overhearing a fight between you and her grandmother, but like I said, she was pretty distraught. I told her we'd get everything straightened out when you got here. After that, she seemed to relax and enjoy the rodeo."

"And you introduced her to your family?" Missy sipped her wine. "Just like that?"

"I wasn't about to leave her on her own to wander around the fairgrounds. I told them she was the daughter of an old friend from high school." He took a swallow from his own glass, the familiar warmth sliding easily down his throat. "As soon as I said your name my folks remembered you. So did my younger brother Bryant. It was my mom who...well, who put it all together, especially when I said you were on your way to Destiny."

"And here I am."

"Yes, here you are." And here he was waiting for his first love to explain how he—they—had a child he'd never known about until today. "After all this time, not hearing from you, I can honestly say I never expected something like...this."

"I can understand. Please, let me start at the beginning. Well, the most recent beginning." She sighed, her gaze lowered. "My father passed away suddenly from a heart attack on August first."

"I'm sorry," Liam said automatically, surprised at how little emotion was in her voice considering that was just three weeks ago. "Was he ill?"

"Thank you, and technically he wasn't, but it was his third attack in the last ten years. Not completely unexpected, especially as he refused to give up his cigars and brandy." She paused and pulled in a deep breath. "I was going through his desk after the services, clearing out paperwork and whatnot, when I came across a file that contained the DNA test we had done just after Casey was born."

"April twelfth, a week after your birthday."

She looked up when he said that. "Yes."

"She told me. That was nine months after we'd last—after you returned home."

"Yes."

"Almost nine months to the day, if memory serves."

"Yes."

"Missy, why didn't you tell me?" Tired of her one-word answers, Liam leaned forward, bracing his forearms against his knees, his fingers laced tight around the glass. "I know things ended badly, but as soon as you knew you were pregnant you should've gotten in touch with me."

"I wanted to, but I didn't... I didn't know if I had the right to."

"The right?" Now he was really confused. "What does that mean?"

"Oh, Liam, I was such a mess when I left Destiny all those years ago." She set her glass on the table, stood and then walked to the porch railing, keeping her back to him. "You and I had that terrible row. All my plans and dreams were gone. I was angry and lonely and..."

"And?" He prompted when her voice faded.

Her shoulders rose and fell as she pulled in another deep breath before turning to face him, her arms tight across her middle. "And I spent the night with my old boyfriend. The lad I was seeing before I came to America. Before you."

The fine Kentucky whiskey now burned in his gut. "Stanley." The name popped out of his mouth before he could think to stop it.

"Stanford. His name was Stanford Dobbs."

He vaguely remembered her telling him all those years ago about a college guy she'd been dating back in London. Hearing his full name—with the same surname as Missy and Casey—had him taking another long swallow of liquid courage. "And this happened soon after you got back that summer?"

She jerked her head in a quick nod, the affirmation tearing at his insides. How crazy was that?

"The following week," she said softly. "It…it was only that one time. After that, I knew I had to pull myself together, get my life back on track. Get back into school. Get over you."

To hear her speak calmly about sleeping with someone else so soon after they—after she returned, despite all the time that had passed, bugged Liam more than he wanted to admit.

Leaning back in his chair, he offered her a casual salute with his glass, his knuckles white. "Well, that was a step in the right direction."

She bit hard at her bottom lip, and then continued. "I didn't realize I was pregnant until almost Halloween."

Now it all made sense. "And you didn't know who the father was."

"No, I didn't." She returned his stare, unflinching. "It took me another month to find the courage to tell Stanford…and my parents. They, of course, expected a hasty wedding, but when I told them that there was no way to be sure—"

"Boy, that must've made Stan a bit upset."

Up went that delicate chin again. "Stanford still wanted to marry me. He said he didn't care if the child was his or not."

Okay, Liam should feel like a louse right about now, but the fire burning in his gut had now spread throughout his body. "That was big of him."

"We had to wait until Casey was born before a DNA test could be done. Before we knew for certain who was—"

"But you *knew* you were pregnant the previous fall."

Liam shot to his feet. "You knew there was a chance—why didn't you at least let me know that the baby might be mine?"

"Oh, Liam, you were on the other side of the world, living your dream. You'd made your decision to be a professional cowboy that summer, and you continued right on with your rodeo competitions after I left. By the time I knew I was pregnant, you were well on your way to earning a spot at grand finals, finishing second your first time there!"

She knew that?

She must've read the shock on his face. "Yes, I knew, thanks to Suzy McIntyre. The girl whose family I stayed with while I was here in Destiny? She told me all about your big achievement in a letter that arrived just after the new year."

"Wait—you got a letter?" The memory returned so strong he dropped back to the chair. "From Suzy?"

"Believe me, no one was more surprised than I to see it in the post."

"That was the only letter you got?"

"Oh, one was more than enough." Missy's voice rose as she paced back and forth in front of him. "Not only did she send me a newspaper clipping of you being a rodeo star, but she also went on about how you and your *bride* were settling in here in Destiny afterward."

Liam closed his eyes and swallowed hard. He hadn't thought about that stupid and reckless decision in a long time. "She told you I had gotten married?"

"Yes! Six months after I left."

The pain in Missy's voice surprised him. He looked at her again. "It didn't last. Six or seven— it was over by the spring."

"Well, I didn't want to upset the newlyweds unless I

had to, so I waited until my daughter was born that same spring." Missy returned to the seating area and grabbed her glass. "When the test results came back that Stanford was a match...we married a month later."

The only sound was the low chirping of crickets now that the sun had set. And there was a distant thunder that could only be the fireworks from the rodeo. It was then that Liam noticed the outside lights on the porch, pathway and the model homes situated in front of the main house had come on automatically, casting muted pockets of yellow glowing here and there, but the end of the porch where they sat was dark.

So dark that he couldn't see Missy's face clearly.

He rose again. Lighting candles on the dresser, he brought back a few and placed them in the center of the table in time to catch the shaking of the glass in her hand.

"I was nineteen years old, a mother, a wife...trying to go to school, to live up to my parents' expectations...to Stanford's." Missy finished the last of her wine. "It wasn't easy."

He was sure it wasn't. At nineteen he'd been concentrating on rodeoing full-time and working for his father, attached to nothing but his horse and trailer. Not even his so-called marriage had rated any importance. One of the reasons it'd ended so quickly.

How long had Missy and Stanford been married? Were they still?

Liam's gaze went to her left hand clutching the glass. No ring. Did that mean anything? "Casey never mentioned her father today."

"Stanford died in a car accident when she was five years old. Before that we were—he traveled a lot. For business. She barely remembers him."

So, she hadn't remarried in the decade since? He tucked

away that question, not wanting to go there. "You started
to tell me about test results. I'm guessing you're referring
to the ones that said Stanford was a match."

"Yes, but what I found in the dark corners of my father's desk were two test results," Missy said, reaching for
an oversize leather tote. She tilted it toward the light and
rummaged around inside, pulling out some paperwork
and thrusting it at him. "The one he showed me all those
years ago and the *real* test. The one that stated Stanford
was not a match. This, of course, meant you were—are—
Casey's father."

Liam took the papers, but kept his eyes on her. "I'm
guessing this is what you and your mother argued about."

"You bet your arse. She admitted to knowing the whole
thing, all this time, when I confronted her." Missy grabbed
her glass, saw it was empty and set it down again. "Like
I said, I had to fly to LA the next day for a work commitment without the chance to talk to Casey. I couldn't have
sprung something like this on her at the last minute and
then left. Not that it mattered. Apparently she overheard
me and Mum and…and took matters into her own hands."

She looked at him then, her gaze steady. "The one thing
I did plan was coming to Destiny. To find you and tell you
everything. Casey got here first."

Liam nodded, certain if he tried to speak right now the
words wouldn't make it past the lump in his throat.

He tried to mentally piece together the jigsaw puzzle
her story created. He believed her, as crazy as it was. He
was angry at her parents for what they had done to both
of them—all three of them. To keep the true paternity of
their grandchild from their daughter because…

He had no idea why. Other than that they must've been
dead set against the plans Missy had made all those years
ago to move to America. To go to college here. To be with

him. Plans he'd stomped all over with his size-twelve boots when he'd announced *his* plan to rodeo full-time instead of going to the University of Wyoming.

So where did they go from here?

"I planned to tell Casey once we were together again. She wasn't supposed to arrive in the States until Monday, meeting me in LA," Missy continued. "She, of course, took it upon herself to change all that."

"Who was watching Casey while you traveled? Your mother?"

Missy nodded.

"I'm guessing she too was in the dark about Casey's plans." Liam leaned forward and set his now empty glass down. "Does she know where her granddaughter is now?"

"Of course. We spoke during my layover. And yes, she had no idea what Casey was up to. She was under the impression she was staying with friends."

"You seem pretty calm about all of this—"

She cut him off with a casual wave of her hand. "Believe me, I'm not."

"Really?" There was that cool British reserve again, and it irked him. "Your daughter changes her international flight plans, arrives alone in a foreign country and hitches a ride to Destiny from the airport and you're just—"

Her beautiful blue eyes grew wide. "Hitched?"

"It was just pure luck that I ran into her at the rodeo at all. In time to get her out of what might've been a... sticky situation."

"I'm not sure what that means, but believe me, I will be discussing my daughter's actions with her as soon as I see her." Missy dropped her hand to the tote in her lap. "And answering what I'm sure will be quite a few questions from her about this entire situation. Thankfully, she and I have plenty of time to talk. We're flying to Hawaii next week for a planned holiday before returning to London next month."

Liam's head spun, his thoughts a jumbled mess of questions, ideas and plans, but her words cut through. "Wait a minute, you mean you *were* flying to Hawaii."

"No, I—"

"Don't think you can just show up, drop a bomb about a long-lost daughter and walk away three days later." Liam's anger was back and it was hot. He got to his feet again. "I don't care who got here first."

"We have plans."

"Plans change."

She stood as well, ready to argue, but then a caravan of cars came down the drive. They parked in the nearby lot and his family spilled out into the night. Moments later they were across the yard and heading up the porch, with Casey leading the way.

"Mum!"

Missy's expression transformed when she saw her daughter, and seconds later they held each other in a tight embrace. When they finally let go, Missy stepped back, running her hands lightly over Casey's multicolored hair as she looked in her daughter's eyes. Then she took in the new boots Casey was proudly showing off.

Watching the two of them, and the private world they created just by being in each other's company, made Liam's chest ache. This was supposed to be his daughter, but he'd never felt more like an outsider despite being surrounded by his own family.

He cleared his throat, catching both of their attention.

"Missy, I think you probably remember my folks, Alistair and Elise Murphy." The sooner they got introductions over with, the sooner they could get back to talking about how long she and Casey were sticking around. "Mom and Dad, this is Casey's mother, Melissa Dobbs."

She took his mother's outstretched hand first and then his father's. "Yes, of course, I remember you, Mr. and Mrs. Murphy. It's good to see you again. And please, call me Missy."

"Oh, it's so nice to see you, too, dear," his mother said, giving her the once-over before sending a wink Liam's way that he hoped no one else noticed. "We remember you as well. You've grown up so nice."

"Ah, thank you."

"And these are two of my three brothers who live in town." Liam waved at the men standing nearby. "I'm guessing Adam took Fay and A.J. straight on home?"

"Only because the baby was fussy. Otherwise they would've been here too. Hi, Missy, I'm Nolan Murphy." Liam's brother stepped forward and gave her a quick handshake. "Adam's our oldest brother and the smart one. He doesn't live here on the compound." He then pointed at the three teenagers lounging on the steps. "Those hooligans are mine. Abby is sixteen and the twins, Luke and Logan, are thirteen."

Missy smiled at the kids and then returned his greeting. "I'm sorry, I don't remember meeting you before. Or Adam."

"That's because I was living in Boston the year you were here. Adam was serving overseas in the military."

After nodding, she then shook hands with Bryant and his wife, Laurie. "Now, you I remember," she said. "You were a wee freshman when I was here last."

"Yeah, that was me." Bryant grinned. "Devlin is only a year behind Liam, so you must remember him too."

"Yes, I do remember Devlin. Popular with the ladies, right?"

"Oh, that's our Dev," Elise said, and then laughed. "Only now he's a one-woman man and living in London, actually, for the next few months, with his lady love, Tanya. And our youngest, Ric—oh, he must've been just six or seven when you were here—is in the air force, stationed in northern Italy."

"Well, it's lovely to meet you all…again…and thank you for taking care of my daughter today. I do appreciate it."

"We enjoyed having her with us." Elise smiled warmly at Casey, waving off Missy's gratitude. "And we're looking forward to getting to know her—and you—better during your stay."

Missy glanced at her daughter for a moment before her gaze flickered in Liam's direction. "Well, we're only in town for a few days," she said, looking back at his mother. "The weekend. Casey and I have a holiday scheduled—"

"Mum, are you daft? We can't go now!" Casey spun around, grabbing her arm. "I just got here. We just got here! There's so much more I want to see and do!"

"Casey, we have reservations—"

"Off the bloody reservations! Everything's changed now!"

Liam couldn't agree more, but from the look on Missy's face, she wasn't buying into her daughter's excitement.

"Why don't we head inside and let these three talk this out," Alistair said, heading for the door with his wife in tow.

"Are you kidding?" Abby leaned in from her perch on the stairs, flinging her long blond hair back over one shoulder. "This is getting good!"

"Nolan…"

Liam sent his brother a warning look, but the man was already corralling his kids off the steps and around the side yard. Bryant and Laurie followed his folks indoors. Then it was the three of them as Casey continued her campaign to change her mother's mind.

It wasn't working.

He could see it in Missy's eyes, hear it in her voice as she laid out the travel plans she and Casey had for spending the next month in a private villa on the beach in Maui. Nice. She'd come from a world of money and power back when they'd first met all those years ago. He guessed she—or her family—was still doing okay.

Either way, she didn't want to be in Destiny. Didn't want to be near him. Too bad. If she thought she could waltz out of the continental US, taking his daughter with her, and expect him to be okay with that, she had another think coming.

His fingers tightened into a fist, crinkling the paperwork he still held. An idea popped into his head and tumbled out of his mouth. "Here's another reason for you two to stick around. We need to do another DNA test."

The two women stopped talking and turned in unison to look at him.

Missy's light blue eyes crackled with fire, but it was the wounded look that flashed in Casey's that got to him.

Damn, what else could he do?

He believed Missy's story about a doctored DNA test, even if it was a bit farfetched. Who knew how long this lie would've gone on if not for her father suddenly dying, Casey overhearing, Liam still living in the same town where it all started…

For whatever reason, the universe had conspired to bring him and Missy back together—to bring them all together—and he wanted them to stay. More than he'd wanted anything in a long time.

"Look, this is a negative report telling us who's not a match," Liam said, gesturing with the paperwork. "A report we now know that has been tampered with. We should have another test done—me and Casey—just so we're all a hundred percent sure."

Chapter Three

Casey was ready to tell her real father what he could do with his suggestion about a new DNA test, and knowing her daughter's temper, it wasn't going to be pretty. Not that Missy blamed her. After his veiled remarks concerning her parenting skills, she was ready to tell him what he could do with his demand for another test herself.

"I think he's right," she said instead, before Casey could speak. She read the surprise on Liam's face at her like-mindedness, but her focus at the moment had to be on her daughter.

Missy reached for Casey's hand, hating that it was ice-cold. A quick squeeze got her attention. "We should have an up-to-date test done. For his sake, sweetie, and ours."

Casey's bravado crumbled and the fire left her eyes. "Why did Granddad do this to you? To us? To Dad?" She bit hard at her bottom lip, and her gaze swung over to Liam. "I mean...you know, my other..."

"It's okay." Liam's voice was gentler now. "Things are a little mixed-up at the moment."

To say the least. The hurt and confusion reflected on Liam's and Casey's faces—feelings that shone brightly in matching sets of dark blue eyes—shook Missy to her core.

Almost as much as the realization that the two of them shared the same eyes. Same shape, same color. A deep cerulean blue she'd once told Liam matched the river-fed lake back behind the Murphy family home. A color she always told Casey was her favorite.

How had she never noticed that before now?

Because you believed the lie you were told years ago. The scared girl deep inside you clung to those test results, filled with righteous indignation that this man didn't deserve to be the father of your precious baby girl.

Missy blinked away that sudden insight, not willing or able to deal with that bitter pill of truth. Not tonight. "I think we should—"

"How did you two hook up anyway?" Casey blurted out. "It's a long way between London and Destiny—oh, wait! I overheard Grandmum say letting you go to America was a mistake. You'd turned nineteen just before you had me... bollocks, don't tell me I'm a souvenir from a one-off during a spring break trip."

"No!" Liam and Missy spoke at the same time, their voices united.

"You were not the result of a one-night stand," Missy continued, aghast that the idea had popped into her daughter's head.

"You never told her?" he asked, taking a step closer. His broad shoulders blocked out the porch light behind him, casting his face in shadows, but the tightening of his jaw was unmistakable. "About your time in Destiny? About us?"

Missy shook her head, surprised at the nuance of hurt in his tone. No, that was impossible. The man had married someone else less than a year after she'd left sixteen years ago. A lifetime ago.

"That's right. You said a few minutes ago you remembered his family!" Casey's voice grew excited again. "So you two were a couple? And you lived here in Destiny, Mum? For how long?"

"A year," Liam said.

"It was more like eleven months." Missy spoke at the same time, overriding him. "As part of a student exchange program when I was in my sixth form. The twelfth grade in an American high school, and yes, Liam and I dated during that time."

"I'd say you did more than date, Mum. A lot more."

Liam let loose a snort that changed to a clearing of his throat, one hand fisted against his mouth, when Missy glared at him. Still, he remained silent, only tilting his head in her direction.

She sighed. She wanted nothing more than to sink up to her nose in bubbles and then collapse into bed, but some private time with her daughter was needed first.

"Sweetie, it's been a long day. For all of us. Right now, I could use a hot bath and we—" she gave Casey's hand another quick squeeze "—need to have a long talk. About everything. Including your clandestine adventure getting to America, which, despite everything, you're not off the hook for."

Her daughter's gaze again flickered to Liam.

"A talk with just the two of us," Missy added, this time looking fully at Liam, half expecting him to argue with her over this as well. "If that's all right with you?"

He returned her stare for a long moment, and then nodded. "If you think that's best." He dropped his hand to his side. "For now."

Meaning Casey and he—or more likely the three of them—would be talking about their shared past, and where they all went from here, during the next few days. At least his anger about their planned holiday seemed to have disappeared, probably because of Casey's vocal objections to leaving Destiny.

Not that agreeing to another test meant anything had changed.

Still, things had gone better than Missy had hoped for tonight. Considering the merry-go-round of memories, emotions and questions that she'd been riding since that night in her father's study, Missy was proud of how she'd handled things so far.

Once she and her daughter started talking? All bets were off.

Casey had never been one to back down from what she was feeling, and like most teenagers, she could get a bit cheeky when her emotions were riled, not holding back whatever she might be thinking. Missy was used to it, even if she did have to pull in Casey's reins from time to time. The truth was she'd encouraged her daughter to always speak her mind and be honest with what she was feeling. A trait that often exasperated Casey's grandparents, especially her grandmother.

It was time to end this evening before she went into memory overload. "Liam, if you could arrange for a car to take us to the closest hotel, perhaps that quaint bed-and-breakfast in town, we'd greatly appreciate it."

Her heart stuttered when he gave a quick shake of his head. "No can do. The inn is full. So are the two hotels out by the highway. With the rodeo in town, there isn't an empty room anywhere. People are staying as far away as Laramie. Even Cheyenne."

"Well, we have to stay somewhere. I doubt we'll be able to do anything about a test until Monday." She released Casey and turned back for the phone she'd left on the table. "Let me do a search and see what I can find—"

"How about we stay here? Who's living in those?"

"Cassalyn Dobbs!" Missy spun back around, surprised by the boldness of her daughter, who was pointing at the nearby log homes. "How cheeky of you."

"She's not being *cheeky*, just curious." Liam again shook his head, this time with a slight smile on his face. "Sorry, but those are only model homes. They have electricity, as you can see, but no plumbing. Since your mother mentioned wanting a bubble bath—"

"I didn't say anything about bubbles," she cut him off, her gaze on her phone, positive she hadn't spoken that desire aloud. "And we can't stay here."

"Of course you can." Elise Murphy's voice carried from the doorway as she came back out to the porch. "You're more than welcome."

Stay here in the Murphy family home? Not bloody likely!

Now it was Missy's turn to shake her head. "Oh, we wouldn't want to impose—"

"It's no imposition, dear." Elise hurried to join them. "We'd love to have you. Now, we do have an empty guest room in the main house, but it only has a queen-size bed. Much too small for the two of you. Nolan's place is out—what with the four of them, it's already crowded and why he turned his guest room into an office I'll never understand."

"He likes to work late," Liam said. "Really late."

"And he can't walk across the yard to his office here in the main house?" Elise harrumphed. "Bryant and Laurie's cabin is too small. And you—" she paused to swat at her son's chest "—if you'd bother to furnish any of the rooms in your new place beside the master suite—"

"My place has furniture," Liam interrupted his mother. "Just not in the bedrooms."

"And aren't you sorry about that now?"

The flash of awareness in his gaze caused Missy's already hastened heartbeat to race out of control. Pressing a hand to her chest, as if that would ease the wild thumping, she tried to put a stop to this. "I appreciate your offer, but we'll be fine in a hotel."

"Wait, I have the perfect place!" The older woman's eyes lit up as she clasped her hands together. "You can stay in the boathouse."

"The boathouse?" Casey asked. "What's that?"

"It's down back, on the lake. Above where we store the boats and canoes and stuff. It used to be a storage area, but a few years ago I came up with the idea of…"

Missy's gaze locked with Liam's, his mother's chatter fading to a dull buzzing. The boathouse. A private sanctuary in the middle of the Murphy family madness she and Liam had often sneaked off to whenever they wanted to be alone.

They'd discovered the secluded setting by accident one cool and stormy spring afternoon after hurrying back from a canoe ride, soaked to the skin and looking for shelter.

Filled with cast-off furniture, old toys and boxes and trunks filled with everything from books to clothes to holiday decorations, the place had had a faint musty smell, but it'd been warm and dry. After realizing no one had found out where they'd gone off to, they'd returned often. Just being together, away from everyone, had been wonderful.

Of course, the intimacy of the space had lent itself to kisses…and so much more. It'd been the first place they'd made love. On a warm night with moonlight streaming through the windows, both unsure of what they were doing, but secure in their feelings and what they wanted.

A wanting that deepened and grew—

"Missy?"

Liam's husky voice broke into her memories, but it was his heated touch on her arm that jolted her out of the past.

She jerked away, refusing to look at him or accept the wild beating of her heart. Thankfully Elise was still going on about the design of the apartment, and her daughter was so enthralled with the description neither one of them had noticed how she had zoned out.

Liam had. Of course he had. He knew exactly why she was about to refuse his mother's generous offer.

"Us dropping in unannounced like this isn't fair to Liam…or to your family." Missy prayed her words didn't sound as distressed as she felt. "We really don't want to put you to any trouble."

"Oh, it's no trouble, dear. We were expecting a visit from friends of Alistair's for the rodeo, but they had to cancel at the last minute. The place is ready with fresh linens and a fully stocked kitchen."

"It sounds perfect." Casey offered a pleading look. "Please, Mum?"

It was late and the constant memories were draining, both emotionally and physically. Besides, after all this time, what did it really matter?

Hating the lump of desperation in her stomach at that thought, she forced a smile. "Thank you. We appreciate your hospitality."

Elise smiled and handed a key ring to her son. "Here, perhaps you should take them around through the back-yard. There's still a group of people in the living room. We'll see you both in the morning."

His mother gave Casey a quick hug, which her daughter easily returned, surprising Missy again. She'd be hard-pressed to remember the last time she saw *her* mother exchange affections that way with Casey.

After the woman went back inside, the teen hurried to the stairs, grabbing Missy's two small suitcases along with a duffel bag she recognized as belonging to her daughter.

"Blimey, Mum…only two cases? I thought you took a whole store full when you departed for California."

"Most of which is still in LA," she quipped, joining her daughter after getting her purse. "I only brought enough clothes for a weekend trip."

"But we aren't—"

She lightly tugged at her earlobe—a familiar gesture between them that had the desired effect of stopping Casey from arguing. For the moment, at least. Her daughter's expression said she was clearly gearing up for round two.

Oh, a tub full of bubbles was sounding better all the time.

"Here, you take the key and let me carry those." Liam relieved Casey of the luggage and gestured for them to head down the stairs first. "Let's get you two settled. Casey, you know the way."

As she followed her daughter, Missy wondered what Liam meant by that last statement.

"We came home earlier for dinner," Liam said, falling into step beside her as they strolled down the lighted stone path that led around the side of the house. "Dad barbecued and then everyone headed back to the rodeo."

Missy nodded, a bit mystified that he'd known what she'd been thinking. "Everyone but you."

"I had a business emergency to deal with." His voice turned low. "And I was waiting for you."

A pang of…something she didn't wish to label hit her

right in the chest. She wrapped her arms across her middle against the chill that danced over her skin, raising goose bumps. The silky blazer and tank top she wore underneath were perfect for southern California in August, but the nights were cool here in Wyoming.

Yes, that had to be the reason for her body's reaction to Liam's words.

"Don't worry, it doesn't look anywhere near the same."

Again, meant for her ears only, and she knew exactly what he was talking about. "It's fine."

"A lot has changed since you were here—"

"Yes, of course, it has." She secretly hoped the attic space had been redone as extensively as Elise Murphy described. "As I said, it's fine. Wait—what is—" She stopped short and pointed at the dark object just outside the reach of the outdoor lighting. "Is that a helicopter on the other side of the lot?"

"It's for the family business," Liam said. "A couple of my brothers and I are the pilots."

She now remembered seeing something about it on the company's website, but she'd had no idea… "You fly, too?"

Liam grinned, gesturing with her suitcase, and Missy started walking again, her heels clicking against the stones. The sturdy pathway continued through the large grassy yard and forest of trees at the back of the house.

She wondered how far it went. Years ago there'd been only a dirt trail that led from the oversize backyard down to the river. When they rounded the corner of the house, Missy stumbled to a stop. "Oh, my."

"I told you things have changed a bit." Liam's voice flowed over her shoulder. "And I wasn't just talking about the boathouse."

She turned to him. "I can see that. I wasn't expecting—"

"Isn't it neat? You should see it in the daytime." Casey

spun around, coming dangerously close to the edge of an oversize in-ground pool. "They've got their own neighborhood back here!"

Yes, Missy could see that. The transformation of the yard was stunning.

"You might remember all we used to have was a simple wooden deck, but my folks wanted a complete outdoor entertainment space. Over the years they added the stone patio, fire pit, pool and the connecting pathways," he said as he led the way. "We boys built the gazebo back there to celebrate their fortieth wedding anniversary a few years ago. Mom said it was the perfect final touch."

Missy tried to take it all in. The care and thought that had gone into renovating the acreage was evident. Outdoor lights offered a soft glow, making it easy to see everything from the landscaping to the entertainment areas. Lighted pathways veered off in different directions through clusters of trees that gave each of the log homes a sense of privacy despite their relative closeness to each other.

"And the log homes," she said. "I'm guessing from what your mother said, you and your brothers all still live here."

"Not all of us. Adam has his own ranch down the road and Ric is currently stationed overseas, but yeah—" Liam grinned, and then shrugged. "I guess the rest of us figured the Murphy ranch was as good a place to settle down as anywhere else in town. At least we're not all still in the main house."

"Well, it's certainly big enough for everyone," she said, eyeing the house more closely.

Missy listened to him describe who lived where as they passed his brothers' homes, Casey a few steps ahead of them. The path sloped downward and led to the lake, and the trees got closer together. When the boathouse with its familiar wooden dock came into view, her stomach clenched.

"So that must leave this one as yours, right?"

Casey's question pulled Missy's gaze from the boathouse to a two-story log home that sat a bit farther back into the trees.

"Yes, that's my place," Liam said.

"Wow, it's big for one person. Since no one's mentioned it, I'm guessing you're not married."

"Casey!"

"It's okay." His gaze lingered on Missy for a moment before he looked at their daughter. "And you guessed correctly, I'm not. I was—twice, actually—but neither one stuck."

Twice? He'd married again? Not an unusual occurrence, but the news still surprised her.

"So do I have any younger half siblings running around?"

"Nope, just a handful of cousins, I'm afraid."

"Bugger, I always wanted a little sister." Casey shrugged and headed for the boathouse. "Used to bother my mum for years over that. Of course there was little chance of it happening. She rarely, if ever, dated after my father died."

Missy gasped and pressed a hand to her forehead, embarrassed at her daughter's directness but also to block out Liam's dark gaze as he turned to look at her. "Cassalyn Elizabeth—"

"Oh, it's never a good thing when she brings out the full name." Reaching the end of the boathouse, Casey jerked her thumb around the corner. "Your mum said stairs would lead up to the flat. Is this them?"

"Yes, a light should come on when you get to the top…" His voice trailed off as Casey disappeared, her footsteps echoing up the stairwell. "Is she avoiding me all of a sudden?"

"No, it's me she's trying to get away from." Missy couldn't stop from stealing glances at the beautiful front porch on Liam's home, so close now that it seemed to tower over them as they walked along the back side of the boathouse. "I apologize for her rudeness."

"Like I said, it's okay. I have a feeling she's going to have quite a few questions for us in the coming days."

"You're probably right." She followed him around the corner of the building, surprised when she saw a second-level porch had been added to the front of the boathouse that faced the water, creating a covered area over the three boat slips she remembered. "My, more changes."

"I told you."

"Yes, you did. Well, I should—" She stopped when the glow from the outdoor lighting suddenly disappeared, leaving them in darkness except for the light coming from the upper landing. "What—what just happened?"

"It must be ten o'clock. The lights are on a timed system with the majority of the accent features going off for the night. Don't worry—the outside lights on everyone's homes, as well as the pathways, are motion activated, in case you need anyone for…well, anything."

Meaning she was to go to him? The queen would give up the throne first. "Well, as I was saying, I should get upstairs and answer some of those questions."

Liam studied her in silence. Was he going to insist on being part of this discussion? Missy honestly didn't think she had the strength to include him, as terrible as that sounded.

Not after everything that had happened today.

Being back in Destiny, staying in the boathouse, standing so close to him she could reach out and touch—

"Yes, I guess you should," he finally said. "Let me take the bags up for you."

"I'll take them." Casey reappeared, clomping down the stairs. "Sorry for popping off like that. I think the time difference has me a bit knackered."

"If memory serves, that means tired, right?" Liam asked with a grin, handing over the luggage. "And apology accepted."

Casey smiled, and then turned to head back upstairs. "You coming, Mum? Wait until you see the loo! There's a giant claw-footed tub that sits in front of a huge glass window looking right out over the water."

Missy faltered, grabbing at the handrail as she started to follow. She swung her gaze back to Liam, even as she called after her daughter's departing figure. "There—there is?"

Liam retreated, the shadows not completely hiding the way his mouth lifted at one corner. "When I said it didn't look the same, I wasn't talking about the *entire* space. Some things are exactly how they used to be."

It was after midnight and she should be lost in dreamland, but Missy couldn't slow her mind enough to allow sleep to come.

Her talk with Casey had gone surprisingly well, her daughter handling the story of what happened all those years ago between Missy and Liam with ease. Of course, her anger with her grandparents was palpable, mixed with even more tears over her grandfather's recent death, leaving the poor girl confused about what she should be feeling.

Still, she seemed more interested in what had happened sixteen years ago here in Destiny. Missy shared some of what her time here had been like. But after one too many yawns from Casey, Missy had pleaded exhaustion herself and shooed her daughter off to the smaller of the apartment's two bedrooms.

After checking and finding her daughter sound asleep, Missy then took that bubble bath she'd been longing for, memories be damned. So what if the tub stood in the exact same spot it had sixteen years ago?

The antique hadn't been in working order back then. Not that they had let that stop them on a stormy afternoon, lining the tub with old quilts and sharing a picnic there, the roomy fixture big enough to fit both of them comfortably. So comfortably that they'd—

Okay, so the bubbles did little to relax her. Nor did the cup of Earl Grey tea she'd made after finding a selection of loose teas and a darling little pot in the cozy kitchen.

Setting the empty cup in the sink, Missy crossed the parlor, drawn to the French doors that led to the covered porch. She hoped a few moments in the fresh air would clear away her whirlwind thoughts as she slipped outside, closing the door behind her.

She tightened the sash on her dressing gown. The air was cool as she walked to the porch railing, drawn by the full moon lighting up the night sky and dancing over the gentle current of the river-fed lake.

Leaning forward, she gazed up at the stars shining overhead, so clear and bright. Not a sight she saw often from her London neighborhood. Years ago, her first glimpse at a Wyoming sky at night had made her feel much as she felt right now.

Lost and alone. Small. Insignificant. The same emotions that had swamped her the day she'd discovered she was pregnant and had no idea who the baby's father was.

She'd prayed it was Liam. Hoped and prayed for weeks, even after her parents and Stanford had learned about the pregnancy. She'd debated constantly over getting in touch with Liam while having no idea how to explain the crazy situation.

Then she'd found out he'd married someone else. Trying not to allow her heart to be filled with pain and sorrow over the news had been hard. She hadn't wanted her baby to be stuck inside a body racked with such intense emotions for the remaining months of her pregnancy.

And she'd stopped hoping.

Now, fifteen years later, those long-ago prayers had been answered and their lives—hers, Casey's and Liam's—would never be the same.

Would it be fair to separate Casey and Liam so soon? Her daughter had pleaded to stay in Destiny, easily brushing aside the temptation of a month on a tropical beach in order to get to know the man who was her father. Her real father.

Casey and Stanford had never bonded, mostly because of his business schedule and a quiet disdain over Missy's refusal to hire a nanny. He had never gotten over the fact she had wanted to be the one to raise their child, even if it meant putting off her own schooling until Casey was older. Putting him and his career ambitions off, too, at times when it came to fancy parties or corporate travel. She had been a mother first, a wife second. Was it any wonder their marriage foundered after such a short time?

Casey had never seemed to miss having a father after Stanford's death, mainly because Missy's father had been such a doting presence in her life, especially when Missy and Casey had moved back home. To learn he'd played with their lives all those years ago damaged the memories both of them had of the man.

Missy sighed. Could she do it? Could she stay here at

Liam's home, where she'd be surrounded by the memories from a lifetime ago?

During her first visit to Destiny, she'd stayed with a family in town. The McIntyres had been nice people, even if their daughter had soon come to regret having to share her room. Not that it had mattered, because from the moment Missy and Liam had become a couple, her life had revolved around him, his family and the Murphy family home.

She'd traveled with the Murphys on weekends to the rodeos Liam and his brothers had competed in, marveling at his strength and commitment to the sport. A rising star on the rodeo circuit, Liam had been popular with everyone he came in contact with but still down-to-earth. So easy to talk to, to be with.

And she'd loved him. Loved all of them.

So much so that she'd turned her entire world upside down, provoking the wrath of her parents with her plan to go to college in America. It had taken time, but she'd managed to get everything in place so that she could surprise him—

"You bloody well surprised him, all right. Then he shocked you." Her whispered words filled the air, her fingers clutching the railing, nails biting into the wood as she rocked back and forth. "And nothing was the same after that."

A chill raced through her, whether from the night air or the fact that she was even more unsettled now than before she came out here, she didn't know. But it was time to head back inside.

When she turned around, a man leaning against a nearby post, barely visible in the dark, caught her eye. Missy gasped and stumbled backward, but then Liam was there, pulling her into his arms, steadying her.

"Are you okay?" he asked. "I didn't mean..."

His voice faded as she clutched at his wrinkled, unbuttoned dress shirt, the bare skin beneath hot to the touch. That same heat flowed through the silk of her gown from where his hands held her, igniting a burst of need deep inside her.

A swift intake of much needed air brought a clean, sharp, yet woodsy scent to her nose. A scent so familiar her stomach tightened at the memory.

"Missy?"

His features were still obscured by the shadows, but she could see a lock of dark hair falling forward as he stared down at her. It was as if the last sixteen years faded away and all she saw—felt—breathed—in front of her was the boy she'd once loved more than life itself.

A foolish love, childish infatuation, a crush.

A mistake.

That's what she'd been told after it ended, by her girlfriends, her parents. Labels she'd repeated often, come to believe, clung to, as the months and years passed. But while they'd been together...

Loving him, being loved by him, had been magical.

He pulled her closer, dipping his head. She responded by pressing up on her toes, her curves aligning to the solid wall of his chest, bringing her face even closer to his.

"Liam."

His name rushed past her lips in a hushed whisper. A low groan escaped from his seconds before his mouth landed on hers.

It was like coming home.

Chapter Four

This was not why he'd come here. He should have made his presence known when he'd first arrived. Surprised when the outside light hadn't come on, he'd paused, ready to call out to her, but had found himself leaning against the post at the top of the stairs as a way to get the crazy beating of his heart under control.

And yeah, so he could look at her, standing there, bathed in the moonlight, dressed in a silky bathrobe.

Then she'd spotted him.

Now, she was in his arms, rising to meet his mouth. She smelled the same, felt the same, and finally holding her caused that familiar electric charge to return, the same one that sang in his veins the moment she'd stepped from the car earlier tonight.

How was that possible after all this time? Why had he wanted her just like this, just this close, from the moment he'd seen her again? A woman who'd kept his daughter from him?

Not her fault. None of it.

Hard as it was to understand why parents would do that to their own child, he believed her story. And yet, she'd kept the possibility she might be carrying *his* child from him.

Shouldn't he be upset with her for that? Never mind that she planned to take Casey away again in just a few days.

None of that mattered at the moment, not when her lips trembled beneath his as he reacquainted himself with the taste of the first girl he'd ever loved.

Her fingers fisted in his shirt as she rose even higher to meet him, but it wasn't enough. He wanted more. Angling his head, he released her shoulders only so he could cup the softness of her cheeks with his palms.

He delved his fingers deep into her hair, itching to loosen the golden strands and see them tumble free. He traced the upper edge of her lips with his tongue, the fullness and shape of her mouth so familiar it was as if he'd just kissed her yesterday.

She gasped at his boldness, but before he could use that to his advantage, she wrenched from his embrace, shuffling backward, putting distance between them.

"What—what are you doing?" She lightly tapped her mouth. "Why did you do that?"

"I'm—" Liam paused, not having a ready answer to a valid question. "I wanted to keep you from falling."

"By kissing me?"

"That wasn't something I planned on happening." He started toward her, but stopped when she retreated again. "Why did you kiss me back?"

Her fingers paused against her lips, and then she dropped her hand. "It's late. Why are you here?"

Okay, no more talk about kissing. That was probably

for the best. "I saw you step outside. I wanted to make sure everything was okay."

"You saw me?"

He debated if he should keep what he'd discovered to himself, but honesty won out. "I never realized until tonight the view from my master bedroom allows me to look down and see much of the apartment."

Her eyes narrowed. "How much?"

"The main room, the kitchen and the porch."

"Did you see Casey and I—did you watch us when we were talking?"

He nodded again, deciding at that moment there'd already been enough deceit between them to last a lifetime. "How is she? She seemed a bit upset at times."

"She was, as I expected she would be, but in the end... I'd say she's handling all of it amazingly well." Missy's shoulders rose in a delicate shrug. "Then again, Casey has always been so easygoing about most things. I see now she must get that from—"

She bit hard on her bottom lip, cutting off her words.

"From me." Liam knew exactly what she'd been about to say. The comparison made his heart pound. "You were going to say she gets that from me."

"Well, she certainly doesn't get it from my side of the family." Missy walked toward the porch railing again, still keeping space between them, her gaze out on the water. "We Ellingtons are as uptight as you Yanks make all British people out to be."

He smiled, glad that she didn't seem to be in any hurry to go back inside. Mimicking her pose, he turned to look out over the lake, too, resting his forearms on the railing. "Oh, I don't know. I seem to remember you loosening up. Eventually."

"Eventually." She brushed back the hair the breeze

swept across off her face. "Being in Destiny was vastly different from what my life was like in London. It took me a long time to feel…comfortable."

"But not comfortable enough to stay." The moment the words popped out of his mouth, he wished he could take them back. The last thing he wanted tonight was to argue about the past. "Missy, I'm sorry. I shouldn't have said that."

"Well, an apology. How nice. Does that make up for the one I never got sixteen years ago?"

He looked at her, confused. "What?"

"Please don't tell me you've forgotten." She faced him. "About the plans I made? To go to college in Wyoming, jumping through hoops to make that happen. Giving up my placement in university back home, applying for a student visa, dipping into my trust fund to pay for it all. Not that any of that seemed to matter to you."

"It mattered. Of course, it mattered." He straightened and faced her. "And no, I never forgot. I also didn't have any idea what you were planning back then."

"I wanted to surprise you with the news that we would be able to be together. Instead, you surprised me—not to mention your entire family—when you announced you weren't going to college after all, but planned to be the next John Wayne."

"John Wayne never rodeoed, except in a movie or two, I think."

Missy rolled her eyes. "You know what I mean."

"Yes, okay, you surprised me that day, but in a good way." The memories of a hot July afternoon, not long after he'd taken the professional rodeo circuit by storm with an unexpected first-place showing at the Cody Stampede, came rushing back. "I wanted you to stay, was happy you were staying. I remember asking you to go on the road with me after I decided to rodeo full-time."

"As what?" Her voice rose, but then she glanced at the glass doors that led to the apartment and inched closer to him. "Your buckle bunny? Isn't that the quaint American saying? Not bloody likely."

Liam copied her low tone, even though he doubted Casey could hear them, as the bedrooms were on the other side of the apartment. "A fact you made very clear that day as you walked out."

"If memory serves, you made it clear you wouldn't miss me if I went back home."

"We were fighting. Hell, we were teenagers. Teenagers say stupid things."

"Yes, like you didn't care about me anymore. You were glad we were through."

"I lied," he shot back.

Taking a step forward, he remembered what she'd said earlier on the porch that triggered a forgotten memory. "Something I made clear in my letters to you."

Silence stretched between them as they stood there, almost as close as they'd been when he'd held her in his arms. Missy was breathing hard, her breasts rising and falling against the edges of her bathrobe.

Liam tried not to stare, but she was beautiful, as beautiful as ever, and a part of him liked that even after all this time, she was still so emotional about their relationship.

"Letters?" she finally asked. "What are you talking about?"

"I wrote to you, after you left." He shoved his hands in his pockets, causing his shirt to open even farther, but he had to do something to keep from reaching for her again. "Steve McIntyre, Suzanne's brother, got me your address from their folks."

Missy started to say something, but then pressed her lips together and remained silent.

"Hell, we were still in the dial-up stage of the internet back then and you didn't even have an email address. So I wrote to you, three times in fact, between July and October, after you left," he continued, remembering how he'd poured out his heart and soul in the same messy handwriting he still used today. "I never heard back from you."

"I never..." She averted her eyes, her gaze landing on his chest for a moment before she turned away. "I never got them. Any of them."

Of course she hadn't. A vile bitterness rose in his throat. He had to swallow it back before he spoke. "Your parents made sure of that."

She nodded, still not looking at him. "Yes, I suppose you're right."

More silence.

Liam dropped his head and closed his eyes. He hadn't planned on any of this—the kiss, talking about the past—when he'd headed over here. He'd been worried about Casey, about Missy, about how their talk had gone. He'd wanted to make sure she was okay, but he should have figured that the way things had ended between them all those years ago would come out sooner or later.

But with such feeling?

Her crack about his apology surprised him. Despite the years that had passed, everything that had happened the day they fought—everything between them during that year—still felt so real. To both of them, it seemed.

"I would've told you." Missy's fingers were cool where she touched his wrist, drawing his attention back to her. "If the test results—if the results I was shown had been different, had been the truth, I would have made sure you knew about your daughter. No matter what my parents might have wanted at the time."

He nodded, reading the truth in her eyes, but believing her butted up against the fact that she'd never had the chance. He'd never had the chance. "I would've done right by you, by Casey. As old-fashioned as that sounds."

"We were both teenagers and living half a world apart. I'm not sure how...what the right answer would have been for us back then." She sighed and dropped her hand. "Perhaps that was the logic behind my father's deceit."

She had a point, but that didn't mean they hadn't deserved to know the truth. "You two could have come back to Destiny."

"And what then? I would have followed you from rodeo to rodeo with a baby in my arms?"

"I wasn't only a cowboy back then. I earned my electrician's license after you left and worked for my father around my training and the rodeo competitions." Her attitude bugged him, even though they were talking about a past they couldn't change. "But your parents thought Stanford Dobbs was a better catch."

"I suppose they did." Missy took a step back, again folding her arms. "His family was in the same social circles as mine. He'd graduated from Oxford that same spring as Casey was born and was working at his father's investment firm by the time we married."

"A proper match for a proper English girl." A thought came to Liam. "Did he know the truth? Did your father ever tell your husband that Casey wasn't his daughter?"

"No." Her response was quick and firm, but then she caught her bottom lip with her teeth for a moment. "I don't think so...my goodness, it never occurred me to ask my mother that."

"Was he good to Casey?" *Good to you?* Liam wanted

to say that second part, but he managed to hold back the words.

"He was, even though he wasn't very involved with her daily care. Stanford worked long hours to provide for us. As he moved up in the company the busier he became and the more he traveled."

"So you were a full-time mother?"

She nodded. "Until Casey started school, which happened to be right about the time of Stanford's death. Casey and I moved back in with my parents and I was able to earn my degree in three years."

Liam added the years in his head. "I was getting my master's degree at the same time."

"Hmm, yes, I know. Casey showed me the write-up in the rodeo program about you. She read to me about both your rodeo career and your time with the family business. I'll admit I was surprised to learn you only competed professionally for three years."

Liam reached inside his open shirt and rubbed at his left shoulder. The phantom burning sensation was in his head—he knew that—but sometimes he'd swear he could still feel the lightning-hot pain.

Even after all this time. Especially now.

"Not even. I was halfway through my third season, holding tight to the number-one ranking, when I shattered my left arm, from the shoulder down past the elbow, after getting thrown by a horse named Destiny Changer, of all things. Sure changed things for me."

"And you never rode again?"

"Not as a saddle bronc rider." He pushed his cotton shirt off his shoulder, baring the rigid scarring to the moonlight. To her. "Took me almost a year just to get full use of my arm again."

A soft gasp escaped past Missy's lips as her gaze flittered over his skin, taking in the evidence of his injury. "Oh, my. It's…it's not what I expected."

"That's one way to put it."

"No." Her eyes flew up to meet his. "I'm sorry, I was talking about your tattoo."

"Oh, that." Liam glanced down at the black silhouette design that covered most of his left pectoral—an image of a saddle bronc rider, right in the middle of the craziness during the eight seconds of a cowboy trying to stay astride the horse. He righted his shirt and closed a couple of the buttons. "Yeah, I got that a few years afterward. I was tired of seeing nothing but scars every time I looked in the mirror."

"But the location—" She paused. "I mean, it's right over your heart."

"Yeah, well, being a cowboy was all I had, all I loved at the time. Even if it was lost to me forever."

It hurt to say the words, but it had been the truth at the time.

That first year in college following his official retirement from the rodeo circuit found him more often drunk than sober, barely getting to his classes and alienating everyone from his family to old rodeo buddies who'd tried to stay in touch.

He'd been lost in a world of self-indulgent pity over the way his life had turned out at the ripe old age of twenty-one, while Missy had been busy raising their daughter as another man's wife.

Damn, they still had so much to talk about, but it was late.

"I should head back," he said, "and let you get some rest."

"Yes, that would be…good. It's been a long day."

He read exhaustion in her eyes, in the drop of her shoulders. The need to pull her into his arms again, to comfort her this time, was so strong he took a step back.

"Well, good night then," he said instead, heading for the stairs. Pausing at the top step, he gestured over his shoulder. "I don't know what happened to the light out here, but I'll check on it tomorrow."

"My fault, I fear. I must have mishandled the switches in the kitchen while learning my way. Will fix that straight away when I go back inside."

"Okay, then. I'll see you both tomorrow." The small talk was inane, but his feet refused to move. "Or rather, later today."

She nodded. "Right. Later today."

Don't look at her and you might be able to get your ass out of here! He listened to the internal command, focused on the stairs and started down. "Good night, again."

"I've decided we're staying."

He froze, his gaze darting back to her. "You are?"

"We have a month or so before we need to be back in London, when Casey's second school term begins." Hands clasped against her stomach, Missy came a few steps closer. "That should be long enough to get back test results... Of course, we can make other arrangements to stay in town—"

"You'll stay here." He cut her off, elation racing through his veins that she and Casey were going to be in Destiny, were going to be at his family's home, at least for now. "The apartment is yours for as long as you want it. Mom will insist on it."

"But most of our luggage is still at the hotel in LA. I'm not quite sure how we go about getting it here."

"I'll get Katie on it," Liam said, adding the item to the mental list of things he needed to take care of in the morning. "First thing tomorrow."

"Katie?"

"She's the office manager for the company. Believe me, the woman can work wonders. You won't have any issues canceling your vacation rental?"

Missy joined him at the landing. With him two steps down, their gazes were even. "The use of the beachside villa was a thank you from a producer friend at the film studio where I work. I'll let him know of our change of plans tomorrow."

Liam brushed aside the flicker of annoyance her words created. So her friend was a man. Big deal. She probably had a lot of male friends.

Casey had made that crack about her mother not dating much, answering his unspoken question about whether she'd ever married again.

Hell, he'd given it a second go himself right after college and failed miserably for the second time. Not that he'd led the life of a monk since then, but after just having this woman in his arms, his mouth on hers, the last thing he wanted to think about was a friendship that netted her the use of a Hawaiian beach house.

No, what he wanted was to lean over the railing, wrap his hand around the back of her head and bring her mouth down to his.

Bad idea. Not when he had just gotten what he really wanted. A chance to get to know Casey. To get to know Missy, again...

Yeah, not helping, man.

He blinked away that thought to find her still standing there, watching him. She had something else she wanted to say. He was sure of it, but her staring at him while swiping at her bottom lip with the tip of her tongue wasn't helping his resolve to get out of here.

"Was there anything else?" he asked.

She nodded, but remained silent.

"What?" he pushed, something telling him he wasn't going to like it. "Missy, after everything we've—said to each other tonight, you can just spit it out."

She pulled in a deep breath, releasing it in a slow exhale before she said, "Destiny seems to be the same quaint small town I remember. I'm sure the gossipmongers are already talking about my daughter's appearance at the rodeo tonight with you and your family."

"You're probably right."

"I wonder whether you've decided what you plan to tell…people. Your family, friends, colleagues. Now that you know everything."

Another good question that he didn't have a ready answer to. "What do you want me to tell them?"

"The truth. All of us have been living with this lie for too long."

Liam admired how she spoke without any hesitation, but the last thing he wanted was to cause her any embarrassment over what her parents had done. To her. To them. Especially since she'd had so little time yet to come to terms with their deception herself.

"We'll tell them…" He paused, and then went with a decision straight from his gut. "We'll tell anyone who asks there was a mix-up with the hospital paperwork and your… husband was incorrectly listed as Casey's father. The mistake wasn't discovered until now."

Relief colored her features, but she still appeared upset. "It won't take a math genius to figure out the time difference between when I left here, Casey's birth and what I did when I got home to create such a…possibility."

"I don't care about that."

When Liam let himself think about it, the idea of Missy getting busy with her ex still stung a bit, but hell, that was

years ago. With everything going on between them now—
especially in the last half hour—her actions back then just
added another twist in this crazy turn his life had taken.

"So, you believe me then?" she asked. "This whole
crazy story?"

Liam looked at her. His first love. Now the mother of
his child. "That's why we're getting a new DNA test done,
right? Don't worry, everything will be okay."

He took a step, intent on heading down the stairs, but
apparently Missy wasn't done.

"I told you earlier how Casey was taking all of this in
stride," she said, "but as excited as she is about you and
what you represent, she has no idea how you feel about
suddenly having a teenage daughter in your life."

The pounding in his chest returned.

All the things he hadn't been able to experience over
the past fifteen years when it came to Casey flashed inside his head. Birthdays. Holidays. Her first words, first
steps, first day of school.

"Seeing how I've only known about her for the last
twelve hours or so, I'm not sure exactly what I'm feeling,
either, but we'll work on that."

"She wants to get to know you, and your family."

"I want that, too."

The words came easily because they were true. He
wanted to get to know his daughter. Wanted her to be a
part of his life, part of his family. What that meant for him
and Missy, he had no idea.

He'd honestly never thought—

Okay, maybe once in a while, especially lately with the
company's business growing in the UK the way it was, he'd
thought that he might someday run into his first love again
on a trip to London. Pass her in Piccadilly Circus. Catch
sight of her in a restaurant or on the subway.

Now she was here, right in front of him.

Now he had the chance to get to know her all over again...

"As for all that happened here tonight, between us—" Missy turned slightly and waved at the porch behind her, before putting her hand on the doorknob "—I know talking about the past—our past—is inevitable. Reliving it, however, is not. I'm only staying in town for Casey's sake. To give her what she wants and needs."

And that was all.

She disappeared back inside the apartment. It was as if she'd read his mind and taken care of answering his unasked question. It was for the best, he decided as he headed back to his house.

All fantasies aside, the last thing he needed right now was to get involved with anyone, least of all Missy. He lived and breathed his position as CEO of Murphy Mountain Log Homes, and now he'd had fatherhood tossed into his lap.

Besides, his track record proved he wasn't a settling-down kind of guy.

But was he father material?

He loved his niece and nephews, enjoyed spending time with them, even the baby. Not that Casey needed him that way, but with the other kids he liked helping with their homework. Taking them and their friends for rides in the company helicopter. Going to their games. He'd even ended up teaching Abby how to drive this past spring after she and her father disagreed over who was at fault for a toppled tombstone in the town's cemetery during one of their lessons.

How hard could it be to have the same relationship with Casey? He had no idea. But one thing he did know was that he only had a month to make that happen.

Chapter Five

They were staying! At least for the rest of their holiday.

Unfortunately, in less than six weeks, she'd be back in London, suiting up in a plaid skirt, navy blue blazer and ugly oxfords.

And she'd have to get rid of the blue and pink streaks. Her piercings would have to go too. Gah. She would be ordinary…again. Worst of all, they'd be back living with her grandmum.

Or maybe not. After everything that had gone on in the last few weeks, Casey didn't have a clue what was going to happen when they returned to London.

For now she was glad to be in Destiny with Liam Murphy. Her real dad.

The man who sat directly across from her with a big smile on his face, stuffing his fourth hot dog into his mouth. Four! Crikey, he was big, but still. He had to be at least six feet tall and sitting there next to her mum, he made her look small and delicate.

She studied Liam while he and her mum chatted. Casey and he looked a lot alike—their baby pictures could have been carbon copies—but she now noticed she and Liam shared height and the same eye color too.

Eyes that were constantly in her mum's direction. Like right now.

"You see, ending a tour of Destiny with a late lunch was the right thing to do." Liam's words cut into her thoughts as he wiped at his mouth with a napkin. "You never could resist a whistle pig."

"It's still a silly name for a food item." Her mum blushed as she lightly scrubbed the crumbs from her fingers over her now empty plate. "Even for the best hot dog I've eaten in years."

"I don't think I've ever seen you eat a hot dog before." Casey finished the last of her own beef frank, deliciously wrapped in bacon and smothered in cheese, then mumbled around the last bite, "Much less two of them."

They sat at a picnic table outside a fast food restaurant named after their lunch, a place that had an oversize dancing cartoon pig with a whistle around its neck on the marquee.

"She's got you fooled. I remember her downing four of these."

Liam grinned as he spoke, sending a wink in her direction that made Casey feel sort of gooey inside.

"I ate those on a dare and I was honking the whole next day." Missy reached for her drink, pausing just before putting the straw between her lips to stare at Casey. "Don't even think about it, young lady, and it's not polite to talk with your mouth full."

Casey swallowed, and then laughed. Blimey, that felt good.

"So, what now?" Liam asked. "Anything you're interested in doing or seeing? Or should we head back to the family compound?"

"Do you have to go back to work?" Not that he'd really been away from it as his cell phone chimed for the umpteenth time since they'd left the house. "Again? That thing is worse than Mum's!"

He grabbed his phone and looked at the screen. "Sorry, but I need to take this. I'll be just a minute."

After a few minutes, Liam returned. When her mum said they should head to the house, he shot Casey a questioning look. She answered with a casual shrug and headed for his truck.

It was bloody hot when they got back to the Murphy compound. Maybe she'd sit on the dock and dangle her toes in the lake. Or perhaps the twins were around and they could hang out, but when they rounded the corner into the yard, they found a crowd gathered on the deck and around the pool.

"Hey, you're back," Adam called from where he sat beneath a shaded umbrella table. His wife and parents were happily passing the baby back and forth between them. Bryant and his wife, Laurie, sat nearby in matching lounge chairs.

"We need a few more bodies if we're going to get up a game."

"Yeah, Uncle Liam! Grab your swim trunks!"

"Yeah, come join us!"

"Your uncle is probably going to disappear into his office, boys." Nolan talked over his boys' excited cries, the three of them already in the shallow end of the pool, setting up a floating volleyball net. Nolan stopped long enough to peer over the top of his sunglasses. "He's a busy man with lots of work. Isn't that right, Uncle Liam?"

Casey looked over at her fath—at Liam. She was ready

to race to the boathouse and slip on her bathing suit, but it sounded as if Liam didn't usually join in the fun with the rest of his family. Did that mean she and her mum shouldn't?

Liam smiled, and then turned to Casey and Missy. "How about it? You two have swimsuits?"

"Packed in our luggage in LA, I'm afraid," her mum said, her gaze unreadable behind her dark sunglasses. "Sorry."

"I've got one with me," Casey piped up, obviously catching her mum by surprise.

"Why don't you and I go and get changed, Casey? Your mother can relax and enjoy the sunshine." Liam gestured toward the deck. "If we can get her to peel off a few layers."

"My layers are just fine." Missy squared her shoulders. "Thank you."

Casey headed for the boathouse, hurrying ahead of Liam, his mobile once again at his ear. It didn't matter now. She didn't want to talk to him, not when it was just the two of them.

Not yet, anyway.

After she'd changed into her suit and lathered on sunscreen, she followed the path back to the pool. She could hear the laughter and everyone talking but slowed when she noticed Abby lying on a lounge chair at the opposite end of the patio area. She wasn't alone. Casey recognized the other girls as the ones Abby had gone off with at the rodeo. They must have just arrived.

"Can you believe they're staying? In the boathouse?" Abby's voice carried over the yard easily enough to hear, but Casey doubted anyone else could at the other end of the pool. "Up until yesterday none of us even knew about her. My uncle has got to be flipping out—"

"Uh, hi there." One of the girls, a pretty brunette, cut Abby off by calling out to Casey while removing her sunglasses to squint at her. "You must be Abby's new cousin."

Should Casey give the girls a simple nod and keep walking? But that would mean giving her cousin and her snarky comments the satisfaction of running her off. Not bloody happening.

She crossed the grass, hoping she looked more casual than the firecrackers banging around inside her stomach. "Yes, I'm Casey Dobbs."

"Abs says you're from England."

"That's right. London, actually."

"Cool accent. I'm Valerie and this is Jannie." The brunette introduced herself and her friend while Abby pointedly ignored her, continuing with her lotion application. "Do you mind if I ask you a question?"

Casey wondered where this might be going. "No, go ahead."

"Did that hurt?" Valerie tapped the side of her nose. "Getting it, I mean."

Ah, the diamond stud. She shrugged. "No, it wasn't too bad."

"What about the rest of the holes in your head?" Abby asked. "You must have at least a dozen piercings in your ears."

Ah, the snarkiness continued. "Thirteen, actually. Seven on the right, six on the left."

"Hey, that's cool."

Casey looked over and saw Logan and Luke had swum down to the end of the pool and propped their arms on the edge, but for the life of her she didn't know which one was which.

"Don't mind Abby," the twin who spoke continued.

"She's pissed our dad won't let her get a third set. Or the belly button ring she wants."

"Zip it, Luke," Abby snapped at her brother and then turned back to Casey. "So, thirteen..." She dropped her chin, pulled the dark shades down to the bridge of her nose and stared. "That's supposed to mean something?"

"It's my lucky number."

"Why am I not surprised," Abby deadpanned, and then hesitated before righting her glasses and collapsing against the lounge chair, stretching out her legs, pointed toes and all.

Her friends giggled. Their dismissal stung. Casey took a step backward, determined to walk away with head held high, but then the twins scurried out of the pool and quickly jumped back in, side by side, causing a spray of water to hit the patio and the edge of the lounge chairs.

"Knock it off, you two!" Abby called out, kicking one perfectly manicured foot at her brothers. "We don't want to get wet."

Casey eyed the trio of American beauties with their perfectly tanned limbs and perfectly coiffed hair. She dropped her stuff onto the last remaining chair, toeing off her shoes. Pulling her shirt over her head first, she reached for the zipper on her shorts.

"Hey, Casey!" the boys called from the water. "You coming in?"

"Of course." A quick shimmy and her shorts fell to the ground. She stepped out of them and before she allowed herself to think twice, raced toward the pool. "Budge up!"

Launching into the air, she tucked her body into a tight ball, wrapping her arms around her knees seconds before she plunged into the water—kersploosh!—making what she hoped was a spectacular splash with far-reaching effects.

Her feet touched the bottom and she opened her eyes, did a swift five count and pushed off, breaking the surface to find the twins cheering for her.

Abby and her crew? Not so much, as their outraged shrieks filled the air.

"Casey."

She spun, surprised to find Liam standing at the edge of the pool.

"Pretty impressive. But was that really necessary?" he asked as he went to rejoin the adults.

She blamed the sudden stinging in her eyes on the chlorine. Pushing her hair back from her face, she schooled her features into a practiced air of innocence. "Oh, bugger, did I do that?" Casey called out. "Sorry, mate."

Abby's glare was lethal, and her friends didn't look too happy either as they toweled off, but then a male voice called Abby's name and the girl's transformation from a wet hen to a purring kitten was striking.

As was the bloke heading toward her.

He was tall and had a killer smile, his cropped straw-colored hair and wide shoulders making him stand out from the two boys with him.

"I found this on the bleachers," the cutie said, holding out a sweatshirt to Abby. "You must've forgotten it after cheerleading practice."

"Really?" Abby reached for the item with what looked like a genuine smile. "I have no idea how that could've happened."

Sincere smile or not, Casey rolled her eyes at her cousin's sickening sweet tone. She climbed out of the pool, the water dripping from her body. "Practice? Don't tell me rodeos have cheerleaders."

Six pairs of eyes swung in her direction. Interest flared

from the boys while the girls' combined glances bordered on wicked.

"We cheer for our school's football team," Valerie said.

"Ah, right." She strolled forward and held out a hand toward the tall lad. "Hello, I'm Casey. Abby's cousin from England."

"Hi." Confusion crossed his face as he glanced between her and Abby, but then he took her hand. "I'm Nathan Lawson." After a quick elbow from one of his friends he added, "This is J.T. and Cody. Abby never said anything about having family from the UK."

"Believe me, she's a surprise. Sort of an oops, you might say."

"So, football." Casey ignored Abby's dig and smiled at the boys after releasing Nathan's hand.

"Well, not the kind of football you're used to," Nathan said. "We're talking American football, not soccer."

"I understand." Casey smiled as a shiver raced through her. "But I did enjoy a game of American football at Wembley. Those Patriots certainly played a good match."

"You went to the NFL game between the New England Patriots and the St. Louis Rams in London?" Nathan asked.

"Oh, yes. My mum and I had box seats thanks to—well, someone she worked with."

"Sweet. What does your mom do that she gets perks like that?" J.T. asked.

"She's a costume designer for a movie studio."

"Really?" Jannie stepped closer, not seeing how Abby's eyes narrowed in her direction. "Have you met anyone famous?"

Wrapping a towel around her waist like a sarong, Casey pushed the water from her hair, squeezing out the ends. "I met Johnny Depp once."

Both Valerie and Jannie gasped.

"You've met Johnny Depp?" they asked, voices in harmony.

"Last summer. On a film location in Paris. He was the one who gave us the tickets to the football game."

"Oh, my God, really?" Valerie asked.

Casey nodded. "He and Emma Watson were—"

"Wait, you met Emma Watson, too?" Cody interrupted her. "That hot chick from the Harry Potter movies?"

"Yes, she was there, too." Her gaze collided with Abby's dark stare and she knew what was coming. "Would you like to see pictures?"

Surprise flared in Abby's eyes. Feeling victorious, Casey got her phone. The kids gathered around as she showed off the images and answered their rapid-fire questions.

Abby joined the circle, but remained silent.

Chapter Six

"She's ignoring me."

Liam's quiet words pulled Missy's attention away from the beautiful open fields and distant thickly forested foothills of the Laramie Mountains that made up his brother's ranch.

It had been sixteen years since she'd last been on a horse, but it felt good, familiar, even, in a way that surprised her more than she expected. Maybe because the cowboy next to her had been the one who'd taught her how to ride.

Earlier today, when Liam had swung into the saddle with a grace and ease that reflected his years as a cowboy, Missy had been as awestruck as when she was a teen. A dark Stetson, similar to the one he'd always worn during competitions, shaded his face. He held the reins loosely in one hand while his powerful legs instinctively commanded the animal beneath him without his having to say a single word.

She'd stared at him like a daft cow!

Thank goodness she'd already mounted her ride. In fact, the places where he'd touched her as he helped with the stirrups still tingled. She rubbed her fingertips across the spot on her jeans-clad thigh again, pausing when Liam glanced her way.

"I don't believe Casey is ignoring you," Missy finally said, purposely laying her hand flat against her leg. She focused instead on her daughter, who rode ahead of them. "She's paying attention to Adam's instructions and trying desperately not to look like she's hanging on for dear life."

Liam turned away, his gaze on Casey now, an easy smile on his face. "She's a natural. Scampered right up into the saddle before I could even help her."

"Eager and determined to learn with a healthy dose of bravado. That's Casey. Besides, you were busy reintroducing me to riding on the other side of the corral while Adam was instructing her."

"You're a natural, too." He looked at Missy again, his eyes warm and the smile still there, but now his lips held a hint of something…more…causing a fluttering deep inside her. "You haven't forgotten anything I taught you all those years ago."

"Well, you taught me a lot back then."

Did he ever.

Being with Liam had introduced her to a whole new world of fun, freedom and the flush of a first love. She'd been surprised to find out he was as inexperienced as she, although having barely kissed a boy until she met him, she had been the real innocent. At least until he'd showed her so many wonderful things with the way he kissed her, touched her, made love to her…

Missy blinked hard, having no idea how her thoughts had gone from horseback riding to…well, to *that*. Then again, in less than forty-eight hours in the man's company, it had only taken one moment in his arms and she'd known exactly why she was having these thoughts, these feelings—

Memories. That's all they were. All they would be.

Giving her head a quick shake as if to empty her mind, she caught Liam's grin, almost as if he knew what she'd been thinking.

Tugging on the brim of the straw hat she'd borrowed from Adam's wife, who'd stayed behind with their napping baby, she planned to blame the heated blush racing across her cheeks on the afternoon sun.

"I meant you taught me a lot about riding back then, when your family still had horses at your place."

Liam looked at her for a long moment. He then leaned forward and gently patted the neck of the beautiful buckskin quarter horse he rode. "Yes, we did have a full stable years ago. Once Adam got his place up and running, he took the few we had left to his ranch. Danny Boy being one of them."

"It was nice of Adam and Fay to invite us for a visit. Their place is lovely."

"Casey told Adam yesterday she wanted to learn how to ride," Liam said, his smile gone again. "After getting Bryant to agree to take her for a spin in the helo."

So they were back to this. Goodness, he sounded almost jealous of his brothers and how they were taking to Casey.

"And when Abby's friends took over the pool after beating us old guys at volleyball and then stuck around for dinner afterward…"

"A teenager choosing to spend time with people her own age instead of her parents," Missy teased when his voice faded. "Shocking."

"Does she think of me as a parent?"

Do you think of her as a daughter?

"Wow, would you listen to me," he said, pulling ahead and guiding his horse across a section of a slow-moving creek with hers splashing right behind. Adam and Casey far ahead now, barely visible in the cottonwood trees that dotted the landscape. "You two have only been here a few days. She doesn't even know me as a person, much less anything more."

She could see Liam's concern was genuine, and it touched her heart. More than it probably should. Then again, everything about Liam affected her more than it should.

Missy thought back to yesterday afternoon, when everyone had gathered at the pool. To how she'd been gobsmacked the moment Liam had returned to the backyard wearing the same polo shirt as earlier but sporting a pair of dark swim trunks that hung low on his hips.

He'd spotted her gawking, of course.

With a grin, he'd walked over to her and they'd talked for a few minutes—about what, she had no idea, as her brain had emptied the moment he stood up, pulled off his shirt and dropped it to the cushion next to her.

A calculated move on his part, she was sure, just as the stop at the eatery they'd frequented as teens had been, but still, she'd been unable to look away as he dived into the pool, disappearing beneath the water before rising again like a Greek god, muscles glistening in the sun, his tattoo standing out in stark relief against his tanned skin—

"Missy?"

She looked up and found Liam pointing at her and then at her ride. "Sorry, woolgathering. Did you say something?"

"You might want to ease up on the bit unless you want

her to stop altogether. You're clutching those reins as if your life depends on it."

Blimey, girl, get a hold of yourself!

Embarrassed at her inability to keep her thoughts centered on their conversation about their daughter, she cursed her fair English skin for the second time today as heat flooded her cheeks.

Easing her grip, Missy dipped her head and offered her riding companion a quick neck rub as an apology. "Sorry about that, girl. I am a wee bit out of practice, and that creek was deeper than I expected."

"You okay now?"

"Right as rain." She took a moment, keeping her attention on the horse as she pulled in a steadying breath before looking up again. "I was thinking about yesterday and wondering if Casey said or did something that makes you certain she's shutting you out."

"I don't know." Liam shrugged, their horses now side-by-side again. "The cheek swab…went okay? You were there. Did she seem bothered by it?"

Missy shook her head.

"And she talked while we drove around afterward, asking us a lot of questions. But once Abby and her friends joined us in the pool, she seemed to shut me out," he continued. "Ah, hell. Maybe that's typical teenage stuff—being embarrassed by the adults—and I'm being stupid."

"No, you're not."

From the moment Missy had found out about the doctored DNA test, a part of her had been worried that Liam might reject Casey, want nothing to do with her. To hear that after such a short time he was worried about her rejecting him, she found herself wanting desperately to make him feel better.

"I know we haven't shared much about our lives in London, but back home, her world is much more…contained. She has just a few close girlfriends, suffered through her first broken heart over a boy last year and other than my parents, I'm her only family. Now, with my father's death and what we've learned since then…it's been a great deal for her to take in. She just needs time to adjust."

"Yeah, I can understand that."

"And like most teenagers, she can go from being cheeky to tears and back again in a matter of minutes. I think she's excited to be here, to meet you and your family, but then maybe she remembers the reason why…"

Missy let her voice trail off when she realized she was talking about herself as well.

"We're going to be around for the next month or so. Give her some time," she continued, her tone gentle. "As I said, being in America, in Destiny, with you…is all new to her. There is so much to see and do and take in. It must be overwhelming. Much like when I took her to Disneyland Paris for the first time, I suspect."

"So I'm being compared to an amusement park?" Liam laughed. "What's that make me? The Dumbo ride?"

Missy was glad to see his smile return. She pretended to ponder his question for a moment, and then grinned back. "I would say you're more like Space Mountain."

"Yeah? Why's that?"

"One part imposing, one part scary and one part thrilling. But in the end I'm sure she'll come to believe the ride was worth it."

Liam reached out and caught Missy's horse's reins in his hand, pulling them to a stop in the dense shade of a grove of trees. "Do I scare you?"

Yes.

She curbed the impulse to go with that answer and instead replaced it with another. "No, not anymore. Perhaps you did at one time, but that—"

"Was a long time ago."

Liam finished her sentence with her, their words tangling together.

Seconds later, he'd maneuvered his horse closer until his leg brushed against hers. "Well, lady, you scare the hell out of me."

She pretended not to notice how her body tingled with awareness at his nearness, how the clean male scent of him invaded her head or how he spoke in the present tense. "Way back when?"

Pushing up the front brim of his Stetson with a finger, he leaned in close and slowly shook his head. "Nope, right now. Right here."

"You know, for a guy who just found out he's a dad, you're handling all of this very well."

Liam looked up from the piles of paperwork littering his desk and found Nolan lounging comfortably on the leather sofa on the other side of his office. A spot where Liam often woke up when his days ended long past sunset and he was too tired to walk back to his place.

Speaking of time…

He glanced at his watch. It was after five o'clock already. End of the workday for most, but not him. He'd planned to go find Casey and her mother at lunchtime today, but then he'd been reminded about the rodeo committee follow-up meeting in town and that had kept him out of the office for the rest of the afternoon.

Now he was playing catch-up by multitasking—sitting in on a conference call, checking email and printing job proposals—while wondering what Missy and Casey had done to occupy themselves on this gray and gloomy afternoon.

He hadn't been able to get them out of his head all day.

"Yeah, how do you manage—"

This time it was Bryant who spoke, breaking into his thoughts, but Liam cut him off with a swift karate chop in the air. When he got a raised eyebrow in return, he tapped the earpiece he wore, signaling he was still on the phone.

Bryant, who had walked in not long after Nolan and now sat with a glass of whiskey in his hand, only shrugged, but Nolan straightened, dropping his feet to the floor.

"That conference call with the Becketts is still going on?" he asked. "What's it about?"

Thankful for the mute button, Liam shrugged and turned to the large monitor on the right side of his desk. "I honestly couldn't tell you. I zoned out after the missus started in on the wall color of bathroom number five."

"Then why are you—"

"Because her husband is a major player in Silicon Valley and we just built them a multimillion-dollar getaway in Jackson Hole, that's why."

Liam put aside his thoughts of Missy and Casey for the moment so he could finish up the two emails he had open and send the latest round of contract proposals to the printer in the outer office.

It was then he realized the silence in his ear meant the tech wizard's wife was waiting for an answer to a question he hadn't heard.

He reached up and pressed a button. "Sorry, but I missed that last part..." Pausing, he listened this time, the question making him scrub hard at the back of his neck. "Well, perhaps you're going about choosing the colors all wrong."

His brothers cringed at the same moment he did. Okay, that came out wide of the mark.

"What I meant was, instead of using a piece of art or fabric as your inspiration, look for something more personal." He then remembered what he'd overheard Missy say to his mother at brunch yesterday while talking about her work. "Start with your wardrobe. You always look fabulous, Felicia. You wear your favorite colors. Why not use the same ones in your home?"

Bryant and Nolan's expressions went from uncomfortable to confused, but the feminine voice in his ear was happy. "I'm glad I could help," he said. "Yes, we'd love to see the place when you and Philip have your open house. Please feel free to add us to your guest list."

He ended the call, yanked the miniature headset from his ear and set his office line to go directly to Katie or to voice mail, knowing the major players had his cell phone number and wouldn't hesitate to call if needed.

Leaning back into his chair, he sighed and closed his eyes.

"Start with your wardrobe?" Nolan snorted. "Where did you come up with a crazy idea like that?"

Before Liam could answer, he heard the distinct sound of high heels on hardwood. He opened his eyes, and for a moment thought it might be—

Katie walked into the office, looking as pulled together as she had at the start of the day, in a dress covered with red flowers that matched the red of her hair. She was carrying his printouts.

"Don't listen to him, boss man," she said. "It was a great idea."

"How did you hear me out in the hall?" Nolan asked.

"Your voice carries. A whisperer you're not." She waited while Liam cleared a space by shoving aside a pile of folders.

"I know that was a last-minute call," he said, taking the

paperwork from her, "but please tell me you had time to record it or listened in to take notes."

"I listened. The transcript is already in their online folder."

Katie stood there, hands clasped, and Liam grinned, knowing the mess on his desk was driving their anal-retentive office manager crazy. Neat and orderly should be the woman's middle name—she kept the inner workings of Murphy Mountain Log Homes just that.

"You sticking around for dinner?" he asked, knowing his mother probably already made the invite.

Katie shrugged and headed for the door. "Sure. I've got nothing else planned." She stopped and then turned around, her expression pained. "I'm sorry. That was terrible of me."

Liam looked at his brothers. Bryant seemed as surprised by her words as he was, but Nolan's gaze was glued to the Persian rug beneath his feet as if he was memorizing the pattern.

Liam swung his gaze back to her. "You're always welcome, you know that, but you don't have to stay for dinner."

Katie's smile lacked its usual brilliance. "I know, but seeing how I've got nothing in my kitchen but leftovers from Sherry's Diner and a half dozen moving boxes, I'll stay."

She left the room, the clinking of her fancy shoes echoing behind her.

"Moving boxes?" Liam turned to his brothers again, but Bryant only shrugged. "Nolan? What's going on?"

"Katie moved out of Jake's place this weekend," his brother said, his gaze now on the empty fireplace. "She's back in an apartment in town."

Liam knew she'd been seeing one of the local sheriff's deputies for over a year and had been excited about moving in with him and his two young girls. "Didn't she give up her place a month or so ago to be with him and the kids?"

Nolan nodded. "Yeah, but I guess Jake and his wife decided to reconcile just before signing the divorce papers. The house is on the market and the man was smart enough to move himself and the girls to wherever his wife went after she first took off."

"What a lousy thing to do." Bryant finished his drink and headed for the bar. "No wonder Katie was in such a bad mood last week, not to mention absent from the barbecue on Saturday."

The anger burning in Liam's gut slowly morphed into guilt. He'd been so busy with the rodeo preparations last week and then with Missy and Casey showing up, he hadn't noticed anything was wrong. Or Katie's absence this weekend—she, Jake and the girls had often joined the family in the past.

"Is she going to be okay?" he asked.

"Oh, you know Katie," Nolan offered dryly. "She always finds someone new."

True, she had dated a number of men over the years, but this time it had seemed pretty serious. Serious enough that she'd moved in with the man. "Maybe she needs some time off."

"I offered. She turned me down." Nolan sat back, leg bent, propping a foot on his knee. "Asked if she needed any help moving, too, once I managed to get her to tell me what was wrong. She said she was all set."

Liam nodded, making a note to keep an eye on her as he stared at the latest contracts, mentally calculating how many he could get through after dinner. "So, is Adam here yet? I'm guessing he went home to get Fay and the baby after work."

"Haven't seen him, but what's with this family dinner?" Nolan asked. "We were all just together two days ago."

"Maybe Mom pulled it together for Katie." If anyone knew about the goings-on in Destiny, it was their mother. She had the town wired, her roots deep in the local gossip, especially now that she'd mastered the art of tweeting.

"Or maybe not." Bryant fumbled the crystal stopper but managed to get it back into the bottle. "You know Mom. Always looking for a reason to have the entire family together."

Liam shared a look with Nolan, who shook his head in reply, showing he was clueless.

Something else was up. Bryant was never nervous.

The man was a freak for numbers, with a laid-back personality that bordered on sedentary. Which was a good thing in his position as the company's chief financial officer. Their folks had always said he was their lull in the storm after the havoc caused by their first four boys. Then, of course, Ric had come along and the family had been complete.

"What's bugging you?" Liam asked.

"Nothing." Bryant stared into the glass for a moment, and then set it down untouched. "How do you do it?"

Confused, Liam glanced at Nolan, who again shook his head. "Do what?"

Bryant turned to face him. "Like Nolan said earlier. How do you stay so effing calm when a daughter you've never met—never even knew about—suddenly shows up at your front door?"

Surprised by his brother's tone, Liam sat back in his chair. Was he pissed? No, Bryant sounded almost anxious.

"Since nothing like this has ever happened to me before," he finally said. "I'm not sure how I'm supposed to act."

"I guess being a father is going to come as easy to you as everything else."

Okay, that was a shot. "What the hell is that supposed to mean?"

"Oh, come on. No matter what you've done—saddle bronc riding, school, running the family business…you never break a sweat." Bryant leaned against the credenza, waving one hand at the bookcases on the opposite wall. The shelves groaned under the weight of ribbons, trophies and prized belt buckles the Murphy boys had earned over the years, the majority of them belonging to Liam. "You set your mind to accomplish something, and bam, you're first in your class."

The sarcasm in his brother's voice made Liam's blood boil. He was proud of what he'd accomplished as a professional cowboy, but he could care less about the display. Their dad had put that together when this office used to be his, long before Liam had taken over as president and CEO, and it remained now as a showpiece for potential clients.

Rising slowly to his feet, Liam noticed Nolan doing the same, but ignored him and turned his gaze on Bryant. "I sweated plenty, not to mention busted my ass, before I turned pro and every day after that when it came to riding."

"And in less than a year you were in the top five. Hell, the top two."

"Again, with plenty of blood, sweat and hard work." Liam was at a loss as to where his brother's resentment was coming from. He walked around the end of his desk, closing the distance between them. "You know that. You were there."

"Yeah, I was there at the University of Wyoming when you decided your rodeo career was over and college was the next step. Believe me, the campus wasn't that big and you cast a long shadow. You still do, Mr. President."

Liam shook his head.

It seemed that out of all of his brothers, Liam's relationship with Bryant had always been the most antagonistic over the years, despite his easy-going nature with everyone else. Adam and Nolan were typical older brothers, bossy and caretakers at the same time. He and Devlin, being born only eleven months apart, should have been competitive as well; instead they'd grown up close, but independent of each other.

Yeah, Liam had finally gone to college the same year as Bryant, but because he'd been twenty-one, he'd been allowed his own off-campus apartment. Liam had also carried a lot of anger over the twists and turns his life had taken at that point and had decided that it was best he lived alone, turning down his brother's offer to be roommates.

The two of them had graduated the same year and had come to work for the family business, but it'd been Liam who'd gone from sales manager to CEO in record time.

He'd always thought Bryant had been okay with that. Each family member was an equal shareholder in the company, and Liam's promotion wouldn't have happened without his brother's vote.

Besides, that had been years ago. His brother was still upset after all this time? "Are you saying you don't like the way I'm doing my job?"

"Guys…" Nolan's warning tone cut the air between them.

Bryant shook his head. "Forget it."

Liam took a step closer. "Like hell. First fatherhood and now this. What is going on with you?"

Bryant opened his mouth, but then Adam strolled into the room with his son, A.J., in his arms, cutting him off. "So this is where you're hiding out. Dad says to get a move on, he and the twins are drowning in all the estrogen out there. Personally, I think he loves being surrounded by the ladies—"

Adam paused then, his gaze quickly darting around the room, from brother to brother to brother. "Whoa, what's going on here?"

"We're trying to figure that out," Nolan said. "Without much success."

"Bryant's evidently got a stick up his butt about Casey—" Liam said, recalling how all this started.

"This has nothing to do with Casey." His brother cut him off, his tone quieter now, his gaze on his boots. "Not really."

Liam looked at Nolan and Adam, seeing that they were as confused as he was. He pulled in a deep breath and took a step back. "He seems to think life has handed me the world on a silver platter and finding out I'm a dad fifteen years too late is just going to be one more smooth ride for me."

"Well, you always were the smart one," Adam said. "Straight A's and barely cracking a book."

"The most popular and always got the girl," Nolan added. "And the best rides."

Yeah, until a horse had damn near taken his arm off and ended his dream. "Geesh, thanks, guys. I really feel the love."

"Hey, you're a hard worker, we all know that," Nolan said. "Even Bryant. But you always were a lucky SOB."

"You scored again with Casey. She's a sweetheart," Adam remarked.

"I know that," Liam snapped.

"But seeing how moony-eyed you've been over Missy the last couple of days, never mind the fact those two are only here temporarily," Adam continued, switching his son from one arm to the other, "I'd say things might not come quite so easy for you this time. In fact, unless I'm reading this situation all wrong, you could be in for the ride of your life."

Chapter Seven

Liam had been ready to tell his brothers what they could do with their opinions of his past and what he faced in the immediate future when it came to Missy and Casey, but then Nolan's twins had barreled into the office, insisting dinner was heading to the table.

The last one to walk into the dining room, he was still fired up over their simplistic view of his accomplishments. He'd worked damn hard for everything he'd ever gotten.

So what if he'd known from the age of ten that he wanted a rodeo career? Yes, he had a natural talent for staying in the saddle from the very beginning, but easy? Hell, it had been anything but, and making the choice to walk away from that dream had been the hardest thing he'd ever done.

Almost as hard as walking away from a future with Missy.

Thankfully his attention was diverted to the women emerging from the kitchen, in particular one beautiful blonde with sparkling blue eyes and a wide smile. She wore a simple sundress that left her arms bare and showed off her tiny waist, but what caught his eye was the way her hair hung in soft golden waves past her shoulders.

Missy laughed at something Fay and Laurie said, and the sweet sound caused the stiffness riding across his shoulders to diminish.

She followed his mother's lead and placed the heaping tray of fried chicken in the middle of the table alongside the rest of the meal. Then she looked up, her gaze moving around the room, across the crowd gathered there, as if searching for...

When she spotted him, the slight tilt of her head, the softening of her smile and the concern in her gaze were so familiar it took his breath.

Back in high school, before he'd summoned the courage to really talk to her, there'd been times when he'd caught her watching him—in class, across the lunch room, by the lockers in a crowded hallway—and a silent communication would pass between them. It had never lasted long, but in those moments, she'd made him feel...

Connected.

It was weird that he could now put a name to that strange feeling. Back then, he'd been cocky enough to think she was looking because he was one of the popular kids, or word had gotten out how well he'd done at a rodeo the weekend before.

After they'd started dating, he'd come to realize it was something else. Something he hadn't been able to describe. He'd never even tried, being a typical self-centered teenage boy.

Until he'd told her he loved her.

Missy looked away and took the seat in front of her.

Casey was next to her and she in turn was next to Luke; he'd wrestled with his twin for the spot.

Liam marched across the room, determined to take the empty chair on Missy's other side. He yanked the seat back, his elbow jostled with another and he looked up at Bryant, who was mirroring his actions for the empty chair next to his.

He froze, and the two of them stared at each other for a long moment.

"What's going on, you two?" Their father's booming voice carried from his place at the head of the table. "Sit so we can say grace."

When Laurie tugged at her husband's arm, Bryant looked away and Liam swore the man looked almost sick as he took his seat.

Liam sat down, thankful for the cold beer that appeared at his place setting. Eyeing Nolan across from him, he offered a quick salute to say thank-you before taking a long swallow.

His mother cleared her throat and Liam realized they were waiting on him. He put the beer down and then everyone bowed their heads. His father gave simple thanks for the people dining here tonight, the family members who weren't and the food before them, the familiar words binding the family together.

Then controlled chaos broke out as everyone started filling their plates and multiple conversations flowed around the table.

"Are you okay?" Missy's whispered question and the gentle nudge of her elbow against his caused Liam to tighten his grip on the platter he held. "You seem distracted."

"I'm fine." The words were automatic. Liam paused, realizing he meant them now that he was with her. He smiled and passed her the chicken without taking any. "Just a long day at the office."

"Don't you want some?" she asked, holding the dish back out to him.

"Ladies first."

Missy smiled, served herself and placed two large pieces on his plate as well. "You look like you've worked up an appetite."

The sudden image of the two of them doing just that flashed in his head.

Not a memory from long ago—fumbling beneath blankets, unsure of what exactly they were doing, but positive it was the right thing—but a vision of her stretched out across the white sheets of his bed, her hair flowing across his pillows as he moved over her—

"Hey, earth to Liam? Yo, man, you want some of this?"

Swearing softly beneath his breath, Liam pushed the fantasy to the back of his mind and took the large bowl of mashed potatoes Nolan offered. This time, he spooned a portion for himself, not wanting Missy to feel as if she needed to fill his plate.

"Would you like some?" he then asked her.

"Oh, no, thank you. None for me."

Before he could respond, Casey leaned forward, peering around Missy. "Oh, mash! I'll take that. Mum's not a big potato fan. Too many calories."

"You like them?" he asked, passing Casey the bowl, glad to see she didn't harbor the same belief. A quick glance at Missy's curves clearly stated she didn't have anything to worry about, either.

"Potatoes in any form are a slice of heaven," Casey said, grinning. "You ever had cottage pie? Minced beef and veggies topped with mashed potatoes. Yum! Our cook makes a smashing good one."

"You have a cook?" Abby spoke up from where she sat directly across from Casey. She then rolled her eyes. "Let me guess. There's a butler, too."

Casey's smile vanished. "Reynolds and Mrs. Mimi have been with us for years. They're terrific. As is Delaney, our maid."

"Casey."

Missy admonished her daughter, but Liam was more interested in the way Casey's eyes narrowed as she leaned forward, her voice a low whisper as she looked directly at Abby. "Guess what? I haven't made my own bed since I was five."

"Oh, that's not true," Missy said, adding a generous helping of green salad to her plate. "Delaney doesn't go anywhere near your room."

Abby's eyes widened and Casey's smile returned as she straightened and then held out the bowl of potatoes. "Mash, cuz?"

"No, thank you. Unlike some people, I try to eat healthy."

Casey shrugged, set the bowl on the table and reached for an ear of buttered corn. "Must be hard making sure you're spiffing in your pom-pom skirt."

Abby stabbed her fork at the salad that filled her plate. "Nathan thinks it's worth the effort."

"Now, I bet he looks cracking in those tight footballer pants." Casey heaved a dramatic sigh. "Wouldn't mind catching a sight of that."

Liam glanced at Missy, wondering if she was taking in this back-and-forth between the girls, but she was now chatting with Katie, who sat across from her, between Abby and Nolan.

"So, what did you two do today?" he asked her when Katie left the table to refill the pitchers of iced tea and lemonade. "I'd hoped to see you before now, but work kept me busy."

"Unpacked, mostly. As you know, our luggage was here when we got back from Adam's last night, but after hours on horseback I was too tired to tackle anything but soaking my sore muscles."

Missy lounging in that claw-footed tub was another mental picture that'd be haunting his dreams tonight. "Nice to know you're putting that antique bathtub to good use."

A light blush colored her cheeks. "Be nice," she whispered.

He grinned. "Anything else?"

"I did some sketching on a few pieces for a potential client while Casey explored the wonders of the American telly. I think she binged on vampires, zombies and police procedure shows."

"I would love to see your work. If you wouldn't mind showing me?"

The blush returned, but Missy looked pleased. "No, I wouldn't mind. In fact, you've already seen some of it. The dress I'm wearing now, in fact."

He allowed his gaze to travel over her again, appreciating the chance to do so. "You look beautiful."

"Thank you. It's one of my favorites."

"I wasn't talking about the dress." He adopted her low tone and leaned in close again, the familiar scent of summertime peaches teasing his nose. "And can I add how much I like finally seeing your hair down? I'd wondered if it was still as long as when I saw you last."

"Oh, goodness, no. I tend to wear it up and out of the way most days."

Liam started to tell her he hoped she wouldn't while staying here, but a noise drew Missy's attention to the far end of the table. He looked as well and found Fay trying to eat while balancing a fussy A.J. on her lap.

Seconds later, Adam noticed and reached for his son, easily cradling the baby's backside with one hand, gently bouncing him against his chest, never missing a beat with his own dinner.

Now there was a father for you.

Liam's eldest brother had taken to fatherhood the minute he found out Fay was pregnant, doing everything he could to make things easy for her, even moving Fay into his place after she'd had a health scare. And that was long before they'd admitted their feelings for each other and married. Even though A.J. was only six months old, Adam was already talking about adding to their family.

The sight of his brother placing a gentle kiss on his son's head as the baby snuggled into his shoulder had Liam suddenly thinking about what it would've felt like to hold Casey like that back when she was that age.

Had she been a fussy baby or more like A.J., who was a happy kid most of the time? Had Missy's husband held her in his arms, soothing her? Had Casey found the same contentment that Adam's son seemed to, with his tiny fist grabbing hold of his dad's shirt?

A sharp sting bit at Liam's eyes and he turned away only to find Missy watching him again, an unreadable expression in her gaze.

"Ah, sh—shoot."

The sound of glass hitting the table came from Liam's other side and he turned in time to see Bryant had up-ended the whiskey tumbler he'd brought with him from Liam's office.

Liam reached for the mess with his napkin at the same time Bryant did.

"I got it, I got it," he said, pushing Liam's hands away

as he mopped up the liquid. "Probably should've stopped at one."

"Yeah, probably."

Bryant's gaze held fire. "You know, you've got—"

"Honey, please." Laurie reached over and laced her fingers with his, stopping whatever he planned to say. "Let's do this."

"You sure?" His tone softened and he brought the back of her hand to his mouth for a quick kiss. "I thought you might want to wait…longer."

She shook her head, lightly cleared her throat and then said, "Hey, everyone. Could we get your attention?"

Silence filled the air.

Laurie smiled, and then looked at Bryant. "Go ahead."

"Well, we asked the folks to pull this dinner together tonight because we have some news to share." Bryant gave his wife's hand a squeeze and gazed into her eyes. "Great news. We're going to have a baby."

And in that instant, his brother's earlier ramblings made sense to Liam.

Happy cries filled the room, led by their mother, who jumped up from her seat to give Laurie and Bryant each a hug and a kiss, followed by their father, who'd also left his place to congratulate the happy couple. Hugs, handshakes and high fives were exchanged and Liam threw his arm around his brother's shoulder, giving him a hearty slap on the back.

"Oh, maybe we'll have another girl in the family and then we'll be even," Elise said, taking her seat again, wiping at her eyes with her napkin. "Three boys and three girls, now that Casey has joined us. For so long Abby was the only granddaughter."

"All the better."

Liam glanced sharply at Casey, wondering if she'd

heard Abby's mumbled words, but with her head bowed, she seemed intently focused on her meal. Where was his niece's animosity coming from anyway?

"So when do we get to meet my newest grandchild?" Alistair asked.

"The end of January," Laurie said.

Liam started counting, but his father was faster. "So, that makes you four months along."

Laurie nodded, her fingers shaking as she tucked a strand of hair behind one ear. "We wanted to wait…well, until…"

Bryant reached for his wife's hand again. "After the miscarriage last year, we thought it would be best if we waited until Laurie was out of her first trimester before we shared the news."

"Makes sense," Liam said, remembering that during Laurie's first pregnancy his brother had shared they'd been trying to start a family since their honeymoon a few years ago. The loss of their child and Laurie's health issues since had hit Bryant hard.

When everyone started chatting again, he leaned in toward his brother and lowered his voice. "So does our talk earlier in my office."

"I'm a jerk." Bryant's mouth rose into a sheepish grin.

"You're a Murphy. It happens sometimes." Liam smiled. "And like the rest of the Murphy men, you're going to be a great father."

"Thanks. So are you, man."

Liam hoped his brother was right.

Despite Missy's assurances and his own common sense telling him it was too soon, he didn't feel much like one at the moment. He and Casey were polite strangers, almost friends, maybe. That was a long way from what his brothers shared with their children.

"Go on, Fay, it's okay." Laurie's words cut into his thoughts and he found his sisters-in-law sharing smiles from across the table.

"Oh, no," Fay said, her curls bouncing as she shook her head. "I don't want to spoil your news."

"You couldn't. Go on."

"But I haven't even told Adam yet."

"So tell him now."

"Tell me what now?" Adam asked, looking at his wife. "What secret are you two sharing?"

"Okay, then." Fay smiled, her gaze moving around the table before it landed on her husband. "Well, I'm afraid the male/female grandkid ratio will still be uneven next year, because I'm pregnant, too."

Adam's mouth fell open, a stunned expression on his face before he gave out a loud whoop and gathered his wife and son in his arms.

More cheers and hugs were passed around by everyone.

When Fay shared she was due only a couple of weeks after Laurie, the remainder of the meal was filled with talk of baby showers, ideas for names and Logan and Luke insisting that another set of twins in the family would be the coolest thing ever, even if their uncles paled at that suggestion.

It wasn't until the table was cleared and his mother put her able-bodied grandkids in charge of kitchen cleanup and then served dessert, that Liam realized Missy was no longer in the room.

She needed a moment.

Walking out on a family celebration was rude. Missy's well-mannered upbringing haunted her with every step, but the love and happiness overflowing in the dining room had been vastly dissimilar from her own experience. And right now it was more than she could handle.

The air was warm here on the front porch, despite it being a cloudy day. Distant rumblings coming from the dark skies overhead promised rain was on its way. A rich scent of earth and grass and trees filled her head, so unlike what she was used to at home, but familiar again after being back here for the last few days.

Seeking peace and quiet to gather her thoughts, Missy made her way to the seating area where she and Liam had talked that first night. Then she would go back inside. She'd rejoin the others and smile and be happy for them because deep in her heart, she truly felt the news of a baby's—or babies'—arrival was wonderful.

But first she needed to deal with the memory of her family's reaction when she'd finally found the courage to tell them…

Oh, it had been far different.

Crossing her arms, Missy lifted her face to the light breeze, her eyes closed in an attempt to hold back the tears.

Even after all this time, she could still hear the distress in their voices, see the disapproval in their eyes as she stood before them in her father's study and confessed she was pregnant and even worse, didn't know who the baby's father was.

"Missy, are you all right?"

Liam calling out caused her to jump, and she hastily brushed at the wetness on her cheeks, erasing the tears that managed to escape despite her best efforts.

"Sorry, didn't mean to startle you," he said as he came closer. "It's just that you left so abruptly—"

"I'm the one who should apologize." She cut him off as she turned around with a pasted-on smile and a determination not to let him see the turmoil crashing around inside her. "It just got too warm—too many people—"

"What's wrong?" His eyes narrowed as he looked at her. "Why are you upset?"

"I'm not. Not really." Surprised at how easily the lie fell from her lips, she quickly dropped her gaze from his. "You come bearing gifts."

Liam held a dessert plate with two forks in the same hand. "It's one of my mother's specialties. Her blue-rib-bon-winning apple pie, complete with a heaping scoop of vanilla ice cream."

"So very American." Happy for the distraction, Missy reached for the plate, but Liam stepped back, holding the treat out of reach. "You don't plan to share?" she asked.

"Of course I do. As soon as you share what's bother-ing you."

"I told you—"

"If anyone knows how overwhelming my family can be at times, it's me," Liam said, putting the dessert on a nearby table. "But I get the feeling it's something more. Somehow related to the happy news?"

"I think your sisters-in-law being pregnant at the same time is jolly wonderful." Missy kept her gaze low. "For them, for your brothers, for everyone."

Bending his knees a bit, he scrunched down, trying to bring his face level with hers. When that didn't work, he gently lifted her chin with his finger and forced her to look at him. "And the family's reaction to that news was noth-ing like what you received sixteen years ago."

She closed her eyes and turned away to look out over the yard, not surprised he had figured out the cause of her distress so easily. He'd always been able to read her.

"No, it wasn't," she finally admitted.

"Tell me."

A shuddering breath escaped her lungs and she shook her head.

"Please." He moved in behind her, so close she could almost feel his warmth. His strength. Then his hands encircled her upper arms, his touch causing a shiver to dance across her skin. "I'd like to know."

"There's not much to tell." She pulled in a deep breath and slowly exhaled. "Picture the exact opposite reaction. My father, sitting in his chair by the fireplace, remaining stoic, even as his eyes raked over me with censure and condemnation."

"Aw, Missy…"

"Believe it or not, that was easier to take than my mother, who didn't even look at me. No, she just cried out and then dropped her crystal sherry glass, shattering it into a million pieces."

"You were alone? That bastard didn't even stand next to you—"

How had he guessed that? "I told Stanford I wanted… needed to speak to them by myself. To explain."

A long silence filled the air before Liam said, "Because you didn't know if the baby was his or mine."

Missy dropped her chin, amazed that the memory of that night still lived so fresh in her mind. That it still hurt so much.

"They, of course, assumed the baby was Stanford's, but then I told them about falling in lo—" She bit hard on her bottom lip, cutting off her words for a moment. "About meeting you. About what happened when I first returned home to London. Why it took me so long to realize…"

"What did they say?"

"Nothing. I was sent to my room. They didn't speak to me for three days."

His hands tightened on her. "That's kind of harsh."

"I'd shocked them, shocked their neat and orderly world. Now, as an adult, I can understand that. My time in America changed me. I was more independent, more vocal in my opinions. At eighteen, I was technically an adult, but in their eyes, I was still a child. Their only child."

She turned to face him, breaking free of his hold. "Oh, this is silly. I don't know why I'm letting this bother me now. It's a totally different situation. Fay and Laurie are grown women, happily married. Of course the reactions would be different."

Liam's brows drew together in a scowl. "That's still no reason for your parents to treat you that way."

"How do you think Nolan would react if Abby came home one day and shared that kind of news? How would I if Casey ever does the same?"

He looked as thunderstruck as she felt, and he backed away, rubbing his hand hard across his mouth. "You wouldn't shut her out," he said. "You wouldn't ignore her and then find a way to manipulate the situation to suit your own needs."

The strength and sureness in his words warmed her. "Thank you for saying that."

"I wish I had known." He came back to her, his hands cupping her face, his thumbs gently brushing against her damp cheeks. "I wish you had told me you were pregnant. That the child might be mine."

"Oh, Liam…what would you have done?"

"I don't know. Flown to England?"

She tried to shake her head at the absurdity of his words, but he held her in place, his eyes boring into hers. "I would've found a way to be with you. To support you until we knew for sure—"

"And then what? My father obviously planned all along to lie about the test results when the time came."

He closed his eyes, a pained expression on his face.

Without thinking, without considering the consequences, she gave in to the need to touch him. Her fingertips scraped the roughness of his evening beard as she touched his jaw.

"After Casey was born, you would've been told the same thing I had…that she wasn't yours," she whispered, her throat tightening as the imagined scene played out in her mind. "And I would've lost you all over again. I don't know if I could've lived through that a second time—"

His mouth crashed down on hers, his kiss raw and unapologetic as he devoured her confession, his tongue sweeping inside.

It was as surprising as when he'd kissed her the other night, but this time she didn't pull away. This time their mouths pushed and queried, relearning, remembering, and when a low groan filled the air, she didn't know if it came from him or her.

The hint of apple and cinnamon on his tongue tasted sweet, the dark sweeping heat of it stroking hers almost savage. His fingers pressed hard against her jaw and then he released her.

She stumbled forward, her breasts brushing against his chest, and his grip returned as the kiss continued. He pulled her toward him until she was flush against his body. She scraped her fingers over his jaw to his hair, her arms sliding up and over his shoulders until they intertwined behind his neck.

The past and present meshed and mingled; she was a girl again in the arms of her first love, her first lover. At the same time his kiss, his touch, his body were new to her in so many ways, and a desire to know him, to be with the man he was now, raced through her.

The kiss seemed to go on forever, a rising desire that

threatened to consume her, consume both of them, until she finally broke free, light-headed and breathless, sure her legs wouldn't keep her upright if he weren't holding her so tightly.

"Liam…"

He pulled her even closer, his arms banding around her as he tucked her head to his shoulder, his face buried into her neck. His lips grazed her skin, his breaths heavy and warm as he whispered in her ear. "Just let me hold you… for a moment."

Knowing she couldn't refuse him—and didn't want to—she relaxed into his embrace and allowed her eyelids to close, the fleeting glimpse of a figure standing in the shadows near the doorway registering in her mind.

Missy gasped and opened her eyes, pushing at Liam's shoulders. He let her go and stepped back, confusion crossing his features.

"Missy—"

"Someone is…" Her words came in a hushed whisper. "Watching us."

"With a family as big as mine, I'm not surprised." He squeezed her hand tightly, his smile unsteady. "This isn't the most private place to talk…or do anything else."

"You don't bloody understand." Panic raced through her veins and she yanked free and stepped away, the cool air now swirling between them. "I think it was Casey."

Chapter Eight

Missy had, as the Americans so often put it, chickened out when it came to asking Casey if she'd been the one who'd seen her and Liam talking—and kissing—out on the front porch a few nights ago.

She'd expected her daughter to come right out and demand an explanation, if not in front of everyone at least with her privately, when she and Liam had sneaked back inside, but the group's attention had been on the large-screen television where old family movies were playing as they ate dessert.

Casey had been sitting next to Liam's mother, watching the telly and listening to Elise's stories about the boys when they were young. Missy had started to go to her when Liam grabbed her hand and pulled her down next to him on a nearby love seat.

After practically landing in his lap, she'd managed to scoot to the far side of the diminutive sofa, shoving a couple of toss pillows between the two of them before Casey turned and sent a big smile her way.

Later, when the evening had ended and the two of them headed back to the boathouse, she'd waited, but again nothing. Deciding it might have been one of his brothers after all, Missy had remained silent on the subject.

In the days since, the three of them had settled into a routine where she and Casey occupied themselves in the morning, but then Liam would join them for lunch at the main house before he went back to his office. Afternoons were spent either poolside or off doing something with Liam's mother, including today, when they had gone to Cheyenne and done touristy stuff with the twins tagging along.

And as much as Missy tried not to impose, Elise insisted they eat dinner at the main house with her and her husband every night. Liam was there, too, of course. More often than not Nolan and his kids joined them, even though at times Abby didn't seem too pleased to have Missy and Casey at the table.

Not that the teen said anything directly to her, but Missy had picked up on the verbal jabs she and Casey tossed back and forth, usually under their breath and the radar of everyone else.

Missy had mentioned it to her daughter the first night it happened as they were heading to bed, but Casey had laughed it off as "not a bloody big deal."

The evenings were nice, filled with watching movies, playing board games—Casey was as cutthroat at Monopoly as Liam—or spending time outside, either taking long walks, being lakeside on the dock or sitting around a fire.

The three of them were always together and often joined by others. Meaning Missy and Liam weren't ever alone.

She'd told him on that first night there would be nothing between them, no rekindling of a long-ago flame. Missy had decided the best way to ensure that was to keep the focus of their time together on Casey, allowing her and Liam to get to know one another. Again, it was something Liam was being a perfect gentleman about.

Oh, she would catch him sending slow, appraising looks her way, his gaze not giving away what was going on inside his head. But then his hand would brush against hers during a meal, or land warm and strong at the small of her back when they walked, sending an all too familiar tingling through her.

But that was as far as it went. It was as if they'd reached an unspoken agreement of what was important. And what wasn't.

After Missy and Casey had spent today shopping and sightseeing with Liam's mother and the twins, Casey had received a text from Liam asking if they were going to make it back in time for dinner. They arrived at the main house in the late afternoon, the twins jumping from their grandmother's car to sprint across the yard toward their own home.

"Where are they off to?" Elise asked.

"Something about who can win a race to the loo," Casey said with a grin. "Uh, to the bathroom, I mean."

Elise laughed. "I guess it's a good thing they have more than one. Come on, let's go inside."

"We ought to take these back to the boathouse," Missy said, lifting the bags filled with the clothes and trinkets she and Casey had managed to accumulate during today's outing from Elise's car. "Perhaps what we should have purchased was another suitcase—"

The tooting of a horn had all three of them turning around.

It was Fay in her pretty personalized van for her flower shop. She parked in an empty space and waved at them through the open window. "Hello there! I come bearing flowers and a baby. You do remember what tonight is?"

"Of course I do," Elise said, and then turned to Missy as they walked toward the van. "She and Adam have standing date nights the second and last Friday of every month. If I'm real lucky, I get to keep my handsome grandson with us overnight."

Missy smiled at Elise's enthusiasm, surprised that August was almost over. She and Casey had been in Destiny a week today and it'd been almost a month since her father died.

And their world had turned upside down.

"Missy, can I ask you a favor?" Fay asked, opening the side door and reaching for her son's car carrier in the backseat. "Would you mind taking this guy into the house and keeping an eye on him for a few minutes? Elise and I have to get the flower arrangements for the model homes."

"Of course I don't mind." Handing off their bags to Casey, Missy looked down at A.J. He was waving his fists in the air, his eyes scrunched up tight against the afternoon sunshine. "Hey, there, buddy. You seem a bit cranky."

"He just woke up from a nap and will probably want a bottle. Don't worry, he can wait until I get into the house."

Missy took the baby's nappy bag from Fay, slinging the strap over one shoulder, the gesture familiar, despite the passage of time. "I think I remember how it's done, if you trust me. Do you have a bottle made up already?"

"Great, go for it." Fay grinned and handed over her son. "The bottles are in the side pocket and Elise has an electronic warmer on the counter. Just pop one in, wait for the ready light and you're good to go."

"Katie's car is still in the lot and the boys should be nearby if you need help," Elise said from the back of the van, where she'd opened the rear double doors. "Oh, Fay, these flowers are gorgeous. Perfect for the coming fall season."

"I was hoping you'd like them," Fay said, and then looked to Missy again. "If you need me, just give a shout."

"We'll be fine," Missy said, hefting the baby's carrier into the crook of her arm. "I've got all the help I need right here."

"Who, me?" Casey's eyes grew wide as she backed away, holding her hands loaded with bags up in mock surrender. "I don't know nothin' 'bout birthin' babies!"

Everyone laughed at her spot-on high-pitched imitation from one of the two classic films they'd watched last night.

"Birthin' and babysitting are two different things." The memory of what she'd said to Liam a few nights ago flashed in Missy's head, but she pushed it away and smiled at her daughter. "Don't worry. I'll talk you through it."

Elise and Fay got to work with the flowers while Missy and Casey headed for the side door that took them directly into the living room.

Missy stopped at one of the leather sofas in the main seating area in front of the fireplace and set A.J.'s carrier on the floor. She easily found a bottle in the baby's bag. "Keep an eye on the little bugger while I warm this up, okay?"

"You better make it fast." Casey stared at the baby with a dubious glare. "With the faces he's making it looks like he's about to go off his trolley."

Bending down, Missy touched the soft brown curls on the baby's head. His dark eyes latched onto the bottle in her hand.

She quickly straightened and tucked his afternoon treat behind her back, but it was too late. "I think you're right. I'll be back in a moment."

Casey dropped the shopping bags on the couch and sat. "So, what do I do in the meantime?"

"Distract him. Try chatting him up," Missy said, heading for the kitchen.

Finding the warming device, she followed the easy directions, wishing she'd had one of these years ago. Hmm, four to six minutes before mealtime. She peeked back into the main room as the baby's fussing got louder. The last thing she wanted was to bother anyone in the nearby offices or send Casey to get his mother.

"Nudge the carrier gently with your foot, sweetie," she suggested, calling out to her daughter. "The rocking motion might calm him down. It's going to take a few minutes before his bottle is ready."

Casey rolled her eyes, but stretched out one foot, the tip of her cowboy boot catching the hard plastic edge of the carrier and setting it into motion. "You know, I'm a bit parched myself."

Missy smiled and then went to work preparing a tray of chocolate-chip cookies and lemonade, not wanting to spoil their appetites.

The moment she heard the clear and pure tone of her daughter's voice raised in song, she froze.

Making her way back to the doorway, she found Casey still rocking the baby's seat with her foot, but she also now had a guitar in her arms as she sang a favorite song of hers about blue skies, wishing on a star and bluebirds flying over a rainbow.

A warm feeling of pride filled Missy, her heart pounding so hard she had to press a hand to her chest.

Music was one of her daughter's passions. A day rarely went by when she wasn't singing or playing. Missy had meant to check with Liam about the piano against the far wall after noticing Casey glancing at it a few times.

She had no idea where her daughter had found the instrument she was playing now. It looked a little beat-up, much like the one Casey had back home that she'd bought last year, after spotting it in the window of a secondhand shop on Rathbone Place.

Could it be— No, she doubted Liam would still have that old thing.

The last rich, mellow notes of the simple melody lingered in the air as Casey finished and smiled down at the baby. "So, A.J., you're a music fan. I like that. Bollocks, don't start fussing again."

A.J. wasn't listening as his soft whimpers started to rise in volume.

"That was beautiful," said a male voice. "Maybe you should try singing to him again."

Casey whipped her head around when Liam spoke. Missy did the same, her wide eyes matching their daughter's startled expression.

At finding him there, Liam guessed, but he'd been the one who was truly surprised.

He'd been ending a phone call when Katie popped into his office, letting him know his mother's car had just pulled into the driveway. Missy and Casey were back. A sudden need to see them had hit him square in the chest and he realized he'd missed them.

Ever since that night on the front porch, Missy had been finding creative ways to stay away from him, or at least ensure they weren't alone again. He could admit he'd gotten a bit carried away with that kiss, but her story—and his frustration over a past they couldn't change—had hit him harder than he'd expected.

Shaking off the memory, Liam decided to concentrate on what was happening now between them. As much as he claimed it was all about him and Casey getting to know each other, he knew there was more to it.

More to him and Missy.

Unfinished business? Something new?

He didn't have any idea. But he was eager to share something he'd come up with today, something he hoped Casey would be excited about.

Something that might give him more one-on-one time with Missy.

"Go on," Liam urged when Casey continued to stare at him while the baby's fussing grew louder. He walked to the sofa opposite where Casey sat, fisting his hands along the back cushions. "He looks like he's about to burst into a joyful noise. Something I'm sure won't sound anywhere near as terrific as you."

Casey's cheeks turned bright pink at his compliment. She dropped her chin and looked away, but the shy smile visible on her face warmed Liam's heart.

She then pulled in a deep breath, slowly released it and started the song again. Her grip on the instrument looked steady as her fingers moved over the strings with a familiar ease. Her voice was solid and unwavering this time as she looked again at her baby cousin, who'd gone silent as soon as she began to sing.

Damn, she was good.

It was obvious she had a natural gift and some training. Much more than Liam. He'd learned to play some when he was a kid from an old cowboy turned logger who used to work for the family business. The rest he'd picked up on his own.

Glancing over his shoulder, he found that Katie and Nolan had followed him and were enjoying the impromptu concert. He then looked across the room and saw that his mom and Fay had come in as well, but it was the delight on Missy's face as she looked at Casey that caused a hard lump to form in his throat.

This obviously wasn't the first time she'd heard their daughter sing.

When had Casey started? Was this something new or had she begun at a much younger age? Then he wondered if someone in her life had discovered and nurtured this talent or if it had come naturally.

Perhaps it was inherited from him?

Damn. How much had he missed out on during the years he hadn't known about his daughter?

He wondered too how she'd known his guitars were kept in a nearby cabinet. He still played every once in a while, and a sudden eagerness to share this moment had him crossing the room and reaching for the second guitar leaning against a low shelf.

He slipped the strap over his head and easily picked up the melody she was playing as he returned to sit on the empty sofa.

She stopped mid-chorus, but Liam nodded for her to continue. Casey returned his nod and moved on to the next line of lyrics without missing a beat, her smile and the slight uptick of her chin an invitation for him to join in. He did, keeping his baritone range low, melding it easily with her sweet soprano, before backing off completely when she softened her tone on the last line, her fingertips drawing out the ending cords.

A light clapping filled the air as A.J. slapped his chubby hands together and gurgled happily.

Liam and Casey laughed; the thrill of achieving an eight-second ride on the back of a bucking bronc paled in comparison to the happiness slamming in his gut at this very moment.

More applause came, this time from everyone else as

they moved farther into the room, gathering around the seating area.

"Oh, sweetie, that was wonderful," Elise gushed.

"What an amazing voice you have," Katie added. "I love your version of that song."

Fay knelt next to her son, unstrapping him from his car seat and lifting him into her arms. "You do realize you've spoiled this young man," she said, giving Casey a smile. "He's never going to be happy with my sorry attempts at bedtime lullabies again."

Missy handed Fay the warmed bottle once she settled onto the sofa, and then she came and sat next to Casey. "That was smashing. I've missed hearing you while I was gone." Then she looked over at him. "It's nice to know you still play, too."

Liam smiled, remembering how he used to serenade her during those stolen hours in the boathouse attic. He'd managed to learn a favorite song of hers, a popular country tune at the time. He was no Tim McGraw, but he'd managed to sing to her about what her love did to him.

And how she made him who he wanted to be.

"Yeah, he still entertains the family from time to time," Nolan said, reaching over and lightly punching Liam on the shoulder. "You two should get together with Abby and do a—"

"Do a what?" Abby asked, interrupting her father as she strolled into the room with Luke and Logan right behind her. "What's going on?"

"Casey and Liam just sang a duet," Fay said. "A lullaby for A.J."

"Oh, really?" Abby walked to the piano and perched on the short end of the bench, one hand lightly running across a few of the keys, the clear notes filling the air. "How sweet."

"She's great," Katie said. "You really missed something."

"I'm sure I did."

Liam studied his niece. Something was bothering her. There was a stiffness in her posture, an indifference that set off his radar. Before he could say anything, Casey spoke up.

"Do you sing?" she asked, directing her question to Abby.

"Are you kidding? She sounds like a bullfrog in heat."

"Logan." Nolan shot his son a warning look. "Knock it off."

"No, I play." Abby turned and faced the piano. Using both hands this time, she played a quick classical piece with precision, ending with a flourish before looking back over her shoulder. "In fact, Uncle Liam and I play together all the time. We're the musical ones in the family."

"I can see that." Casey's voice was flat as she placed the guitar on the sofa next to her and got to her feet. "Well, I better tote our bags to the boathouse."

Liam blinked; the quicksilver change in Casey's demeanor surprised him. Gone was the beaming girl he'd just had an incredible moment with. In fact, her face was wiped clean of any emotion at all.

Missy reached out, placing a hand on her daughter's arm before the girl could grab the first bag. "Casey, what's wro—uh, I thought you wanted something to drink."

"I'll get something for all of us," Elise said. "Katie, would you like to help me?"

The two women disappeared into the kitchen, but Liam was more interested in the abrupt tension in the air, not to mention the nonverbal conversation going on between mother and daughter.

Casey stared at Missy for a long moment, blew out a dramatic puff of air and flopped back to the couch. "Fine."

Missy grabbed for the guitar before it toppled to the rug, handing it to Liam. "Here, you might want to put this away for safekeeping."

"But I thought she might—" His gaze moved from her to Casey. "I thought you might like to keep it. Take it back to the apartment with you."

Casey shrugged, not looking at him, her focus now on the silver rings decorating her fingers. "I know where it is if I want to play again."

"How did you know where to find these in the first place?" he asked.

"I noticed the door to the cabinet was open and spotted the buggers." She finally looked at him again. "Why? Can't I touch them?"

The chill of her tone surprised him. "Of course you can."

"Hey, you never let us play with them," Luke said.

"Because they aren't toys." Liam softened the words with a smile. "Casey knows how to play, quite well, I might add. If I were to guess, I'd say she also knows how to take care of guitars because she has one of her own?"

The hardness eased from her eyes. "It's nothing special. A secondhand Cordoba C5."

Liam nodded. "Nice. These are both Fenders, not new by any stretch, but they do hold value to me, especially sentimental. And you're free to use either one. Any time you want. Any place you'd like."

A flicker of a smile returned to Casey's face as his mom and Katie came back into the room with a tray of glasses, pitchers of iced tea and lemonade, and a large platter of homemade cookies that the twins immediately dug into.

Picking up both guitars, Liam returned them to the cabinet and then took his seat again, noticing Casey's gaze following his every move.

"So what are everyone's plans for dinner?" Elise asked. "I know Fay is heading home for her date with Adam, but who's interested in homemade pizzas?"

The twins' hands shot up, Nolan's, too, but it was the shared glance between Missy and Casey that had Liam speaking up. "None for us, Mom," he said. "I thought I'd take these two ladies to the Blue Creek Saloon tonight."

Casey's eyes sparkled with life again. "Really? We can eat at that place that was once a real Old West saloon?"

"Sure." Liam caught Missy's eye. "Don't worry. It's changed from the rowdy bar you might remember. Well, somewhat. It doesn't get crazy there on Friday nights until later. It's very much a family restaurant. At least until the band kicks in."

"Band? They have live music? That's dench!"

Liam laughed, glad to see Casey's good mood was back. "I take it that's a good thing."

Casey nodded. "A cracking good thing. Let's go!"

"I think we should take our purchases back to the flat first. I'd also like to grab a shower and change," Missy said. "If that would be all right."

Liam nodded, fighting off the urge to picture her doing both of those things in vivid detail. It took a moment, but he got his head back on straight and held out his hand when they started to rise. "Before you go, there's something else I'd like to talk to Casey about."

"Can't we chat over dinner?" Casey asked.

"Well, sure, but this includes Nolan." Liam looked at his brother. "At least partially."

Casey's gaze flickered to Nolan for a moment, then to Abby, who'd left the piano to perch on the arm of the chair where her father sat, before coming back to Liam.

She shrugged. "Okay. What's up?"

A sliver of caution sliced through his chest as he looked at the curious expressions around the room. Hell, maybe he should have waited until they were alone to bring this up. Too late now.

"I want you to know I'm really happy you and your mother still have a few weeks in Destiny with me—with all of us—but I'm worried you might find your days...boring, especially after next week, when Abby and the twins head back to school."

"Man, don't remind us," Luke said.

"Yeah," Logan agreed. "Back to having tons of homework coming out our as—ah, ears."

Casey smiled at that and Liam took that as a good sign. "So, I thought maybe we could get you permission to attend classes at the high school," he continued. "To let you see what life is like at an American school, which I'm guessing is somewhat different than the private all-girls academy you go to."

"Is that possible?" Missy asked.

"Well, we've got an inside track." Liam glanced at his brother. "Nolan's been dating the vice principal for the last month, so I thought he could talk—"

"What!"

Abby's outcry and the jarring clunk of a glass against wood cut Liam off midsentence. He—and everyone else—looked first at Abby and then at Katie, who'd righted her drinking glass but was hastily wiping at the spill she'd caused on the large hand-hewn coffee table with a handful of napkins.

"Oh, I'm sorry. I didn't—" Katie jumped to her feet, tossing the wet mess onto the tray. "How clumsy of me. I'll just take this into the kitchen. Please, don't let me interrupt...your plans."

Katie hurried from the room, tray in hand, but Abby wasn't finished.

"Dad, you can't be getting serious with Ms. Elan," she cried, jumping to her feet. "Just because she won you at that silly bachelor auction? And as for her going to the high school—" Abby waved a hand in Casey's direction "—forget it! She was bragging the other night how she has nothing to do but laze around because she's on a holiday!"

"Hey, back up a minute." Nolan pointed at his daughter. "I've been out with MaryAnn twice since the auction date. That's hardly getting serious. And what Casey does or doesn't do during her stay isn't your call."

"Oh, she doesn't have to get her knickers in a twist." Casey stood as well. The anger flashing in her eyes as she glared at Abby told Liam his idea was shot all to hell. "I'd rather be bloody bored out of my skull than go to the same school as her. And I'm quite sure the feeling is mutual."

Chapter Nine

Trying to find a spot for a moment of privacy wasn't easy around here. Casey could only stay holed up in her room for so long. Thankfully everyone seemed occupied on Sunday afternoon, including her mum and Liam, who both had work-related issues to deal with, so she'd grabbed an apple, bottled water and her journal, thinking maybe she'd find some solitude here in the boathouse to put her jumbled thoughts down on paper.

She thought back to the night Liam and she had played guitar together. She'd been tempted all weekend to grab one. Then she'd spotted that piano and remembered what Abby had said to ruin the moment.

Trying to find common ground with Liam wasn't as easy as she'd thought it'd be.

The horseback riding had been fun, something she'd never been interested in despite her grandmother's attempts at getting her into lessons. But finding out that her real father was a former champion cowboy had changed that. And she was good at it. Liam had come right out and told her so.

Still, the moment he'd picked up that second guitar and started playing alongside her…

That simple act had caused a rush of powerful emotions. Then when their voices had blended in almost perfect harmony, all those crazy bounding sensations had boiled down to a simple longing she'd never felt before.

Longing to be connected.

It was the same—and yet different—feeling that she had toward her mum. The bond between them was as natural to her as breathing. But for the first time Casey had felt a link, even if it was fragile, between her and the man who was her real father.

Until that blonde prig had come along and ruined everything.

Not wanting to relive that memory again, Casey stepped out of the sunshine and into the cool, shadowy interior of the lower level of the boathouse, drawn by the sounds of the lake gently lapping against the boat slips.

Pushing her sunglasses to the top of her head, she looked around, debating if it'd be okay if she curled up on the bench seat of the wooden powerboat that sat bobbing in the first slip. It wasn't as if she planned to power that baby up—

"We've got plenty of kayaks, singles and doubles, not to mention a few—what are *you* doing in here?"

Casey whirled around. Blimey, just what she didn't need. Abby stood just inside the arched opening of the boathouse near the first slip, surrounded by a half dozen hangers-on this time.

The princess and her minions. Geesh, did they multiply?

"Looking for a little peace and quiet, but I guess that's

a bust." She hiked her drawstring bag higher on her shoulder. "Don't worry. I'll get out of your way."

"Good." Abby's voice dropped away, but she wasn't done. *You're not wanted*, she added, mouthing the words silently.

Biting her tongue because it just wasn't worth it, Casey settled for an old-fashioned eye roll as she brushed past her cousin, refusing to back down when Abby didn't move aside. Her minions scattered, so there was some satisfaction in that.

"Hey, Casey. I was just thinking about you. What are you doing?"

Her footsteps faltered and she looked up into familiar green eyes, but even the appearance of that good-looking lad she'd met last week couldn't save this moment.

"Leaving," she said.

"Wait." Nathan reached for her as she started past him, gently grabbing at her elbow. "Don't go. Stick around. Hang with us."

Casey stared at him. She could almost hear her cousin's head exploding behind her at the invitation. "No, I don't want to get in the way."

"You won't. Right, guys?"

Nathan let go of her and looked at his buddies, who all either nodded or shrugged with indifference as they walked past her and deeper into the boathouse.

Casey made a quick count. Seven lads, including Nathan, and six girls, not counting her. She wouldn't be the odd one out this time. At least not numerically. And she did have a good time when they all hung out at the pool, as long as she kept blinders on where her cousin was concerned.

Still, she wasn't sure—

"Don't tell me you can't swim?"

Nathan's question pulled her from her thoughts. "What? No, of course, I can swim." Casey looked over to where the crowd was putting kayaks in the water, slipping into the seats and heading out into the sunshine. "I've just never done that before."

"Oh, that's too bad." Abby called out in a false voice from where she sat on the edge of the dock, holding a double kayak in place with her feet. "All we seem to have left are singles."

Meaning Nathan was going to be getting into hers.

Casey gave what she hoped was a casual shrug. "Maybe next time."

"What next time?" Nathan walked backward toward the boat slips with a cocky grin. "You and I can take one of the rowboats. How about this blue one?"

Abby's eyes grew wide as she got to her feet. "Nate, wait."

"Don't worry, Abs, I can handle getting this thing off the storage rack—hey, what's this doing in here?"

Liam's guitar! Casey couldn't believe Nathan had it. Her gaze flew to Abby, catching the fleeting guilt in her eyes before it disappeared. She'd done it! Abby had taken one of Liam's prized possessions and hid it out here—for what?

Everyone had heard his offer that Casey could use one any time she wanted. Had Abby hoped someone would notice it missing and assume Casey had taken it without asking? Or worse, that the instrument would get damaged and she'd be blamed?

"I brought it." The words popped out of Casey's mouth before she could stop them. She had no idea why. She walked to Nathan and took the guitar from him, grateful to find it unharmed. "I was looking for a quiet spot to practice."

"You play?" he asked, easily maneuvering the rowboat

into the water and tying it to the slip. "Cool. Maybe you can serenade me once we get out on the water."

Casey turned and narrowed her gaze at her cousin. "Maybe. But I wouldn't want to get distracted and fall in. You might have to rescue me."

Abby returned her look for a moment, and then wheeled her attention back to the kayak, calling out to one of the other lads, who quickly abandoned his single to join her.

Casey looked back to Nathan, wondering if seeing Abby with someone else would bother him. No matter how fun it was to tease the priss—who didn't deserve any leeway after the stunt she'd just pulled—the last thing Casey wanted was to get in the middle of a teenage romance.

Been there, done that, never again.

"Don't worry, you're safe with me," Nathan said, grabbing a couple of life vests from a nearby shelf. "I spent the summer working at the local kids' camp as a lifeguard. But to be safe, let's put these on."

"Do you mind if I run upstairs and put these things away first?" Wow, did she sound like a breathless twit. "I mean, I trust you to save me, but I wouldn't want anything to happen to the guitar."

"Sure, I'll wait right here."

Casey gathered her things and started to walk around him when he stopped her. "Hey, Abby said you're here until the end of the month," he said. "What are you going to do while the rest of us are back in school on Tuesday?"

A zing raced through her when she realized he'd asked her cousin about her. "Going to school with you, I hope."

The feminine shriek and subsequent splash from behind her were music to Casey's ears.

"What do you mean you're going on a date?"

Missy bit back a smile at Liam's incredulous tone and

watched his gaze move from Casey to her and back again. The three of them sat at the huge center island in the Murphy kitchen, eating a late dinner of takeout pizza.

"Did you know about this?" he asked, looking at Missy again.

His surprised expression was so genuine, she almost felt sorry for him.

"Of course," she said. "Casey told me two days ago."

"She didn't tell me." Liam turned back to their daughter. "You didn't tell me."

Casey shrugged. "You've been busy."

"I told you," Missy said, stealing a piece of pepperoni from a half-eaten pie still in the box, "that same night."

"You did?" This came from Liam and Casey at the same time.

"Yes, I did." She lifted one shoulder in a casual shrug. "You replied with a mumbled 'that's nice' while your nose was stuck in a financial report. I figured you were—as Casey said—busy."

Too busy to care?

Missy hadn't wanted to think so, but a part of her had worried that Liam didn't think the news of Casey going out with a boy was a big deal. In his defense, he didn't have much experience at this, and the last two weeks had been hectic for all of them.

Her boss had pushed up the deadline for a design concept for a new film, a period piece set in the 1940s, due to start filming in the US next year, and Liam had had to deal with one work crisis after another, most of which kept him at his desk or on the phone long after the end of the workday.

Other than an overnight trip to Jackson Hole last weekend in which he'd flown the three of them in the company's helicopter—an amazing experience even if the trip had been business related for Liam—they hadn't seen much of each other.

Especially with Casey now attending Destiny High School.

She'd surprised them when she told them two days before school started that she'd changed her mind. Missy didn't have any idea how he'd arranged it—maybe with his brother's help after all—but Casey was now a full-time student with the understanding that she was expected to follow the same rules and guidelines as the other students, especially when it came to classwork.

Thanks to a review of her school records from London, she was allowed to take many of the same classes as Abby—something the young lady wasn't pleased about at all, at least according to Casey, who shared some of the snarky comments and subtle digs she'd been dealing with, both here and at school, all the while insisting her cousin's attitude wasn't a big deal and she didn't want anyone to know about how Abby was treating her.

Especially Liam.

"So where is this date taking place?" He dropped his uneaten piece of pizza to his plate and instead reached for his glass of wine. "And more importantly, with whom are you going?"

"The Star-Lite Drive-In and Nathan Lawson."

Liam choked on a mouthful of wine and both Casey and Missy slapped him on the back until he slipped off the stool and out of their reach.

"The d-drive-in?" he sputtered.

Casey nodded, confusion in her eyes. "Down near Laramie. Nathan says they close for the season at the end of the month and I've never been—are you okay?"

"Y-yeah." Liam pounded at his chest with a closed fist a few times, and then cleared his throat. "Yes, I'm fine."

"You look a wee bit pasty."

Missy had to agree with her daughter, but she wisely kept her mouth shut. Hmm, it seemed that the man did care that Casey had plans with a young lad for the evening.

That meant more to Missy than she'd thought it would.

"Sweetie, it's after seven," she said, noticing the time. "Didn't you say Nathan would be picking you up—"

"Bollocks! I've got to change my clothes, do my hair!" Chugging down the last of her milk, Casey raced for the door that led to the back deck and then stopped and spun back around. "Hey, we're not going to make a big production out of this, right?"

"If you mean do I want to meet him, then yes, we are," Missy said.

"Damn right we are." Liam's muttered words reached Missy, but thankfully they didn't seem to carry across the room.

"But that day in the pool—"

"He was just one of the crowd." Missy cut off her protest before it even began. "We were never introduced. You know the rules, Casey."

She sighed. "Fine, but please, let's keep this chill."

"In a house with this many people? We'll do our best."

Another eye roll, and Casey was gone. Missy turned around, glad to see that Liam had retaken his seat and regained his coloring. "Are you sure you're okay?"

He nodded. "I honestly didn't hear you the other night. Please, next time, make sure I respond to news like that with a comeback more intelligent. Like *not until she's thirty* or something."

That was sweet, but with just a couple of weeks left to their stay, Missy didn't think there would be a next time.

She ignored the pang in her chest and busied herself with cleaning up their mess. "Will do."

"Are you really okay with this?"

"I'll admit I was surprised when she first told me, but she has been out on group dates back home. She didn't mention it just now, but there are a bunch of kids going tonight. It's not like she's going to be alone with this Nathan." Missy put the box of leftover pizza in the refrigerator and tossed their used plates and napkins in the trash. "Besides, it seems the boy is a regular here at the house and he's a friend of Abby's. That's in his favor."

"The name sounds familiar."

"According to Casey he's the star quarterback of the football team and his father works for you."

Recognition shone in Liam's eyes. "Yes, Bill Lawson. One of our construction foremen. He's a good man."

"That's good to know."

"But Nathan is a senior. He might be eighteen already."

"He's not. His birthday isn't until next spring."

"And you know this how?"

Missy smiled. "Mothers and daughters do talk, you know. She's been bubbly about this boy since the group of them went out on the lake the Sunday before last."

"She's never mentioned him to me." Liam lifted a hand, cutting her off. "I know, I know. I've been busy."

"We all have been. The last two weeks have flown by."

As scared as Missy had been in coming here, even though she'd known it was the right thing—the only thing—to do, the last month had been wonderful...for Casey.

Liam and Casey seemed to be slowly finding their way with each other, especially since he'd found out Casey was keeping one of his guitars in her bedroom. And she'd surprised him in Jackson Hole when she sat at the baby grand piano located in their suite and gave a beautiful performance of a Mozart favorite.

But had they had enough time? Would the remaining days make their connection strong enough to survive being separated by so many miles? Being on two different continents?

How would she survive—

No! Missy blinked back the surprise sting of tears, refusing to allow her thoughts to even stray in that direction. She busied herself at the sink so as not to let Liam see her silly reaction.

This—none of this—was about her. Her and Liam.

There was no her and Liam.

He got to his feet and seconds later was at her side, leaning against the counter. "You know, spending twelve or fourteen hours buried in my work is the norm for me. Ever since I started working for the company full-time out of college. Especially after my dad semiretired and I moved into his job."

Thankful he hadn't picked up on her warring emotions, Missy could only nod, not trusting her voice yet.

"The last couple of weeks aside, I've gotten used to taking a lunch break every day, ending the workday in time for dinner."

Missy grabbed a towel and dried her hands. "Spoken like a man thinking with his stomach."

He leaned over and bumped her shoulder with his. "I was thinking about the people I've been sharing those meals with, and the times spent together afterward. I like having the two of you around."

And they liked being around him. More than they should.

"I think it's time we head outside to the deck so I can meet this young man," Missy said. "We wouldn't want Casey to sneak off on us."

"Would she do that?"

Missy grinned at him and, walking backward, headed for the door. "What were you doing when you were a teenager?"

Liam frowned, following her. "Yeah, that's what worries me."

The night air was warm as they stepped outside, even with the sun gone and twilight casting a glow over the yard. Casey was heading back toward them along the pathway, when a red pickup truck pulled into the lot.

"They're going in a truck. To the drive-in."

Missy looked at Liam, not surprised to find his arms crossed over his chest and a frown creasing his brow. "How did you think they were getting to the drive-in?" she asked. "On a bicycle?"

He remained silent, but at least he dropped his arms when the lad got out of the truck and headed toward them, nervously smoothing his hand down the front of his shirt as he approached the deck.

He smiled at Casey, but then turned to Missy and said, "Hi, you must be Casey's mother. I'm Nathan Lawson."

She took his outstretched hand, impressed that he'd spoken first. "Hi, Nathan. It's nice to meet you. I'm guessing you already know Casey's—"

The widening of her daughter's eyes conveyed an unspoken panic.

"Uh, Liam Murphy." Missy quickly amended the introduction, surprised that she'd been about to introduce him as Casey's father.

Casey had yet to call him that in front of her—in front of anyone—so Missy made the effort not to do so as well.

"Yes, ma'am, my father has worked for the Murphys for years." Nathan released her, and then held out his hand toward Liam. "It's good to see you again, sir."

Liam's shoulders relaxed a bit as he took the boy's hand. "You, too. What are your plans for the night?"

Casey sputtered, but Nathan shot her a quick smile and said, "We're meeting some friends at Sherry's Diner in town and then caravanning to the drive-in. There's about ten of us going in three cars."

"What time do you plan to have her home?"

"Crikey!" Casey managed to find her voice, and it was edgy. "It's a double feature! We'll be back after the movie ends."

"Well, actually, Coach has the entire team on a curfew, so we'll have to leave before the end of the second movie. She'll be home by midnight." Nathan looked at his date again. "Hope that's okay with you."

Casey's blustering vanished and she smiled shyly. "That's fine." She then turned imploring eyes to Missy. "We should go. Like Nathan said, there are others waiting for us."

Missy glanced at Liam, who seemed ready to say something else, but she placed a hand on his arm and turned back to her daughter. "Have fun."

The two kids nodded and headed for Nathan's truck. Missy couldn't hear what her daughter was saying—probably apologizing for putting him through that—but the lad only laughed. He walked Casey to the passenger side, held the door for her as she climbed in and then jogged around the front and got in behind the wheel. Nice touch.

"I wasn't done with him yet."

"I'm sure. What were you going to do next?" She could feel his muscles clenching beneath her fingers and she dropped her hand away. "Ask to see the lad's driver's license?"

When Liam remained silent, Missy turned to face him, but he was watching the pickup as it left the parking lot.

She could see the worry on his face and found his concern for their daughter endearing.

"She's going to be fine."

"She's in a truck. With a teenage boy."

"So?"

"So I—we—that used to be me. Used to be us." Liam looked at her, his expression different now, his eyes taking on a darker emotion. "Please tell me you remember what we were doing in my pickup when we were seventeen."

A heated flush stole over her cheeks. Of course she remembered. "That was different."

"How so?"

"For one, Casey isn't seventeen, and this is a first date." Missy fought against the flood of memories filling her head. Her heart. "You and I had been together for a while before things got…involved."

"A couple of months." Liam reached for her then, putting one hand at her waist and cupping her cheek with the other as he stepped closer. "If memory serves, we couldn't seem to keep our hands off each other."

"Hey, don't mind us," came a male voice, the words laced with laughter.

Missy sprang back from Liam's touch, surprised to find Adam and Fay heading toward them, smiles on their faces. "Oh! Hello…we didn't know you two were here."

"Yeah, we can see that."

Fay swatted at her husband. "We just dropped off A.J. and we saw you two out here and wondered if you have plans for the evening."

"I think we're going to the drive-in," Liam said.

"We are not," Missy countered, knowing Casey would be horrified to find them spying on her. "We most certainly are not."

Adam threw them a questioning look before saying,

"Okay, then come with us. Bobby and Leeann Winslow are officially closing the camp tonight with a bonfire." He glanced at Missy. "Leeann said we should invite the two of you. Do you remember her? She was Leeann Harris back then. She graduated with you and Liam."

"Yes, of course, I remember her."

Missy had run into a few former classmates over the last weeks: Racy Dillon, now married to the local sheriff, who owned the Blue Creek Saloon, and Maggie—whose last name Missy couldn't remember. Maggie had happily introduced the handsome cowboy with her as her husband, Landon Cartwright.

As for tonight, Missy had planned to get some work done while waiting up for Casey, but now she thought a distraction for Liam, one that involved other people, was probably a good idea.

"I think a bonfire sounds like jolly fun," she said with a smile. "I haven't been to one since...well, since I was a teenager."

"Well, I guess that's settled." Liam stepped in close again, one hand to the small of her back, his words a low whisper in her ear. "I, for one, am all for reliving *our* youthful past. Each and every moment of it."

Chapter Ten

"Are you having fun?" Liam asked.

Missy peeked at him over the rim of her red plastic cup, the glow from the roaring campfire highlighting the mischievous sparkle in her eyes.

"I've asked you that before."

She lowered the cup, a soft smile on her beautiful lips. "A few times, and the answer is still the same. Yes, I'm having fun."

Liam returned her grin, feeling foolish and happy at the same time. Unbelievably happy. Despite the nagging irritation over Casey being out with that boy tonight, he was finally alone on a date himself, with Missy.

Well, as alone as one could be in this crowd.

He looked around at the group sitting around the outdoor fire pit at Camp Diamond, the kids' camp his friends Bobby and Leeann Winslow had opened this summer. Liam and his family had been contracted to construct all of the buildings, and from what he'd heard tonight, the camp's inaugural season had been a big success.

With the sun long gone, there was a hint of fall crispness in the air as the dark sky put on a show with an abundance of stars and a full moon shining overhead. Except for the office, the rest of the camp buildings were dark, allowing the fire to create a warm beacon that gave off just enough light to see the water lapping at the edge of the lake a few feet away.

There'd been quite a crowd here already when Liam, Missy, Adam and Fay showed up. Maggie and Racy, Leeann's close friends, sat in folding chairs next to Missy, along with their husbands, while Gina and Justin Dillon were beside him.

Family and friends, gathered together. Just as it should be. And somehow it felt right having Missy here with him.

Bobby and Leeann had seats on the opposite side of the fire pit with Dean Zippenella and Priscilla Lennox next to them, but at the moment Bobby's best friend, Dean, was chasing after a couple of four-legged guests. The camp's official mascots were dogs that belonged to Dean and Priscilla, who'd come to town this past summer to help with fund-raising for the camp. Last month's bachelor auction had been Priscilla's idea.

The funds raised that night hadn't been substantial, less than five thousand dollars, and a good chunk of that had been from Priscilla bidding two grand to win a date with Dean. She'd been competing with her own sister, no less. The important thing was the event had brought the town together to support the camp—and had brought Dean and Priscilla together, too, as they were now living in Dean's log home along with their pups.

In fact, Liam noticed all the couples here tonight were married, except for Dean and Priscilla.

And him and Missy.

Leaning forward, he propped his elbows on his knees and poked at the fire with a long stick, sending a shower of fiery sparks into the air. He looked at Missy, enjoying the view of her profile and how her hair and skin glowed in the firelight as she talked with Maggie and Landon. He wondered if she too had noticed how everyone sat boy-girl-boy-girl around the fire. It hadn't started out that way.

When they'd first arrived, Leeann had taken her on a quick tour of the camp, most of the ladies tagging along while the men argued good-naturally over the best way to get the fire going. But once everyone gathered at the fire pit, they naturally paired off and Missy had come to sit beside him, accepting the cup of wine he'd poured for her and the old plaid blanket he draped across both their laps to ward off the night's chill.

"Hey, how about some music?" Racy asked. "I bullied Gage into bringing his guitar, as he only seems to serenade our babies nowadays."

"That's not true," Gage protested with a wide grin, reaching for the instrument stowed beneath his chair. "I sang you an Elvis tune in the shower just this morning."

"Which I had to listen to over the baby monitor while changing a pair of stinky diapers. So romantic!"

Everyone laughed as Dean and Priscilla came back to join them, along with their worn-out pups, a wiry terrier mutt and a Chihuahua wearing a bright red sweater, both of whom curled up beneath their chairs.

Liam set aside the stick to grab his own guitar, glad he'd thought to bring it along as well. But doing so had his thoughts turning to Casey.

Maybe getting her enrolled at the local high school hadn't been his best idea. He'd wanted her to have fun during her stay and get to know some people her own age, and yeah, he'd hoped for some alone time with Missy.

That hadn't worked out so well due to one work crisis after another, until tonight, but even that was only because Casey was out on a date.

With a boy.

Correction, with a group, much like the crowd here, but had those kids paired off as easily as the adults? What exactly was going on at the drive-in?

If personal experience served, he knew exactly what was going on.

Damn. He rubbed at his chest.

The heaviness that had settled there as he'd watched that boy's pickup truck drive off now seemed to have doubled in weight. It wasn't painful, but definitely unfamiliar.

He wasn't used to...well, worrying about someone.

He had a normal concern for his folks, especially when they took off on one of their cross-country adventures in their tricked-out RV, and caring about his brothers and their families was as natural to him as breathing, but this wasn't the same.

Not nearly the same.

"I'm glad you brought your guitar, too." Missy gave his knee a nudge with her own beneath the blanket. "It'd be nice to hear you sing again."

Liam grinned, her words pulling him from his thoughts. "I'm afraid I'm not much better than I was years ago. Which we both know wasn't that good."

"You were great with Casey."

"That was all her. I just tried to keep up."

"Your daughter plays?" Racy asked, and when Missy nodded, she continued, "I guess she gets that from Liam, huh?"

"Yes, she does," Missy said. "My creativity begins and

ends with my design work, I fear. I have zero talent when it comes to music."

Liam managed to keep his gaze on Gage, joining in when the man started strumming a classic Johnny Cash tune, but inside he was bursting with pride at Missy's words.

Not just over the connection she'd made between him and Casey, but the ease with which she'd spoken about their daughter. He'd figured there'd be questions. Missy had told him the ladies had asked about Casey when they first arrived. Nothing invasive, just a natural curiosity over an unusual situation, especially for a town the size of Destiny.

They'd somehow managed to keep the whole truth from everyone, including his family. Things were going well and the last thing he wanted was any upheaval when he was making so much headway with Casey and Missy.

The sound of applause yanked Liam from his thoughts and he found the first song was over. The sheriff gave him a quick nod that meant it was his turn to pick the next one. He went with another classic, this time one from the Fab Four, earning a big smile from Missy, who joined in as they sang about welcoming the sun after a long winter. After that they went through a half dozen tunes until he and Gage begged off, insisting they needed some liquid refreshment.

"I was wondering something," Missy said to Liam after he refilled her cup. "How did the camp get its name?"

"Ask those two." Liam pointed across the fire as he called out to Bobby, "Hey, Missy wants to know about Camp Diamond's name."

"It's all Leeann's fault," Bobby said.

"It is not!" Leeann protested. "Who told you to toss it in the lake?"

Bobby barked out a quick laugh and then turned sober.

"Okay, that was all me. It's amazing to hear us joke about it now. You see, I'd asked Leeann to marry me during our senior year."

"Really?" Missy looked surprised. "I don't remember that."

"We tried to keep it a secret. Our parents weren't happy about us being together back then," Leeann said. "But just before graduation I panicked and broke things off. I gave the ring back—"

Bobby cut her off. "More like chucked it at my head. But she's right, I was the one who heaved the ring into the lake on my way out of town. It wasn't much, barely a chip, but after that, I always called this place Diamond Lake."

"And the ring is still down there?"

Leeann nodded. "As far as we know. After Bobby told me what he'd done all those years ago, I gave him the lake, and the land around it, for the camp. Before I even knew if he'd decided to go ahead with building it."

"What a wonderful story."

"Yeah, just not one we share around the fire with the campers," Bobby added, with a grin. "No need to give them any ideas."

"Well, you've done good here, Winslow," Liam said to his friend. "This camp was just what the town needed."

Everyone joined in while Bobby tried to wave off the praise. Then he placed a hand over Leeann's rounded belly and cradled her on his lap. "If it wasn't for the love of my life coming back *into* my life, none of this would have happened."

"Let's hear it for the ladies," Justin Dillon said, coming up behind Gina, wrapping one arm around his wife's waist while raising his beer in the air with the other. "If it wasn't for them, we'd all be lost and lonely bums."

Everyone joined in on the toast and then Gina said,

"Looks like the town is going to have one less bum running around. Or one less bachelor."

Liam wasn't sure what she meant, until Landon pointed toward the water's edge in time for everyone to watch Dean drop to one knee before what appeared to be a very surprised Priscilla.

Moments later, she was in his arms with Dean shouting at them, "She said yes!"

There were more cheers, congratulatory hugs and handshakes when the couple returned to the fire and Priscilla showed off a large diamond solitaire on her finger. Liam placed a quick kiss on her cheek and then shook Dean's hand, offering his best wishes.

"I thought they'd only just met."

Missy's words were quiet, meant only for his ears as Liam returned to the bench and sat next to her.

"Priscilla came to town just after July Fourth, so yeah, it's only been a couple of months." He turned to her, threading his fingers through hers, noticing how warm, how right, it felt to hold her hand. "When it's the right person, why wait?"

The party broke up an hour later. Liam glanced at the clock on the dashboard as he drove back to the ranch. It was almost eleven thirty. Missy hadn't said anything, but he guessed she wanted to be home before Casey got back from her date.

Hell, he wanted to be there as well to make sure their daughter arrived home safely.

On the other hand, he hated to see this night end.

Being with Missy tonight was like old times. Familiar, comfortable. But at the same time a thread of a new awareness, a new excitement, coursed through him every time he looked at her. Touched her. When she'd rested her head against his shoulder and looked up at him with a riot of emotions reflected in her eyes, he'd almost said the words aloud.

She was the first girl he'd fallen in love with. She was a woman he desperately wanted now in his bed. In his home. In his life in every way possible.

She was breaking his heart all over again.

Not really, not yet, but tonight made him realize his time with her and Casey was quickly coming to an end. Or was it? He had to admit the crazy idea of the two of them making the move to Destiny a permanent one had been gaining traction for the last week.

He just wasn't sure how to make the suggestion, how Missy would react or if she was even battling the same needs and wants as he was.

"You made a comment back at the fire tonight that has me wondering about something."

Missy's quiet words filled the silence of the SUV, and he immediately started to mentally backtrack.

They'd talked about a lot of things. Memories from high school. How the town had changed over the years. The bachelor auction. Liam had made it clear his date had ended with nothing more than a simple kiss—

"When you said time didn't matter. Is that what you felt before?"

Okay, he was totally lost. "Before?"

"When you proposed? I guess you believed those women were right for you…at the time."

Her question floored him. They hadn't talked about his previous marriages at all after the first night she'd arrived. And it wasn't exactly a topic he wanted to bring up now, but since she'd asked, he said, "I honestly don't remember. The first time was a crazy, stupid, alcohol-laced quickie in Vegas. I figured out not long afterward how unfair our marriage was…to her and to me."

"Unfair?"

He glanced at her. "I was trying to get over losing you. And failing miserably."

She gasped softly and the glow from the dashboard allowed him to see her press her fingers to her lips.

He focused again on the road as he turned onto the lane that led to the compound. "When I decided to marry for the second time," he continued, "it was right out of college. Nicole and I had dated for a couple of years, so marriage seemed like the next step after we graduated."

"What happened?"

"After a year we finally admitted we wanted different things." Pulling into his usual parking spot, he turned off the engine and cut the lights, his hands gripping hard at the steering wheel. "She hated the fact that I chose to stay in Destiny and work for the family business. She wanted bigger and better things. So she left to find them."

Making him a loser twice over. Three times, actually, counting Missy.

He dropped his hands, curling his keys into his fist as silence again stretched between them. For such an intimate setting, it felt as if she was now farther away from him than just the next seat.

Almost as if there was an ocean between them.

"And you never found the right person after that?"

The dull ache in the center of his chest returned, but he refused to acknowledge it, no matter how desperately he wanted to rub the pain away.

"Nope. There was no need." He opened his door. "I'd already found the right girl, but I wasn't smart enough to hold onto her."

He got out of the truck before she had the chance to say anything.

By the time he made it around the back end to Missy's door, she was already standing outside. She remained silent as they started walking along the pathway through the yard, passing by the gazebo.

"It's still so bright out here," she said. "Shouldn't most of the accent lighting be off by this time?"

After what he'd said to her back at the truck, this was what she wanted to talk about?

Liam sighed. Not that he was interested in talking anymore tonight. No, what he wanted to do was grab her, pull her into his arms and find other uses for that pretty mouth of hers. Find out if his feelings were all one-sided, or if she was trying to sort through some crazy emotions as well.

He shoved his hands in his pockets to keep from doing what he desired. "I overrode the shutdown remotely from my phone while we were out."

"Why…oh." She looked at him, her lips pursed as if she was attempting to hold back a smile. Or blow him a kiss. "You didn't want Casey to be alone in the dark with her date."

"Damn right I didn't."

Her soft laughter rippled over his skin like caressing fingers. "You know, she might be home already."

Liam looked up as they approached the boathouse; the apartment was still dark except for a small glow from the living area. "Are you kidding? If she's anything like we were, she'll push the curfew right up to the last minute."

"Well, since there's plenty of light out here, you don't have to see me back to the flat."

They stepped onto the path that led along the side of the boathouse, the shadows darker and deeper here. "A gentleman always sees his date to her door."

"And you're a gentleman?"

"I'm trying my best."

She stopped, her touch warm on his already heated skin. "What if I don't want you to be?"

Hoping he was reading her words correctly, he gave in to the need raging in him. He stopped too and reached for her, one hand landing on the small of her back, anchoring her against him. He cupped her head with his other hand, his fingers digging into the soft strands of her hair, holding her in place as his mouth came down on hers.

A spike of heat started low in his gut. A moan escaped Missy's lips as she parted to accept his kiss.

She grabbed at his arms, not to push him away but to hold on as they stumbled backward together, deeper into the darkness, into the corner, until the rough texture of the log wall scratched the backs of his hands.

Longing that had been building since the last time they kissed twisted in his gut. She had to feel the same, with the way she met the forceful demand of his kisses with demands of her own. He moved his hand down past her hips to cup her perfect backside. But only for a moment—then he slid them up again along the softness of her shirt until he found her breast, his thumb automatically scraping lightly across the hardened tip—

She stiffened and broke free from his mouth. "Liam, wait."

He lifted both his hands from her and moved to take a step away, but she stopped him. "No, I don't—I thought I heard—oh, my, headlights."

Liam looked over his shoulder in time to see the harsh glare, but then it was gone. Seconds later the sound of a vehicle engine being shut down and doors opening and then closing filled the air.

"It's Casey," Missy's words came out in a whisper. "She's home!"

And she wasn't alone. Liam could hear his daughter's sweet laughter, and unintelligible words in a lower, masculine tone. They were headed this way, cutting through the yard on the far side of Nolan's place, taking the most direct route to the boathouse.

Meaning they would be here any minute.

He grabbed Missy's hand. "Come on."

"What—"

Yanking open a nearby door, he stepped inside the small space, pulling her behind him. "In here."

"Where are we?" she whispered.

"The outdoor shower." The door gently bumped closed behind them and Liam receded as far as he could, until he felt the cold metal pipes and fixtures pressed against his back. Missy followed, her backside against his front. He tightened his hands on her waist, biting back a groan at how perfectly she fit there.

"Liam, we shouldn't…" She leaned her head back into his chest, her words still a low whisper.

"Shh, they're right outside." He dipped his head, his mouth at her ear.

Moments later, they clearly heard two sets of footsteps as Casey and Nathan walked past them.

"You know, you don't have to walk me all the way to the flat," Casey said, sounding just like her mother a few minutes ago.

"Sure I do," Nathan replied. "My dad taught me I should always make sure my date gets safely home."

Missy looked over her shoulder at him and smiled.

Yeah, okay. The kid got points for that.

"That's sweet, but I'm sure my mum is waiting up for

me. I can go from here. The last thing you'd want is to be…" Casey's voice faded as they continued walking.

Although Liam could hear a deep chuckle that had to be Nathan's, they were too far away now for him to hear what they were saying. Setting Missy aside, he stepped toward the door, easing it open a crack. Just enough to—

"What are you doing?" She hissed in his ear. "Spying on them?"

"Yes."

She rolled her eyes, but then moved in front of him again, crouching a bit so both of them could look at what was happening out there.

Liam spotted his daughter and her date standing in a pool of light at the far end of the boathouse. It was a familiar scene, as if he was seeing himself and Missy, just like that, years ago. Needing to say good-night, but not wanting the night to end. Neither of them sure of what the next move should be.

Nathan stood with his thumbs tucked into his back pockets, Casey rocking up on her toes a bit. Their voices were too soft to hear. Then, all at once, Casey placed her hands lightly on her date's shoulders and reached up, giving him a kiss on the lips that lasted far longer than Liam liked before she spun away, her footsteps echoing on the stairs that led up to the apartment.

The boy remained rooted to the spot for a moment. Then he shook his head and headed back toward them. Liam wasn't sure he liked the goofy grin on Nathan's face, but he allowed the door to shut again when the kid got close, staying perfectly still until he heard the sound of the boy's truck starting up and leaving the parking lot.

"That was sweet," Missy said.

That was close.

Their daughter had almost found her parents making out

right outside the boathouse. Then again, if he and Missy had made it up to the apartment, she might've walked in on them necking on the sofa like a couple of teen—

Liam slammed a lid on that thought, raking his fingers through his hair.

"Hey, are you all right?"

No, he was far from all right.

Liam looked down at her, surprised that his emotions had switched so fast from worrying about their daughter to wanting nothing more than to pick up where he and Missy had left off.

He wanted her in his arms, wanted his mouth, his hands, on her. Wanted her hands on him.

Missy must've been able to read the desire in his eyes, because she turned, pushed the shower door open and stepped back into the cool night air. He followed, taking her arm to stop her when she started to walk away.

She stilled, pulling from his touch, but she did turn back to face him. "I should go. Casey is probably wait-ing for me."

"And worrying?"

Missy shook her head. "I left her a note."

That surprised him. "Telling her you were out with me?"

"Telling her that you and I went to see some old friends and I would be back around the same time as she."

And she would've been if he hadn't given in to the crazy need to have this woman in his arms again. But it wasn't just him. Missy had been willing, too; she wanted that kiss as much as he did.

Why was she now acting as if nothing had happened between them?

"I want you."

She slowly lifted her gaze to his, the astonishment in her eyes cutting him.

"Please don't tell me that surprises you."

"We can't…we can't let the past—*our* past—affect our lives now."

"Why not?" he demanded.

She took a step back, pulled in a quick breath and squared her shoulders, her posture perfectly ballerina straight now. "I've already told you, I'm here because of Casey, to give her a chance to get to know you and your family."

"Do you really believe that? You were the one who put out an obvious invite a few minutes ago. Now you're giving me mixed signals."

"I'm sorry. I shouldn't—we shouldn't have—"

"Oh, yeah, we should." He stepped closer. "Are you going to hide behind Casey and deny you still have feelings for me?"

"Of course I have feelings for you. How could I not?" Missy's response came in a cool, distant tone, despite how much her admission surprised him. "But this trip isn't about me, about us. It never was. The last thing I'm going to do is to let myself think, to dream… I did that once and I got my heart crushed. I won't do it again. Not even for you."

"Missy, I would never—"

"Please…don't." She moved back again, holding out a hand this time to ward him off from following her. "Please don't make a promise we both know you can't—that neither of us can keep."

Chapter Eleven

Liam stared at the envelope in his hand, his heart beating so loudly in his chest he was certain it could be heard even here on the sidewalk outside Destiny's medical clinic on a busy Friday afternoon.

"I was about to head out to your place when I saw you drive by." Dr. Ronald Cody, the only full-time physician they had in Destiny, looked more like a cowboy in his worn leather boots and white Stetson instead of a stethoscope and a white jacket.

Dr. Cody had just flagged Liam down as he drove along East Main Street. When Liam had first seen the doctor waving at him, he'd feared the worst. That something had happened to someone in the family—to Missy or Casey—while he'd been on a return flight from a two-day business trip in Denver.

He'd hated leaving on Wednesday, but he hadn't been able to reschedule the meeting. The crazy idea of asking

Missy to come with him had crossed his mind during one of his many sleepless nights since their date, but he knew she'd never agree to go.

Hell, they'd barely spoken to each other in the last week.

Short of coming right out and demanding time with her, he couldn't get her alone so they could continue their unfinished conversation about the two of them.

At least it was unfinished on his end.

Missy had that British stiff-upper-lip thing so down pat no one else seemed to notice how she was being aloof, even when it was just him, her and Casey.

Not that there'd been many of those times recently.

His fingers tightened around the envelope, remembering the fleeting glimpses of confusion he'd seen in Missy's eyes over the last few days when she thought no one was looking.

And he'd put them there. His fault. He hated that and they needed to talk—

"Liam?" The doctor's voice cut off the memory. "You okay?"

"Yes, I'm fine, and thank you." Forcing a smile, Liam relaxed his grip and held out his other hand. "For getting this back to me."

"I'm sorry it took so long, but a computer glitch caused quite a backup at the lab." The doctor returned his handshake. "I'm sure you want to open that somewhere more private. It's pretty self-explanatory, but if you need to talk, just call the office."

Somewhere more private.

An image popped into Liam's head, so clear it was like looking at a photograph. Him, Missy and Casey. Yeah, as much as he wanted to get Missy alone, he wanted even more to share this moment with their daughter, too.

Especially because of what he planned on *not* doing.

Heading back to his truck, he checked his watch. There was still time to make a few stops. The grocery store, the butcher shop. And he'd swing into Fay's to grab a bouquet of flowers before heading home.

But he was going to need some help, and he knew exactly whom to ask.

He pulled out his cell phone as he slipped behind the wheel. "Hey, Mom," he said after the call went through. "Yeah, I'm back in town, but keep that to yourself, okay? And I need a favor."

Less than an hour later, he arrived at the house, surprised at finding a group of all-terrain vehicles sitting in the parking lot, one with a trailer attached to the back.

After exiting his vehicle, he grabbed his bags from the backseat as Nolan came around the side of his house, the twins with him, their arms loaded with boxes, a couple of axes and sleeping bags.

"You're back. How did the meeting go?" Nolan asked.

"As expected. The deal is closed." Liam joined his brother and nephews at the three-wheelers. "What's going on here?"

"The boys and I are going to winterize the north cabin this weekend." Nolan secured a crate he'd been carrying in the trailer. "Lay in supplies, chop a few cords of wood, the usual."

Liam nodded. He'd forgotten that was this weekend. The cabin was used year-round, as it was situated right in the center of their woodland acreage. With only one bedroom, it was small, but bunk racks in the main living space allowed for up to six people to stay there as long as they didn't mind roughing it. Other than a small generator, the place was pretty much off the grid when it came to modern amenities.

Because of the cabin's remote location, ATVs and horseback were the only ways to get there. In the past, at least two of the Murphy brothers had gone, Devlin usually being one. Of course, he was in England now. Getting Bryant away from his pregnant wife was probably going to be a tough sell. That left Liam or Adam.

"Hey, you aren't looking for company, are you?" Liam asked.

Nolan grinned. "Why? You want to get out of that suit and rough it for the next couple of days?"

Not really. "Ah—"

"Don't worry, I think I've got all the company I need," his brother said, slanting his head in the direction of the twins. "It's about time these Muggles earned their keep."

"Well, have a good time."

Liam started for his place, thinking he should get the steaks he bought into the refrigerator when the sight of Casey and Missy heading his way stopped him. They were talking and neither saw him standing there, but the same duffel bag Casey had had with her the day they met was slung over one shoulder.

"Oh, hey, you're back." The smile that lit up Casey's face when she spotted him pierced straight through the envelope tucked away in his inside jacket pocket and smacked him right in the heart. "I was hoping I'd see you before I left."

He glanced over his shoulder at the ATVs again, counting the vehicles parked there. Yeah, her plans weren't hard to figure out, and there went his.

"Left?" he asked anyway, hoping he might be wrong.

"Just for the weekend." This came from Abby, who skipped down the steps from her house, a similar bag over her shoulder and another in her arms. "We're still lucky enough to have her company for another ten days. What fun!"

Liam caught his niece's bright smile from the corner of his eye as she walked past, but his gaze was on Casey, who turned her back to her cousin and rolled her eyes. "Did I mention she's started a countdown?"

"Are you sure you want to go?" Missy asked.

"Of course. I'm not going to let some nippy—" Casey glanced his way and snapped her mouth closed for a moment before she sighed. "I never should've told her that you got our tickets. She caught me in a moment of weakness after tipping me off about Nat—the jerk who shall be nameless. Besides, I want to drive that ATV again."

"With a helmet," Missy added.

Again with the eye roll. "Of course."

"Wait a minute," Liam said, feeling the need to catch up as Casey switched from topic to topic. "What is Abby counting down to, what tickets are you talking about and why is Nathan now a jerk? Did he try anything with you—"

"Ah, look at the flowers. Yellow roses, nice." Casey cut him off, placing a hand on his arm as she pushed up on her toes and peeked into the top of the grocery bag he carried. "Crikey, you got a bunch there. Planning something special?"

Liam tried hard to keep up with his daughter. "Actually, I was hoping to cook dinner for you and your mother tonight."

"That's sweet. I didn't know you cooked."

"I can manage a barbecue grill as well as the next guy."

Casey's gaze flew from him to her mother and then to where Nolan and his kids were milling around the three-wheelers. "Well, I guess I could cancel my plans…"

Her voice trailed off, but he could see how much she wanted to go to the cabin. It meant a lot to him that she'd offered to stick around. They'd had a great time last weekend when he taught her how to ride the all-terrain vehicles his family kept at the compound. He didn't want to be responsible for her missing the chance to ride again.

The test results could wait. He'd already accepted the truth.

"No, don't do that." Liam said. "We can do this another night."

"You sure?" Casey asked.

"Very sure." He grabbed one of the bundles of roses from the bag and presented it to her. "Here, something to decorate the cabin."

"Cool!"

"And please, do what your mother said. Wear all of your protective gear while driving and listen to—"

"Yeah, I know. Do everything Uncle Nolan says, stay on the trails and no going over the designated speed limit." Casey buried her nose in the flowers for a moment, and then gave him another big smile. "You know, you should still cook for my mum. She got some great news today!"

Liam enjoyed the pink blush on Missy's cheeks. Maybe his plans for the evening weren't a total bust after all. "Really? What's that?"

"Oh, it's nothing." Missy shook her head. "Just something related to my clothing line."

"Hey, finding out Princess Kate purchased one of your formal frocks isn't nothing," Casey said, caressing one of the rosebuds. "Can you imagine what's going to happen when the future queen shows up at some high-society fling in a Melissa Ellington original? Your sales are going to go through the roof!"

"I agree with Casey. That sounds like a pretty big deal." Liam grinned at Missy, happy when she returned his smile. "And a perfect reason for us to celebrate."

She almost hadn't come.

Foolish as that seemed now, walking along the pathway

from the boathouse to his place in the soft, diffused twilight, Missy had been tempted to call Liam and tell him getting together was not a good idea.

Especially after his mother had made a big deal about her, Alistair, Bryant and Laurie going out tonight for dinner and a show in Cheyenne. With Nolan and the kids gone, that meant she and Liam were the only ones in the compound.

A fact that made it clear why canceling their plans would have been the right thing to do. For her. For him. For everyone.

But she couldn't do it.

Tired of debating with herself when deep inside she'd already accepted the fact she wanted to be with him tonight, she'd taken a quick shower and then slipped into a simple top, a long, flowing skirt that reached her ankles and a pair of flats. She'd studied her reflection in the mirror after applying her makeup, and thought about leaving her hair loose, but ended up putting it in the familiar chignon style she normally wore.

Yes, normal was what she was going for.

Tonight was just another normal night. Dinner with a man who just happened to be the father of her child…and the only man she'd ever loved.

Past tense, of course.

"Oh, you're a bloody liar," she whispered, her words floating on the cool night air. "Why can't you just admit what you want?"

Lifting the hem of her skirt to keep from tripping, she took the stairs to Liam's front porch. A quick intake of breath and she knocked before she could think about it.

Nothing. She knocked again and thought she heard him call out her name. She opened the door and peeked inside. "Liam?"

"Yeah, come on in. I'm—" A loud clanging filled the air. "Damn! I'm back in the kitchen."

Stepping inside the front foyer, Missy closed the door behind her, the sight of bright yellow roses in a vase on the entry table making her smile.

She'd only been inside Liam's home once before, when he'd given her and Casey a tour one afternoon, but she remembered the kitchen ran along the back of the log house. There was a wide timber stairway directly in front of her that led to the second floor, and his office and an empty guest room were on the right. She turned left and walked into the living room.

A fire was already lit in the fireplace, reflecting off the leather furniture arranged in front of the stone hearth. She headed for the dining area that opened into the oversize kitchen, noticing the large table was beautifully set at one end with matching place mats, cloth napkins, sparkling dishes, tapered candles, an open bottle of wine and more of those beautiful roses.

And the distinct odor of something…burning?

"Liam? Is everything okay?"

He slammed the lids on a couple of stainless steel pots and spun around from the stove, looking adorable with a dishcloth tucked into the waistband of his jeans as a makeshift apron. "Define okay?"

She moved to the counter that separated the two spaces, noticing how his dark hair stood in spiky tufts, as if he'd run his hands through it a few times. His white T-shirt hugged his muscular chest nicely, highlighting the dark shadow of his tattoo and the splattering of multicolored food stains across the front.

"Is that our dinner I smell?" she asked.

"If it smells like burned rubber, then, yeah, I guess it is."

"It's not that bad," she said, noticing that the two sets

of French doors that led out to the rear deck were open, along with the windows over the sink, allowing the night air to clear out the kitchen. "Can I do anything to help?"

"Yeah, pour us a glass of wine. I need it." He grabbed a wooden spoon and turned back to the stove.

Missy tried to hide her smile as she did what he asked, but the furrow of his brow made it hard to resist as she joined him again, two glasses of wine in her hands. "Here."

He reached for one, and then paused and wiped his hands across the towel at his front before taking it from her. "Thanks, I really need this."

"I can see that." She started to check one of the pots, but his fingers, warm and firm, landed on hers before she could lift the lid. "What's in here?"

He took a large gulp. "Burned rice."

She slid from his touch and this time only pointed at a second pot. "And that?"

"Broccoli." His tone was unforgiving. "Also burned."

She didn't ask about the third pan. A quick sniff spoke of extra-crispy carrots, and not in a good way. "Please tell me you haven't gotten the steaks on the grill yet."

His sharp gaze swung to her, but then a moment later humor replaced the hardness in his cool blue eyes and he grinned. "No, not yet."

"Well, thank goodness for that."

Liam sighed and looked again at the mess on the stove. "I don't know what happened. I came home, put the groceries away, grabbed a quick shower and then started getting things ready."

The smoothness of his jaw told her he'd shaved again as well. The familiar scent of his woodsy cologne made it through the lingering kitchen odors to tickle her nose and dredge up old memories.

Taking a step back, she sipped from her wine. "So, what happened? Trying to do too many dishes at once?"

"No, I think I was distracted."

Missy looked around the kitchen. "By what?"

"The thought of you and me. Alone. In my house."

His words brought her gaze back to his, and the intensity of his look made her fingers tighten around her glass.

"I kept waiting for my phone to ring," he finally said. "For you to back out on dinner."

She closed her eyes, nibbling on her bottom lip to stop herself from confirming his suspicions.

"I'm really glad you didn't."

His words were soft, but she could hear them clearly, feel the warmth of them on her face, telling her he'd closed the distance between them.

She opened her eyes to find him right in front of her. "I'm glad I didn't, too."

He grinned and she noticed a smudge of something—mashed carrots, maybe—on one cheek. "So, I guess I should get back to figuring out what we're going to eat tonight."

She had a better idea. "How about we get a little teamwork going?"

"What do you mean?"

"Do you have the makings for a salad? Maybe a couple of potatoes?"

He nodded. "In the fridge."

"Why don't you get cleaned up?" Unable to resist, she brushed the small orange blotch from his face with the tip of her finger. "And then you can concentrate on the steaks. I'll see what I can do about side dishes."

He grabbed her hand, brought it to his mouth and placed a kiss at her wrist. "Don't touch anything. I clean up my own messes."

Her breath caught, rendering her speechless. All she could do was nod and tug her hand free, oddly disappointed when he let her go.

"I'll be right back."

"I'll be here."

An hour later they sat at the dining room table, lingering over what had turned out to be a great meal. Liam was now wearing a pale blue button-down shirt hanging loose over his hips with the sleeves rolled back, but was still in jeans and barefoot.

He'd proved to be as skilled at manning a barbecue as he'd claimed; the steaks were perfect. The simple garden salad and grilled potatoes she'd whipped up while he'd filled the dishwasher with the remnants of his culinary disasters had been good complements, if she did say so herself.

Their conversation while they ate had been easy. She'd shown him the text from Casey letting her know they'd arrived at the cabin. He'd told her about getting a call from Nolan and then shared funny stories about trips to the cabin over the years with his brothers and friends.

He'd then told her about his successful meeting in Denver with a well-known political figure they were going to build a home for. She had in turn confessed her joy over a member of the royal family buying one of her designs and what it might mean to her business.

Now as they sat here after dinner, he asked about the tickets Casey had mentioned earlier, a shadow passing over his eyes when Missy told him that their return flight to London was all set for a week from Monday.

Then the subject turned to Casey and Nathan. Missy relayed why their daughter now considered the lad a jerk—

apparently she'd caught him kissing someone else, a former girlfriend who'd moved back to Destiny just this week.

"And it was Abby who warned Casey to this kid's two-timing?" Liam asked.

Missy nodded. "Apparently she pointed out the two mid-kiss to Casey during the school day, which does surprise me, as the two of them haven't actually gotten along too well during our stay."

"Yeah, I noticed her attitude a few times, but then again, Abby's always been…opinionated."

Spoiled was more like it, but Missy kept silent about that assessment. Casey had made it clear from the beginning she'd wanted to find her own way when it came to her cousin.

And now they only had ten days left in their visit.

Then what? Surely Liam would want to continue the relationship he'd forged with their daughter. Would he expect Casey to fly to Destiny for her school breaks? What about next summer? Would he want her here the whole time?

Missy had never been apart from her daughter for more than a few weeks, and knowing Casey would be here in Destiny with Liam while Missy was back in England would be a tough pill to swallow.

"Hey, where'd you go?"

She blinked, his words causing the empty plate in front of her to come back into focus. "Oh, sorry. I got lost there for a moment." She looked at him now, hoping her smile appeared easier than it felt. "I blame the wine."

He reached for the bottle of merlot, the second one they'd opened, and filled her almost empty glass again. "No sense in letting it go to waste."

"It's a good thing neither one of us has to drive home."

His hand stilled for a moment before he emptied the remains of the bottle into his own glass. "Yes, a good thing.

Just like this dinner. Thank you for rescuing me from my cooking calamity tonight."

"I'd like to think tonight was a joint effort."

Liam smiled and lifted his glass. "Here's to working well together."

Missy lifted hers and they gently clinked them before each took another sip.

"Why don't you go and enjoy the rest of your wine in front of the fire," Liam said, "while I clean up in here."

"You don't want help?"

He got to his feet, shaking his head. "I'm going to let the dishes soak in the sink. I'll join you in a minute."

Missy rose as well, automatically reaching for her plate, but Liam got there first. She returned his smile and headed for the living room, taking her glass with her.

Walking around the room, she let her fingers trail over the soft leather of the love seat before settling on the matching couch. She noticed that like the rest of the house, this room was beautifully put together. The furniture, lamps and art worked well together, masculine in style with rich earth-tone colors that fit Liam's personality and the ruggedness of the log home. Still, the place needed a hint of something soft as well as brightening—

"Hey, you're frowning," Liam said, coming in from the kitchen. "What are you thinking so hard about?"

She offered another smile. "Your place. It's lovely."

"You can thank my mom and Katie. It was only finished this summer, and I was so busy I gave them free rein when it came to getting the main rooms done." He joined her on the couch. "But your frown tells me your designer's eye has found something wrong."

"Not wrong," she said, looking around again. "But a few things might make it more personal. More you."

"Like what?"

"Maybe a cerulean-blue cashmere throw, some golden sandstone-colored pillows, a plant or two." The list rolled off her tongue as she easily pictured the items in selected spots. "A favorite book or two for the tables and a few family photos…"

Her voice faded when her gaze caught on the grouping of simple black frames centered on the fireplace mantel.

Unable to stop herself, she placed her glass on the large square coffee table and rose, drawn by the photographs of her and Casey. And Liam.

One was of him and Casey, smiling, heads tucked in close, their faces filling the frame. Another was of her and Casey sitting next to each other on the dock, talking, their feet dangling in the lake.

There was Casey playing the guitar, not even aware of the picture being taken, and the smallest frame held an old black-and-white photo of Missy and Liam taken years ago. Dirty from a rodeo competition, Liam stood, grinning, a trophy held aloft in one arm while the other was wrapped around her, holding her close to his side. Her head was tipped back at she stared at him in utter adulation.

"When did you—how did you—"

The fact that he had photographs of her—of all of them—so prominently displayed threatened to take her strength. She grabbed onto the mantel. How had she missed seeing these when she'd first walked in tonight and just now, as she'd analyzed the decor of this room?

"Hey, are you okay?" He left the couch and stood in front of her, one hand touching her shoulder. "Missy?"

She shook her head, gulped in a deep breath and somehow found her voice. "I'm sorry. These—the pictures surprised me, that's all. When did you do this?"

"Just last week." He reached for the frame that held the image of him and Casey. "She took this one of us on Sunday morning and sent it to me. I printed it out, and later that day—I think you were in the kitchen or something—she helped me pick out the others, and we found a few frames in the main house for them."

"And this one?"

Liam put the first frame back in its place. His mouth softened, his lips hiking at one corner as he reached for the old photograph of the two of them. "Casey spotted this when I showed her our old senior yearbook. I remembered how I snuck into the graphic arts room at the high school and *acquired* the actual photograph after you and I had... well, the September after you returned home."

His story surprised her. "You did?"

"Took me a couple of days of searching through my old stuff to find it. I thought I'd give it to Casey. She got such a kick out of seeing us as teenagers."

Trying desperately not to get caught up in a haze of memories from years past mixed with the moments they'd spent together over the last weeks, Missy took a step back. Then another, needing space between her and Liam before she did something stupid.

Like throw herself into his arms.

She blinked away the image, noticing for the first time the long envelope tucked in behind the picture frames, the return address for the genetic testing center in the upper corner.

"What is that?"

Liam returned the picture to the mantel and retrieved the envelope. "*This* is the reason I asked you and Casey to dinner tonight."

"The DNA results?"

He nodded.

"But it's not opened."

"Nope."

Understanding dawned. "You were planning to open it tonight, while the three of us were here together."

This time he shook his head, his gaze on the packet as he turned it over repeatedly in his hands. "No, actually I planned to toss it into the fire."

She gasped. "What?"

"I don't need to see in black and white what I know in my heart—what I've known from the moment she told me—to be true." He looked at Missy then, genuine certainty in his blue eyes. "She is a part of me, a part of us. Casey is my daughter."

A warmth that had nothing to do with the fire radiated throughout Missy's body. A sharp sting soon had her vision wavering and she had to close her eyes, but a tear escaped anyway.

"Hey, what's this for?" Liam whispered, his hand cupping her cheek, his thumb brushing the moisture away.

"That's—" her voice broke and she had to swallow hard before she could continue "—the first time you've said that."

"Huh?"

She opened her eyes, her smile wobbly as she took in his puzzled expression. "Tonight, right now, is the first time you've actually said Casey is your daughter."

"No."

Missy nodded. "At least to me, and you've never said it directly to Casey. Believe me, she's been waiting."

This time it was Liam who closed his eyes, dropping his hand from Missy's face as he turned away. "Are you kidding me? Damn, could I be any more stupid?"

"Hey, you're not—"

"I could've sworn I've told her." He cut her off and pressed his fist with the crumbled results against his chest.

"I know it in my head. I feel it in my heart. I have from the beginning."

She believed him. She could see it on his face, hear it in his words, and her own doubts about him accepting her story as the truth released their last hold on her. "I think when you insisted on the test…"

"It was the first thing that popped into my head that night on the porch. To keep both of you here longer than a weekend." He dropped his hand, the paperwork inches from the flames. "I'm getting rid of this—"

"No!" She grabbed his wrist, stopping him. For good measure, she tugged the envelope from his fingers, pressing it to her chest as she backed up a few steps. "No, don't do that."

"Missy—"

"I know you believe." She moved back farther when he headed for her, stopping only when she felt the couch at the back of her legs. "You believe in me, believe in her, and that means everything…to both of us, but this is tangible proof. We'll need this paperwork in order to change her birth certificate."

"Change…" This time it was Liam's face that registered his shock, his voice gone as he stumbled past her and sank into the cushions. "Are you serious? You would do that? For me?"

Missy joined him, setting the test results on the table, so that she could take his hand in hers. "Casey is your daughter. Our daughter. Your name deserves to be on her birth certificate."

Chapter Twelve

Her words froze him in place, but at the same time Liam felt as if he were flying. The last thing he'd ever thought he would hear Missy say was that his name should be on Casey's birth certificate.

Would that change her last name, too?

He didn't have any idea how that worked, especially in the UK, but in this day and age, a name change was probably a separate action requiring more paperwork. Was that something Casey would be interested in?

The idea of her being a Murphy by name caused his chest to swell, but that would mean her last name and her mother's wouldn't be the same anymore. Unless Missy would consider—

"Liam?"

The way she whispered his name sent a flash of hot need racing through his veins. Then he noticed how tightly he was squeezing her hand and realized that she was just trying to get free from his grasp.

He eased his hold but didn't let go. Instead, he cradled her hand in both of his and gently rubbed her fingers. "Sorry. I didn't mean to hurt you."

"You didn't." Her lips curved in a gentle smile. "I surprised you."

The back of his throat burned, a sensation that quickly made its way upward as his eyes moistened. "I'm stunned. Flabbergasted."

She rested her free hand against his cheek. "I can see that."

Right here, right now, he wanted nothing more than to haul her into his arms. He wouldn't do it, of course. As astounded as he was over how this night was going—from the burned dinner to this startling conversation—he suddenly couldn't think about anything else other than kissing her.

Kissing her and holding her and making love with her.

The last three times they'd kissed, she'd been willing, but he'd been the one to make the first move. Even when she had practically come right out and asked him to.

This time, it had to be from her.

He could see the longing in her eyes, feel it in her touch.

Swallowing hard, he stared at her.

Please, Missy, please come to me.

She leaned forward, bringing their bodies closer, hesitating when her breasts brushed against his arm.

Forcing himself to stay completely still, he kept his gaze on her as she inched closer again, her fingers tightening around his this time. But she stopped when her lips were a hairbreadth away from his.

He didn't close his eyes as he bowed to the slight pressure of her fingers against his jaw, allowing Missy to bring his mouth to hers. Her initial kisses were cautious. As if they were kissing for the first time, both with their eyes wide-open, innocent and unsure. Her soft, sweet breath was warm against his mouth and his muscles hardened everywhere when he refused to let his body do what it wanted.

She pressed her mouth to his more firmly, and then he felt the tip of her tongue trace the edge of his bottom lip. A low growl escaped his throat. Her eyelids closed, but not before he saw the victorious flash in those blue depths.

He tunneled his fingers into her hair, tipping her head back as he claimed her, opening his mouth to welcome her in.

Releasing him, she grabbed at his shoulders as he pulled her onto his lap and sank back into the leather cushions, their kisses growing hotter, wetter and frantic.

It wasn't enough. Wasn't nearly enough.

Both hands at her waist now, he lifted her while stretching out completely on the oversize couch, fitting her perfectly against his body as she blanketed him.

"Oh!" she cried out as their mouths broke free and her hands landed on either side of his head.

"It's okay. I've got you," he whispered against her neck, before she drew back to look down at him. "I mean…is this okay?"

Her smile was like a liquid arrow straight to the part of him nestled against her. "It's very okay."

Two soft thuds caught his attention for a moment, but then the cool touch of her toes tangling with his bare feet felt as intimate as if they were lying here totally naked.

Which wasn't a bad idea. But for now, he wanted her like this.

Lifting his head, he placed his lips just below her collarbone, nipping soft, wet bites as he moved south to the swell of her breasts. She rose up on her arms, scooting forward so that he could lie back down and still have her right where he needed her to be.

Her low moans filled the air as his hands reached beneath the edge of her top and traveled to the lacy cups of her bra.

He nosed the neckline off one shoulder at the same moment his hand peeled away the delicate material covering her. As he sucked her nipple into his mouth, she arched against him, rotating her pelvis as instinct took over. The heat of her melted through her skirt and his shirt, reminding him how long it'd been since he'd made love to a woman.

This woman.

No one else mattered except her.

No one ever would.

He released the tiny nub and started toward the other, but she slid down his body, crushing her mouth to him again in a rush of wild kisses. Her fingers were just as busy at the buttons on his shirt and soon she had it opened almost to his waist.

Pushing the material to one side, she released his mouth and pressed hot, openmouthed kisses down his throat and across his chest. Over his heart. She traced the outer edge of his tattoo with the tip of her tongue, leaving behind wet heat as she neared his left shoulder.

"Missy…"

"Am I hurting you?"

Yeah, she was killing him, but that's not what she was asking. "No, but you don't have to—"

"I want to."

Her words were whispered against his skin, but still, he reached for her. She grabbed his hand and pushed it up and back until it was shackled beside his head by her fingers. Breaking free of her hold would have been easy, but he let her keep him there as her mouth danced lightly over the puckered scar tissue.

He groaned, loving the feel of her lips on him there and wanting her to do the same to him everywhere. But the way she was moving against him, hip to hip now, was going to end things before they even began.

He broke free and rose up on one elbow, opening his legs wide. Capturing her between them, he squeezed. "Missy, wait."

Her kisses continued as she scooted farther down his chest. "Don't want to."

Hell, he loved hearing her say that. "I'm not going to… last. And I'd rather we continued this in a bed. My bed."

She looked up at him, her chin resting high on his stomach. Bright pink highlighted her already flushed features. "Do you remember the last time we did it in a bed?"

He chuckled at the memory and flopped back down to the couch. "You mean the only time? You lied to your host family, I lied to my folks and we snuck off to that shabby motel on the outskirts of Cheyenne the weekend before graduation."

She crawled back up his body until they were face-to-face again. "We were so nervous about getting caught."

"Yeah, until we weren't."

Nodding, she looked away, her eyes taking on a faraway expression. "You know… I was going to tell you that night. About the plans I'd made to stay in Wyoming. Go to school here."

His smile faded as he looked up at her, wanting nothing more than to tighten his arms around her. Instead, he kept his hands loose at her waist. "Why didn't you?"

"I was still waiting on the final word about getting money out of my trust. Without that, there was no way I could afford it, but I think now that was just an excuse."

She hitched her shoulders in a tiny shrug and looked back at him. "You were so excited about high school being over in a few days. The entire summer was already planned when it came to your rodeo competitions."

The hurt in her voice, even after all these years, tugged at him. He brushed a strand of her hair from her cheek. "Plans for us. Plans to be together."

"Plans for your future." She looked at him again. "I should have known something was up when I couldn't get you to talk about going to college in the fall."

"I can't say that rodeoing full-time hadn't crossed my mind. Heck, it'd been a dream since I was a kid, but I didn't want to think about packing off to college mainly because you were going to be gone by then."

Missy nodded and he could almost see her turning over his words in her head. He couldn't believe how fast they'd gone from being on the brink of making love to talking about the past.

It was the future that he was interested in, especially when it came to where they were headed tonight.

"I want you to stay," he said, "but if you'd rather not…"

Her breath hitched. "Stay?"

"Here, tonight." Didn't she understand what he was saying? "With me."

Silence stretched between them for a long moment. So long, he was convinced she was going to turn him down. But then she said, "I want that, too."

His heart raced again at her words. He wanted nothing more than to grab her and head upstairs, but first things first.

"Ah, can you give me a few minutes?" he asked.

Confusion filled her eyes. "For…"

"I wasn't expecting this. I mean, I'd hoped—okay, fantasized about you and me being together, but I didn't want to…"

"Jinx anything?" she said when his voice faded.

"Exactly. And I didn't want to presume."

He returned her smile, and gently easing her off his body, moved to the edge of the couch. "So I need to check the upstairs. Light a few candles. Make sure I don't have any dirty socks thrown around. That kind of thing. I'll be right back."

"That's what you said earlier."

He remembered. "And you said you'd be here."

"Do I have to say it again?"

Yes, she did. He wanted her promise that she wasn't going to change her mind. But deep inside, he knew if at any point she decided that being with him wasn't what she wanted, he'd let her go.

It might kill him, but he'd do it.

She cupped his face, pressing her lips to his in a quick kiss. "I'll be here."

As much as he hated to, he turned away.

Straightening took a bit of effort, considering his condition, but he headed for the kitchen. There were emergency pillar candles in the pantry. Not purchased for an occasion like this, but it was the best he could do on short notice. He grabbed a few, a couple of drinking glasses to use as holders and a box of matches.

Then he remembered the trio of vintage Old West–style oil lamps on the fireplace mantel in his room. Katie had teased him about how he'd be all set if the power ever went out or he had a lady friend stay the night.

"Not just a friend," he whispered to himself. "More like the love of your life."

He started to leave, but then turned back and grabbed the vase filled with roses off the table. Heading down the side hall by his office, he paused when he got back to the foyer, glanced into the living room and found Missy sitting up, facing the fire, wineglass in hand.

Taking the stairs two at a time, he prayed she wasn't having second thoughts.

Was she doing the right thing?

This evening had already been so amazing. Finding Liam fretting over his attempts at cooking had eased her nervousness, and just the two of them sharing a meal and talking about everyday things had felt…familiar, comfortable, with a hint of something simmering between them at the edges.

Something that exploded once she'd made it clear to him what she wanted this time. She wanted Liam. Wanted the two of them to have this night together.

Not that she would have deliberately tried to create a chance like this, despite her feelings for the man. Their lives were too different; they lived on two different continents, for goodness' sake.

But for whatever reason, events had conspired to bring them to this moment. No strings, no plans. No thoughts about anything or anyone outside the warm timbered walls of his spectacular home.

How could she walk away from this?

A single yellow rose appeared before her and she jumped when it brushed her cheek. Then she tipped her head back and found Liam standing behind her, leaning over the back of the sofa.

"I called your name. You must've been lost in thought."

"I was."

"Good thoughts, I hope." He held out his hand.

She stood up, set her empty glass on the table and

walked to him, lacing her fingers with his. "Very good thoughts."

He smiled and stepped backward into the foyer. She followed, her breath catching at the sight of rose petals scattered on the stairs. "Oh, Liam. How sweet. You didn't have to do that."

"Yeah, I did."

He pulled her into his arms and drew her close. The kiss was soft and gentle, but only for a moment. Then that hunger returned as she became aware of him, his strength and the urgency in his hold when the most intimate part of him pressed against her.

He released her but kept one of her hands in his. He started up the stairs. She kept pace, the petals cool beneath her feet. At the top, she smiled at the trail continuing down the hall and into his bedroom, where more surprises waited. A wash of candlelight filled the space. On his dresser, the bedside tables, the rough-hewn beam that served as the fireplace mantel, sat glowing lanterns and candles. Soft instrumental music came from an unseen source and rose petals decorated his king-size bed.

She flattened her hand to her chest; the wild beating of her heart matched the speed with which she blinked, fighting back tears. "Liam, this is so beautiful."

"You're beautiful." He turned her to him, taking her face in his hands, and gently kissed her lips, her cheeks, along her jaw and just below her ear. "*You* are so beautiful," he repeated, the lightest whisper into her hair. "And I'm so happy you and I are finally here, together, like this."

She reached for him, popping the last button on his shirt. Desperate to feel the heat of his skin against hers, she pushed the soft material from his shoulders, forcing him to let her go so that she could rid him of the clothing entirely. After his shirt fell to the floor, her fingers lightly danced over his skin, over the beautiful tattoo that represented the heart of this man.

Strong, determined, courageous.

She laid a hand there, barely covering the intricate tattoo, loving that his heart was pounding out a cadence that matched hers.

Looking up and finding him watching her with a slow, sexy smile set off a wave of need and desire inside her. She reached for the bottom edge of her shirt, but he gripped her hands, stopping her.

"Let me."

Lifting her hands high over her head, she kept them there as he eased off her top. Once it was gone, she lowered her arms, but he had his fingers in her hair.

"Can you please take this down?" he asked. "I love it when it's loose and flowing over your shoulders."

With the removal of a few pins, it was done. He found the simple elastic waistband of her skirt and slid it easily over her legs until it pooled at her feet, pausing to leave an openmouthed kiss on the scrap of lace that rode high on her hips before he eased her panties from her body as well.

"Hey, you've got a scar of your own." His fingers lightly traced the thin line that ran low on her abdomen.

Sending a silent thank-you for years of yoga classes, she still constricted her stomach muscles and tried not to squirm under his close inspection. "Yes, but mine's only fifteen years old."

He looked up, understanding in his eyes. "You had Casey via cesarean?"

She nodded. "I was quite a bit tinier back then, and she was just over nine pounds when she was born."

Keeping his gaze locked with hers, Liam leaned in and placed his lips over the faded blemish, leaving a trail of kisses that brought tears to her eyes.

When he dropped his head lower, his mouth and tongue loving her where she throbbed, she tunneled her fingers into his hair, holding him there as she spiraled up and out of control. When she came, she cried out.

He rose, swearing under his breath, both of them reaching behind her to unhook her bra. Their hands tangled before she brushed him away to pull the straps from her shoulders. Raw, naked desire filled his gaze, causing her breasts to tingle, her nipples to harden all over again.

He yanked her into his arms, and they were finally skin to skin, as their mouths came together in heated, devouring kisses. Grabbing at his waist, her fingers fumbled with the edge of his jeans. She managed to get the top button undone, but it wasn't enough, especially when she could feel the hard length of him pressing against her belly.

Missy gasped, tearing her mouth from his. "Jeans. Off. Now."

"Hmm, where has my proper little English lass gone?" Liam teased.

"She's right here. Wanting desperately to make love to you."

A low growl filled his chest as he stepped back, ridding himself of his jeans and boxer briefs at the same time. His body was perfection and she wanted to feel him against her desperately. She reached out to touch him, but he took her hand, bringing her around to the side of the bed. With his free hand, he yanked back the dark blue comforter, sending rose petals flying in the air, and Missy couldn't help but giggle at the sight.

Seconds later, he had her flat on her back, pinned beneath his hard body as he kissed her, his hands roaming over her, reigniting her arousal all over again. She cupped him in her hand, loving his moan as she caressed him while he, in turn, lavished attention on her breasts with his lips, his fingers slicking across the most sensitive part of her.

"Ah, you are so wet," he rasped against her throat. "Wet for me."

"Yes, thanks to you. *Liam, please...*"

He rolled away from her then, reaching for the drawer on the bedside table. She debated telling him that wasn't necessary. She was on birth control and her last steady relationship had ended three years ago. She was healthy, but she had no idea when he'd last been physically intimate with someone.

He sat back on his knees, put on the protection and then moved between her open legs. "It's been a while...since I've done this. I'm not going to last long this first time."

"It's been a while for me, too," she confessed, thrilled at his words. Then she caught what he'd said. "First time?"

"Oh, yeah." He grinned, but then his smile slipped a bit as he looked down at her, an unspoken question in his gaze.

"It's been a few years," she said.

"I don't want to hurt you."

She wrapped her hands around his waist, pulling him closer until she felt him right where she wanted him. "You won't."

Still, he went slowly, a tremble coursing over his muscles as he eased inside. She was tight, but arching her body, she opened, making room for him as she rose up to meet his kiss.

When he was finally deep inside her, he broke free from her mouth, tucking his head next to hers, his lips at her neck. "You...okay?" His words were guttural and strained.

She tightened her hold on him. "I'm wonderful."

"Ah, Missy..."

Proving it, she rocked her hips, urging him to move as well, and he did. He reached one hand beneath her, cupping her backside as he lifted her, giving her more and more, meeting her thrusts with his own until her entire body tightened and she clung to him and shattered.

He followed, repeating her name again and again as he found his own release before covering her body with his. Joy filled her. She'd gotten what she'd wanted, but everything was now changed.

She was in love. And scared to death.

So scared, Missy tiptoed around Liam's bedroom, getting dressed with the hope of not waking him after an incredible night. She hadn't planned on sleeping over, but whenever she mentioned going back to the boathouse he'd kiss her, and before she knew it they were making passionate love again.

At some point, he'd gotten out of bed, extinguished the candles and lanterns and gone downstairs to make sure the fire was out as well. He'd come back with her phone, the two-way radio and a crystal decanter of ice water and glasses, smiling indulgently as she'd checked to see if she had any text messages from their daughter, which of course she didn't.

She'd then clicked on the email button, noticing her inbox was full to bursting, but Liam had relieved her of her phone and proceeded to make her forget about anything outside the cozy confines of his bedroom, time and time again.

So thoughtful, so loving, so—

No. She had to put a stop to her crazy and out-of-control emotions before she started to believe what she felt meant anything.

It didn't. It couldn't.

The last month had been a world of make-believe for her and for Casey. Missy had put their lives on hold because of the amazing truth she'd found out, but in a week the fantasy was coming to an end. She would go back to her life, Liam would go back to his and somehow they'd find a way to make it work for their daughter's sake.

"Hey, what are you doing?"

His rough, sleep-filled voice stilled her hands as she attempted to make order of her messy hair.

"Getting dressed," she said, stating the obvious before glancing his way in time to watch him roll onto his back. The sheets tightened across his lower half, highlighting his washboard abs and an impressive morning erection that reminded her of all the wonderful things they'd done last night.

"Why?" he asked, rubbing at his eyes.

She blinked and forced herself to look away. "I should head back to the boathouse. Someone might—"

He dropped his hand, his gaze focused now. "Casey won't be back for another day and a half."

"Your mother?"

"She usually doesn't show up this early uninvited."

Missy waved at the bright sunshine pouring in through the windows. "It's almost nine o'clock."

"Why are you running away when we have so much to talk about?"

His question caused her heart to race. "We do?"

"Of course." He yawned and pushed into a sitting position, stopping suddenly when things got a bit uncomfortable, she guessed, but then he bent one knee and tugged the sheet back over his lap. "We need to make plans. For the future. For getting you and Casey in Destiny on a permanent basis."

Shocked filled her. "What?"

"I know this is kind of sudden, but I want you here, both of you." He leaned forward. "You said you were here on a work visa. How long is that good for? And Casey is half American. We'll need to find out how we can get her dual citizenship. You said your company has offices in LA, but you do most of your design work from home and you can travel whenever you need to. Casey loves it here and I know she'll be happy—"

"Wait just a bloody minute!" Missy held up a hand, cutting him off. How could he make assumptions like that? "I can't just up and move to America! My home, my career, my mother—despite our current relationship—are back in London. My *life* is in London. So is Casey's with her friends and her school."

"She has friends and school here. Family, too, and her father. I'm just trying to figure out a plan—"

"Blast it, it's like nothing has changed." Missy reeled from his words. "You're doing the same thing you did years ago. Making plans based on your needs and wants. You've always had that luxury, but that's not how being a parent works."

She paced the area at the end of his bed. "If it was just me…if I only had myself to think about, I might be temp—" She cut off her words, refusing to allow her emotions to get in the way. "I can't uproot my life, and my daughter's, because you and I rekindled a teenage passion into one night of great sex."

One night? Liam had just experienced the most amazing night with the woman he loved—the only woman he'd ever truly loved—and she was calling what they shared a fling?

Being with her had been a dream come true, every moment of it, and long after she'd fallen asleep in his arms in the wee hours of the morning, he'd started—well, making plans.

The last thing he'd expected was this reaction or for

her to throw his immature behavior from sixteen years ago back in his face. This wasn't like then. He wasn't the same person. He had responsibilities that went far beyond himself or even his family.

"Missy, I'm the CEO and president of my family's company. I can't just move to another continent—"

"Exactly. No one is asking you to. Or telling you to, for that matter."

"That's not what I'm doing."

"Really?" She folded her arms across her chest. "That's what it sounds like to me."

He opened his mouth to set her straight on a few things—most importantly, how he felt about her and their daughter—but the two-way radio on the bedside table chirped, and then Nolan's voice came over the airwaves.

"Liam? Come in, Liam. You there?"

Damn! This was the last thing he needed right now. Leaning back, he grabbed the radio, pressing the receive button. "Yeah, I'm here. What's up?"

"Casey's missing."

Missy's gasp filled the air, and Liam's stomach fell to his feet. He reached for her with his free hand, but she shook her head and stayed where she was, panic now etched on her face.

"What do you mean missing?" Liam asked.

"She and Abby got up early…took a couple of the ATVs to the ridge to watch the sunrise. According to Abby they had…words, and Casey told her she was going back." Nolan's voice broke, static marring his description. "Abby thought she meant the cabin, but by the time she returned, Casey still hadn't shown up."

"You're out looking for her now." It was a statement, not a question. Liam knew his brother well. "Where are you?"

"I've been doubling back on the three possible trails, but

you know as well as I do how many offshoots they have. I haven't found her. I'm thinking if she stayed on the main road, she'd be back to the house by now. Have you seen her this morning?"

Liam got out of bed, radio in hand as he reached for the clothes he'd tossed on a nearby chair at some point during the night, but Missy was already gone. His front door slammed as she raced outside, yelling their daughter's name.

His heart froze when he heard nothing in response.

Chapter Thirteen

She had to be out here. Somewhere. It was almost noon, just after their self-imposed two-hour search deadline, and no one had found Casey.

Liam rode the all-terrain vehicle along the trails, moving slowly as he searched the dense forest. He could hear the company's helicopter overhead and knew Bryant was doing what he could from the air, while Adam and his dad were on horseback, taking the less-used road from Adam's property, with Fay staying behind just in case Casey somehow found her way there.

Nolan worked the trail that led farther up into the mountains, and Abby and the twins stayed at the cabin if she returned. His mom and Laurie had the formidable task of keeping Missy calm back at the main house. She'd only agreed to stay behind when Liam reminded her that Casey might get past him and make her way home.

Find my daughter.

Missy's parting words this morning had cut deep. Liam had wanted to point out that Casey was *their* daughter, but the pain and fear in Missy's eyes had held him back from saying or doing anything, other than laying a hard kiss on her mouth and promising to bring Casey home.

Concentrating on the search helped a little, but his mind still replayed the argument he and Missy had had this morning. Where had he gone wrong? He wanted them in his life, wanted them in Destiny. He'd been so sure Missy felt the same way. To hear her say differently tore at his heart.

After finishing a trek on a rarely used dead-end trail deep in the woods, he pulled to the side of the road and let the vehicle idle. Then he checked in with everyone at the twenty-minute interval they'd agreed on. Still nothing. His last transmission was to Missy, as he'd insisted no one contact her but him. He didn't want a million voices coming at her with the same bleak news.

"Missy, it's Liam." He didn't waste any words. "We're still looking."

A long pause filled the air, but the static told him she was there. "It's been two hours," she finally said. "Where could she be?"

He wished he knew.

Wiping the sweat from his brow, Liam pressed the talk button. "We'll find her."

"She must be hurt. I keep trying her cell phone, but... she wouldn't ignore my texts. She just wouldn't. I can't bear to think of her lying somewhere...alone."

The heartbreak in Missy's tone had Liam fisting his hand and jamming it into his thigh. Missing the mark, he hit the ATV's kill switch instead, shutting the machine down. Dammit! As he blinked hard, the woods turned into watery shades of green and brown and silence enveloped him.

He swallowed a few times before he trusted himself to talk. "I think we should—"

A faint noise, a mechanical whine, carried on the breeze, stopping him cold. He lowered the radio and, concentrated on the sound, wanting to be sure. Yes, that was man-made. It had to be.

"Liam?" Missy's voice came back. "Why did—"

"Give me a minute. I think I heard something."

Missy's gasp filled the air, but she remained silent. He climbed off the ATV and hurried to the side of the road he'd avoided, due to the soft mud and the steep decline into a gully.

No tracks, at least not at this end.

He stood still, straining to hear—yes, there it was again. Heading back up the way he'd just come, he walked farther into the woods, peering down into the dark undergrowth filled with fallen logs and shrubbery so thick the filtered sunlight bounced off it.

"Casey!" He called out. "Sweetie, can you hear me?"

Something—instinct, awareness, a father's love—called to him now in a way that it hadn't before. She was here, she was close.

He tried again. "Casey, where are you?"

Then he saw it—a rear wheel, spinning upside down in the greenery, the rest of the vehicle barely visible in the dense woods.

His heart vaulted into his throat. "Casey! It's Dad! Are you okay? Can you answer me?"

A long moment passed and he searched for a way down to where the ATV lay, his boots catching and sliding in the sodden earth. Then a few feet away, a dark glove rose into a patch of sunlight, and stayed suspended there for a moment before it disappeared again.

"I see you! I'll be right there. Hang on!"

Liam reached for the closest tree branch, broke it into three pieces to form an arrow and laid it in the road. Racing back to his ATV, he grabbed a coil of rope and the emergency backpack, thumbing the button on the radio. "I found her!"

"Oh, Liam!" Relief flooded Missy's voice. "Is she okay? Is she hurt?"

"I don't know. I'm heading there now."

"Did she call out to you?"

"She only responded with a wave when I yelled. Probably due to her helmet." He prayed it was her gear that kept her silent. "Tell everyone I'm on the main trail, at the second fork from the mountain base. About two hundred yards in. I marked the spot on the road. There's a steep ravine on the left. She's down there."

"Oh, my God."

"Tell Nolan to take care of his kids, but send Adam and my dad this way in case I need help hauling her out of there." He started back up the road. "Have Bryant land, but keep the helo live...we might need to get her medical care in a hurry."

"Liam—"

"Do it, Missy. I have to sign off. I'll need both hands to get to her." He regretted his harsh tone, but he didn't have time to spare. "Let me bring our daughter home."

"Please, as soon as you can...call me back."

He promised and then pocketed the radio. Reaching the marker he'd left, he easily spotted the overturned ATV this time. He slung the backpack over his shoulder, tied one end of the rope to a tree, tossed the rest into the foliage below and started downward.

"Hang on, Casey," he yelled. "I'm coming."

It seemed to take forever to get to her. He kept a running commentary so that she'd know he was there, but honestly it was probably more to keep himself from falling to pieces. Finally, he reached her. She was laid out flat on her back next to a fallen tree that completely blocked her from the road.

Kneeling, he almost lost it again when he saw her staring at him through the cracked shield of the helmet. "I know I've been asking this for the last twenty minutes," he said, "but are you okay?"

She started to nod and then stopped, grimaced and mouthed something.

He lifted the shield, hating the tear tracks that stained her cheeks. "What is it, sweetie?"

"God, I'm a stupid wanker." Her words came out in a rough whisper. "I'm okay, but I ache from my teeth to my toes."

"Anywhere specific?" He leaned back, wondering what that fall must've been like and if she'd broken anything. "Any part of you that you can't move?"

"Everything seems to be working, except my right arm hurts bloody awful. Is Mum furious?"

Liam noticed that Casey was cradling her arm against her chest, the protective glove missing. She had a long-sleeved jacket on, but he could see her wrist was swollen badly, with dark color marring her skin. "Not furious. Worried. Just like the rest of us. That's some bruise you've got there."

"It's from an earlier tumble," she said. "Before I got myself into this mess. How did you know where to find me?"

"We've been looking for you all morning. Abby told us you took off after the two of you drove up to the ridge for the sunrise."

Casey's mouth pressed into a hard line, her eyes going cold. "Is that all she told you?"

A feeling of dread came over Liam. "What else is there?"

"We argued, got into a tussle." His daughter's words came out cool and collected, but he heard anger in her tone. "I landed hard against the rocks, banged up my wrist, but not before I landed a solid right hook to that pretty face."

Surprised filled him, but now wasn't the time to go into details of whatever had been brewing between the two girls. "Why don't you tell me about that later? I want to concentrate on getting you out of here."

"Come to my rescue again, huh?" Casey offered a half-hearted smile. "Bit more trouble than a blister this time."

Leaning in close, Liam brushed away a new tear from her cheek. "I'll always come to your rescue, sweetie. You're my daughter. That's what dads do."

Her eyes widened. "You...you truly believe that? Even without the test results?"

Now wasn't the time to reveal that he had the results or how badly he'd screwed things up this morning with his plans for the future. Thank goodness he still had a week to convince Missy the three of them belonged together.

"Yes, I believe that." He reached for her uninjured hand, his heart skipping a beat when she clung to him. "I knew from the beginning. I'm sorry I didn't make that clear to you. I love you, Casey. You're my daughter and I love you."

Every time the doctor touched Casey's arm, she winced despite the pain medication she'd been given and Missy's heart broke a bit more.

"As I suspected, you've got a couple of hairline fractures in the radius bone, located just above your wrist." The doctor laid Casey's arm gently back down on the gurney. "We're going to put you in a fiberglass cast."

"Really?" Casey asked. "For how long?"

"Minimum four weeks, maybe six. You're young. You'll heal nicely."

That would put them almost at Halloween, and of course, she and Casey would be back in London long before that. Wondering if there might be an issue, Missy opened her mouth, but Casey spoke up first.

"Can I travel? I mean, this won't stop me from flying, will it?"

Liam's head jerked up at their daughter's questions. Missy could see why. Casey sounded anxious, even eager to leave.

He sat on the other side of the room, having given up his spot at Casey's bedside when the doctor came back with the X-rays.

Except for explaining to the staff, and the sheriff, who happened to be at the clinic, what happened today, Liam had remained silent as Missy spoke about Casey's medical history and answered what seemed like a thousand questions.

"No, you should be fine," the doctor said. "I'd recommend taking along a pillow to keep it elevated. Now, let's get you fixed up, and yes, your mother can come with you."

Casey nodded, her gaze straight ahead and her brows furrowed in a way that was so familiar, Missy realized it was the same expression Liam often used. In fact, he had the matching look on his face right now.

What was he thinking? Was he upset that the doctor hadn't invited him along as well?

He'd been so calm when they arrived at the main house, Casey riding in front of him. Other than a quick hug and a fevered thank-you, they'd barely spoken to each other in the ensuing chaos.

Was it just this morning that she'd awoken in his arms?

"Mum? You ready?"

Missy started, realizing Casey and the doctor were waiting on her. "Yes. Of course." She looked at Liam again and decided to say what the doctor hadn't. "Do you want to—"

"I'll stay here," he said, cutting her off. "It'll be too crowded. Besides, there's paperwork to be taken care of."

"I have health insurance."

He got to his feet, something heartbreakingly haggard in his expression. "Don't worry about it."

"Liam—"

"Just take care of Casey, okay?" He walked over and laid a hand on their daughter's leg, below her knee and far away from her injured wrist. "I'm glad you weren't hurt even worse. You gave all of us quite a scare."

"Well, thank you. For saving me."

Liam gave a quick nod and then stepped away.

Missy was amazed at how they were acting toward each other. It was as if the closeness they'd found over the last five weeks had disappeared.

This was not the same man who'd had tears in his eyes when he spoke last night about knowing in his heart Casey was his daughter.

Or the one who'd passionately stated his case this morning for having her—both of them—move to Destiny. Now was not the time to talk about that, but they needed to soon. Missy hoped they'd find a chance. For everyone's sake.

In less than an hour, Missy had the pain medication in her purse and Casey sported a bright pink cast on her right arm. Liam stood when they walked into the waiting area, but when they headed out to the parking lot, Casey switched sides so that it was Missy's hand she held tight.

Missy could see her daughter was exhausted and still in pain. Getting her back to the boathouse and into bed was the best thing—

"Casey!"

The three of them stopped and turned. Casey's grip tightened as Nathan Lawson jogged toward them. Missy glanced at Liam, not liking the way his eyes narrowed on the young man.

"What's he doing?" Casey started to say, and then stopped and addressed the boy directly when he joined them. "What are you doing here?"

"I heard about your accident."

Casey turned to her, rolling her eyes. "Bugger, this is a small town."

"Actually, my mom works at the clinic. Are you okay?"

Casey waved her cast-covered arm at him and then winced.

"Ah, yeah, that was a stupid question." Nathan's gaze flew between Missy and Liam, but since her daughter hadn't let go of her, Missy wasn't going anywhere. Neither was Liam, from the stormy look on his face.

Quickly figuring out he wasn't going to get her alone, Nathan continued, "Look, I'm happy we got things straight between us last night."

"Last night?" Liam asked, before Missy could.

"Yes, sir. I knew Casey was up at your family's cabin, but it seems her cell phone gets reception there. We texted and I explained about what she saw at school yesterday. Or what she thought she saw."

"What Abby *told* me I was seeing," Casey said, her words spoken with a bitter tone. "She's your ex-girlfriend, she's staying that way and she kissed you. Don't worry, Nathan, everything's fine."

The boy didn't look convinced, nor did he seem as if

he wanted to leave, but Missy's main concern was getting Casey home. "We should be heading back. Casey needs to rest."

"Right, sure." Nathan took a step back. "You're probably not going to want to hang out or anything this weekend, but I'll see you in school on Monday?"

"No, you won't. I'm going home. To London."

Shocked, Missy stared at her daughter. "Sweetie, we don't leave until next Monday. That's a week away."

Casey shook her head, her gaze rooted to the ground. "No, I want to go home. Now. Tomorrow. As soon as we can."

Silence filled the air. Missy sneaked a peek at Liam and the misery on his face at their daughter's declaration caused her stomach to clench.

He looked so lost and alone, even though he stood right here with them. Unlike this morning, when he'd looked ready to fight for his cause, now he appeared to have had the wind knocked out of him.

"Um, okay." Nathan took a few steps back, picking up on the tension. "I'm sorry to see you go. We'll stay in touch? Maybe you'll come back to Destiny for Christmas?"

Casey shrugged. "Maybe. I don't know."

Looking almost as dejected as Liam, the boy only nodded, said goodbye to all of them and turned and walked away.

Confused, Missy placed her fingertips beneath her daughter's chin and gently forced her to look up. "Hey, what's going on? Where did this come from?"

"Nowhere. I just want to go home."

"Because of what happened today?" Liam asked softly, drawing Missy's attention. "No one blames you, Casey, for any of it. It was an accident, that's all."

A tiny hiccup squeaked from Casey, and Missy looked back in time to see her daughter's eyes fill with tears.

"No, it's not…about the mess I caused. I'm glad we came here, glad we all know the truth, glad that we met." She spoke to Liam, but kept her back to him, her eyes pleading with Missy. "But I've had enough. I miss our home, my room, my school, my friends. I just want to go home. Please? Please, can we go home?"

Pulling her daughter gently to her, Missy tucked Casey's head beneath her chin and began swaying back and forth, an instinctive gesture of comfort instilled in her the first time they'd placed Casey in her arms as a wee babe.

Missy looked up, her heart breaking for the agony Liam was going through, but she'd been serious this morning when she'd told him that she couldn't just up and move her life—their lives—to Destiny.

Especially now, when she had to do what was best for her daughter. For their daughter.

"I'm taking her home."

Liam's world was falling apart and there was nothing he could do about it.

In the span of just over twenty-four hours, he'd gone from the high of being a man in love, overjoyed at the idea of making his claim to fatherhood official and planning for the future, to standing here at the security gates of the Cheyenne airport saying goodbye to the two women he loved most.

They'd returned from the clinic yesterday afternoon to a quiet homecoming as everyone stayed out of sight. Missy had gone to get Casey settled while he had the un-happy task of telling his family they were leaving, a full week ahead of schedule.

But first he'd had a talk with Abby.

She'd owned up to what had happened between her and Casey, even though Liam wasn't convinced he had the whole story. The side of Abby's face was swollen, and he was sure she'd have a souvenir from her English cousin that she wouldn't soon forget.

When he'd gathered everyone together in the main house, he'd explained what happened at the clinic, and Casey and Missy's decision to leave early, as best he could. He'd then tried to deal with their questions, most of which he didn't have any answers to.

Missy had shown up with the news that she'd been able to get them on a late-afternoon flight to New York and then a red-eye to London the next day. He'd insisted she upgrade their tickets to first class on his dime. He wanted Casey to be as comfortable as possible.

When she and Casey had said goodbye to everyone earlier, Missy had been gracious and kind, especially to his parents, which meant a lot to him. Casey had seemed genuinely upset about leaving and he'd kept hoping she'd announce she'd changed her mind and wanted to stay, even if it was only for the additional week, but now that they were at the airport, she looked excited about heading home.

And Missy? He couldn't quite figure out how she felt about all of this.

"Don't be mad at me."

Casey's softly spoken request yanked Liam from his thoughts. He looked at her, still amazed that this wondrous creature was now a part of his life.

"I could never be mad at you," he said.

"Only because you haven't known me that long." She smiled and he was glad to see the spark back in her eyes. "Just ask my mum."

Liam glanced at Missy, loving the all-encompassing

way she looked at their daughter and wishing desperately she'd look at him that way, too.

"Okay," he said, turning his attention back to his daughter. "How about I promise that I'm not mad about this?"

"Truly?"

He nodded, pushing the words past the lump in his throat. "I know I told you yesterday, but I'll keep saying it. I love you, Casey, and I only want what's best for you. You're the most important thing in my life and leaving doesn't change that fact."

"Oh, Dad, I love you, too!"

She flew at him and Liam caught her, taking care with her injury as he pulled her into his embrace.

He had to close his eyes, wanting to commit this moment—the first time she'd used the familiar moniker so many men took for granted—to memory, knowing he'd replay it over and over again in the coming days.

Opening his eyes again, he found Missy standing there, her fingers pressed to her lips and a bright sheen in her gaze as she watched them.

He gave Casey an extra squeeze before releasing her, and then reached inside his jean jacket and pulled out the stuffed buffalo he'd picked up at the gift shop while they'd been checking in. "Here's a new friend to keep you company on the plane."

"Oh, he's bloody cute!" Casey squealed and gave him another quick hug. "And he's the official state mammal for Wyoming. I love him, and I love you!"

She dropped to her knees, busying herself with finding room in her bag, allowing Liam to make his way to Missy.

"That was wonderful," she said when he stopped in front of her.

"It's just a stuffed toy."

"I was talking about what you said to our daughter... and when she called you Dad."

Damn, the lump in his throat was back and this time it matched the two-ton rock in his chest. "Yeah, I was pretty happy about that. Wasn't sure I was going to hear that before—well, I thought the first time might be via a text message."

Missy smiled, but the emotion didn't reach her eyes, which remained solemn. "Liam, we need to talk, to fig- ure out—"

"We will, just not here. Not now."

He didn't wait for her to come to him. Pulling her into his arms, he held her close, brushing his lips at her temple. Holding her felt perfect. As perfect as having his daughter in his arms a moment ago. There had to be a way to make sure this wasn't the end for them. They were a family and families should be together.

His mind whirled, an idea catching hold so fast it stole his breath. Could he—?

Yes, he'd find a way.

"You need to get a move on." His voice was tight with need. "Your plane is going to be boarding soon."

Missy nodded in agreement. She got that familiar blush on her cheeks as she stared at him, clearly surprised by both his words and his actions.

Yeah, well, she hadn't seen nothing yet.

Chapter Fourteen

A video chat? Abby was freaking daft if she thought Casey was going to click on that link. Home for three days and every day there'd been a friend request she'd ignored, an email that got sent to the trash folder or now, an invite to talk face-to-face.

As if she was going to give that prissy American princess the chance to torture her from across the pond!

Hitting the cancel button gave Casey a bit of pleasure as a knock came at her bedroom door.

Her mum peeked her head inside a few seconds later. "Hey, there. Just checking in. How's the arm?"

"It's fine." Casey spun her desk chair around and studied her mum more closely, noticing how tired she looked. Was that from sitting up with her?

It was taking Casey a bit longer to get her body back on London time, and the busted arm that ached like a son of a biscuit wasn't helping. The two of them had been watching the telly late into the night, especially now that they had an on-demand streaming media account.

"How are you doing?" Casey asked.

Her mum looked down at the envelopes she held in her hand with a smile that seemed equal parts happy and sad. "I'm doing okay."

"What's that you've got?"

"Oh, just some…mail." She paused for a moment. "Old mail…your grandmum has been holding onto for me."

Casey thought her mum had gone through the stack waiting for them when they got back Monday night, but maybe she'd been wrong.

To say that things were a bit strained between her mum and Grandmum was putting it mildly. It still felt strange to be back here, knowing her grandfather was no longer around. Casey hadn't yet said anything to her grandmum about the secret her grandparents had kept from her, only because her mum had asked her not to for the time being.

"So, any big plans for the night?"

Casey thought about the chat request she'd just deleted and wondered if she should suggest it the next time she spoke with Liam. It would be great to see him again. "I don't know. I'm waiting to hear from Li—from my dad."

Her mum raised an eyebrow. "You've talked to—uh, your dad? I mean, since the first night we got back?"

"Yeah. Every day. We either text or email or he calls." She looked closer at her mum. "Is that a problem?"

"Of course not. I think it's great." She pressed the letters she held close to her chest. "Tell him h-hello from me the next time you talk."

Casey nodded, wondering about the hitch in her mum's voice but stayed quiet. And then she was alone again.

Swinging back around to her laptop, she found another video chat request, but this time it was Luke and Logan.

She grinned. Now, this one she'd accept. She missed those guys more than she'd thought she would.

When she clicked on the link, the video opened and there sat Abby.

"You!"

"Please don't hang up." Her cousin held up a hand as if she could wave off Casey's anger. "Using my brothers' names is a crappy thing to do, but I couldn't think of any other way to get you to talk to me."

It took Casey a minute, but she found the button to end the call. "I'd think you would've gotten the hint by now."

"Maybe I'm just stubborn." Abby leaned in closer, her face filling the screen. "Or maybe you knocked something loose with your right hook."

As much as she wanted to shut down the screen, Casey couldn't look away from the multicolored bruise that marred the left side of Abby's face. It ran from her brow to her jaw and Casey clenched her fingers against her cast at the memory of the pain when she hit Abby.

She hated to ask, but she had to know. "Did I...did I hurt you? The way your eye is swollen—"

"No. My eyesight is fine. It's just the outside that looks bad." Abby reached up and gingerly touched her cheek. "You should see the amount of makeup I need to cover this. I look like a cartoon character."

Casey breathed a sigh of relief that she hadn't done any damage. Then she remembered all the things Abby had done to her. "Well, what's that American saying? If the shoe fits? Look, I've got to go."

"Wait! Please, just give me five minutes."

"For what?"

"To apologize."

Surprised, Casey sat back in her chair. "You're joking."

"No, I'm not. I was a real...witch to you while you were

here. Please, feel free to respell that. I was petty and jealous—and not just because Nathan chose you over me. He
really misses you, by the way, and asked me to ask you to
get in touch if I ever spoke to you." Abby sighed. "Anyway, I want you to know that no one put me up to apologizing. What I did—everything I did to you—was wrong.
I'm sorry."

Was this for real? Casey didn't know what to believe.
Never in a million years had she expected this. Abby was
a topic that she and her dad didn't talk about at all. No one
really knew the bullying her cousin had done during her
time in Destiny.

"Do you think it's going to be that easy?" Casey asked.
"That I'm just going to forgive you?"

"No, I don't, but I wanted you to know how I feel. I
know I've got…some issues. I've been talking to…some-
one, but apologizing is completely my idea." Abby tucked
her long hair behind her ear, but then quickly pulled it
back out as if trying to hide the bruising. "You should also
know that everyone here misses you. Nathan, the kids at
school, my brothers. My—our grandparents. And Uncle
Liam—your dad, most of all. He seems really lost without
you and your mom around."

Casey's throat tightened. She'd gotten that feeling too
when she and her dad talked, but he never said anything.

"Look, I know you're probably ready to hit the end
button on me and I wouldn't blame you. I've said what I
wanted to say. I don't know if you and your mom left because of me, but I'm sure my actions made the decision
easier. Again, I'm really sorry. I hope you two don't stay
away from Destiny forever because of me."

The screen went blank before Casey could say anything else. Not that she had any idea how to respond to
everything Abby had just said. It was nice to hear that ev-

eryone there missed them, though. As comfortable as she was being back here, surrounded by her own things, she missed her dad terribly.

She got the feeling her mum did, too.

Abby had been the one who'd told her about catching the two of them kissing on the porch and yeah, at first it had seemed a bit strange. But the more Casey had seen them together, heard about what their relationship had been like all those years ago—

The special ring chime she'd assigned to her dad filled the air.

Casey grabbed for her phone and connected the call. "Hey! I was just thinking about you."

"Well, this is good timing, then." His low-timbered voice sounded happy. "How are you doing? How's the arm?"

"I'm fine, every bit of me is. Oh, and before I forget, my mum said to say hello for her."

Silence filled the air for a moment. "She did?"

"Yep, just a few minutes ago." Casey decided the video chat between her and Abby was going to stay private for the moment.

"So, you're both at home, then?" Liam asked.

"It's almost ten o'clock on a Thursday night. Of course, we're home. Grandmum is out with her bridge club and won't be back for hours," Casey blurted out, and then bit hard on her bottom lip. That was the first time she'd mentioned her to her dad, not wanting to upset him. "I'm sorry. I didn't mean to—"

"Don't worry about it. Hey, did you get the package I sent?"

Confused, Casey looked around her room. There was nothing here. Maybe Reynolds had left it downstairs in the pantry. "No, I don't think so. Let's keep talking while I go check."

She told him about the sleepover with her friends planned for tomorrow night as she walked downstairs. Nope, nothing in the pantry, kitchen or entry table in the front hall. "I don't see anything. Do you know when it was supposed to arrive?"

"I'd think it could show up any minute. Maybe you should see if it's on your front stoop."

Casey giggled at his cryptic tone, and grabbed the door handle and pulled it open. "Well, seeing how I'm right here, let me check—Dad!"

Liam caught his daughter as she launched into his arms.

"I can't believe you're here! This is so cool!" Casey tightened her grip on him. "I've missed you so much."

Liam returned her embrace. "I've missed you, too, sweetie."

Simple words, but the truth.

It had been four long days since he'd said goodbye to her and her mother, and they had been the loneliest and emptiest days of his life.

Busy, hell, yeah, especially when he told his father and his brothers about the plan he'd come up with at the airport and fleshed out on the way home from Cheyenne the day Casey and Missy flew out. Things had been crazy around the office and they still didn't have everything figured out, but nothing compared to the ache he carried from the loss of the family he'd found with Missy and their daughter.

An ache that disappeared the moment Casey opened the door.

"Hey, you're wet. I didn't even realize it was raining. Come inside." Casey stepped back but didn't let go of him entirely as she grabbed his hand and led him inside the posh town house that spoke of the wealth and dignity of Missy's family. "Here, let me take your coat."

Liam took off his raincoat, knowing his business suit looked as if it had spent the better part of the day on an airplane, which it had. He'd stopped at his brother's flat after getting out of the airport, but only stayed long enough to greet Devlin and Tanya, drop off his suitcase, and grab a taxi.

"When did you arrive? How long are you staying? Are you here for work?"

He smiled at his daughter's rapid-fire questions. "Just a few hours ago, I don't know and no, I'm not here for work. I'm here for you."

Reaching for Casey's good hand, he held tight, knowing everything was *almost* right.

Something told him Missy was going to be a harder sell than his daughter. Still, it was important that their daughter know how he felt. "I've missed fifteen years of your life. I'm not going to miss another moment."

Casey beamed. "So is it just me or do you feel the same way about my mum?"

"Hmm, another direct question. Do you mind if I answer that by speaking directly with her?"

"Straight down the hall. Last door on the left is her office." She reached up and kissed him on the cheek. "I'll be upstairs in my room. Best of British to you!"

Liam smiled, watching her go. He didn't know exactly what she meant by that last phrase, but he guessed she was wishing him luck.

He wondered if he was going to need it.

Unlike his daily interactions with Casey, he and Missy hadn't talked once since they'd parted ways at the airport. He had no idea what kind of reception his unexpected arrival would get him. Being prepared to meet Missy's mother, Elizabeth Ellington, for the first time had him feeling like a teenager again, but it was just him and Missy here.

If she was half as happy to see him as Casey had been, he'd consider himself a winner.

Liam loved her.

At one time, he truly had, and she now had the proof she'd once so desperately needed all those years ago.

Missy sat curled up in her favorite chair, in front of a low fire, with the three long-lost letters he'd mailed her resting in her lap. Her mother had shocked her tonight when she'd handed them over before she'd headed out for the evening, as casually as if they'd arrived in the post just today.

She'd told Missy that her father had instructed her to burn them, but she never had. She'd tucked them away, just in case. Just in case the secret they'd concocted ever came to light.

What exactly her mother knew and how Missy's father had kept her quiet all these years were topics they still hadn't discussed. Only four days home and with her clothing design business exploding thanks to the princess attending a charity event in the dress she'd designed, Missy was still trying to get her spinning world under control.

A feat that seemed impossible with Liam so far away.

But now he was here—or at least the boy she'd known, the boy she'd loved, was in his letters. Finally opened, finally read. Words written in his familiar scrawl about how they'd met, how they'd fallen in love and that last terrible fight.

In the first letter, he'd begged her to come back, to find a way to forgive him for hurting her, promising they'd figure out how to be together.

The second had been more subdued. He hadn't heard from her. Did she still love him? Had anything he'd written to her meant anything? He'd told her about his victories on the rodeo circuits, but they were hollow without her there to share them.

The last one had been short, barely filling one page, written almost three months to the day after she'd left. He said he'd gotten the message. Her silence meant she'd moved on and he had to do the same. He wished her well, told her he'd never forget her and hoped she was happy.

"Happy? Am I happy?" Missy brushed the wetness from her face, her question echoing off the walls of the room. Her private sanctuary, decorated in her favorite colors, with cherished collectibles and floor-to-ceiling windows that flooded the room with natural light, even on the dreariest English rainy days. "I don't know anymore."

"Then perhaps you'll let me help."

Missy gasped at the words, the sound of his voice. She whipped around and saw the shadow of a man standing in the darkened doorway.

"I don't—you can't—" She stumbled over her own words, refusing to believe until he stepped deeper into the room. "Liam? What are you doing here?"

The small lamp on her desk was just bright enough to show his smile and the easy shrug of his powerful shoulders. He glanced down at the yellowed pages in her hand. "You never seem to get my letters. This time I decided to come in person."

"Can you believe she kept them all these years?"

He stepped farther into the room. "I'm glad you finally got to read them, but I'm here to do what I should've done before you left."

"What?"

"Tell you that I love you." He crossed the room then,

and seconds later knelt in front of her chair, his face fully lit by the glow from the fire as he took her hands in his. "That I never stopped. I'm hoping you feel the same. Tell me and we'll find a way to make this work. To be the family we—you, me and Casey—were meant to be."

"But my career… Casey's education…my mother." Her mind whirled as she tried to wrap her head around what was happening. "What about your family's business? Your career? Your life in Destiny?"

"My life is wherever you are, where you and Casey are." His fingers gave hers a gentle squeeze. "I've already started on a plan—a new one—with my dad and brothers. Restructuring within the company, spreading out job duties, digging deeper in our business interests here in the UK. Traveling to Wyoming, to wherever, as needed. My brother Devlin is heading home in a month. I plan to take over his flat, or I'll find somewhere else to stay in London. Whatever it takes, I'll do it. For you, for our daughter."

"You love me. You love Casey." Not questions this time, simple facts that made her heart soar. She didn't even have to ask, knowing he'd already stated his case to their daughter and she'd told him where to find her. "It took us a long time to find each other again."

"Too long, but we were destined to be together."

She couldn't stop from reaching for him, laying a hand on his cheek. "You were destined to be a dad."

"I already told Casey I don't want to waste another moment, miss another moment of her life. I feel the same about you. About us." Liam looked at her, his eyes bright with everything he had inside him, there for her to see. "Let me make you happy."

"You have always made me happy, Liam. The happiest I've ever been was with you," she whispered, lowering her forehead until it touched his. "I love you, my Wyoming cowboy. I always have and I always will."

* * * * *

MILLS & BOON®

Cherish™

EXPERIENCE THE ULTIMATE RUSH OF FALLING IN LOVE

A sneak peek at next month's titles...

In stores from 18th September 2015:

- **The Tycoon's Proposal** – Shirley Jump
  and **A Proposal Worth Millions** – Sophie Pembroke

- **Soldier, Hero...Husband?** – Cara Colter
  and **Betting on the Maverick** – Cindy Kirk

In stores from 2nd October 2015:

- **The Baby Who Saved Christmas** – Alison Roberts
  and **The Good Girl's Second Chance** – Christine Rimmer

- **Falling for Mr December** – Kate Hardy
  and **The Boss's Marriage Plan** – Gina Wilkins

Available at WHSmith, Tesco, Asda, Eason, Amazon and Apple

Just can't wait?
Buy our books online a month before they hit the shops!
visit www.millsandboon.co.uk

These books are also available in eBook format!

0915/23